THE
QUANTUM
AWAKENING

DAVID ALLAN HAMILTON

DeeBee

THE QUANTUM AWAKENING
Copyright © 2021 by David Allan Hamilton

For information contact :
Davidallanhamilton00@gmail.com
http://www.davidallanhamilton.com
ISBN: 9781896794440

First Edition: April 2021

10 9 8 7 6 5 4 3 2 1

For David "Artie" Langdon, 1965—1992
My first friend at Laurentian University

Through faith we understand that the worlds were framed by the word of God, so that things which are seen were not made of things which do appear.

Hebrews 11:3

PROLOGUE

Kirkland Lake, Ontario
September 2007

"SAY, YOU NEED A HAND?"

It became terrifyingly clear to Grey Dawson that the immense ruffian posing as a miner used his massive hands not only for heavy machinery at a rock face but also for a darker kind of physical extraction.

Jerry rummaged in the back of his pickup, then wrenched open the cab's rear door and spun around. For a big man, he moved like a cat and in one deft motion, he'd seized Grey by the neck and threw him into the truck. Another thug, hidden in the shadows, struck him in the stomach before covering his head with a thick wool hood. A chemical inside the fabric caused him to fade. Before he *lost consciousness, the stranger growled, "Let's get out of here."*

When Grey awoke, his brain buzzed, and his body ached as if he'd gone ten rounds with a dozer. He slumped, tied to a chair in a gloomy basement, and remembered nothing about the trip here. As his vision sharpened, he recognized Jerry slouching by a closed door, arms crossed over his chest. A second man wearing a lab coat fussed at a kitchenette, and a third—a woman—petite with reedy, short hair and dead eyes, watched from the corner shadows, straight as a sentry. A fragrant scent of lilacs lingered in the musty air.

"Wh—where am I?" he asked, finding the sound of his voice distant and unfamiliar.

"Ah, welcome to the land of the living, Mr. Dawson. So glad you're presentable. Jerry here," he motioned to the brute by the door, "sometimes gets excited and, well, feed him a beer or two and bad things often happen."

"Who are you?"

The man in the coat washed his hands and toweled them dry. He turned. "My name is unimportant. I am simply The Technician, and I'll take care of you, fix you up, and return you to your survey and family as soon as our business here is completed."

Dawson pulled on his restraints, but his arms were bound tightly behind him. They'd also roped his legs to the massive wooden chair.

"I demand to know what's going on here," he croaked, his voice cracked and dry.

"You are in no position to demand anything." The fellow approached him, holding a clear beaker in his gloved hands. "Yes, it's quite simple. You have an item that I and my colleagues covet."

"Like what, money? I have little of that."

The Technician glanced at the woman. "No, not that

of all things."

"What, then?"

"A photograph, Mr. Dawson. I believe you know the one I'm talking about."

Grey closed his eyes, squeezing the pain from his throbbing head and screaming chest muscles, suggesting he'd suffered a cracked rib at some point. But what photo? His mind turned to his fieldwork in Boston Township. Perhaps these thugs belonged to one of the active mining companies and wanted early access to his findings. But the results would soon be available in the public domain, so it made no sense. Unless...

"Ah, the lightbulb flashes."

Dawson cleared his throat. "Are you talking about the picture of my grandparent's farmhouse?"

The fellow grinned at the young woman. "Well, the man wins a prize. He got it right away." Then his eyes narrowed. "So where is it, Mr. Dawson? At your hotel? Back home with your pretty wife?"

He instinctively yanked at the ropes. "Don't you dare!"

"See, if you tell me where it is, I'll send Jerry to retrieve it and once it's in our possession, you're free to go. Quite simple, yes?"

"Why is it so important to you, anyway?"

The man rocked on his heels. "I think we both understand what that print represents." His eyes widened and his thin lips curved into a reptilian smile.

Dawson had no desire to give this photograph to anyone. He'd only found it a few days ago while rifling through the old field notes in his survey documents. But he understood why someone might be interested in it. The mysterious way it glowed when he held it just so... how the eyeless apparitions in the image gaped and beckoned him to follow, imparting a sense of danger. He had shrugged it off as a hallucination and overwork.

But whatever the photo represented, Dawson had no intention of giving it to anyone. This is what the surreal warning must have meant.

"I have no clue how you came to know about it, but if you figured I had it, you'd also realize I threw it in my campfire on the trail with a bunch of other useless crap I didn't need. Stupid old farmhouse. Means nothing to me."

The Technician raised his hands in front of his chest. The glass jar contained a clear liquid with a brush standing in it.

"Do you know what this is?" He sneered.

Grey Dawson gulped. He'd worked in the mineralogy labs long enough to know the harsh smell coming off the beaker anywhere. "Please…"

"You recognize sulfuric acid." He nodded to Jerry. The big man dropped his hands, thumped across the concrete floor, his heavy boots threatening violence with each step. He clenched Dawson's right hand and forced the fingers open against the arm of the chair.

"Oh, God…"

The Technician withdrew the brush, wiped the drips on the side, and painted a thin line over Dawson's knuckles. The pain was immediate as the caustic liquid seared through his skin, filling his nostrils with a nauseating scent of burning flesh and bone. Dawson shrieked.

"Where is the photograph," the man said.

Dawson's eyes bulged as the acid bubbled through his fingers. He sucked the putrid air through his teeth, unable to stop the tears rolling freely down his cheeks.

The young woman glared from the shadows. She had the most alluring, deadly, beautiful black eyes, and she approached him as quietly as a morning mist. Then she leaned close to his ear and whispered, "Last chance, Mr.

Dawson."

Grey Dawson was hardly impulsive. He preferred reasoning things out, whether on a geological survey line or playing the stock market. But with his mutilated hand screaming at him, he abandoned rationality. Instead, he launched himself awkwardly against the trio, striking The Technician's chest with a shoulder before crashing to the floor in a tangle of furniture and bodies. What he saw next—and heard—made him gag. The impact sent the jar of acid flying, spilling its contents over the woman's face. She shrieked—an unholy, desperate wail—and stumbled to the sink. Jerry immediately kicked Dawson in the head.

Then again.

And again.

The last thought he had before death mercifully snatched him from this life was of his mother in his childhood home, baking bread.

ONE

London, Ontario
September, 2020

DESPITE THE URGENT DESIRE TO MAKE HEADWAY ON HIS analysis of the latest quantum topological encoding data, Matt Dawson simply lost the motivation to plant his butt in a chair and get to work. How much longer would he have to wait before he had sufficient numbers analyzed to finish up his PhD? And then what? Where to next? He'd studied so long, he didn't know how to live any other way. Twenty-four years old and mired in a full-blown existential crisis. That's all he needed.

He slumped at the flimsy dining room table in his beat up, north end apartment, anticipating the arrival of that elusive, fragile inspiration.

Thick, heavy air ran hot in this place. The way his windows were set in the building, cross breezes rarely appeared. Instead, no matter the weather outside, his one-bedroom home baked. Not that he should complain much. Some of his colleagues suffered worse conditions in musty basement rooms and were scattered all over the city. At least he could walk to campus. He had that to be thankful for.

He sighed heavily, sipped his ice-water, and stared at the blank computer screen. In front of him lay several notebooks and snippets of paper on which he kept ideas and thoughts and other mental flotsam. He shut his eyes for a moment as a fresh wave of sleep fluttered over him. The dense night air clung to everything in his room, including him, drenching his shirt in a foul-smelling sheen even though he'd changed it only a couple hours ago. A cool shower would help him relax.

Dawson yawned and closed the laptop nestled in front of him and gathered his notes. Tomorrow would be another day, a fresh start. His thesis advisor had found a rare mid-term Masters student from Boston College to join the lab and push through the last suite of experiments. This, the professor assured him, would provide sufficient findings to write up into a dissertation. He may even graduate in the spring if everything went well.

So he needed sleep and to show up bright and early in the morning. Mondays were tough on some, but Matt looked forward to seeing other students on campus. Ever since his split with Linda a couple months ago, life in the apartment was quieter. And lonelier.

He rubbed the back of his neck and glanced outside the balcony window at the cityscape. Over by the TV, poking out from under an old shirt and some dog-eared magazines, the parcel his mother had sent caught his eye. It arrived last week, but he'd been preoccupied organizing the lab for the new girl that he hardly had time for anything personal. Tonight, though, he picked it up, grabbed a pair of scissors from the kitchen, flopped onto the sofa and broke it up.

She'd said it was an odd assortment of bits and pieces from his dead father's workshop. Nothing special, but she didn't know what to do with it, so rather than toss it out, she passed it on to him.

Matt flipped open the crushed corners of the shoebox and poked around inside. She was right: this collection was mostly dusty, random junk… some odd-looking trinkets… a postcard of Paris with no writing… a dog-eared hockey card… and a jumble of things that came from a desk: pens and pencils, erasers, a pencil sharpener, some paper clips, postage stamps, thumb tacks… He was about to toss the package aside when he saw the corner of something poking out.

He dumped the contents onto the coffee table. A marble rolled off and plunked on the carpet. In the bottom were some papers (personal accounting of trips, with dates, destinations, money spent on lunches) but underneath those sat a ragged black-and-white photograph. Matt pulled it out and placed it on the table in front of him.

Odd. It was an image of an antique farmhouse. In fact, as he studied it more, he realized the building was partially constructed out of sod. He'd heard the stories about some of his ancestors on his father's side emigrating from Scotland and settling on the prairies, and how the pioneers typically constructed their shelters from available local materials. How on Earth did people survive? When he'd spoken to some old-timers, they told him how solid and warm those homes were, despite their appearance. And they were simpler to maintain than the more contemporary, flashy, pre-fabricated garbage being built now. Of course, indoor plumbing and the niceties of a modern home were non-existent then. Townspeople often had those luxuries, but not those living on the land.

There were no people in the photograph. He ran his

fingers through his thick, curly hair, picked it up and flipped it over. But nothing on the reverse side indicated when the photo was taken, or exactly where. Although, he guessed it must have been from the western side of the clan. Some distant relative in his dad's ancestral line, perhaps.

He rubbed his eyes and was about to call it a night when warmth suddenly tickled his fingertips. He glanced at the image in his hand. Something wasn't right. Overwhelming dread rose in him like he'd never experienced before.

The edges of the photograph shimmered.

Dawson swore the photo had come alive. All along its boundaries, waves appeared in grey, fluid motions, like water or sand in the wind. Then, the movement spread across the entire image so the farmhouse itself became washed out under a wave of monochromatic ebb and flow.

At that moment, unsure of what he was seeing, burning heat coursed through his fingers. His mind told him to drop the picture, but he couldn't release the grip it held on him. He sat on the sofa's edge, sweat dripping from his face, mouth agape, unable to breathe.

But the pain soon overwhelmed him and the spell clutching him was shattered in a strained gasp. He dropped the photo, curling his hands into fists.

His eyes squeezed shut as his body relaxed. Dawson fell over on the sofa, clutching his wounded fingers, incapable of processing what had happened. Black invaded his vision, smothering his mind, and the image he saw before passing out was the photograph lying face down on the coffee table, a soft, faint orange glow framing its edges.

A powerful force overwhelmed his senses, intangible and unidentifiable. An underlying fright running deep through his bones. Visceral fear laced with terror.

A warning.

Then, nothing.

TWO

THE RUMBLE AND BELCH OF A TRANSPORT TRUCK ON THE street below shook Dawson from his dreamless sleep. After a moment, he realized he'd slept on the sofa all night. The lights remained on in his apartment, and that photograph—the one that sent him spinning—rested on the top of his coffee table. No strange glows. No strange noises. Just an ordinary photo.

Yet it wasn't. His fingertips stung and when he brought them up to his face, pinprick blisters on the index and middle fingers of both hands were unmistakable. He also had a nasty red patch on the left thumb pad.

So I wasn't dreaming or hallucinating.

He kept a first aid kit in his bathroom and rummaged through it until he found the aloe cream, which he then rubbed gently over his fingers. He bandaged the blisters—a delicate one-handed operation—and made a pot of coffee.

Dawson poured himself a mug and returned to the living room. Standing above the coffee table, staring at the photograph carefully, he saw nothing unusual and snorted. "Yeah, fatigue. That's what gave me these blisters."

He found a pencil and flipped it face up. The farmhouse appeared like any other nondescript old homestead. But two questions screamed for him to consider. Did he imagine or truly witness the grains move last night in his hands? And, the burns were obviously real: his fingertips smarted, and he struggled to manage the hot cup of coffee. So where did they come from?

Another thought tapped him on the shoulder: the sense of being in danger, that this photograph contained a warning. But the message was nebulous, and slipped away.

Dawson kept watching the photo, waiting for it to shimmer again. It didn't. After five minutes passed, he picked it up, awkwardly at first, but since no burn appeared, he shrugged and dropped it back in the box. Then he shoved the remaining odds and ends into the package and dumped it on the dining room table.

Time to think about that later. Now, he needed to shower, and dress, and head to campus. He'd abandoned the lab in mid-experiment and wanted to clean up before this—what was her name? He checked the email from Dr. Gunar. Oh yes, Wendy Sakamoto from Boston College. Scheduled to arrive at 8:30. He downed his coffee and in fifteen minutes, left his apartment and jogged off under a warm September sun on the half-hour walk to campus.

But as he marched along sidewalks and side streets to the university, the only thought haunting him was how to solve the riddle of the old photograph, and determining if his experience really happened.

If it had, then what caused it?

THE EXPERIMENTAL SUBATOMIC PHYSICS LAB ON THE second floor of the Physics and Astronomy Building at the University of Western Ontario was well beyond its prime.

The stone building originally housed all the sciences in the early 1900s, and now comprised a jigsaw of labs and lecture halls, seminar rooms and faculty offices that were regularly sprayed for cockroaches and reeked of body odor and dust. Still, his lab was magical, a rectangular enclave, large enough for a couple of students to work comfortably and containing highly advanced imaging equipment. He wouldn't trade it for anything in the world.

Maybe that's my problem.

He swiped his access card across the reader and the heavy steel door clicked and swung open. After flicking on the fluorescent lights, he dropped his backpack on the desk and surveyed the area.

"What a mess."

The main work table in the centre of the room supported two stations for running subatomic imaging experiments. Both were quiet now, but when operational, the hum and purr of various power supplies and powerful computers filled the space with relaxing white noise. He toggled the switches on the primary lines and the equipment jumped to life.

On the right, beside his desk, sat another makeshift work area covered in his textbooks and paper copies of dog-eared journals. Wendy would sit here, so he gathered his materials and shoved them in a box on the shelf overhanging the two.

A monitor on the other side of the lab glowed with streams of scrolling data. He methodically inspected the operating parameters to ensure everything worked properly. The information being collected here came from one of the long range experiments, investigating optical anomalies of thin film surfaces in the upper EM band. The trial would continue another few days before completing its run. To date, the results held no interest for him, but Gunar wanted it done and so he would oblige. He pulled his hand across his face, the bandaged fingertips scratching his cheeks and chin.

After spending a few minutes clearing the table tops and organizing the equipment in a more coherent way, he grabbed the straw broom from the coat closet and swept the floor, then sprayed some air freshener throughout, a bit too much perhaps, and smiled approvingly. *Good as new.*

A knock at the door sounded.

He opened it and an athletic Japanese woman with shoulder length dark hair met him with a nervous, crooked smile. Dr. Gunar loomed behind her.

"Wendy, I presume? I'm Matt. Come on in."

She held her bag in front of her chest and stepped into the lab with an evaluative stare. Gunar squeezed around her and marched to the monitor displaying the streaming lines of data.

"Dawson, how's it coming along?"

"The EM band experiment? Still running normally, sir. Nothing of significance yet but it has another couple days to crunch numbers. I can show you both the findings to date if you like."

"No need. Ah, but where are my manners? Matt Dawson, meet Wendy Sakamoto."

They shook hands.

"Wendy comes from Boston and we're lucky she could join us mid-semester. Great timing."

She nodded sheepishly.

"Well," Gunar said, "I've got a faculty meeting in a couple of minutes so I'll leave you to it. Dawson, show Wendy the equipment and review the experimental design with her. I want these trials finished up as quickly as possible so we can meet our milestone targets."

"Of course, Dr. Gunar."

The professor slinked out the door in a waft of cheap aftershave. Dawson smiled and said, "So, what do you think?"

Wendy dropped her backpack and small purse on the empty desk and sighed. "This is it? I was expecting something a little more... contemporary."

Dawson bit his tongue. "Sure, well don't let this place fool you. We've done some outstanding work here over the years. Dr. Gunar was one of the brightest physics minds of his generation."

She stood across from him and placed her hands on her tiny hips. "Yes, he told me on the way over. Anyway, I'm here to learn, Matt, so shall we start?"

Dawson furrowed his brow and forced the rising resentment away. A year had passed since another student worked here, and sharing the space would require an adjustment period. But if she was all business, they'd get along fine. "Over here. I'll show you." He pointed to a stack of storage units and grabbed his notebook.

"Did those injuries come from the experiment?" She motioned to his bandages.

He shook his head. "Nah, let's get to work," he suggested, and directed her to follow.

THE REST OF THE MORNING UNFOLDED IN A QUIET, professional manner as the two scholars tested each other. Dawson showed Wendy the inventory of equipment, briefed her on the mind-numbing projects he ran for Gunar, and provided her with a series of journals and links to papers related to the work. She spent most of her time reading, peppering him with questions when she needed to clarify something.

His attitude improved as he slipped into the work and, he admitted to himself that he didn't mind the lab company. Plus, no doubt she was smart, and he recognized her knowledge helped fill in some gaps in his own understanding of light waves and optical surveying.

At 12:30, she left to grab some lunch and Dawson relaxed, pulling out the notes he'd made about the farmhouse photograph. He grabbed his phone and punched in his mother's number. In a moment, she appeared on the screen from her kitchen.

"Matt, well this is a surprise! What's up?"

He pulled a sandwich from his backpack and placed the phone in a desk holder. "Not much. The new assistant started today, so I spent most of my time reviewing things with her."

"Sorry, *her*?" she asked.

"Yes, she's a *she* from Boston. Her name's Wendy and it's not like that, Ma. We're both here to work."

"But you're all right, hm?"

"Yeah, sure, I'm fine. But I want to know about this photograph in Dad's stuff you sent."

"What photograph is that?" The tone in her voice shifted slightly.

He described the homestead and the odd fact that no one was in it. Only a sod house surrounded by endless prairie.

Her expression changed. "I don't think I've ever seen a picture like that, although your relatives settled in Saskatchewan and their first home was likely built out of sod. That's the way it was. Crazy settlers, eh?"

"Look, can I ask you a few questions, because the photo did something to me... or at least I thought it did, and I want to check it out."

His mother glanced off to the side, fidgeting with her hair.

"Is that okay with you?"

"Well, I'm not sure I can be any help. Like I said, it was just some extra stuff from your dad's workshop in the basement. I was going to chuck it but figured you might like some of it. That's all."

"So you know nothing about the photo?"

His mother paused. "Probably came from your dad's relatives and got stuck in a bunch of his papers and notes. What's with all the questions?"

"Mum," Dawson said in a low voice, "something happened."

"Hm?"

He retold the story of his experience, how he'd been working on his research all weekend and quit around 11:00 last night, and opened the parcel. He described the photograph and recalled every detail he could about what transpired when he held it. How the images shifted like rolling waves, and his fingertips burned, and a peculiar foreboding came over him.

"You sure you weren't daydreaming? Your dad used to get that way when he worked on his geology surveys. His mind would wander off and he'd go all squirrelly quiet and—"

"If that's all it was, sure. But how do you explain these blisters?" He pulled back a bandage on his finger and held his hand to the screen. The pad had bubbled into a dark purple sore with white in the centre.

"Oh my god, what happened to you?"

"That's what I've been trying to tell you. I don't know, Mum. But something did, so if you have any clues about this photo, please say so because it sure as hell hurt and I can find no logical explanation for it."

Despite her protests, he continued. "Maybe I was, like, way tired or something, but I felt what I felt, and this morning I woke up to this. Can't figure it out."

Her brow furrowed, and she spun away, shifting her weight.

"What is it, Mum? What do you know about this?"

"Nothing, I swear, Matt. I—I just don't know what to tell you and now you got me all worried." She dipped closer to her camera. "Are you okay otherwise, though? Anything else going on?"

"You mean like with school?"

"Sure."

"I guess everything's good. Nothing out of the usual."

She paused. "Well, I have no more to say. I've heard of nothing like that. Should you see a doctor or something?"

"Nah, it's not that bad. I'll live."

The apologetic tone in his mother's voice hinted that she knew more, but refused to open up.

"Mum, come on. I'm your only son. I can tell when you're hiding things from me."

"Sorry, I just can't."

The lab door pinged and swung open. Wendy appeared with a coffee and a bowl of soup and returned to her desk.

"Listen, I gotta go, but we'll continue this conversation later, okay?"

She hesitated. "Sure, well, have a good rest of the day, Matt. I love you."

"You too, Mum."

He punched the phone and stared at the papers on his desk.

"Everything okay at home?" Wendy asked while slipping the plastic lid off her soup.

"Yeah, thanks."

He threw her a wan smile and plugged his earphones in, flipped on some music and blocked out the sound of his racing heart.

THREE

SEVERAL DAYS PASSED SINCE THAT FIRST ENCOUNTER where the mysterious photograph blistered Dawson's fingertips. The healing had begun—he no longer required bandages—but despite concerted efforts to focus on Gunar's experimental trials, his mind raced with this bizarre phenomenon. He quit the lab early on Thursday afternoon, emotionally spent and desperate for sleep, strolled home to his apartment and flopped on the couch.

His mother hid something from him, and it festered like an unspoken lie. Despite chatting several times during the week, she refused to budge, changing the subject until he finally let it go. *She's never kept secrets from me before. Why now?* He rested his eyes, listening to the jumble-song traffic below and the rattle-clack of his balcony screen door in the wind gusts.

The challenge of concentrating on his lab work crushed him. Wendy turned out to be a real help and knew her stuff. She engaged in the experiments immediately and fed Gunar bits and pieces of the preliminary results... just enough to keep him happy and out of their way. But the project couldn't continue like this while he struggled with the photograph that now gripped his full attention like a vise.

Dawson raised his head and stared at the lonesome box taunting him from the bookshelf. What harm would one more look do? If new blisters appeared, he'd conclude that what he experienced was real, but if nothing happened, he'd be able to sweep it from his mind and continue with his work—no matter how boring—and chalk the experience up to some kind of brain malfunction brought on by stress gremlins.

He seized the box and dumped its contents on the coffee table. The photograph fluttered on top, face down, where he'd left it Sunday night. He discerned nothing odd, no glowing edges, no squirrelly vision seeing things that simply weren't there. Dawson lifted the photo out by a frayed edge and placed it beside the container. He felt no fire on his fingertips. The image appeared the same: a sod farmhouse, dark against a bright prairie landscape that ran into the horizon. Haunted? Not at all. No sinister happenings here. Off to the right, he caught a shadow, possibly a person standing there outside the frame. Curious why no people posed in serious silence against the house. He'd seen many of those in the family archives.

But not this one.

"Well," he spoke aloud, "here we go."

Matt lifted the photo in both hands, running his fingertips along the creased edges.

5 seconds...

10 seconds...

He held it up against the muted light spiralling in from the balcony window, flipped it over a few times.

Nothing unusual happened.

Dawson scratched his thick hair, then chucked the photograph back in the box and stood, arms akimbo. The stupid thing had rented precious space in his brain these past few days, and now he needed to re-engage with his actual work. He stretched and drew the laptop from his backpack, glancing one last time at the cause of his obsession.

That's when it flickered to life.

A faint glimmer along the top edge.

A subtle shift in the grey hues, from monochromatic spatter to a hint of fiery oranges, the colour of pre-dawn sky.

He ditched the computer on the floor and grabbed the photograph, instantly feeling warmth surge through his fingers and up his arms.

It was happening again.

Or was it?

Dawson dropped the picture on the coffee table, and the glow disappeared. He studied it from various angles, focusing on the edges, peering into the shadowed crevices. But the photo now remained inert. He raised a hand over it, hovering a few centimeters from the farmhouse.

Nothing.

Dawson's mouth dried up.

He lowered his hand, almost touching the image, and held it there, trembling.

At first, he believed the warmth emanating from the photograph was a residual memory, an echo. Until the light appeared. Dawson summoned courage from the depth of his soul, and picked it up by the edges again.

This time, mesmerized by the fiery glow along the margins, he discovered something more. The farmhouse shimmered, like heat waves off a summer highway, until the building disappeared in a haze of swirling eddies, replaced by images of hands in the grains of the photo itself. Dozens of them. Small, large, some in a swiping motion, and others resting. One hand raised a finger, as if imploring him to follow.

"What is going on?"

The ambient noise from the traffic faded, supplanted with the hush of wind and water. He couldn't tell if the sounds emanated from his mind or were living spirits; all he felt was the authentic rush. He fixed his gaze on the photograph and gasped when distorted faces appeared. Some were children with closed eyes. Others, adults.

But they were not closed... they lacked pupils. Like statues.

A stinging burn forced him to release the snapshot, and it drifted to the floor. When Dawson recovered and exhaled, his head spun and stars pin-pricked his vision. He dropped to his knees, gulping deep breaths, and waited for the sensation of losing consciousness to pass.

When his senses returned, the sky hues had shifted, and glancing at the wall clock by his dining room table, he realized a couple of hours had passed.

But it felt like seconds.

His palms and fingertips screamed with searing pain. Fresh blisters peppered his skin. Still, he remained on the floor with the photograph, returned to its inert condition, in front of him.

Despite his hope that this was all his imagination or stress-induced hallucinations, he recognized that whatever happened was real and no science he understood could explain it.

Dawson accepted that his desperate search for knowledge often tumbled down crooked goat paths toward the truth, and now, undertaking his normal pedestrian work as if everything was fine seemed ridiculous.

His entire life had changed.

FOUR

THEIR EYES GLAZED OVER. TEN MINUTES REMAINED IN her lecture, and Hannah King silently implored her young scholars to pay attention to the ultimate point in her presentation. Some always did, those true believers comprising five percent of the class, typing copious notes on their laptops, nodding when she made the briefest of eye contact. But most could not care less about *Topics In Paranormal Experiences.* Most students viewed her course as fringe neuroscience in their psychology programs... something to fulfill degree requirements and nothing more.

Hannah glanced at the time on her laptop, fussed with an errant strand of hair, exhaled, and reflected on another tough sleep.

The tap-drip nightmare that awakened her at 3:00 this morning refused to dissipate, but in ten minutes, she'd dismiss the fourth-year students and deal with the darkness then.

I can do all things through him who strengthens me.

She cleared her throat and continued. "So once this electromagnetic field has been produced from some charge distribution, other charged or magnetized objects already in this field may also experience a force. If these other charges are comparable in size to the sources producing the above EM field, then a new net electromagnetic field will be formed." She paced in front of the class, leading them toward the crucial point. "Do you see the importance of classical EM field theory to parapsychology?"

More blank stares, some shuffling of papers, eyes diverted to their screens or their shoes. One keener sitting by the window overlooking a pristine garden raised his hand and mumbled. "Is it because there's a measurable interaction between the fields themselves and biological organisms in those fields?"

"Correct. The electromagnetic field is dynamic. That means it causes other charges and currents to move, and simultaneously, it's also affected by them. Remember from last class when we discussed Maxwell's equations? The Lorentz Force law?" Groans drifted forward from the back of the lecture hall. She forced a smile. "Okay, we won't go through the math again, but look at the theory underlying EM fields and make the connections. The calculations can be a challenge, but the concepts are elegantly simple."

"Ms. King?" A blond-haired girl raised her hand. "I'm not sure I follow. Are you saying *we're* affected by these current fields all the time?"

"Yes."

"And we can actually measure these effects?"

"Most times, yes."

The curious student nodded and tapped a note on her laptop before speaking again. "So are you suggesting these fields *cause* paranormal experiences?"

Their eyes focused on her, and her throat tightened. "Well, that's what my research is all about. Searching for, and understanding the mechanisms at play, to determine if there are physical, measurable processes behind phenomena like ESP and spoon-bending."

Joe Skeptical cocked his head and squinted. "Sounds a bit late-night voodoo to me."

Others nodded and smirked.

"Perhaps I can remind you what Arthur C. Clarke said about science. You know *2001: A Space Odyssey*?" She posted the last slide. Clarke's famous quote appeared beside a black-and-white photograph of the man: *magic's just science that we don't understand yet.*

She paused, sipped her lukewarm coffee, grimaced and glanced again at the time.

"Anyway, please give that some thought over the coming days and don't forget your mid-term assignments are due next week."

Students broke out into conversations, checked their phones and gathered their books and bags, existing the hall. The regular group of keeners lingered to ask some other questions and then departed, leaving her in the quiet of the room. The next lecture wasn't scheduled for a couple hours, so she closed the door and slumped on the stool by the lectern, gathering her thoughts.

The Lord is on my side; I will not fear.
The Lord is on my side; I will not fear.

Hannah closed her laptop and turned off the projector, leaving her with the gentle, muted sounds of laughter and movement from the hallway, and the whirring equipment fans. She sighed, dropping her chin to her chest, and closed her eyes, recalling the all too familiar terror from last night...

...The nightmare, fresh in her memory, flowed into her thoughts and replayed in her mind. A summer day, bright blue sky speckled with random puffs of clouds. She hiked along the well-trodden path through the woods surrounding her childhood home, filled with the buzzing and drone of insects, distant airplanes, and her own footfalls on the hard ground.

She turned a corner on the tangled trail by a granite outcrop and he appeared, a beautiful man with broad shoulders and calm smile, leaning like a cowboy against the thick trunk of an old maple.

"I know you. You are not real," she whispered.

"Hannah, don't make this so tough on yourself. Come join me." He extended a white hand toward her. "There is danger here... in these woods. I will help you through. Come."

Hannah averted her gaze. Her legs froze, and she tried screaming, but nothing came out of her mouth.

He approached, tall and stunning, with brilliant green eyes and a determined look. "Stop playing, Hannah. Come join me." He added, "I could never harm you."

She fought the urge to give in. Her feet inched forward, and the scream remained strangled in her throat.

"That's it." He reached out his long arm.

Hannah stared at his outstretched palm, the crooked fingers, then saw his face. In that instant, she glimpsed the familiar evil, felt the shame that haunted her in this twisted never-ending dream.

The burning eyes.

The sardonic grin.

Pure malevolence hissing from every pore.

He snatched her hand and pulled her close. Hannah struggled against his arms in vain, his hot breath on her neck. And still the screams would not come.

"No one will hear you, Hannah. Stop fighting. You'll

see it's futile in the end."

When her voice finally escaped, she bolted upright in her bed, gasping. The dreamscape vanished into the misty recesses of her mind as the recognizable setting of her bedroom revealed itself. Sweat dripped off her forehead, soaking through her drenched nightshirt. Hannah flicked on the light, grabbed a notebook, and scribbled as much as she could remember about him, the trail, the colour of his eyes, the endless blue sky, his breath on her neck. Instinctively, she touched her temple and brushed the memory of it away...

"Ms. King?"

How long must this continue?

"Excuse me, Ms. King?"

Hannah opened her eyes and snapped toward the voice. One of her students stood beside her, clutching a backpack draped over his shoulder.

"Sorry, I didn't know if you were asleep or something."

She collected herself and smiled. "Just caught up in a research problem. What can I help you with...?"

"Ah, I'm Brian. I could come back another time, if—"

"No, it's alright. What's up?"

The young man pushed his glasses up on his flat nose. "Well, I was thinking about your lecture, and these EM fields, and I was, like, wondering if they're always around? Like, are we affected even if we're unaware of them?"

Hannah brushed her hair back and tackled the rogue strand again. "There are man-made sources, like your phone, but also natural processes within the Earth, so I'd say yes." She cocked her head, thinking he might be an interesting fellow to share coffee with some time. "Why do you ask?"

"Oh, because I think it's pretty cool how there's this entirely invisible world around us we know so little about." He paused, as if debating whether to say more. "Well, that's all I wondered about, Ms. King."

"Please," she said, "call me Hannah. No need to be so formal."

He smiled. "Okay, Hannah. Thanks." He pivoted and shuffled out the door. Hannah finished collecting her materials and, before she turned off the lights, she hesitated.

The nightmares can't go on forever.

She drew an imaginary slipknot around the ugly dream, then tugged it tight until the memory became an infinitesimal speck that she blew into oblivion. Then she slung her messenger bag over her shoulder and disappeared into the jostle of the crowded hallway.

FIVE

"I CAN'T DO THIS ANYMORE."

The mewling scientist struck a childish, defiant pose, if that was even possible in his carry-on state of emasculation, sitting across from Cornelius Stone in a darkened booth at the back of Denver's most innocuous watering hole, O'Malley's Bar. His chin protruded forward, his eyes narrowed, and he held his hands together on the table in front of him like a school boy expecting a gold star. The man's body odour hovered over their corner like an unspoken threat.

What is it with scientists and their disregard for personal hygiene?

Stone shrugged and snorted, admired his manicured fingernails, and brushed a speck of lint from his tweed jacket.

"I'm serious," the man spat under his sour breath. "I

asked to see you tonight because I'm afraid someone will discover who I really am. A coward. An imposter." He inhaled sharply. "I want out."

The buxom server swooped by, clearing the table of their empty coffee cups. Muted voices and soft music floated up from the gathering area of the bar which enjoyed a modest degree of subdued, if desperate, patronage for this time of night.

Closing time.

No one remained but the chronic drinkers, the incessant babblers, the broken women... and the guilt-ridden, useless scientists. All the beautiful losers.

Stone said, *sotto voce*, "Jamieson, we both realize that's impossible. What you ask is out of my hands."

"Nothing's impossible."

"Says the failed psychologist who couldn't string together a coherent line of enquiry if his life depended on it." He smiled at his own wordplay, glimpsing himself in a sidebar mirror. "You seem to forget, dear Dr. Jamieson, that unlike other contracts and promises on which you give your word, our agreement *is* fully binding. It cannot be changed. Not by me, and certainly not by you. The covenant will remain closed to negotiation. As such, it behooves me to understand what we have left to discuss."

The scientist squirmed. A bead of sweat trickled down his puffy cheek. Stone wondered how a man could care so little about his appearance as to leave the house unshaven, unbathed. The mealy-mouthed idiot had a good life now and wanted to renegotiate the deal? Pah. He offended Stone on a level too intimate for words.

Jamieson's demeanour changed, and he ditched the false bravado for straight up despair. "You don't understand. I can't sleep anymore. I can't live this lie."

Stone raised an eyebrow. "You did not receive what you coveted?"

"I… at first, I got everything I dreamed of, and more." He chewed his lip.

"Then what is the problem?"

Jamieson pulled his palm over his mouth, avoiding eye contact. He lowered his voice. "I simply cannot continue living a lie, pretending to be something I'm not. When I approached you at that conference, I had no idea what I was looking for. Oh sure, the money has helped, don't get me wrong. But now…"

"Ah," Stone mused, "your guilty conscience keeps you from enjoying a good night's sleep, hm? Your wife… does she not like her new clothes? Are you not happy driving around in that fancy automobile?"

"That's not—"

Stone bristled, placed his hand on Jamieson's fleshy fingers and squeezed. "Silence. I'm speaking."

The man recoiled, eyes searching the room.

"Our business has concluded. May I suggest you and your pretty wife take a vacation? Go visit Italy. I hear it's beautiful this time of year. You'll see. Your need to feel guilty for finally getting what you deserve will soon pass, and no one's the wiser." He narrowed his gaze. "As long as you ditch the diapers and keep your end of the bargain. Otherwise…" Stone played with the edges of his napkin, hanging his sentence in the air.

Jamieson shouted, "Okay!" Then, realizing he'd raised his voice, he whispered, "Okay, I got it." He grabbed the car keys from his pocket and scooted to the edge of the banquette. Before hauling himself up, the scientist turned. "I wish I'd never met you, Stone."

Stone smiled and flicked the round-framed glasses from his face. "Oh, trust me, Dr. Jamieson. The good times have only just begun." He reached out and grabbed the man's forearm in a vise-like grip. "We're going to see a lot of each other for a very long time."

"I hope you roast in hell."

Jamieson adjusted his jacket and snatched his overcoat, then waddled off into the night.

The server floated by again. "Anything for last call?"

"If it's no bother, I'd love a glass of brandy." He smiled.

"No trouble at all. Be right back." Halfway to the bar, she turned with an odd look on her face. Stone described it as being *smitten*, not so much by his striking good looks as by the promise of possibility, the strongest intoxicant. He shook his head. The poor girl was not part of his work.

Moments later, brandy in hand, Stone pulled his leather-bound notebook from his attaché, and reviewed his list of clients and their locations. His agenda filled up quickly this time of year as the failing professors, returning from their summer barbecues and booze-fests, realized they'd grown a year older... a year closer to complete irrelevance.

He ran through the names with the tip of a pen: Margaret Spencer, Epidemiology, Hudson...William Knapp, Computer Programming, Kent...Diana Shelton, Dean of Arts and Sciences, SFU.

I have not met with Diana since the spring. Two years ago, Diana Shelton was a mousy piece of dusty toe jam occupying space in the Library Sciences program at Morgan College when she approached him at that Albany conference on the future of IM. A shitty little three-day self-congratulatory gabfest, but never mind; he'd connected with half a dozen hot prospects leading to a couple of contracts and a rare note from The Whisper herself.

A lucrative get-together with the self-important and the dreamers.

Stone made a note to book a flight to San Francisco

next week and to give Dr. Shelton a heads up about his visit. He mused over the extensive data she'd collected for him, and what that information might fetch on the black market. The latter was not so much his business. Others would take care of the marketing and distribution to global buyers. Still, as a way to keep score, he enjoyed thinking about the money passing hands so useless sacks of useless knowledge could enjoy their useless and filthy lucre. Hypocrites.

His smart phone pinged with a familiar ringtone, signifying someone new had sent him a message. After he'd opened up the screen and swiped to his email, the sender's name appeared and he pulled a curious face.

Stefan Gunar?

Stone recalled where they'd met. It was a few months ago at the annual American Geophysical Union conference in Tucson. He'd been watching this Gunar fellow circulating through the booths, picking up free swag from the commercial vendors, and avoiding chatting with others.

Looking for something he'll never find here.

Stone did his homework, researching Gunar's background, and on the last day of the conference, outside one of the stale breakout meeting rooms where some idiot student puffed up his findings on the effect of *god-knows-what* on the displacement of *who-gives-a-crap* in igneous intrusions, they met. Stefan Gunar ate a sugar donut and stared out a massive window at the distant, purple hills. The lost expression on his face suggested resignation more than anything else.

Stone struck up a mindless conversation, pitched him on the heady vision of possibility, and let the man's own mind fill in the gaps.

He handed him a business card and grinned, wondering what this failed piece of dog turd truly desired… and what he was willing to pay for it.

LUSH FERNS DRAPED FROM TIRED COPPER POTS ACROSS the open industrial ceiling of the university's Grad Lounge. Dawson carried a couple of beers over to a small round table near the massive picture windows overlooking the park-like campus. Few patrons gathered in the pub on this cool Thursday afternoon, and Matt recognized most of them: some students, some professors, and the cheery stout bartender who was rumoured to be a philosophy student once.

He placed the drinks on the table and passed one to his friend, Tony. "Here, get this into ya."

Tony thanked him and took a long pull.

"So what's new?" he bellowed in a hail-fellow-well-met voice. Tony was an extrovert's extrovert—the exact opposite of Dawson. He made friends wherever he went and always had a smile and joke for whoever would make eye contact. Dawson liked Tony, even though he was a mathematician.

"Not much. I got this assistant Wendy working in the lab now. Remember, I told you about her?"

"What's she like?"

He sipped the foam from his beer. "Nice. Smart. All business."

"Ha! Well maybe you'll finally get your thesis done."

"What are you talking about?"

Tony slapped him on the back. "My friend, you're not exactly a go-getter. You've been stuck with Gunar for how long now, still farting around with bullshit physics. You need someone in there to kick your ass and get going." He glanced about. "Living in your head, man, that's what you do. By the way," he whispered as he leaned in, "I bet you didn't even notice Claire over there checking you out, hm?"

Dawson innocently peered toward the corner of the pub and locked eyes with Claire from applied chemistry. They'd survived Chow's course in Advanced Statistics for Scientists together. She raised her glass of wine at him and he hoisted his mug, then turned back to Tony, frowning.

"I guess not."

"Like bro, what is *up*? Still grousing over Linda or something?"

"It's not that."

"Come on, so you guys dated since forever. but you gotta move on. Get out of your head, bud."

Matt smiled. Tony was probably right. He was miserable and still couldn't understand why Linda felt compelled to move on, but he was determined not to let that interfere with his research. If only he could focus on it. Yet, after many years of withering in classrooms and smelling the dust and mould of experimental labs, he struggled with accepting that this current project with Gunar was the apex of his journey.

Tony took another sip and wiped his mouth. "So tell me more about this assistant? Is she cute? Where's she from? Perhaps I should swing by and meet her."

Matt cocked his head and filled him in. "Yeah, she's wicked smart. Showed up from Boston College with a degree in experimental physics and a couple of papers to her credit already. I'm totally grateful for the extra set of hands and all, but I really want to pick your brain about something else."

"I figured. You've been incommunicado the last few days. I assumed you finally got your shit together and got down to business. Or not?" He burped under his breath.

"No, but you have to promise not to laugh, okay?"

Tony leaned back and chuckled. "What the hell, of course! Serious times, serious subject." He adopted a scowl. "Let's go!"

"All right."

Dawson recounted the story of the photograph and showed him his healing fingertips from that initial encounter. Residual scars from the blisters remained, but the colour had changed to normal and they didn't sting anymore. He also mentioned the second time when nothing happened, and the third when the eddies of hands and apparitions appeared again. Then, after he spoke with his mother, she became distant and aloof.

"So what you're telling me is…what exactly?" Tony asked, his brow furrowed as he cradled his beer. "If I can summarize, you get this strange, old photo, pick it up, the thing starts swirling around like a whirlpool or something, and the edges burn your fingers. The next morning, nothing. Except a few days later, it happens again. Is that about it?"

Dawson nodded. "I don't know what to make of it. It's sitting in a box with some other junk from Mum's basement. Maybe I was hallucinating, but I sure didn't imagine the blisters. They hurt like hell."

Tony pursed his lips for a moment, and lowered his voice. "Okay, well this sounds completely weird and I'm afraid I got nothing to say about it."

"Nothing? I thought that massive brain of yours could figure out anything. You know, bore me with second order differential equations and mechanisms and such."

"Normally I'd agree with you, but in this case, given I can't break out laughing, I got nothing."

"Not even a remote, off the wall idea? Come on, Tony, this thing's eating me up."

"Yeah, you're a freakin' dog with a bone when you set your mind on a project. I wish I had that persistence." He drained the rest of his beer. "If we assume something mysterious really happened, then there's got to be a logical explanation, right?"

"It *did* happen. I'm not making these things up." Dawson said, wiggling his fingers in the air.

"Sure, sure, I get it. But maybe there's an alternative explanation. Perhaps your fingers touched the stove when you were making supper and you didn't notice till after. That can happen. Like a sunburn, you know? Anyway, I gotta run. I've got a student coming to see me about his tutorial grade, blah blah blah."

"Yeah, well thanks anyway," Dawson said.

Tony stood and gathered his laptop. "Maybe take another look at the photo and call me if you start spontaneously combusting. That would be cool. Be sure to record it, because I'd pay a nickel to see that." He held a serious face together for a moment, then smiled mischievously. "Sorry, Mattie, it's too much! Haunted photographs, yeah right. You're pulling one on me, I just know it, but I'm telling you, my friend, you can't trick a trickster." He touched the side of his nose, took a couple of steps, then turned, pointing at him. "Wait a sec, there is something."

"Come on, Tony, enough with the sarcasm."

"No, man, I'm serious. Perhaps you experienced a psychic phenomenon."

"Tony, please…"

"Hear me out. There's a team of researchers in the Psych department investigating different crap like this. Seems all weird and out there on the fringe of legitimate science, but one of them might have an explanation for what you saw."

Dawson grinned like a polite man being served a meal he couldn't eat. "Great. Pseudo-science at its finest."

"Just a thought. Anyway, I gotta book."

Tony darted toward the main door, stopped to chat briefly with a couple of profs, then left. Matt peered over to Claire's table, but she'd already disappeared too.

Considering what Tony said about Gunar's research project and his own future, he figured if he was going to solve the mystery, he'd have to do it on his own. But what would be the harm in chatting with the Psych folks? He knew no one in that department and rarely set foot in their building for fear of losing his science cred, but this might be the right time to check out what the fringers did.

SIX

Near Rosetown, Saskatchewan
1911

GARETH SUTHERLAND STEPPED BACK A FEW PACES AND mopped his forehead with a tired handkerchief. The new sod house, for all intents and purposes, was finally completed. A blazing mid-afternoon prairie sun pierced the deep blue sky, casting a blinding glare on him and his family. Only a whisper of a breeze tumbled across the surrounding fields of barley and oats, acres he and the family planted in the spring. They'd lived in the covered wagon for the most part since early May, but now, with the roof complete, they could move into the house and make it their home.

His three daughters hopped and skipped around him. They ranged in age from two-and-a-half to eight, and all helped in their own way to build the homestead. His wife, Kathleen, jumped down from her work in the wagon and cleaned her hands on her apron, beaming with pride at the finished building.

"The photographer from town is a-comin', Gareth. I seen the dust bloom."

Gareth squinted against the harsh rays of the sun and shaded his eyes. In the distance, along the trail from Rosetown, a dusty plume kicked up against the sky.

"Ah, so he is. Quick now, girls, stay out of the mud. Go wash yourselves up an' all and get ready. Becky, mind the young'un."

The trio giggled and ran to the well to draw water. Kathleen joined Gareth at his side. He slid his arm around her waist and gave a delicate squeeze and a wink.

"We have ourselves a home, love."

"Aye, that we do," she said. "And it won't be long before it's filled with the family's laughter." She faced him, staring up with large blue eyes. "How's the furniture coming?"

"Oh, always lots to do, but the cabinet's almost finished. Come, I'll show ya."

They sauntered over to the makeshift workshop built from packing crates and a lean-to for protection against the western wind, where he uncovered the progress of his carpentry. A few minutes later, the photographer arrived. He dismounted and pulled his equipment out of two heavy saddle bags and set up facing the home.

Kathleen rounded up the children and ushered them in front. She and Gareth stood behind the kids.

"Smarten up now. This'll be an important occasion. Sunday best manners an' all." He nodded at Becky, the oldest. "Keep the young'uns in line, now."

"Yes, Pa."

It took close to twenty minutes before the last shots were taken and the photographer announced, "All done, Mr. Sutherland. My boy will deliver them within a week."

He began tearing down his equipment, folding the rickety tripod and lashing it to his horse. "Congratulations. That's a fine-looking home." With a tip of his hat, he mounted, clicked the mare into action, and cantered back to the trail.

Six days later, a boy on a handsome white steed arrived at the homestead. Kathleen offered him a cup of cool water from the well, and Gareth filled his canteens.

"Can you stay for a bite to eat?" Kathleen asked. Becky giggled behind her, smiling sheepishly at the teenaged rider.

"Afraid I can't, ma'am. I gots a few more deliveries to make before I'm done for the day. But thank you for the offer. Right kind."

He handed the flat package to Gareth, smiled at Becky, and rode away to the west.

Inside the sod house, the air was hot and thick. He'd punched temporary windows in three of the walls to allow for circulation while he finished building the proper frames. Kathleen pulled the covers back and a cooling breeze wafted through.

The middle child, Rachel, bounced around singing while Gareth untied the package and placed the photographs on their eating table. He spread them out one by one in a checkerboard pattern: the sod house, some closeups of the family, even a picture of Megs the dog which sent the children into whirls of laughter.

Then Rachel picked up the photograph, the one with the solitary farmhouse, that the photographer took as a test for whatever magic he needed for the equipment to function. But as she held it to her face, she immediately shrieked and dropped it, as if bitten by a snake, pulling her hands back and staring wide-eyed at her mother.

"There, there, Rach, let me see," Kathleen said. "Becky, fetch me a cloth and some fresh water, girl."

Becky bolted to the well and returned a moment later with a soaked cloth. Kathleen wiped Rachel's fingers and glanced at Gareth. "Better look at this."

Gareth approached them and sighed. "Show me, Rachel, let's have a look-see."

Rachel, fighting back her sobs, held out her trembling palms. Gareth took them in his large, calloused paws and caught his breath. He stared at his wife and clenched his jaw.

"Oh, we've seen this before," he whispered.

"What is it, Pa?" young Rachel said between gasps.

Gareth frowned. "She's the one, Kathleen. The story what I told ya."

Kathleen hugged the child, massaging her hands with the damp cloth. "We canna let anyone know about this, Gareth. Mark what your mother said."

He remembered all too well. Growing up the youngest of the brothers in Nova Scotia, he saw details that weren't there, visions that appeared only to him. When he was a youngster, other kids were frightened that Lucifer had grabbed his soul. The townsfolk in Lawrencetown murmured. And Gareth continued seeing things whenever he touched certain objects: a blue cup, a ragged blanket passed down from his family.

"Aye, Kathleen. No one must know about this." He towered over his other children, who stood dumbfounded and dead still. "Do ye hear me an' all. Not a word."

SEVEN

HANNAH SLUMPED AT HER DESK IN THE DEPARTMENT'S
windowless graduate student ghetto, reading the same
paragraph over and over in the *International Journal of
Neuroscience*, without grasping what the author argued.
Yes, the article on weak complex magnetic fields and their
influence on the limbic system proved challenging, but
what prevented her from moving forward was nothing
more complicated than lack of sleep.

She released an audible groan and slammed her laptop
closed.

"Hey, Hannah, everything okay over there?" Peter's
nasal voice rose over the baffles. He sat two desks down,
closer to the door, and ate the nastiest microwave dishes
for lunch. She could almost hear his acne oozing.

"Yeah, sure. Just need to take a break from this
reading for a bit."

Peter stood and inched his way toward her, carrying a
half-filled coffee cup from the cafeteria. He'd tucked a

pencil behind his ear. "Roger that," he said. "Nothing a good night's sleep or a long weekend can't fix, though, am I right?"

"That's right," she sighed, stretching her arms over her head. Then a thought occurred to her. She pushed back her chair and rose. "You're a clever sort, Peter. You've been around here a while, right?"

"10-4. Not quite a lifer, but I came here for my research about 4 years ago. Why?"

Hannah parsed her words with care. "You ever ask yourself why you study these fringe phenomena? I mean, we get ridiculed about our work all the time, and I'm just wondering... well, do you ever tire of it? Think of switching into a more mainstream program?"

Peter sipped his coffee and cocked his head. "Once in a while, I guess, but I'm cool with the program. I couldn't care less what others believe, so perhaps I'm not the best one to ask."

Curious George swung the office door open and sauntered in with a backpack over his shoulder, Starbucks in his hand, and nodding to whatever metal tune screamed in his earphones.

"He might," Peter smiled. They turned to George until he pulled his ear buds out.

"Yo, what's up, brainiacs?"

"Not much," Hannah said, her mood lightening. "Radioboy and I were just chatting about fringe science."

"Oh, yeah?" He dumped his pack on his desk near the coat rack. "Isn't that what we do here?"

"Uh-huh. Say, you ever get sick of others making fun of your work?"

"What do you mean?"

She shoved her hands into her back pockets and rocked on her heels. "Some of my students chatter in the hallways. I hear things like *Twilight Zone* and *X Files*.

They've recently given me a nickname too."

"No way," Peter laughed.

"Unfortunately, way."

Curious George scratched his stubbled chin. "Can't be worse than mine."

"Tell all, Hannah!"

"Okay, relax. So the other day I'm gathering my stuff and overhear a bunch of students refer to me as *Spoonbender*."

They roared with laughter. George almost lost his coffee through his nose, adding to the moment.

"Spoonbender...I like that," Peter concluded, and wandered back to his desk.

After George sleeved his face, he said, "That reminds me, Hannah. I bumped into this Masters student from Physics at the coffee stand. She arrived a week ago. Anyway, we're chatting away there and when I told her about my research, she mentioned the guy she worked with just experienced major league weirdness with a photograph. It sounded like something up your alley."

A flush of excitement flooded Hannah's mind. "What was it, George?"

"Oh, seeing images shifting. I don't really remember 'cause I was putting sugar in my cup at the time and I can't multi-task." He paused a moment. "But she said it burned his fingers. Got real blisters and everything."

"Really? She saw them?" She sidled up closer.

"That's what she told me. Apparently he had bandages on his fingertips."

"What area of physics? Did she say who this guy is? And what about—"

George smiled. "Hang on, Hannah, we didn't get that into it. Her name's Wendy something. Shorter than you with long black hair. Japanese origin, I'd guess." He checked the time on his phone. "Anyway, I gotta run to class." He grabbed a notebook and headed out, stopping at the door. "Subatomic physics? Particle physics? Something like that."

"Thanks George, I'll look into it."

He whirled away, and his pack caught an empty drinking glass perched on top of one of the carrels. It tumbled to the floor, smashing into a hundred fragments. Hannah sighed, then grabbed the community broom and dustpan to help clean it up. As she stooped to gather the piled pieces, she caught her reflection in each shard and shivered.

Hannah returned to her desk and pulled her laptop open with renewed vigor. The physicists could be the cruelest of the bunch with their insistence on pursuing "real" science, but if what this student said was true, she'd risk the ridicule if it meant bringing her closer to her own truth.

My help comes from the Lord, who made heaven and earth. Thank you, Lord, thank you.

The Western website was a fount of information, but a challenge to navigate. Hannah stumbled into various rabbit holes around the research areas being investigated in the Physics department, and few of them held any obvious clues as to the phenomena that piqued her curiosity.

She looked under "Graduate Students" for Wendy, but no one appeared with that name. Probably too soon if she just started. Then she surfed to the areas of interest and pulled up the lines of enquiry in experimental condensed matter physics which, she read, dealt with surfaces and their composition. While some of them held possibilities (photonic materials, pattern formation), she found nothing obvious. Same with theoretical matter. Space physics? Not likely. Medical physics? Definite possibility, but again, no direct connection presented itself. She didn't recognize any of the faculty names, and knew no one in that building.

This could take longer than I thought.

Curious George suggested subatomic physics was the area that this Wendy person mentioned, so rather than focus on the research topics, she began exploring the equipment and there were definite pieces of gear worth noting. She found some that other researchers in the neuroscience journals had used: atomic force microscopy, variable-energy positron beam for defect analysis…focussed ion beam/scanning electron microscope… nanoscale patterning capability. No shortage of potential, but nothing led her to a name or where this gear resided.

An hour flew by and she needed to prepare for her weekly meeting with her thesis advisor, so she clicked on the staff link and found the department's admin assistant. *If she's anything like ours, she'd know everyone and everything going on there.*

Out of nowhere, the image of the man from her nightmares appeared in her mind. Hannah stopped typing and closed her eyes. Her throat constricted, and she shuddered.

Heal me, O Lord, and I will be healed; save me and I will be saved, for you are the one I praise.

She placed the creep in an imaginary circle and squeezed it smaller, repeating the prayer again and again until the dread dissipated. Then, inhaling deeply, Hannah crafted a simple email to the admin person, introduced herself, and asked about a new Masters student named Wendy and how she might contact her. Then she fired it off, grabbed her research folder and notebook and raced down the hall toward her supervisor's cubby hole, repeating to herself *Heal me, O Lord, and I will be healed…*

STEFAN GUNAR'S OFFICE OCCUPIED A DUSTY SPACE HALF-

WAY down the eastern corridor with the rest of the oddball professors and lecturers. Only the most political, longest-tenured profs had the prime real estate on the western side.

Dawson slunk around the corner, acknowledging the other students and researchers milling about, and waited outside Gunar's closed door. A sliver of light from the window at the end of the hall cut a sharp geometrical design across the tiled floor. He used to dream about someday being here, or at least at a similar institution, where he could teach and conduct his own research, follow his own interests, and not have to perform the soul-crushing bidding of a once up-and-coming physicist who, for whatever reason, failed to reach his potential.

Tony often warned, "Don't be like Gunar". He took that to mean closed-minded, but perhaps what his friend meant was not to be a scientist in decline, living on yesterday's possibility of breakthroughs until age overtakes you. He'd ask him about that.

In the meantime, he ached to get this photo business off his mind and he wagered the best way to do that—and to refocus on Gunar's project—was to spend a couple weeks researching the phenomenon, investigating it, talking to his mother more, and coming up with an explanation that he could live with, even if it meant delving into the fringes of ineffectual scientific methodology.

He knocked on the door at precisely 10:15.

"Enter."

Matt pushed it open. Gunar sat at his desk poring over a stack of ubiquitous papers. Cardboard boxes were amassed against the far window wall, choking out much of the light that struggled to pinch into the confined space. Piles of old journals and hardcover theses from previous students occupied several rows of a bookshelf. A half-eaten donut teetered on the edge of Gunar's desk.

"Have a seat, Mr. Dawson."

Matt squeezed into the wooden chair at the side of the room, avoiding the sticky arms, and opened his laptop.

"We've got 15 minutes."

He cleared his throat. "Okay, well here's the update. The project's moving along okay, sir. Unfortunately, we're still running the analyses on those new trials so I don't have—"

Gunar looked up sharply over his reading glasses. His dark eyes narrowed. "No results yet?" He tossed his pen on the stack of papers. "What have you and Ms. Sakamoto been doing? I was under the impression you'd be finished with those runs this week and moving to the next phase."

"Well, that's just it, sir. We haven't found any significant anomalies, or any sign of underlying patterns in these tests. The findings you'd talked about, at least, the *anticipated* findings, simply refuse to reveal themselves."

"I see." Gunar peered down at his desk. "So what can I help you with this morning if there's nothing to report?"

Dawson pulled the photograph from a folder in his backpack. "Something else has come up that I need to discuss with you. It's unrelated to the project."

"Go on."

"Strangest thing happened a week ago or so. I was going through a box of desk jam my mum sent me and in it was this photo." He lifted the folder to show him.

"I see. Well, what about it? An old farmhouse, eh? What could that possibly have to do with our project?"

"That's the point, sir. It doesn't have anything to do with our work, but I observed something really bizarre and I'd like to pursue it as a new line of enquiry."

Gunar leaned on his elbows. Dark circles appeared under his eyes and the lines on his face were more pronounced than usual. He hadn't shaved either.

"Tell me again, how does this innocuous photograph relate to our project?"

"Well sir, it doesn't, but I want to take a couple of weeks to investigate it and the phenomenon I experienced. Perhaps there's a connection. It's a real mental puzzler, and keeps pulling me away from the work."

"Let me see it."

Dawson passed the material to him without touching the photo itself. Gunar held it in his hands, studied it a moment, and said, "What could possibly be so interesting here that you want time off from the project." He dropped it and the folder on a pile of papers. "You realize we're already behind schedule by almost a month. I specifically brought Wendy Sakamoto in to kick start the results, run more trials and move this work forward. Excusing you from it now would be completely irresponsible, don't you think?"

Dawson brushed some rogue locks of hair from his eyes. "Sir, it would only be a couple weeks, maybe shorter if I can track down what happened and put an end to the mystery."

"And what exactly is this riddle, Mr. Dawson? I see nothing here."

Dawson briefly recounted his two paranormal run-ins with the photo, showed him his healing fingertips, and asked again for time away to pursue his observations.

Gunar remained stone-faced behind his desk until Dawson finished. "Well. That's quite a story. My first thought is you're seeing things. A hallucination. Nothing more. So unless you've got more compelling evidence to give me, I want you back in the lab working on my trials with Sakamoto and getting some results that I can publish."

Dawson sighed heavily, took the folder from Gunar

and returned it to his backpack. "There is one more thing, sir."

"I'm waiting."

"Well, the second time I experienced the phenomenon, the time with the swirling hands and apparitions, I felt an overwhelming sense of... er..."

"Come on, Mr. Dawson, spit it out. We all have work to do."

He looked into Gunar's cold eyes and blurted, "A sense of danger, sir. Like somehow this photo, or the energy connected with it, was warning me. I don't know what to make of it, but it's in my head and I really must solve the mystery before I can focus on the project."

An unexpected look crossed Gunar's face, as if his mind extracted valuable hidden nuggets from Dawson's words and turned them around. He said, "Although this is intriguing, Mr. Dawson, and as you say, it is a curiosity, it seems to lean more toward paranormal pseudoscience rather than to the serious physics we do here. And, if I may remind you, the reason why you're here. I don't pay you good money out of my research grant to spend time in the airy-fairy realm of ESP or other psychic phenomena. So, to answer your question about taking time off to investigate what may have happened to you, it's a hard no." He lowered his head and picked up one of the papers on his desk.

Dawson's jaw dropped. At the back of his mind, he understood selling his supervisor on his wish was a long shot, but he still hoped that with Wendy on board, the project would continue and right itself.

"Is there anything else?" Gunar continued making notes on his paper without looking up.

"I guess not, sir." He wedged out of the confining chair, picked his backpack up from the floor and headed to the door.

"I suppose," Gunar added, "that what you do on your own time is your own business."

"Sir?"

He peered up at him. "If, after giving me your 60 hours per week on the project, you still have time and energy to pursue this, er, investigation, then I won't stop you. But," he lowered his voice, "I need the trials completed, and those data analyzed. Remember, I've made a commitment to publish those results—even if they're interim findings—in the coming weeks, and I won't allow anything to impede that. Understand?"

Dawson chewed his lips. "Yes, I get it."

"Excellent. Good day, then."

STONE FOUND CASEY'S BAR ON A SIDE STREET IN downtown London half an hour before his scheduled meeting with the professor. He picked a booth in a quiet corner and ordered a herbal tea and a glass of ice water. Once settled, he opened his notebook and reviewed the file he'd put together on Dr. Stefan Gunar, the middling physicist from Western.

The photo he'd downloaded from the university website was dated. It showed a young, vibrant, clean cut man with a thin face, thick eyebrows, and arrogant air. Not exactly the same fellow he'd befriended at the conference in Tucson, but definitely the same self-confidence bordering on aloofness.

I'll fix that up for him.

His accomplishments as a graduate student were remarkable. Several published papers in the areas of quantum optical networking, two of which were consistently cited by others in the literature. However, now as a man in his forties, he hadn't lived up to his potential. A smattering of B grade letters and half-baked publications in tertiary journals was all Stone needed to peg him as yet another failed, falling star. The perfect candidate for the services he offered.

He closed the notebook, squeezing the profile details inside, and slid it off to his right. As he sipped his tea and considered an opening offer, the man himself appeared like an apparition by his table.

"Excuse me, Cornelius Stone?" He reached out his hand. "I'm Stefan Gunar from Western. We met in Tucson at the—"

"Yes, yes, hello again, my dear Dr. Gunar. Please have a seat."

They exchanged small talk about the weather, Stone's flight into Canada, and then touched on the state of subatomic particle research in North America.

When the conversation took a natural pause, Stone cocked his head and asked with a lilt, "So. The once great Dr. Gunar."

Gunar's eyes widened.

"There, there, no need for alarm. If you have something I can use, then I'll change your unfortunate reputation and restore you to proper glory."

Gunar scowled and wrung his hands. "Frankly, Mr. Stone, I'm not even sure what we're talking about here. I thought, based on our chat on the phone, that you could help me stickhandle my findings through some A list journals... that you were personal friends with several referees in my field and could, you know, grease the machinery as they say."

Stone smiled coldly. "Yes, I can do all that, but only if you have something of value for me. You see," he mused in a self-effacing manner, "the help I provide is not typical. And it's definitely not for everyone."

"So what are we talking about here?" Gunar's scowl morphed into an expression of scrutiny. He repeatedly wrung his hands, stopping only to sip the water that the server had left with him.

A small group of boisterous office workers entered the pub, laughing and shouting as they headed to the bar. Stone watched them with a constrained look on his face. "Dr. Gunar…"

"Please, call me Stefan."

"Very well, Stefan. What we share is the making of a profitable partnership where we both get something we covet. You, for example, wish more than anything to regain your academic swagger, yes?"

Gunar paused, then nodded.

"You want to feel the thrill of being on top of your game, respected among your peers, contributing to the body of knowledge in your chosen field."

Gunar stopped wringing his hands. "Yes."

"And I? Well, I want something, too. I'm what you might call a data merchant. My employer, The Sodality, has existed for a very long time, and we're interested in helping societies around the world find the truth in their trade. You like truth, don't you, Stefan?"

Gunar sneered. "Truth. For what it's worth, I see it as just another ridiculous word, like love or honesty… loyalty."

"Just another word," Stone mused. "That makes it challenging, but I understand your frustration. You feel that if truth is relative, anyone can make any truth claim they wish. So ultimately, it means nothing."

"Yes, I suppose."

Stone watched his client, studying him in the dim light and airy shadows of the upscale bar. *He may have something we can use.* He leaned forward, noting Gunar's hands.

"Stefan, I like you. But if you keep wringing your hands like that, they're going to fall off. Listen, do you want a drink? Maybe settle your nerves a bit. People inform me I can sometimes be a tad… off-putting, at least when they first meet me. What do you say?"

Gunar dropped his hands to his side and shook his head. "I'd like to hear more about your proposal."

"Ah yes, down to business then." Stone flipped open his notebook and removed a yellow sheet of paper with a few words and glyphs written on it he knew Gunar would never understand. After a quick glance, he spoke. "I am familiar with your research area into subatomic coding. You basically are doing the grunt work that Stanford spearheaded several years ago, yes?"

"Well, I wouldn't categorize it as grunt work. If you mean it's important, methodical science designed to infill our knowledge gaps, then yes, that's what we do. My grant is predicated on this necessary research."

"Of course, I meant no disrespect. But tell me, Stefan, the last paper of actual value you published was how many years ago now? I believe it was 1998 when you were cleaning up your PhD thesis. How old were you then?"

"Twenty-four."

"So… twenty-some years ago." He narrowed his gaze. "What happened?"

Gunar grew silent and stared off into the distance. Stone knew everything about his career: how he came to be a rising star in quantum physics circles… how he and a handful of others from that time at Hamburg were crushing it in the scientific community, pursued to speak at international conferences, talk about their findings, yes, but also methodology and philosophy. And now behold the poor man. A shadow of his former self.

Gunar looked up. "I guess it is about 20 years, sure. Dammit, Stone, I don't know what happened. By the time I turned 30, my peers from the Hamburg Lab were tenured or working on rocket propulsion systems or what have you."

"Well, regardless. I'm here to help you regain that path and get your career on track. The only problem, though, is your research itself."

"Wh-what about it?"

Stone played with his teacup. "I've reviewed it thoroughly, and unless you've got something I'm unaware of, I'm afraid there may not be much I can do. Please, Doctor, tell me about your research, your findings, and then I'll have a better idea about whether I can use you."

Gunar leaned in and recounted the various projects he ran under his grant. He emphasized the important, if not pedestrian aspect of the work, how he and his students contributed to the body of knowledge in quantum encoding. Stone studied the man's face, his hands while he spoke. He took no notes, only sipped his tea. When Gunar leaned back, he asked, "Is that everything?"

"Yes, that's everything worth talking about."

Stone pursed his lips, reflecting on what he'd heard. "I'm sorry, Professor, there's nothing here I can use."

"But you said—"

"I said I'd love to help you out, but only if I think there's value in what you're doing. My stock in trade is information. Specifically, ground-breaking, innovative, game-changing, leading edge information. What you've described here is consistent with my knowledge of your work, and I simply don't believe any buyers would be interested in quantum encoding the way you do it. That game's ten years old now. Stanford is—

Gunar flinched.

"Well, never mind."

He sank into the seat, working his hands again. And with every word that Stone uttered, the colour faded a little more from Gunar's face.

Stone narrowed his eyes. "But let's keep going. What else are you looking into? Tell me about something you're working on outside the realm of your public research areas."

"That's all there is, I'm afraid," Gunar whispered. "What a waste."

"How about those ideas you play with off the side of your desk; the ones you doodle about on napkins and such... the ones that nobody would take seriously."

Gunar shook his head. "I have nothing."

Stone sighed and checked his watch. "Then our conversation is over. I'm sorry, Stefan, but—"

"Wait, there may be something else." Gunar's eyes lit up.

"Continue."

"I have this one student, Matt Dawson, who talked about a photographic phenomenon in which he sensed hidden messages, saw apparitions and such."

Stone straightened his back, senses on full alert, eyeing Gunar carefully. "Are you talking about psychometry? Sensing psychic impressions?"

"Not sure what it's called. He wanted time off his project to investigate. Claimed this photo burned his fingertips or something. I don't know, it all sounded airy-fairy to me, like *The Amazing Kreskin*, remember?" He fell silent a moment. "Would that interest you and your buyers? If we uncovered the mechanism behind this?"

Stone let the failed physicist stew in his own juices as he considered his answer. Indeed, psychic phenomena were part of all cultural backgrounds. Most of which had been revealed through improved scientific knowledge or outed as shams. Regardless, mysteries remained, especially those of a spiritual nature, and if Gunar's student had an ability to not only see psychic impressions, but sense messages contained within them, well, that may be worth the risk.

Moreover, there was something familiar about a

psychometric photograph and that name *Dawson*... an echo from his early days in The Sodality... something near and dear to The Whisper's heart.

He stretched his neck and grabbed the pen and notebook. "Tell me more about this student and his work."

EIGHT

LATER THAT EVENING, DAWSON PACED THROUGH HIS apartment like a particle in an excited quantum state. The small lamp on the dining table he used as a desk cast an eerie, yellow flush across the gloom.

He ran his fingers through his tangled hair and sighed. It wasn't bad enough that Gunar had crapped all over his request for some time off so he could investigate this phenomenon, but Wendy too asked a ton of questions when he returned to the lab. All good queries, to be sure, but his head and his heart were not in the work and the last thing he needed was to get swept up in the deluge.

Dawson needed time away.

Well, Gunar allowed him to review whatever he wanted as long as he made the project his priority. He seemed overly antsy about publishing some results, and that's the way of academia, but he hadn't pushed him like this before. Dawson suspected his overseers were pressuring him. A tough problem to have, he mused sarcastically.

His phone pinged from the other room and at first he wished it would go away. It chimed again, so he picked it up, scrolled through the various messages and found the last one. Wendy asked how he was doing, thanked him for his help in the lab, wondered if he was progressing on the photo. Dawson swiped the phone to erase it when another text caught his eye.

Wendy: *someone's looking for you. Message me back for deets.*

Dawson: *Hey, thanks for checking in. What's up?*

In a moment, Wendy responded.

Wendy: *Got an email from admin in Neurosciences on behalf of another student. Asked about me, but really wanted to find out who you are.*

Dawson: *Sounds intriguing. What's it about?*

Wendy: *No idea. Here's a name. Hannah King. She's a grad student there.*

Dawson: *don't know her... any ideas?*

Wendy: *I had a chat with a guy at coffee earlier and told him about you and the photo. He's in psych or something. Maybe it's related?*

Matt looked around the dim apartment. Traffic noise rose from the street and a couple of horn blasts took his attention away from Wendy for a moment. He didn't like that she blabbed about his experience to strangers.

Dawson: *Thanks. Gotta run. Chat soon.*

He dropped the phone in his pocket and grabbed a beer from the kitchen. Hannah King... the name rang no bells, but he wasn't surprised. Not only were there thousands of grad students at Western, but he also kept pretty much to his own little circle in the Physics department. Tony and a few others from math and chemistry were the exceptions.

He took a long pull from the bottle and sat at the

dining room table. After opening his laptop and logging on to the campus intranet, he clicked to the Neuroscience grad student site and found Hannah King. A PhD candidate, fields of interest include psychometric encoding, EM field influences on psychic interpretations… basically what Gunar said: pseudo-science.

But he was drawn to her profile photo, the friendly smile and soft features, her shoulder-length brown hair running in twists and curls. Yet, something else about her struck him. A haunting in the eyes muting their brilliance. The listed phone number was for the Neuroscience switchboard. He didn't want to call anyway; not a fan of talking on the phone.

So he tabbed over to social media and dropped her name in a bunch of different apps. Nothing appeared on Instagram or Snapchat. She had an account on LinkedIn, but it contained little information either.

He pulled his phone out and texted Wendy again.

Dawson: *sorry Wen, did Hannah King leave an email or number?*

Momentarily, Wendy responded and passed along Hannah's UWO email address. He thanked her and set the phone aside.

Hannah did have an account on Facebook with a few photos, but no recent postings. In fact, she'd hardly posted anything at all.

Another mystery.

Her research page on the Western website outlined her areas of interest. Dawson had no understanding of these, but several journals published this subject—journals of international reputation—so there must be some scientific basis underpinning it.

Could she help me learn about this phenomenon? Is that why she reached out?

He tabbed to his mail browser and typed in her

address. Added a subject line: *reaching out*, then crafted a quick email. Before sending it, however, he walked over to his coffee table and opened up his research folder—the one containing the photograph that Gunar looked at earlier in the day. Strange, perhaps, that when the professor touched it, nothing happened.

The temptation was tremendous. Dawson slipped it out and held it in his hands. The photo reacted like any other he'd seen. Inert. Lifeless. A simple black-and-white image.

Perhaps it only reacts under certain conditions? He took it with him to the dining table and placed it beside his laptop, then opened up a new folder: *Photo Phenomenon*. After taking a picture of it and loading the copy into the digital folder, he created a new document for his notes and quickly typed in the two dates when the object had glowed.

The observations would be qualitative, something he preferred not to admit, but in the absence of any physical mechanism to explain what happened, his experiences would have to do. He noted the size, the texture, the unusual shadow on the right side of the farmhouse. He recounted what he'd been doing and thinking about both occurrences, the time of day, meals and breaks, and his state of mind.

Nothing may come of this, but he knew enough from his courses in the history of science that the ancient philosophers recorded everything. He would too.

Time flew by and, when he finally finished, he'd written a dozen pages outlining everything he remembered about how his interaction with the photograph led to the mysterious blistering and the overwhelming sense of dread... the same feeling he experienced as a child when he got lost in the woods near his home, only for a moment before a friend found him, but long enough to frighten him to his core.

Dawson checked the time on the computer: 11:43 pm. Sleep crept over him, blanketing him in a fog. He yawned and, as he closed the various apps and files, he read the drafted message to Hannah King. He considered adding to it and even attaching his notes and a copy of the JPG file. Another minute passed, and he changed his mind.

Too early.

He deleted the email and shut the laptop lid.

THE NEXT DAY, POLLY WINDELL, THE DEPARTMENT'S administrative assistant, talked to her contemporary in Physics and came up with a handful of information related to Wendy Sakamoto, her office and email, and the project she worked on with Matthew Dawson, PhD student in Subatomic Encoding (*whatever that is*). So this Dawson fellow was the guy who apparently experienced a psychometric event by interacting with a photograph. Most intriguing. Hannah wrote the details on a piece of paper in the main office, grabbed her backpack, and wandered across campus to the Physics Building.

The sun shone brilliantly that afternoon, and even though the temperatures remained late summer—short-sleeves other than mornings and evenings—a hush of the coming fall floated through the air. Hannah loved this season from early September to the end of October. The vibrant, changing colours, muted sunlight, and the cerulean blue of the sky comforted her and energized her soul. So with a peaceful heart and cheery disposition, she pulled open the thick wooden doors to the building and climbed the staircase to the second floor in search of Matthew's lab.

It took her a moment to get oriented through the nooks and crannies of the department, but shortly stood in front of a blue steel, windowless door with a notice announcing "Subatomic Particle Physics—Authorized Persons Only" pasted on it. An additional sign showed Matthew Dawson's and Wendy's names scratched in marker, and Dr. Stefan Gunar's contact information for enquiries.

She tucked her hair behind her ears, inhaled deeply, and knocked. A few seconds passed, and no response came. Hannah glanced up and down the hallway, self-consciously conspicuous, like an imposter. *Perhaps they're in class?* She tapped again, waited, then turned away.

Hannah had taken a few steps down the corridor when a door opened and a friendly voice asked, "Hey, are you looking for someone?"

She recognized Matthew Dawson from his photo on the grad student site, but what she didn't count on was how tall the young man stood. His hair was longer and bushier than his photo, too, bordering on dishevelled. The mad scientist look.

"Yes, are you Matthew Dawson?"

"Live and in colour," he replied, holding the door open with his foot. "And you can call me Matt. Only my mother calls me Matthew." He grinned.

"I'm Hannah King, and I believe one of my colleagues ran into Wendy yesterday and mentioned something about a strange photo. Is it true?"

His smile disappeared, and he stepped forward, now propping the door with an outstretched arm. "Well, that depends. Actually," he confessed, "I heard you were looking for me. Wendy texted me."

Hannah stuffed her hands in her jeans pockets and approached him. In a lowered voice, she added, "If you have time, I'd like to know more about it. I'm a grad student in Neurosciences, and my research focuses on psychometric events. I'm curious about what you experienced. George, my colleague, said something about blisters?"

Matt scrutinized her in a friendly, firm way. "Well, I don't know. I thought I saw some weird stuff, but I doubt it's much." He turned back toward the lab. "We could grab a coffee sometime, if you like." He nodded as if the conversation had ended.

Hannah quickly added, "I don't want to take you away from your research, but how about right now, if you're not too busy?"

Matt hesitated.

"It's a beautiful day. You wanna grab a coffee and find a bench outside?"

"Just a sec." He stepped into the lab, said a few words she didn't make out, then reappeared and let the door swing shut. "Sure, I can spare a half hour." He muted his phone and stuffed it in his pocket.

They walked in silence out of the building, made small talk while they grabbed a Starbucks from the coffee stand outside the science food court, then found a picnic table under one of the massive oak trees that dotted the campus.

Matt pulled the lid off his cup. "So... Hannah King from Neurosciences," he said, tapping the drops off the lid. "What exactly is the research you do?"

Hannah told him about her focus and investigation into electromagnetic fields, how they influence organic matter, and how they may reveal underlying physical psychometric mechanisms. She discussed the other topics her peers studied, and ended by saying she hoped to graduate in another year, but lacked an interesting application for the theoretical model she'd constructed.

"I see." Matt gazed across the campus.

"What's your project about?"

He chuckled. "Nothing like yours, I'd say. Dr. Gunar has me working on experiments involving the coding of subatomic matter. Came out of Stanford a few years back—the foundation of it, anyway—and there's a genuine need to infill some gaps in the knowledge." He pulled an apologetic face. "Yeah, so that's what I'm doing."

Hannah caught that familiar look, one she'd seen in her own department. She understood academic disappointment, like when she first attended university expecting exchanges of Big Ideas and poetry, only to find out that myths played a massive role in the university narrative, too. "Is it my imagination, or are you less than thrilled with your work?"

Matt smiled and took a sip. "Put it this way, what I'm doing isn't exactly what I had in mind when I switched into physics years ago."

"You weren't always in this field?"

"No, I started out in geology. I wanted to be a geologist like my dad. As a kid, I dragged my mum out into the bush, banging on rocks along the country roads for my sample bag. Yeah, that was the dream."

"So what made you switch?"

Matt watched a group of students walking in the distance. "It was the second year of my undergrad. I got curious about the processes giving rise to ore deposits and tectonics and such. I wanted to understand the Earth, and then discovered I liked how math could be used to describe it. That, and a good physics prof in first year, pulled me away."

Hannah brushed the hair from her cheek. "Subatomic particle encoding is a long way from hammering on outcrops in the bush, isn't it?" She immediately regretted saying the words, concerned he may take it judgementally, but Matt simply smiled. Sunlight danced in his eyes.

"Perhaps," he said, "but I'm sure you didn't track me down to talk about my academic journey."

"No, you're right." She paused. "Let me tell you more about my research and then I'd love to hear about what you experienced with this photograph of yours."

Hannah recounted her investigations into psychic phenomena, particularly how weak EM waves are used to manipulate brain functions. "You may scoff, because most people do, but some experiments performed in the 70s and 80s, especially with the CIA, might sound familiar."

"You mean like telepathic abilities? Spoon bending?"

Now it was her turn to smile as she recalled the nickname her students gave her. "Well, sure, there's the spoon bending thing but a lot of that has been debunked. No," she said, "I'm talking about the apparent psychic powers that some people had where they read documents from miles away... saw an individual's thoughts."

"Like a mentalist."

"Mm, not quite." She shifted her weight and played with her cup. "Have you heard of the God Particle?"

"Bose-Higgs? Sure, what about it?"

"Well, what may surprise you is that psychometric researchers were investigating the so-called God Particle long before Bose-Higgs came along. Matter of fact, if what I suspect you experienced is true, you may have come across it yourself."

"What are you talking about?"

She sipped her drink. "Just because we don't understand something doesn't mean it isn't real. Your focus appears to be on the physical nature of matter. Mine is too, except mine is harder to measure because we don't fully understand the mechanisms behind it. Some argue the physics and math haven't caught up yet." She looked into his striking eyes. "Doesn't mean it's not legit, though."

Matt grew silent, so Hannah changed the subject to his vision. "Tell me about this photo of yours."

"Okay, as long as you don't think I've gone nuts," he chuckled.

"I don't consider any honest experience crazy."

Matt rolled up his sleeves and told her about the photo, the blisters, and then the second time it happened when he sensed a warning.

Hannah knew the psychometric ability to see or sense things by touching objects was well-documented, and more common than many people realized. But what intrigued her most was this threat he felt after his second encounter. That's what she wanted to investigate. "Matt, I'm serious. I'd like to work with you on this investigation and find out more about your background and this photograph. Is there any chance I can see it?"

Matt frowned. "Yeah, but I'm overloaded with work for Dr. Gunar and already behind. Even with Wendy helping in the lab, there's only so much I can do after hours. I just can't afford to spend time on this until, well, possibly after my thesis is completed."

"Oh," she said, unable to hide her disappointment, "is there nothing we can do? Like, don't you want to get to the truth?"

Matt finished his coffee and put the cup back down on the picnic table. "I'd love to know, but I—I can't. I'm afraid I just don't have the time, and besides, I really do need to focus on my research." With that, he stood. "It sure was nice meeting you, Hannah King. Perhaps we can hook up again sometime and see what we're up to?"

Hannah remained sitting, gathering her thoughts and wishing she could find the right words to make him reconsider. She pulled her legs out from under the table. "Before you go, Matt, if you're sincerely interested in what happened to you, I urge you to google the science of noetics and psychometry. You might be surprised by what you discover."

"Noetics," he said and shrugged. "Maybe someday."

He wandered back to the Physics building, and Hannah arrived at the only conclusion she could reach: Matt Dawson wasn't ready for the truth. Especially not hers.

NINE

"SO WHAT'S SHE LIKE?"

Dawson immediately checked the equipment when he returned to the lab. Wendy still monitored the trial runs by the scanners, smiling mischievously.

"Hannah King? Yeah, well, I know little about the so-called science she studies, but she seems nice enough. Really wanted to help with the photo phenomenon." He leaned against the desk.

"And?"

"And what?"

Wendy removed her glasses and approached him. "Is she going to?"

"Nah," he said, staring across the gloomy lab. "Listen, I realize I've been preoccupied with this photo business, and I appreciate how much work you've been doing—much of it stuff that I should have done—but I'm dropping the mystery picture and focussing on Gunar's experiment here."

"So… no more photo?"

"Correct. Gunar's right: we're already falling behind schedule, and I've been dragging my feet on this for a long time now… since well before you arrived."

The primary data-processing computer pinged and Wendy returned to the equipment, checked a run, and pressed some keys on the keyboard. "That works for me. To be honest, I'm like flying solo and I'd appreciate more guidance."

"Sorry about that. It'll change from here on out, promise."

For the next few minutes they circulated through the experimental runs, checking data and ensuring the equipment continued working as designed. Dawson reviewed a handful of random interim results that scrolled up on the main monitor, searching out any patterns, any hints of coherence in the raw findings. None appeared.

"Still, though," Wendy piped up as if the conversation hadn't ended. "I saw her in the doorway. Seems cute."

"Wendy," Dawson sighed, "It's not like that. She wanted to help investigate the phenomenon. That's all. I told her I couldn't because of the project and my need to focus on that first."

"Ah."

A frantic knock sounded on the lab door and he opened it. Joan, the Department Head's administrative assistant, stood outside, red-faced and flustered.

"Joan, what's up? You okay?"

"Yes, just a little out of breath. Matt, listen, your mum's been calling the office trying to contact you. She'd like you to call straight away… says it's super urgent."

He'd forgotten to turn his phone back on after meeting Hannah.

"Okay, thanks. Did she say what it was about?"

"No, just that you needed to call." Then, touching his arm, she added, "Your mother sounded distressed... out of sorts. I think you'd better phone soon."

"Of course, thanks Joan."

She turned and waddled down the hallway.

Wendy said, "I'll leave and give you some privacy."

"No." He grabbed his backpack. "I'll go so you can hold the fort."

He wound up sitting at the same picnic table where a short while ago he'd met with Hannah. Dawson punched his mum's speed dial into the phone and plugged his earphones in. She answered on the third ring.

"Oh, Matthew, thank God. I've been worried sick."

"Hang on, slow down. What's going on? You all right?"

Her voice quivered, and a dish rattled in the background. "Oh yes, I think so... well, I don't know. Mattie, I must share this. Please don't hate me."

Dawson raised his voice. "Mum, don't be ridiculous. Come on, what's going on."

She sniffed in the background. Dawson softened his tone. "You know you can tell me anything."

"Oh, please, please forgive me, I should have said something earlier. But... but I just couldn't."

Dawson paced around the table, dread racing through his veins. "Mum?"

"Well, you remember about two weeks ago when you first talked about it?"

"About what?"

"That photograph. That awful photograph. I had no idea that you—" She caught her breath. "Remember the box with Dad's old junk?"

"Sure."

"Well, I didn't realize it was in with all that stuff. The thing is, oh forgive me Matt, I should have said something when you raised it." She burst into tears.

"Mum, what's up with the photo?" *She's not even listening to me.*

"It's just that... if I'd known the photo was in that box, I would never have sent it."

"This is the same one that gave me blisters? But why wouldn't you tell me?"

"Son, you don't get it. Your dad saw the photograph, too. He experienced the same visions you did—the exact same thing. Burned fingers, fiery edges, all kinds of other weird stuff with ghosts. Even had this ominous feeling that something dreadful was about to happen. It was all so strange, and he didn't explain it very well. He told me when he got home from the bush one weekend. I had no idea back then—how could I? But here's the thing."

She inhaled sharply with stuttering breaths.

"A few days after Grey told me about the photo, about his experience... a few days later, he—he had a heart attack."

Dawson's throat seized, and his jaw dropped.

"Matt," she whispered, "that's when your father died."

TEN

GREY DAWSON DIED SHORTLY AFTER MATT'S TENTH birthday in the fall of 2007, and, despite his questions and fear over losing his dad, no one talked much after. He assumed Beth and others in the family were silent because they were in pain. Now he wasn't sure.

"Good God, Mum, are you saying this stupid farmhouse had something to do with Dad's death? I thought his death was from natural causes, like working too hard in the bush, or maybe heart disease from smoking. Isn't that what you said?"

Beth whimpered in the background on the phone. "Please don't get mad."

"I'm not angry," Dawson replied, voice dripping with frustration, "but what happened? I've got to know, Mum."

She blew her nose again and in a more relaxed tone, said, "Dad came home from a big survey in Kirkland Lake. He was down for a couple nights, then returned to the project. Anyway, that's when he told me about that photo. Apparently he found it tucked inside some old maps."

Dawson inhaled deeply and sat down at the picnic table. He leaned forward, holding his head. "Did he know where it came from?"

"Oh yes. The photo belonged to his mother, and it's a picture of the first house some ancestor built in Saskatchewan. He'd seen it before, but the minute he got home, he couldn't wait to tell me about... his vision."

"So what happened?"

"I remember little, Matt. He wasn't making sense, and his mental health suffered from being in the bush most of the summer. To be honest, I'd forgotten all about it until you brought it up a couple weeks ago."

"Yes, when I got those blisters. Why didn't you say something then?"

"I wanted to," she offered, "but I was totally overwhelmed with these awful emotions flooding back. And you have enough worries, Matt. God, I'm so sorry."

Dawson exhaled and gazed around the campus. The afternoon sun continued shining brilliantly like a star, casting soothing shadows across the pathways and lawns.

He realized what he had to do.

"Listen, I'm coming home this weekend and we can talk more then. I need to understand everything about the history of the photo and what Dad was doing... all of it."

"Okay," she whispered. "It'll be wonderful to see you. I miss you so much."

"Yeah, you too, Mum. Anyway, I gotta get back to the lab. Talk soon."

He ended the call and slumped at the table. The additional information about his father's death and the strange photograph troubled him more than he let on to his mother. *How am I going to deal with this and keep Gunar off my butt at the same time?* But a way forward suddenly appeared. The more he considered it, the crazier it sounded, but he also realized how helpful it could be. He had to talk to Wendy and tell her his plans.

WENDY BIT HER LIP. SHE STOOD IN THE LAB NEAR HER desk, arms folded across her chest, staring at the grey-tiled floor. "What should I say, Matt?"

"Sorry to dump the trials on you, but I need to get home and make sure my mother's okay."

Disappointment overwhelmed her concern. "And the photo? What are you planning to do about that?"

Dawson clenched his jaw. "There's only one thing I can do. I've gotta sort this out. Look, I'm scared about this cryptic warning I... *felt*... and if my dad experienced the same effects, maybe there are other clues in his gear. My mum's basement is full of old junk: bags of specimens and folders and all his survey equipment. I could be grasping at straws, but I want to review it all and see."

"And you'll be back on Monday? Like, I hate to pressure you, but Dr. Gunar's been asking about results and I'm still learning how to manipulate the software. I mean, I can run the trials—that's no problem—but the analysis is, well..." Her words dangled in the stale air. "Oh, he was in here a few minutes ago. Says he must speak with you but wouldn't tell me why."

"Probably wants to chinwag about interim findings. But look, I won't abandon you to do all this yourself. I'll be back Monday and then we'll tackle the number crunching together. Promise."

She smiled thinly and gazed at the monitor. "What about asking that Hannah person to help you now? She might provide some insights."

Dawson mulled over the suggestion. Wendy was right: he needed her assistance. Especially if this phenomenon occurred in the realm of fringe science. He wouldn't know where to start. "But I told her I didn't have time. Guess I blew that."

"Call her, Matt. Explain the new info about your dad. If my instincts are correct, she'll still want to help."

"Let me think about it. In the meantime, we've got trials to run."

The next few hours flashed by. After completing a long session, Dawson offered to get coffee and stepped out of the lab. On his way to the stand, he pulled up Hannah's coordinates and sent a text:

Dawson: Time for a quick chat? New facts have come up.

Once he'd collected the drinks, his phone pinged.

Hannah: I do. Got time for a quick chat now?

He called immediately, and she picked up and blurted, "So what happened?"

Dawson explained the call with his mother. Hannah remained silent while he reviewed their conversation. When he paused, she asked, "How can I help?"

He juggled the cups as he opened the door to the Physics building. "What are you doing this weekend?"

DAWSON ARRIVED AT THE SLEEPY, FERN-FILLED GRAD Lounge a few minutes before he and Hannah agreed to meet there early that evening. He hadn't contacted Gunar yet and wanted privacy for that and to assuage the nagging hope that his supervisor had changed his mind about time off. A weekend off the academic clock would help, but a couple weeks invested strictly in the phenomenon would be ideal. He punched the professor's cell number and waited.

Gunar answered after a few rings. "Ah, Mr. Dawson, I was looking for you earlier."

"Yes," he said, while picking out a quiet table by a scenic window, "Wendy mentioned you'd been by.

What's up, sir?"

"I was chatting with an… acquaintance last night about our project, and he seemed confident that once the preliminary results are ready, he'd be able to stickhandle the referees and get them published."

"Excellent news!"

"Yes, well, there's more." Gunar paused and cleared his throat. "I really wanted to suss out your, ah, paranormal experience with that photograph. This fellow was extremely interested in what happened. He asked for more information, but unfortunately, I don't have any other than what you told me."

Dawson found a table with a couple chairs around it and sat. Gunar sounded different. Anxiety and suspicion rose from the pit of his stomach.

"Oh, well sir, there's not much else, and besides, I've put that away. Your project—my thesis—is way more important than chasing minor mysteries like this. I'll look at it some other time, after we're done and I've graduated."

"Ah," Gunar replied. He signalled disappointment.

"That is what you told me, right, sir? To focus on the actual experiment, finish the trials and get the analysis completed as quickly as possible?"

"Yes, yes, that's true and I haven't changed my mind on that. The scheduling of the project is critically important for maintaining my grant conditions and meeting the needs of various journals. It's just that…"

"What, sir?"

Hannah entered the Lounge, halted, and looked around. He waved her over.

"Well, I was hoping you had more information on that photograph." He paused, inviting Dawson to respond, but he refused to offer anything. "Listen, I'm setting up a time for us to meet again soon and I'd like all the details.

Everything you say that happened. If you've got any notes, please send them my way."

"Ah, yeah, sure. Are you thinking next week?"

"Yes, Monday or Tuesday latest."

"Okay, I await the meeting request. Is there anything else?"

"No, I suppose not. Better get back to work." He ended the call.

Hannah approached the table and threw her backpack on one of the empty chairs. "Well, this is a surprise. I thought you weren't interested in my help."

Dawson muttered something lame and then asked if she wanted a drink.

"Oh, no thanks. I'm seeing a student shortly."

She studied his face, making him uncomfortable with the attention, and for a moment, he wondered if he'd made the right decision about asking her on a trip to his hometown. "So Hannah, are you sure about coming with me this weekend? It's a big ask and I totally understand if you'd rather not. Like, it's my mum's place. There's a spare bedroom, and she'll make you feel really welcome, but don't worry about it if you're busy."

"Are you kidding," she said, "this is fascinating. I tried not to get way excited when you told me about your vision, but I've never come this close to someone who's actually experienced a true psychic phenomenon. So yeah, I'm down." She played with a band on her pinky finger. "When do you want to go?"

Dawson leaned forward and spoke in a low voice. "What about tomorrow afternoon? It'll take about seven hours to get there, so if we leave by three we'll miss a lot of traffic through Toronto."

"Exactly where are we going?"

"A little town in northern Ontario called Haileybury."

"Never heard of it, but sure, I can be ready at three." She twirled the ring. "You have a car, or…"

He chuckled. "Yeah, it's not much… a 2002 Toyota Yaris with a billion miles on it, bald tires and a rattle that just won't quit. I hit a raccoon last summer, and the old car's been on the limp ever since."

Hannah smiled and waved a strand of hair from her face. "Alright. Let's meet outside the Physics building. Three o'clock."

Dawson nodded, and they finalized the plan. They'd start with his dad's survey files in his mother's basement Saturday morning and go from there. Then, as Hannah collected her bag, he said, "I made some notes about what happened that I can send you."

"Awesome, shoot them to me right away. The more I learn, the better prepared I'll be."

"Sounds good." Dawson paused as she stood. "Hannah? I'm really sorry about earlier. I kinda dismissed your research and offer to help because, well…"

She touched his forearm, smiled, then turned and strolled out of the Lounge.

Dawson ordered a draft from the bar, leaned back, and stared across the campus contemplating the possible intersection between the photo and his father's death.

ELEVEN

"DR. GUNAR, THANK YOU FOR RETURNING MY CALL IN such a timely fashion. I like it when my clients are organized."

Stone leaned back at his temporary desk in Richmond, Virginia, and stared absentmindedly out the massive picture window overlooking the bustling city below.

"Yes, well, your voicemail said it was urgent, so here I am. Did you get a copy of the signed contract I sent earlier?"

"Indeed," he responded, checking under his fingernails, "and I'm happy to report that everything is in order. You provide me with your research papers, and I ensure they're published in renowned journals."

"Perfect, yes, that's what we agreed to. Is there anything else? I'm really quite pressed for time, as I'm teaching in a few minutes."

Stone smiled, raising his eyebrows. "You are pressed

for time. *You* are pressed for time. My Dear Dr. Gunar, I forgive you because you are new to The Sodality and we have not worked together in the past, but—"

"What do you mean, *you forgive me*?"

Stone rolled his eyes. "See, that's another example of a misunderstanding. Make no mistake, Professor, now that we have a signed agreement, I call the shots. When I require something from you, your job is to get to it. Remember our discussion the other night?"

Silence permeated the line. Stone heard papers shuffling and Gunar's ragged breathing. "Very well, whatever. Are we done here?"

"Tsk, such hostility for no reason. No, Dr. Gunar, we are not done yet. There's this minor matter of your student Matt Dawson and his fringe project... the one with the photograph."

"Look," Gunar snapped, "I tried getting more information from him and we're meeting on Monday to discuss it. I'll let you know what I find out. Satisfied, Mr. Stone?"

"Oh, hardly. No, you see, it takes more effort to fulfill my needs than you may be accustomed to. As it happens, my superior is particularly keen on this project, based on what you shared with me, and when she demonstrates an interest in something shiny like Dawson's little fiery photo, an observation such as this, well, you understand she will not be deterred."

"No, I don't follow what you're saying," Gunar chuffed. "I said I'm meeting with the student on Monday and I'll apprise you then."

Stone clicked his tongue and sighed. "Very well, I shall have to wait, but I'll expect your report by Monday evening at the latest. FYI, it could be worth a lot to you." He rearranged some papers on his desk. "And Doctor, don't disappoint me."

"I'll get what you're looking for, but I still figure it's all that namby-pamby pseudoscience crap the astrologers like to fuss about. Not genuine science at all. You realize what that can do to my reputation if you reveal I'm part of it."

The poor professor could be excused for his cultural ignorance this time. "The validity of the science is not for you to judge, Dr. Gunar. There's so much more happening that you have no clue about. So much, I wish I could show you. Some other time, perhaps?"

"I have to go, but promise me this: you won't pursue Matt Dawson or talk to him about this."

"You depend on him."

Gunar hesitated. "I need him to finish his work, provide me with the results so I can get them to you for publishing. That's all."

Stone snorted. "Well, since my superior has raised the profile of your research, I'm afraid what happens is out of my control. However, it is not in my best interest to see any harm come to you or your bootlick student. So, we'll talk more on Monday."

"Yes," he sighed, "Monday."

Stone ended the call and picked up one of the papers in front of him. He ran his fingertips over it and punched in a new number on an encrypted line.

A man answered. "Florian Lamont speaking."

"Are you ready?"

"I am. Where would you like me to begin?"

Stone rose and faced the window. "Get on the next flight to London, Ontario. I want you to target Matthew Dawson. He's a graduate student at Western in the Physics department. I'll send you all the information I have on the young man from the university database."

"Shall I detain him, sir?"

"Patience, Mr. Lamont. At this point, it's unclear

how much he knows. Let's not put it to the test. I simply want you to watch him closely and report to me daily. I'm most interested in anything he does related to a family photograph. It's not part of his ongoing thesis project, so be prepared."

He gave the man additional instructions and ended the call.

Stone caught the glint of a paperclip that had fallen beside his desk. He retrieved it and put it back in place. Then, he hit one last number before calling it a day.

"Yes?" The woman's soft, hollow voice was barely audible.

"It's me... Stone."

"And?"

"We're in play with the Dawson file."

"Excellent. Keep me apprised."

THE ODDBALL GRAD STUDENT WITH THE CURLY HAIR AND handsome smile pulled up to the Physics Building in a beat up Toyota and leapt out of the car. Hannah checked the time on her phone: 3:20. She rose from the concrete stoop and stretched, relieved that Matt Dawson had actually appeared, assuaging her deep fear that he'd abandoned her.

Or stood her up like other jerks had in the past.

She adjusted her plaid shirt, trotted down the steps and threw her overnight bag into the trunk of the Yaris, and a few minutes later, they eased out of the campus onto Western Road, heading south toward Highway 401. Matt apologized for being a bit late. He had to check several items in the lab with Wendy that Gunar was on him about. She wondered why he hadn't texted her, then shook her head at her own insecurity.

Do not fear, for I am with you; do not be dismayed, for I am your God. I will strengthen you and help you; I will uphold you with my righteous right hand.

Because they were late getting on the road, they ran into Friday afternoon traffic through Toronto, which slowed them down to a crawl. During that drive, they discussed their work, the campus, what they liked to do when not teaching or working on their theses. Dawson told some funny stories about his first year physics labs and fried equipment and such. Hannah laughed more than she had in months, and for a couple of hours, the thought of her crippling nightmares seemed a lifetime away.

They stopped in Barrie for a quick bite at a greasy burger stand and got back on the road, heading north along Highway 11. She'd never been to northern Ontario, so this leg of the trip was a new experience. Soon, the sun dipped over the trees and hills to the west, pulling with it the last breaths of the day, and plunging the world into darkness.

Hannah's mood shifted with the night. Strange things happened in the dark. The mind easily expanded like an iris, drawing matter in from every little hidden memory corner, and turning once-pleasant thoughts into nightmares. She forced herself to focus on other subjects— Matt's psychometric experience, for example. He was no fool, even if he couldn't yet appreciate her chosen field. If nothing else, she'd be able to help him understand what happened, even if it turned out to be a dead end. And this journey with him was at once exciting and frightening as hell. As the night folded around them, she debated about asking him to stop at the next town so she could grab a Greyhound back home, then realized the attraction of a shared adventure with this confident young man.

Besides, what would you be doing at home, Hannah? Spending another lonely Friday evening listening to 60s music and watching reruns of Gilligan's Island with the lights on?

After several minutes of silence, Hannah thought they'd avoided his experience too long. She said, "Matt, I've gone through the notes you sent."

"Oh, yeah?"

"Uh-huh, and I studied the photograph. I hope you brought the actual one with you."

He shoulder-checked as a car passed him on the left. "Yep, got it in my backpack. I guess the pic I took of it wasn't great, eh?"

"It's not so much that," Hannah said. "The phone shot is a simulacrum, not the real thing, so it wouldn't contain any psychic impressions if, in fact, that's what you experienced."

The thickening darkness squeezed her, causing her toxic anxiety to rise through her entire body. She pushed herself into the lumpy seat and gripped the seatbelt that crossed her chest.

Thank God for the dashboard lights.

Dawson drummed his fingers on the steering wheel. "Whatcha think about it? I mean, the notes I made. Helpful?"

"Oh yes, I wish others would do this. You discussed lots of details about what you saw and felt when you held the photo and sensed its message, and—"

"Wait, what? You think there's a hidden message in there?"

Hannah adjusted her grip on the seatbelt, staring straight ahead. "Matt, these events don't happen randomly, so yeah. The big question is: if you put on your researcher's cap for a sec, what's the secret in the photo, how did it get there and, most importantly, how are *you* able to read it?"

Dawson chuckled. "What, like I've got some kind of alien superpower? Yoda or... or..."

Hannah smiled and felt her body relax. "You don't

watch a lot of movies, do you?"

"Nah," he said, "I haven't even seen Star Wars."

"That explains the Yoda bit."

"Hm?"

"Never mind," she snorted. "You're suddenly capable of seeing visions in a material object that can't be explained by your scientific knowledge. Now you're wondering what else the universe holds that can't be seen or measured. But there has always been more unfolding behind the scenes of our lives than we've been led to believe." She turned to him, watched him driving, and clenched her jaw.

"We'll chat about this tomorrow when we go through your dad's notes." *Is this a good time to tell him?*

The nightmare would visit her again, she knew, and sleeping in an unfamiliar bed in a stranger's house would compound the apprehension that gripped her. But she had told no one about the ugly dreams, except her mother when she was young. That hadn't gone well. Still, something about Matt drew her close and if she planned to help him with his investigation, she didn't want this darkness getting in between them.

"Hey, you okay?" Dawson asked, glancing over.

"Oh, sure, Matt, sorry. I was just thinking about things." She was confident he couldn't see her face in the dark, which brought her no small measure of relief. Hannah gazed ahead, locking on taillights.

Do not be afraid, she prayed, you will not be put to shame.

"Listen, can I ask you a few questions about this psychometry thing?"

"Of course," she said, thankful for a distraction and delay. "What's on your mind?"

"Well," he began, "you mentioned it's the study of psychic impressions… reading them and such. So this may be what's behind my photograph, right?"

"Could be," she replied, struggling to keep her breath and focus steady. "It's a type of extrasensory perception—ESP—where you get historical insights about someone else by touching objects that the other person handled."

"Okay, but I heard about guys who can read things over great distances, like finding lost kids in cornfields, or locating other missing persons. Is that true?"

Hannah inhaled sharply. "Not quite, but I know what you're talking about. There's anecdotal and circumstantial evidence for some ESPers having that ability, yes, but it's not as simple as determining a physical mechanism that's repeatable on a consistent basis. Not like what you and Wendy are doing in the lab, for example, where you constantly test theory with observation."

"Right. We pose an argument, or build on one in our case, arrange an experiment to investigate it, run it and see what happens. The foundation of what we do is repeatability. If someone finds an interesting result, researchers in other labs should be able to reproduce those findings by following the exact procedures." He thought a moment, and asked, "Wait, your own research focuses on reading impressions from objects, correct?"

"Uh-huh."

"Have you ever held an object and felt something from it? Like, is there a standard process for doing that?"

Hannah bit her lip and stared at the glove compartment in front of her as she wrestled with her mounting anxiety. *This moment will pass. This moment will pass.* "Depends who you follow."

"What do you mean?"

"Different schools of thought on that one."

"Well, I gotta be honest. I'm not convinced your science is real. Maybe I've seen too many of those tricksters on TV, you know, mediums and the like."

Dawson kept his eyes on the road.

"Oh, yeah, the clouds without rain."

"But I'm keeping an open mind because, er," he glanced at her, "I'm a bit messed up over my father's death and how this photo business might be related." He turned back to the road and ran his hand through his hair. "Truth is, Hannah, I'm scared."

And this is as good a time as any.

Hannah inhaled deeply. "If we're being honest, Matt, I have to tell you something." She waited for a response that never came. "See, I have these, er, these… "

"What, Hannah? What's going on? Should I pull over, or—"

"No, keep driving. Please." She swallowed hard as panic set in. "I've never told anyone about this except my mum and a couple others years ago, and I hope you don't get all creeped out, especially if I'm staying in your mother's house and we're gonna work together and—"

"Hey," he said in a soft voice, "slow down. You can tell me later if that's easier."

"No, I want this out of my head now." She told him about the recurring nightmare of the demon in the woods, the one she'd experienced since she was a young girl, and that no matter what actions she took, she found no peace. "The creeper tries luring me somewhere, keeps taunting me to follow. They are super intense and so real. Inevitably I wake up in a panic and spend the rest of the night recovering." She dared not look at him. "I've even given myself to God hoping he'll protect me. That's helped, but the evil remains and comes out to play almost every night. Every night, Matt. Every night."

For the next twenty minutes, neither said a word. Hannah listened to the rhythm of the road, the rush of tires. They stopped on the opposite side of North Bay for a break and got some snacks separately.

Hannah regretted opening up to him and vowed not to mention her fears ever again. Her mother was right: no one wanted to hear this. She ached for this night to pass quickly so she could numb herself with work on his dad's notes.

"HEY, WE ALL GET NIGHTMARES," HE FINALLY SAID, breaking the awkward tension, "but it sounds like yours are what I get on steroids, so let me know if there's anything I can do to help."

They pulled up in front of his mother's—and his childhood—home on the shores of Lake Temiskaming. A couple of lights burned inside. The Yaris sputtered as Dawson shut off the engine, and before exiting the car, Hannah said, "Sorry I brought it up, Matt. That wasn't fair, and you don't need to be concerned. I've lived with this for a long time." She smiled and opened the door. "Just wanted you to know if you hear things in the night."

After retrieving their bags from the trunk, they walked over the flagstones toward the front step. Dawson's mother, wearing a housecoat and slippers, opened it and greeted them.

"Matt!" she cried, hugging him closely. "So good to see you again." Turning, she beamed. "And you must be Hannah. Welcome. I'm Beth."

Hannah nodded, clutching her bag in front of her with both hands.

They entered the modest bungalow. Beth showed Hannah her room, then they sat together in the dimly lit kitchen.

"Are you hungry at all? Can I fix you something?"

"Not for me, Mum."

"I'm good, Mrs. Dawson. We ate a little while ago."

Beth almost seemed disappointed. "Well, there's plenty here, so don't be shy and help yourself."

"Thanks."

"And call me Beth." She furrowed her brow as she turned to her son. "Now tell me, Matt, you're sure you're okay? I got so worried."

"Yeah, fine. No different, except I'm bound and determined to figure out the mystery of this thing. Hannah knows more about the phenomenon than I do, so we're gonna start tomorrow with Dad's notes and whatever else he stored in the basement. See if anything down there could help."

Beth nodded. "Okay, well, he stored a bunch of stuff in the workshop. He's got old journals, prospecting equipment, rock and mineral specimens and remember all those testing machines he tinkered with? It'll take you a while."

Hannah found her voice and said, "We have all weekend, if it's okay with you, Beth, to search for clues."

"What exactly are you looking for?" Beth asked, cocking her head.

Dawson glanced at Hannah with a confused look. He didn't know the answer, figuring that if anything looked odd, they'd recognize it. But Hannah had different ideas.

"We need to do a couple of things. First, is to review the notes that Matt's dad wrote about the photo, if any, or another event he experienced."

"Wait," Beth asked, "You mean there could have been other... *happenings*?"

"It's possible. With psychic impressions, there's often a dance between several objects and the individual. Yes, the photograph is important, and we'll study that closely, but there may be other items your husband read psychometrically, and he might have written about those."

"I don't remember him talking about any others..." Beth stared absently at a spot on the kitchen table. "What can I do to help?"

Dawson yawned and covered his mouth.

"Oh, what am I thinking? It's late and you two must be exhausted from all that driving. You should get some rest."

"Sounds good, Mum." Dawson rubbed his eyes.

A hint of trepidation crossed Hannah's face. She brushed her palm against her thigh.

"You want to hit the sack, Hannah?" he asked.

"Sure, that's a fine idea." She paused. "I'll read for a while in bed first." She pushed her chair back, and it scraped across the tiled floor. "See you all in the morning." Hannah shuffled out of the kitchen and down the hallway toward the bedrooms.

When her door closed, Beth whispered, "She's very nice, Matt. How long have you known her again?"

"Only a couple days."

"Hm," she said, brushing the tabletop with her fingers. "Seems you've known each other a lot longer." She hesitated. "Do you ever wonder about—"

Dawson cleared his throat. "Let's not go there, Ma. Linda and I have been apart for six months, and that's not changing."

"Oh," she answered, "I didn't mean to pry or anything. Linda was sweet."

"I know."

"But I suppose since she's working and living in a different city, well…"

He pursed his lip. He and Linda had drifted apart and eventually broke up, and he'd pretty much gotten over the split. The last time they'd seen each other was in London when she'd visited for a weekend. Linda taught at a public school near Cornwall and pushed him to hurry up and finish, and join her in the so-called real world.

But there was nothing in that town for him other than her. No research facilities, very few science jobs. And something held him back from wanting to complete his degree requirements early. Besides Gunar's boring project, he was in no rush to finish up only to be unemployed.

"That's okay, Mum. Listen, I'm heading off to bed." He stood and kissed her on top of her head. "Thanks for making Hannah feel so comfortable. She's, er…"

Beth craned her neck and looked up. "Yes, son?"

"Never mind. Not for me to say. I think she's grateful you made her feel welcome, is all."

"Of course." A line of wrinkles crossed her forehead. "Well, see you in the morning."

"Good night."

Dawson padded down the hall toward his old room. After preparing for bed, he sat at the desk for a few minutes. It seemed so tiny now. He traced his fingers along the top. This relic had been through the wars. A pet at some point had chewed on one of the corners. Pencil marks and tiny gouges made from a sharp instrument, probably a compass, scarred the top. A tangle of lines where a pen had left the page and trailed off on the wooden surface. Random cigarette burns.

He pulled the folder out of his backpack and opened it, staring at the lonesome farmhouse.

But he dared not touch it.

And his thoughts shifted to Hannah across the hall in the spare room. They'd shared a lot in the seven-hour drive from London, and he liked the vibe between them. *Maybe it's time to consider a relationship again?* Not necessarily with Hannah—far too soon to even approach that—but perhaps his mindset was opening up to the idea. Although he remained unsure about what career lay ahead of him in physics—and this farmhouse had thrown a wrench into his research plans without question—he'd soon be ready to meet someone.

Dawson closed the folder, shutting away the photo

and notes, and turned out the bedroom light. As he climbed into bed, a thin glow spilled in from the hallway under the door. He wondered if his mother left a lamp on. He rose to check.

The flicker came from Hannah's room across the hall. Dawson thought nothing of it since she'd mentioned reading for a while, but as he turned back, he heard a stifled whimper. He froze and listened again, but it had stopped. Then, as he prepared to return to bed, it came again.

There was no mistaking it. In the magical hush of midnight, the muffled sound of Hannah softly crying filled the empty spaces. Dawson considered knocking on the door to make sure she was okay. He raised his hand, but without understanding why, he whirled away, crept back to his own room, and clicked the door shut.

TWELVE

Lawrencetown, Nova Scotia
May, 1896

MAGGIE SUTHERLAND WIPED HER HANDS ON A FRAYED
*apron and stood on the porch overlooking the north
section of the farmstead. Gareth, the youngest, slowly
made his way to the barns, driving the oxen. He had such
a deft touch. His father would have been so proud.*

*The family settled near Lawrencetown in the
Annapolis Valley when she was a child. Her mother
Bonnie, still living, met Ash Robertson on the Telegraph
sailing from Scotland in 1843. From what she remembered
of her father's story (he died in a farming accident shortly
after Gareth's birth), he'd left Edinburgh during the
Disruption in search of a new life in Glasgow, but
suddenly changed plans and traveled here. After arriving in
Halifax, it wasn't long before they fell in love, and a few
months later, journeyed deep into the valley, married in*

Bridgetown, moved west through the lowland to farm, and establish a household.

Her two eldest sons and their families farmed up the road, close enough to keep an eye on the daily operations here, and Gareth had been her godsend, working the orchards and the vegetable crops, making sure the animals were cared for.

Now he and the new wife prepared to leave the valley, but unlike his brothers, they weren't staying here. Instead, they decided on the territories in western Canada. He'd already secured 160 acres from the local government office by paying ten dollars, and had gathered his belongings.

Although she'd miss him—for he was her favourite—he had to find his own way. Besides, the farther away from the old country, the better. The safer. For he was the sole child of her brood showing signs of the gift.

Gareth marched up to the porch. His sweat-laden face glistened, and his blue shirt took on a grey hue from working the dusty fields. He washed up in the tub designed for that purpose, grabbed a towel and dried his hands.

"So," Maggie began, "two days away. And you're still excited to leave?"

The youngest pushed his hat back on his head and smiled. "You know, Ma, it ain't like that at all. I'll surely miss you and the brothers. But you'll be fine here. Jason'll work the land. The wives'll take care of anything else around the house." He kissed her on the cheek.

"Oh, I appreciate that," she smiled, "and I'm sorely happy for you and Kathleen, but a mother has a right to be sad sometimes and feel sorry for herself." She burst out laughing, masking an overwhelming grief like a lover's secret affair.

Gareth dragged the rocker from the porch corner into

the shade and sat. Maggie did the same. She stared across the valley at the hazy dark green mountains to the north. "I hear the winters be mighty cold, and longer than here."

"Aye, that's what they say."

She began rocking. "Well, and you'll be taking the railway and all."

"Ma," he said, with an exasperated look, "we've been through this. Kathleen and I leave the day after tomorrow. We'll stay in Toronto for a spell before catching the train to Winnipeg. Then, find and drive a team to Saskatchewan."

"It seems so far," she whispered.

"Yes. But it's where our hearts are pulling. We'll arrive sufficiently early to build a temporary home, and we have enough provisions to survive the winter. There's hunting too, Ma, and other homesteaders. We're gonna be fine."

Maggie continued staring at a speck of black on the horizon. The bundled blackness of a lonely figure walking out along the crooked path. A man. Her eyesight wasn't quite as good as before. She didn't wish to admit the years were creeping up.

"I know, Gareth." She paused rocking and stood, catching her youngest by surprise. "Wait here. I'll return in a moment."

She ducked into the simple home that now moaned in solitude. In her living room, she walked to the bookshelf beside the piano and found a wooden box tucked away behind some books. She brought it back to the porch.

"What is that?" Gareth asked, leaning on his knees.

Maggie placed the container on her lap and smiled. "This is a wee keepsake, just for you and, someday, for a child."

The lid was stuck. Between time and humidity, the

wood had warped and now required prying. Maggie yanked sharply, and it finally sprung wide, revealing a tiny piece of material about the size of a towel that had seen better days.

"This," she said, holding it up by the corners, "is a wee blanket cut from a cloth that belonged to your Grampa Ash's kin in Scotland." She turned it around. There was no pattern, save for a slight discolouration along one side. The cloth may have once been white, or perhaps a cream colour, and the band appeared to be blue or turquoise—impossible to tell. What she held now had tilted toward monochromatic, various shades of time and age, and ragged at the edges.

Gareth's brow furrowed. "I don't understand. Is this here some family heirloom, Ma?"

"Aye, son. This piece, well, I cut this from a larger cloth when I left home and married." She dropped the blanket to her lap and peered across the land again. The black speck had moved closer. Or did she imagine that? Hard to tell now.

She turned to Gareth. "I want you to have this. Maybe Kathleen can clean it up a bit for whatever babies may arrive, God willing." She offered it to him and his eyes immediately lit up.

"Ma, what is this?"

He fingered the material, and suddenly straightened his back. He stared into the cloth, turning it over and over. "Ma…?" Suddenly, he dropped it on the wooden floorboards and gawked at his mother, wide-eyed, mouth agape. His hands trembled.

"You see, Gareth, you recognize what this is now."

"I—I'm speechless."

Maggie reached over and held his hands. The trembling moved through her forearms, and she squeezed tight until the tremors stopped.

"I figured you had the gift when you were a wee bairn," she said.

"What are you talking about?"

"Oh, Gareth, make no mistake. You're like me in many ways. Kind, strong-willed." She smiled. "Seems Father had a true ability, though, a special way of seeing the world. He wouldn't talk about it much, and Mother refuses to even acknowledge any correlation." She narrowed her eyes. "But you have it, too. Do you ever notice a deep connection to things? To other people?"

Gareth stared in silence.

"That's the gift."

He gulped and continued searching her face.

"He told me it was unheard of, allowing a young fella of sixteen to roam the countryside by himself in those days. Far too dangerous and all. But he never worried about that... never feared for his life. Just like he never fretted about crossing the Atlantic and encountering the northern storms. Just like I never doubted finding an honest man to farmstead and raise a family with."

"You—you have it, too?"

"Oh yes. I noticed at a young age I were—was—different, and that cloth held some spirit." She nodded at it on the porch floor. "And I believe you knew it all along, too."

Gareth gazed across the land. When he peered up again, his face had lost all tension. "Those many times," he whispered, "when I'd touch something and see things... that was all real?"

"Aye. I could tell you had the gift."

"And my brothers?"

"No, none of them."

"Pa?"

"This comes through me only."

He paused, scrutinizing the cloth. "My hands warmed

all over, like I'd put 'em in front of a cheery fire, when I handled this thing. What's it mean, Ma?"

She shifted in the rocker to behold him. "You have the special sight, Gareth. Use it wisely. When the time comes, you'll know exactly what to do." She reached over and retrieved the cloth, folded it up neatly. Then she offered it to him, and he held the gift reverently in his palms. Maggie searched his eyes. "But beware, son, what you have is powerful and sought by many. Including our enemies."

Maggie returned her gaze to the horizon and squinted, her mouth set hard in a line, scanning the newly planted fields. The black speck had disappeared.

THIRTEEN

THE NEXT MORNING, DAWSON AWOKE FIRST AND CREPT to the kitchen to make coffee. The sun peeked out from behind a few scattered clouds, casting long shadows across his mother's dew-laden backyard. When the coffee maker chimed, he poured a cup, threw on a jacket, and eased into the garden to sit under the massive willow tree and inhaled being home again.

Shortly after, the back door creaked open and Hannah appeared with a mug. Dark circles framed her eyes. She joined him on an Adirondack chair.

"How'd you sleep?"

"Meh… you?" She embraced the cup in her hands.

"Oh, great. It's always easy coming here."

They spent the next couple minutes in tangled silence. Nuthatches chattered above with their cheerful song, and a distant raven squawked.

Dawson asked, "Are you okay, Hannah? I hate to pry, but you were crying last night, and—"

"Sure," she snapped, "I'm fine."

He dropped that line of enquiry. After observing the sun rise over the misty green hills and listening to the awakening world, Dawson caught Hannah staring off toward the horizon. There was clearly more bothering her than a recurring nightmare.

"To be honest," she finally whispered, "as I lay in the dark, wrestling demons and trying to keep quiet so as not to disturb anyone else, something outside the bedroom window moved. I peeked around the curtain, but couldn't see anything. Then I saw movement in the shadows. Like, I have this strange feeling someone's watching me. Weird, eh?"

Hannah straightened her back and sighed. "Actually, I didn't sleep much at all."

"Probably some animal, a racoon or a skunk?"

"Well, I was afraid of the nightmare returning and I had no energy for that, so I dozed until you got up."

He placed his mug on the chair's arm. "Anything I can do to help?"

"I doubt it," she said, "I've been this way for many years. The dream comes and goes. Sometimes it's so powerful. Debilitating. And I wake up with night terrors. Other times, not so bad, and on rare occasions, I remember nothing at all." She paused, sipped from her mug. "Those are good nights."

He wasn't fooled. Something else raged inside her, demanding more than the nightmare. He wanted to press about her crying, but decided against it. "So, like, you're my guest and we can chill if the pressure's too much. I can rummage through my dad's stuff and—"

She smiled and shook her head. "I'll be fine, Matt. In fact, I'm really looking forward to today. Like I said before, for me this is legitimate investigative research and you're giving me a real-life experience I've only ever imagined."

"Can you use it in your thesis?"

"Oh, too soon to tell. But regardless, and as cheesy as this sounds, I'm exactly where I want to be." She gazed up into the trees. "Funny, those birds... they sound like they're mocking us."

"Yeah, the nuthatches are always cheerful."

After a few silent moments, Hannah spoke. "I continue living with this foreboding that I've forgotten something important, as if all my life I've tried hard not to remember something that happened when I was young." She met his eyes. "But the memory's not completely buried, know what I mean? It skulks around in the murky depths beneath my conscious thoughts like a demon. I wonder if the nightmares are part of that? A reminder of unfinished business."

They polished off their drinks and strolled inside where Dawson made toast and they enjoyed a light breakfast. Beth entered the kitchen in her housecoat and greeted them. Then the time to work had arrived.

"Is Dad's stuff in the same place?"

"Yes," his mother yawned, drawing an arthritic hand through her greying hair, "in the storage area by the workshop."

He led Hannah down the rickety basement stairs and flicked on a light. Cobwebs had taken over most of the corners and walls. The cellar had that familiar musty, damp stench that reminded him of his childhood when he'd watch his dad build things. Back then, he pretended to help, but really, he spent most of the time keeping him company, chatting about school and sports.

"It's all over here," he said, pointing at the ceiling high wooden shelves stuffed with overflowing boxes. A large olive green filing cabinet leaned off to the side. His personal survey equipment—an old VLF receiver and a portable magnetometer, anchored the floor under the shelving.

"I don't know where to begin, and I'm not sure what we're looking for, but we should start with his notebooks." He stood with his hands on hips. "If we can find them."

Hannah pulled down a couple of cardboard boxes and opened them up. She tossed through some bagged rock specimens, old geological maps, and pocket tools. "What are these?" she asked, holding up a handful of gadgets.

Dawson reached out and studied them. "This," he said, lifting it up, "is a scratch plate, a piece of ceramic. Minerals leave different streak colours when you scratch them, so in the field you get an idea of what you're looking at based on colour." He returned it to her. "And this is an inclinometer, for measuring dip angles of geologic features relative to the surface. Things like fault planes."

"Sure doesn't seem sophisticated."

He laughed, "You're right, but for prospectors and surveyors, these tools are light, small, and generally reliable." He opened up the cabinet. "Here," he said, "these look like notebooks."

They pored through the folders and reviewed reports, handwritten journals tucked into the back of field books. Other bits of paper with checklists on them, dates, locations, expenses.

After several hours going through them all, Hannah sighed, "Nothing jumped out at me here. This is all his work stuff, eh? I see nothing of a more personal nature."

"Me neither, which is kinda odd given the journals he kept," Dawson agreed. Then he had an idea. "Perhaps there's more after all."

Hannah looked at him quizzically.

"Check this out." He pulled one of the project

memos from a pile of papers. "See all these names and emails here? Researchers and students working on that big survey—the last one he did. Some of them may still be around." He entered their addresses into an email on his phone and wrote a message explaining who he was and if they remembered anything about his dad and the survey. Then he hit the send button.

"Bit of a longshot," Hannah said, "but definitely worth pursuing because right now, we have little to go on."

The pleasant aroma of home-made soup filtered down to the workshop, and they grinned and trundled upstairs.

Beth had prepared a spread of sandwiches and had a stew pot bubbling on the stove. They sat at the kitchen table and, as they ate, Dawson noted something different about Hannah. He'd grown accustomed to her demeanor, a sense of profound sadness and struggle since they'd met, but now another expression poked its way through her mask and this was far more sinister. *For someone who claims to have the peace of God, she doesn't look too happy.*

Shortly, they returned to the basement, uncertain about what to investigate next.

"Should we go through these files again," he asked?

"Not sure how much good that'll do," Hannah replied, "but could we study the photograph now?"

"Oh yeah," he said, grabbing his research package from the workbench. He cleared some room on the surface and placed it on top. After opening the folder, he pointed and stepped back. "Voila."

Hannah picked up the photo and held it to the light streaming in from a basement window. She turned it over a few times, then placed it on his notes.

"What do you think?"

Hannah shrugged and said, "It's bigger than I

imagined from the description you sent me, and yeah, not exactly a remarkable building." She faced him. "Have you tried reading it here?"

"Nah."

"She stepped closer. "You wanna try now?"

Dawson hesitated and clenched his jaw. Hannah may have her nightmare to contend with, but he had this. While curious about the message it might hold, he anticipated that handling the thing would lead to more painful blisters. But what he dreaded most was the connection this photo held with his father's death.

As if reading her mind, she said, "Your dad passed away after telling your mother about it, right?"

"That's the story she told me."

She placed her hand on his forearm. "Perhaps he didn't appreciate what he was looking at. If the picture held psychic messages and warnings, how could he have known? But you, Matt," she continued, "you *know* what this is. If you want to leave it here untouched, I totally understand."

Dawson inhaled deeply and searched her blue eyes. He felt safe with Hannah beside him, and if anything developed, she could intervene.

"Okay, let's do this."

He gently picked up the photograph by the edges and closed his eyes, anticipating the burn, and held his breath.

Nothing happened.

Another couple of minutes passed, then he looked at Hannah. "Strange."

She stared at the farmhouse. "Have you drawn a dud before?

"Yeah, there doesn't seem to be a rhyme or reason as to when it works."

"My presence might be an influence," she wondered out loud. "I've read about that happening, that sometimes

ESPers only see these impressions when they're alone."

Dawson's skepticism rose. "Uh-huh, and I suppose—"

Heat suddenly shot through his fingertips, stealing his breath, and he stared transfixed at the swirling photo.

"Sweet Mary," Hannah murmured.

It had begun.

FOURTEEN

THE FIERY GLOW SHIMMERED ALONG THE MARGINS OF the photograph like a summer highway heat mirage. Dawson continued gripping the photo in his fingertips, ignoring the burn, mesmerized by the dynamic vision.

The apparitions returned. Eyeless creatures floating over the surface. Ghostly hands grasping at boundaries and swirling across from one side to the other, top to bottom in vast sweeping motions. The farmhouse was now completely replaced by this spectacle of strange characters in the monochromatic mix.

"What are you seeing?" Hannah asked, sounding as if she spoke from deep within an endless tunnel.

Dawson's jaw moved, but he failed to voice any words.

The sea of faces gave way to an apparition arising and dominating the scene. He couldn't tell if it was male or female, but this apparition's eyes were open and its forehead tilted in a questioning glance, as if recognizing him. Dawson sensed a presence in the room, and that's when the message crystallized.

Danger. Go.

His heart sank and a terror threaded its way from the cold pit of his stomach to the back of his neck.

Danger. Go. Go now.

"Matt, what's happening?"

The ghostly figure glanced left, as if watching something outside the frame, then stared at Dawson with a set, firm face, mouth gulping like a dying fish.

As quickly as it began, the vision disappeared, washed clean by the return of the farmhouse and the barren prairie landscape.

"Matt?"

Hannah grabbed his shoulder. He dropped the photo on the workbench and stumbled back. His throat was dry and the hairs on his neck strained against their tethers.

"What happened?" Hannah's voice had returned from the mysterious echo tunnel and sounded normal again. He faced her, holding his fingers.

"Did… did you see it?" he mumbled.

"I saw the glow and felt heat.

He stepped away from the bench, and Hannah guided him to an old, dusty chair. She dragged up another and sat across from him.

"Tell me everything you saw and felt, Matt."

Dawson took a moment to collect his thoughts. *What did I see?* He walked through the vision, noting the sequence of observations. He shared it all with Hannah, who picked up a notebook and jotted it down.

He described the flying hands, the eddies, and the faces, and she'd interrupt with a question, but when he mentioned that last figure imparting this sense of dread, she put her pen down.

"I had this overwhelming sensation," he rasped, "that

the ghost was warning me. Not in words though; it just stared right at me. And... and, the notion of *danger* grew immediately."

Hannah searched his eyes. "What else?"

"The second half of the message said *go*."

"Where?"

"No idea, the impression I got overwhelmed me with this compulsion to disappear somewhere, that there's imminent danger, and to leave immediately."

Hannah picked up the notebook and wrote.

"Hannah?"

"Yeah?"

"You saw it, right?"

"I saw something, yes. Not to the same extent as you, but the image came alive."

"Thank God," he said, bringing his fingers up in front of his face. "Thank God you witnessed it, too."

"Hm."

A moment passed as the old house creaked and groaned. The rustle of his mother watching TV upstairs filtered to the basement. He glanced at Hannah, and noticed her eyes were closed and, yes, her lips moved ever so slightly.

IN THE LATE AFTERNOON, ONCE THEY'D TALKED THE event through several times and reviewed Hannah's notes, they sat at Beth's kitchen table and discussed what to do next.

"If we put some of these clues together, what do we get?" Hannah taped bandages on his fingertips.

"The same message as the last one. There's no more to it."

"But it's not the same. According to your notes, the previous encounter left you with an impression of a warning. But I don't recall this sudden urge to leave." She paused. "Think back. Was disappearing part of the last message?"

Dawson concentrated and recalled that second episode in his apartment. He concluded that, no, the only sense he got was the warning of danger.

"Then that's something new." She rubbed her temples and stifled a yawn. "There's also my paranoia of being watched."

"Right. Could that be related, too?"

"Possibly, or I could've just imagined movement in the shadows. You know how the night can play visual tricks when it's so quiet."

Dawson recalled several times walking across campus around midnight after a marathon session in the lab, and how the thick darkness teased his fatigue, causing him to imagine all kinds of movement.

"Matt," Hannah said, leaning forward, "if the photo is urging you to leave, we'd better ask ourselves *where* that could be."

He agreed, and they reviewed her notes again, mining for other clues. Nothing obvious jumped out, but Hannah had a thought.

"So your dad experienced the same visions, right?"

"Yeah, that's what Mum says."

"And he was surveying in the field, then raced home with this story, and returned to the bush a couple days later?"

"Yes."

"Do you mind me asking how your father died?"

Dawson chewed his lip, remembering how he found out as a naïve child of ten. Beth had fallen into a deep depression, and he spent a lot of time at the neighbour's house.

"Mum knows those details, but I'd rather not drag her into this. She's shaken up enough seeing me going through the same thing." He straightened up and leaned in, speaking in a conspiratorial tone. "But from what I gather, after he'd gone back to the bush, he did his work, taking measurements along a survey line, and suffered a heart attack."

She thought a moment. "But, he would've been quite young."

"Yes, that's what everyone kept saying. Mum said the doctor asked about a genetic heart defect, because there was no doubt his ticker gave in."

Hannah pursed her lips. Her unsettled look betrayed the lack of a decent sleep, and her dark eyes were bloodshot. She stared at the table and asked, "Where was this survey line?"

Dawson ruffled through a folder of his dad's notes. "Here's the schedule from the project he worked on. It says *Boston Township*. That's near Kirkland Lake." She threw him a confused, cursory smile, and Dawson grinned. "It's about an hour and a half's drive north from here." He studied her reaction. "What're you thinking, Hannah?"

She rubbed her eyes and whispered, "We must investigate where he worked and what he was doing. Perhaps the photo is trying to tell you there's danger *here*, and to return to his lines for additional clues."

"Bit of a stretch in logic, don't you think?"

"Yes, and that's precisely why we should retrace his steps."

He sighed, remembering his promise to Wendy that he'd be back at the lab on Monday. "All right," he said, "let's drive up early in the morning. But then we'll have to book it to London right after."

LATER THAT NIGHT, AFTER A QUIET SUPPER AND SOME laughs looking at photo albums of Dawson as a child, Hannah lay in bed, staring at the dark ceiling, fighting the sleep that washed over her.

The Lord is my light and my salvation; whom shall I fear?

Beth had gone to her room a couple hours ago. She heard her turn the TV off and close her bedroom door. Then Matt shuffled around before his light switch clicked. But Hannah remained awake, dreading the return of the nightmare that patiently awaited her on the other side of consciousness.

A sliver of moonlight sliced across the bed. She'd tracked its movement over the last two hours as Luna danced with the Earth. To avoid sleep, Hannah reviewed the events of the day, from investigating Matt's basement to the encounter with the photograph and, despite the note-taking, no real pattern emerged to show how this farmhouse played out in the family's lives, and what kind of danger or warning he was meant to heed.

What was that?

Hannah froze. Movement outside the window. A shadow floated across the covers and disappeared.

I'm going crazy with fatigue. Seeing things again.

She tilted her head toward the window and the open strip between the curtains where moonlight entered. After several tense minutes, she saw nothing else. Then, slipping out of bed, she crept to the side of the glass pane, mindful of the creaky floorboards, and slowly inched the curtain back just enough to see. She stared into the gloomy yard and its conference of shadows.

After watching the trees and bushes for anomalies, she concluded her imagination had indeed played tricks on her, and she returned to bed.

The Lord is the stronghold of my life; of whom shall I be afraid?

Over the next hour, sleep pounded at her brain and she caught herself dozing until she could fight it off no longer.

Within moments of closing her eyes, the nightmare began...

...Another beautiful summer day and Hannah, younger in her early teens, hiked through the woods near her home with her best friend Kim. They laughed and joked around. Hannah picked up an old branch to use as a walking stick.

After leading in silence, Hannah twisted around to find Kim gone. Panic set in. She shouted her name, but only the curious sounds of nature responded.

Until she heard the voice.

"Lose something?"

She turned slowly, and he stood there, hands behind his back in an at-ease stance, his shoulder-length black hair flowing. He wore a friendly, alluring grin, but his green reptilian eyes shone dark and hypnotic.

"I don't know you," young Hannah said. "Kim!" she yelled, looking through the woods.

"Oh, not something... someone. Well, your friend went home. I ran into her on the trail and she asked me to tell you."

Hannah didn't know what to believe.

"You want to come see? I'll show you where." He reached out his thin, bony hand and his dark eyes pierced into the depths of her soul. She at once felt an attraction to him, and an overwhelming fear that if she took his hand, she'd never be safe again.

She stepped tentatively toward him, stared into his angular face, the passion in his eyes. He smiled and Hannah froze. A scream rose from her gut and caught in her throat. She tried again. And again. The beautiful stranger approached...

Hannah bolted upright in the bed, panting, sweat pouring from her head and dripping down her cheeks. She fought to control her breathing and relax. The moonlight in front of her had shifted. A measure of time had certainly passed, and she peered at her phone.

3:07 am.

Always around the same time.

Hannah had to do something, and what teased her mind was waking Matt and asking him to keep her company until morning. Sleep would be impossible now, and she hadn't slept nearly enough. She stood and, after wrapping the bedding around her shoulders and grabbing a pillow, she clicked open her door.

No lights appeared, but she glanced down the hall bathed in shadows toward Beth's room, afraid that she may have screamed in her nightmare and awakened them both. All was quiet. Shards of moonlight glittered randomly from the kitchen windows at the end of the hallway, casting a haunted, sparkling slash.

She tapped on Matt's door, but no answer came. Riddled with anxiety from her dream, Hannah swallowed hard and turned the handle.

He slept on a small twin bed against the wall by a window. He hadn't pulled the curtains closed and moonlight flooded the space. She crept in slowly and, near the desk, dropped her pillow and gently lowered herself to the floor, settling down on the thin rug beneath her—a hard spot, and she'd pay for it in the morning with stiffness in her back and neck—but she immediately felt safe closer to him.

Fear not, for I am with you. Fear not, for I am with you.

As she lay on her side, staring off toward his bedside window, she settled down under the rhythmic sound of his slow, deep breathing. In a moment, she closed her eyes. Her mind had cleared and simply being near him allowed her to force the vision of the nightmare away into the corners of her thoughts where she slipped a line around it and pulled the dream to oblivion.

The dying thought she had before sleep claimed her was tomorrow morning's adventure, and the rush of sleeping in her own bed by nightfall.

FIFTEEN

DAWSON HAULED THE LAST BOX OF HIS FATHER'S NOTES up from the basement and dumped it in the Yaris' crammed trunk. He checked the time on his phone. A few minutes after 7:30. After slamming the trunk closed, he returned to the house, kicked off his shoes, and met Beth in the kitchen for some coffee.

Hannah had yet to awaken.

"Oh dear, I hope she's not sick or something," Beth fussed, fingers wrapped around a mug. "She was up in the middle of the night, eh." She paused. Dawson stared at a topographic map he'd spread out on the table showing Boston Township and various mine sites either in operation or abandoned. His father's survey lines had been pencilled in. "And you found her on the floor this morning?"

He nodded.

"Well, that's not good at all. If there's a problem with the bed…"

"Mum," he said, sipping his coffee, "The bed's fine. Look, she didn't sleep the night before, so this is actually amazing. She was exhausted."

A hollow thump down the hallway startled them.

"See? She's getting up now."

Several minutes later, Hannah presented herself at the kitchen entrance, hands in the back pockets of her jeans, wearing a sheepish, sleepy grin. She'd pulled her hair into a ponytail that hung over a dark green blouse.

"Oh," said Beth, scraping her chair backward, "are you okay, Hannah? I hope that bed wasn't too hard or, well, it couldn't be harder than the floor, but never mind—"

"Mrs. Dawson, I'm fine. Actually, I had a wonderful sleep." She glanced at Matt, met his eyes, then spun away.

"Come have some coffee," Beth insisted. "Can I make you some breakfast?"

"If it's all the same with you, Matt, I'd rather get to the survey area and see what's there. We don't have a lot of time today, got a big drive back to London coming up, and I slept longer than I'd intended."

Matt wiped his lips. "Sure thing. I loaded some of Dad's stuff in the car in case we need it later."

She studied the map on the table. "This is where we're going?"

"Yeah, let me show you."

They passed the next ten minutes exploring the terrain in Boston Township, figuring out which roads would take them to the old survey lines, then gathered their overnight bags. Dawson hugged his mother goodbye.

On the front doorstep, Beth said, "Please be careful, Matt. I worry so much about you."

"I will, Mum. We'll sort this out soon enough."

They hopped in the Yaris, pulled away from the house and drove north on Highway 11 toward Kirkland

Lake. Hannah had folded the map up as best she could, pouring over the terrain, tracing his dad's parallel lines over hills and around marshes with her fingers.

"You say this was part of government research project?"

"Yeah," Dawson said, eyes watching the road. "The Geological Survey was the major partner, and a bunch of universities were involved too. McGill, Queen's, Bishops... some others. Anyway, from what I read, the work centered on mapping detailed information about the underlying structural formations. Near surface terrain. The mining industry sponsored portions of the research, too."

After driving several minutes in silence, Dawson finally asked the question he'd been mulling over since waking that morning to find her curled up by his desk. "Hannah, why were you asleep on my floor?"

She bowed her head and closed her eyes. *Praying.* He remembered discussing her faith on the trip up, and how it eased the dread of the nightmares.

A few seconds later, Hannah responded. "I slept in my bed at one point. Not sure for how long, though." She turned to him. "I had another nightmare."

"Oh, I'm sorry."

"Yeah, well, it wasn't anything new. It's repeatedly the same, sometimes with different people in it, slightly varied settings, but this particularly creepy guy always shows up. I suppose it means something on a subconscious level, but I'm too frightened to go there."

A minute of silence passed. Dawson focused on the road ahead, unsure of what to say. Her crying alone the first night still festered, but he decided to let that go. Few vehicles traveled this morning, but he noticed a car some distance behind keeping pace, the same red vehicle he'd seen leaving Haileybury with them.

"The truth is, Matt, I hope I didn't make you feel

uncomfortable. I—I thought knowing someone else was close would help me survive the night. And it did." She faced him with the map on her lap. "Thank you."

"Sure," he said, uncertain what else to say. He liked Hannah, no question. Something about her fascinated him and she had a pretty smile, but she was also elusive and challenging to understand at the level of depth where he could completely trust her. Perhaps in time.

And there was the praying thing.

"Were you always a religious person?"

She smiled patiently. "I'm a Christian, Matt, but not like the whackos you see on TV."

"I could tell."

"And you aren't a believer."

"No," he said, smirking. "No, I'm an atheist. I put my faith in science, in physics."

"I see," she said pointedly. "But you enlisted me to investigate a phenomenon that apparently has no genuine scientific basis. So, do you think it's magic?"

"Nah, but I'm trying to keep an open mind. Truth is, I don't know what to make of it. Not yet. But I firmly believe there's a cause behind what's happening." He licked his lips. "See, I like to imagine that the world is one big machine, with delicate jewelled movements and bone-crunching pistons working in tandem. And our only task as scientists is to reverse engineer the whole damn thing. Figure out how it works."

Hannah cocked her head. "Is that how you see a sunset? Nothing more than an intricate mechanism with brass gears and springs and ridiculously annoying equations?"

"Well…" He thought of a counter argument, but realized he had no worthy reply.

Who is this woman?

The trip to KL passed quickly as Dawson and Hannah

continued chatting about various subjects, including where to begin once they found his father's lines.

They pulled off the highway on the outskirts of town and traveled along a twisting gravel road that grew increasingly narrow and bumpy the farther they moved into the bush. Dawson slowed as the route jackknifed around a corner. He peered out the driver side window at a slight opening in the woods and eased on to the tight shoulder.

"Is this the place?" He asked.

Hannah studied the map for a moment, checking the landscape. "Sure looks like it according to your dad's field notes." She gazed ahead. "Yep, right after the sharp turn in the road... west side... entrance way with barely enough room for a vehicle." She unlashed her seatbelt. "Let's go see."

Tangled shrubs and tall grasses licked at the Yaris as they nosed into the opening that resembled more of an overgrown, abandoned trailhead. They exited the car and breathed in the cool, clean fall air. Dawson was immediately struck by the silence of the forest. No traffic appeared along this old goat path, and he didn't expect any either. There weren't even any visible hunting cabins. It was merely an access point to the Crown lands for hikers and prospectors, and hunters in the fall.

Hannah pulled a light jacket from her bag and slung her backpack over her shoulder while Dawson rummaged through his own, double-checking he had all the notes he needed to find his dad's trail. Surely any remaining markers from the major project would have disappeared by now, and the lack of cell coverage meant no GPS mapping, so he made sure he had the trusty Brunton compass with him.

"Ready?" he asked.

Hannah, relaxed and bright-eyed, answered, "Let's

get going!"

After they'd hiked into the woods following an established path for a few minutes, Hannah suddenly stopped. "Did you hear that?"

Dawson froze in place and cocked an ear. At first he thought it was the wind in the leaves, but realized the sound was a vehicle approaching along the gravel road.

Instinctively, he crouched and pulled Hannah close beside him. From a narrow clearing in the trees, they watched the hairpin turn and within a moment, a red car appeared running at a good clip. It slowed to take the curve, then briefly sped up before gearing down again to a snail's pace. The driver crept along momentarily, then finally accelerated and drifted out of sight.

Hannah glanced at Dawson. Her eyes widened and her adventurous demeanor had been replaced with trepidation. "Maybe I'm paranoid for a reason."

THEY REMAINED HIDDEN IN THE TANGLE-BRUSH, GLANCING at the gravel road, ears alert for the car, but after a few minutes, the calming silence of the forest returned.

Hannah crept about, craning her neck to see farther away.

"Maybe it was a hiker or some birdwatcher," Dawson said in a low voice.

"Yeah, you may be right." She adjusted the pack on her shoulders. "I guess my imagination is still running on hyper-drive."

They continued along the twisting pathway, Hannah studying his dad's notes and checking off trail markers. Several tags had long since been swallowed up by the overgrowth, but outcrops and lone trees and other singular flags appeared, and Dawson's confidence grew that they were on the right path.

After several minutes of tough hiking, they rested

beside a small creek in a clearing amongst the pines, a shallow oasis in the woods.

"This looks like the starting point for one of the survey lines, if these notes are correct."

"We'll assume they are," Dawson said. He gazed across the terrain. "But which way do we go?"

Hannah juggled the papers and the folded topographic map in her hands, orienting it several directions. "This way," she pointed. "It should be northeast."

Dawson checked the compass and confirmed the route.

"It's a line about 500 meters long. At the end, according to this, Dad veered east and circled back along another parallel line."

He wiped his brow. The hiking had burned off the chill in the air and in his bones, and he removed his jacket. "All right, let's take a look. You lead so I can follow with the compass and make sure we're on track."

Hannah marched out through the clearing. Dawson periodically took a bearing, and they adjusted their path wherever the trail grew murky. After they'd traveled a hundred meters over relatively flat terrain, he asked, "What are we actually looking for?"

She turned as he caught up to her and took a sip of water. "Yeah, I don't really know, but I'd say anything that's odd, extraordinary. Like, I doubt we're going to find some physical object, but I'm more interested in the feel of the place."

"The *feel?*" Dawson snorted. "Sorry, but that sounds a little woo-woo to me."

She smiled. "And you said you'd keep an open mind, eh?"

He grimaced. Hannah was right. He'd already conceded that this hike appeared to be a waste of time except getting some fresh air with a curious girl. Still, an attitude change and renewed focus on his dad's work was desperately needed. Most importantly, he obsessed on the potential triggers giving rise to his dad stopping, finding the photo in his notes, and experiencing the phenomenon that somehow contributed to his death.

"Touché," he conceded. "Okay, let's finish this line and go from there."

After tramping along several more parallel lines, noticing nothing strange, they rested on an outcrop for some lunch.

Hannah doled out a couple of sandwiches that Beth made for them and then sat cross-legged facing the trail.

"I wonder if this is where your dad stopped and looked at the photo," she said, between bites. "I couldn't find anything that specific in his notes, just that he'd taken a break, found the photograph in his kit, and that's when it happened."

"Yeah," Dawson mused, untying his shoes and airing out the dogs. "All a big mystery, for sure." He sipped his water. "Hannah, is it possible something else took place here?"

"What do you mean?"

"Well," he began, "not only did he handle the photo, but he also died out here. I couldn't find exactly where on the map, and the coroner's report didn't give a precise location, stating only that he'd been surveying in Boston Township as part of this major project."

She twisted around and gazed off through the woods. "True. And it was a heart attack, eh?"

"That's what the medical examiner concluded, but I don't know."

"Tell me more."

"For starters, he was relatively young, in his mid-thirties. How many thirty-something fit men have heart attacks, unless there's something genetic going on? But the medical report mentioned nothing about any pre-existing defect."

"Yeah, that doesn't sound right. But what else could have caused it?"

Dawson shrugged. He'd been wondering this himself. Could the image have awakened a dormant, underlying condition? When he'd seen the glow and the apparitions himself, he hadn't been physically at risk other than receiving burns on his hands. "Perhaps the danger, the cause, is the photo itself?"

They finished the rest of their lunch in silence.

"Well," Hannah said, taking her last bite, "let's keep going. There are another half-dozen lines to cover, and we can talk about this more on the drive back to London." She brushed the crumbs off her jacket and legs, stood and stretched.

Dawson caught himself watching her when she didn't notice, and a wonderful, ancient flutter of a perfect moment rose within.

THE SUN DIPPED LOW IN THE SOFT, WATERCOLOUR SKY as the tandem finished the last survey line. Throughout the afternoon, Hannah had taken more notes, observing curiosities on the trails and in the woods, talking about her studies. Nothing had jumped out at her, but she made copious notes, regardless. They'd agreed to review it all on the long journey back to southern Ontario, to see if any patterns emerged that could be clues to not only what happened to his father, but possibly more.

As they bushwhacked toward the first line by the creek where they'd started, a twig snapped in the woods. Now it was Dawson's turn to freeze.

Hannah, walking ahead, noticed he'd stopped. "What is it?"

He raised his hand and listened. "Thought I heard

something back there." He peered into the shadows of the trail they'd cut and waited. She joined him.

A couple of minutes passed in silence other than a distant jet, the gurgle of the nearby creek, and birds.

But as he took another step, it happened again. This time, there was no mistaking the crack of twigs and branches.

"There," he whispered.

Hannah nodded and knelt down. He wondered if a moose or bear was tracking through—his dad noted seeing wildlife along these lines in his notes—but a moose would make a hell of a racket. This sound was lighter. Like that of a—

The heavy set man appeared not ten meters away on the trail when Dawson saw his piercing eyes. He stood about six feet tall, wide as a truck, dressed in camo fatigues. In his right hand, he twisted a machete.

The man paused a moment, then narrowed his eyes before charging straight toward them.

SIXTEEN

"GET TO THE CAR, HANNAH!"

Dawson tossed his backpack to her, then faced the aggressor. But she didn't move. "Go!"

Hannah, jolted into action, raced up the trail and disappeared.

The man slowed as he approached. His eyes darted up the path, then back to Dawson, like he was unsure whether to follow Hannah or remain.

"Who are you?" Dawson demanded, placing himself in the middle of the clearing, striking a defensive posture.

"That's no concern of yours, Mr. Dawson."

"You know me? What the hell?"

The figure approached cautiously, waving machete in slow, menacing twirls. Dawson stepped back, throwing cursory glances at the stones and roots on the path.

"Why are you here?" the bush man growled.

"That's none of your business!"

The blade glistened in his hand.

"Stupid fool," he hissed. "I was instructed not to harm you, but I don't follow orders too good." He grinned, displaying a set of crooked teeth.

Dawson scanned the trail for anything he could use as a weapon.

"But here's what we're gonna do. You'll come with me, then we'll find your little sweetheart, and go for a nice drive." The man raised the knife and lunged, but Dawson was too quick. He swung behind a tree trunk and evaded the thrust.

"What do you want!" he cried. "We're just trying to—"

The dark figure recovered and moved to a more open space, slashing his arm down, narrowly missing Dawson's wrist.

Adrenaline kicked in and Dawson bolted. He crashed through the brush along the creek until he arrived at the trail leading to the road. The aggressor followed right behind, grunting hard.

Dawson raced over the pathway, looking for a makeshift weapon to stop the man, but there were no loose stones, just thick grass and branches clawing at his legs.

The man's sharp breath grew louder, closer, and he hoped Hannah had already found the road.

Dawson rounded a bend in the trail, but his foot caught on a root and he tumbled forward in a heap, scraping his arms. Turning on his back, he saw the man pull to a stop and sneer; the blade glistening in the late afternoon sun.

"You're mine now, you little bastard. Make this easy on yourself and come peaceful-like. Perhaps if you give me the photo and notes, I'll spare your miserable lives."

"Go to hell!"

"Very well, I'll inform Mr. Stone about your unfortunate... accident."

He stepped forward. Dawson scrabbled away, struggled to rise, and fell into a thick stand of pines.

Suddenly, a rock hit the man square in the chest and he staggered back, flinching and cursing. Then another skipped off his head, and he fell to his knees, dropping the knife.

"Come on!" Hannah screamed from behind him. She helped him to his feet, and they tore down the trail. Dawson glanced over his shoulder several times, but the aggressor didn't follow. They pushed through the rough patches, twigs and branches scraping at his face and clothes. With panic-driven strides, they soon arrived at the trailhead.

Dawson fumbled for the car keys. Snapping twigs and grunts echoed through the woods as their pursuer approached. He unlocked the Yaris, and they dove inside. Within seconds, he'd slammed the old beast into reverse and screamed from the access point onto the road, gunning through the gravel toward the highway. Hannah prayed out loud, and after a hundred meters he checked the rear-view mirror. The dark figure exited the bush and stood in the roadway, holding his head.

"O Lord, my God, I come to you for protection; rescue me and save me from all who pursue me." Hannah repeated the prayer as they roared down the access road. She suddenly grabbed the dashboard, as if bracing for impact. "Slow down, Matt."

Dawson checked the mirror. No vehicle followed. He braked and, as they approached Highway 11, glanced both ways. No traffic appeared from either direction, so he rolled through the stop sign and squealed onto the road heading south.

After several minutes of wide-eyed silence, his hands

finally relaxed on the wheel and his breathing stabilized. He turned to Hannah. "Are you okay?"

She stared straight ahead. "I—I think so. Oh, Matt, who was that?"

"I've no idea, but it's clear he's after the photograph and us, too."

"The photo?"

"Yeah, that's what he told me he wanted. Definitely something else going on." He continued checking the mirrors. Near the horizon, a transport truck appeared, but the red car they'd seen earlier that day was nowhere to be found.

"We should call the police," Hannah stated, her voice frail and shaken.

Dawson hesitated. What would the stupid cops do? Take a statement, get a description of the man, keep an eye out for him? Nothing that could really help. No, somehow this dude knew about the photo, and had followed them into the bush. But he resolved not to turn it over to anyone.

"Maybe, Hannah, but not now. I want to know who this jerk is."

She silently moved her lips.

"Listen, what you did back there…"

Hannah nodded and choked back tears.

Approaching the outskirts of Haileybury, Dawson asked, "Do you want to stop at my mother's, or keep going?"

"Let's carry on. Put some distance between us and that creep."

Dawson breathed a sigh of relief. Beth wasn't expecting them, and if they showed up in this condition, he'd have to tell her what happened and she'd worry even more. No, continuing on to London made sense.

He pulled his phone out and handed it to Hannah.

"Can you send a text to my mum?"

"Sure." She opened up the screen. "What do you want to say?"

"Yeah, just say we're on our way to Western. Found nothing along the trail, and that I'll talk soon."

Hannah thumbed the message, read it back, and sent it off.

In a moment, her reply came: *thanks for the update. Drive safe xx oo.*

"Can you check the emails too? In case there's anything from Wendy?"

Hannah scrolled through the messages. There was nothing from Wendy or Gunar, but one caught her attention. "Hey, Matt, you got a message here from Charlie Denton at McGill. Want me to read it?"

"Charlie Denton? He wasn't on the project list, was he?"

"Can't remember."

"Okay, read it anyway."

Hannah shifted in the passenger seat to face him.

"Matt, Professor Watanabe passed your email on to me. The one you sent the other day about Grey Dawson, your dad, and the multi-partner survey we did together. I was a tech on the survey, and I knew Grey quite well. We'd hang out whenever he was in town. Anyway, most of the remaining journals, notebooks and equipment from the project are stored on campus in the geology building. Some might belong to your dad, so you're welcome to have a look."

Hannah scrolled through the message. "He leaves his coordinates at McGill." She looked up. "What do you think?"

Dawson checked the rear-view again. Several cars followed at a respectful distance, and in the dusk, he couldn't tell whether any were red.

"I'd love to see what's there," he mused.

"Me too. I thought we were missing something from his stuff in your basement."

A pained look grew on his face, but he buried it. "Yeah, and I want to know more about the bush man, who he works for, and why he wanted the photo." He smiled across at Hannah. The fading wisps of light caught the highlights in her tousled hair and reflected off her deep blue eyes. He reached over and pulled a tiny yellow leaf from her shoulder. *She's beautiful.*

"Let's go, Matt. Right now. I'll email this Charlie guy and see if we can meet tomorrow."

Dawson furrowed his brow and clenched his teeth. "No, we both can't go."

"Why? What about—"

"Hannah," he said in a low voice, "No, I'll drop you off in London and head to Montreal myself. I can't put you in any more danger."

SEVENTEEN

HANNAH STRAIGHTENED UP, FOLDING HER HANDS IN HER lap as they drove south in the dark, quelling the anger and scorching frustration that bubbled in her. "So that's how it's going to be? You get to decide whether I can look after myself?"

"It's not that I—"

"Whoa, hang on a second. Did you not see what I did to that creep? Remember who saved you?"

She saw that Matt felt responsible for bringing her into this madness, the photo, the man in the bush, and mysteries behind the phenomenon. But she joined him with her eyes wide open, and desperately wanted to be part of his adventure, not only because of her professional interest in psychometric events, but also because there was something different about the young man himself. Something oddly comforting that she wanted to explore.

He worked his jaw muscles. The conflict raging in his mind was palpable.

"If something happened to you..."

She bristled. "Two things, Matt, okay? First, while I appreciate your concern, it's not your choice to make. In case you've forgotten, I'm totally committed to finding the truth. Second, you may not be a believer, but I am. I put my faith and trust in God that everything will work out exactly the way it's supposed to. Doesn't mean I'm reckless or that I don't get scared because, believe me, I do. But I recognize a lot of things are outside my control no matter what we do."

He stared into her eyes a moment, then his look softened. "All right, we'll both go."

"Glad that's settled. I'll craft an email to Charlie then."

She recited the message as she typed into the phone. Then hit send.

"So, straight to Montreal?"

"Yeah," he grunted, but his face showed no peace.

"What's up, Matt"

"I'm worried about leaving Wendy on her own to manage Gunar, and I'm gonna have to blow off a meeting he desperately wanted with me to discuss the photo, too. But this is more important despite the consequences of being a no-show on Monday." He thought a moment longer. "I'll message them both next time we stop. Let them know I won't be back for another day."

"That's the spirit," she smiled.

"Hey, something's bugging me," he wheedled mischievously. "I assumed you Jesus types were against violence. Like, turn the other cheek and feed my fluffy lambs and rainbows and unicorns?"

Hannah snorted and rolled her eyes. "I'm a Christian, Matt, not a wallflower. I take no joy in hurting a fellow human being, but sometimes it's called for. Oh, and if you actually read the Bible, you'd understand that God and

Jesus were hardly emasculated do-gooders like some folks want you to believe. Try reading about the birth of Jesus in the Book of Revelation. There are no fluffy lambs or gentle wise men in that account. No contemplative *Silent Night.* More like an all-out Battle Royale between God and Satan for the souls of the world that would put *The Avengers* to shame."

She recognized the idea of violent Bible-thumpers wasn't new. The media was full of far-right paradoxical whackadoodles. But she had no issue reconciling *love thy neighbour* with souls roasting in Hell. Perhaps one day he'd be more open to discussing that with her.

But, whatever. Hannah's conviction seemed to calm Matt as they continued driving, and she could tell he'd taken an interest in her above and beyond helping sort out the psychometric responses. She smiled in the dark, then considered her own optimism. She'd often faked being happy and hopeful—a ploy to trick her mind into supposing that all was well, that God's plan unfolded naturally with purpose.

It hadn't always worked.

The image of the creep in the woods standing over Matt with a massive knife haunted her. But her strength came from elsewhere and provided her with the wherewithal to double back along the trail and grab some rocks to defend herself. Growing up playing competitive sports had given her plenty of life skills, including firing stones at psychotic bush people. Still, she worried over exposing herself too much, too soon. The nightmares couldn't be helped since they stayed in his mum's house. Hard to hide that. But the other darkness... that would have to wait. Perhaps never to see the light of day.

The unearthly, dusky landscape blurred by. When they approached the town of Temagami, Matt pulled over at a roadside grocery store and picked out some food while

Hannah wrestled up a couple of coffees. She offered to pay, but he refused, and they quickly exited. Then, standing beside the beat up Yaris, they stretched and had a snack. Matt busied himself firing silent notes to Wendy and Dr. Gunar.

His phone pinged and he looked up, frowning. "Wendy's nervous about handling the experimental runs and analysis. Says Gunar's looking for me." He grimaced and thumbed a response.

Hannah placed her coffee on the car's roof and sent her own messages, including one to Curious George, saying she'd be out of the bullpen for a couple more days. Another to her advisor. That finished, she said, "There. All good to go."

Complete darkness was almost upon them now, and the traffic through the town eased. Hannah grabbed her cup and tumbled into the passenger seat. Matt opened his car door and a revving car caused him to look over his shoulder. A red sedan screamed by, hit the brake lights, and slid into a gas station a couple hundred meters ahead.

He jumped in, startling her. "See that car, Hannah? The one that just pulled up ahead?"

"Uh-huh." Then she understood. "Oh, no."

"Let's get out of here."

Instead of turning south on the highway, Matt veered north and circled around the side streets of the village until he'd passed the station. Then he squealed in front of a transport almost cutting him off, and howled away in a southbound direction.

They drove in silence. The eighteen-wheeler pulled over on the shoulder at one point, revealing a car's headlights trailing in the distance. Matt glanced at the mirrors. "We've got company. That's the same car that followed us to the bush."

"Looks identical." Her cheery mind tricks failed to

work now, and terror rose inside.

Protect me, God, because I take refuge in You.

Dawson remained calm. "I know this road, Hannah. There's a spot ahead to pull off and let this guy pass unnoticed. Just after that long bend in the highway. He'll lose sight of us for a moment."

The slow curve appeared with numerous caution signs to reduce speed. But Matt gunned it as soon as the trailing car's headlights sank behind the hills and trees. He raced to an intersection, veered left onto the side road, and immediately spun around to face the highway. He killed the engine and the lights and waited.

The sedan hurtled past and disappeared, showing no signs of stopping.

"Let's wait awhile," he said. "Don't want to take any chances in case he circles back."

Several tense minutes passed. A transport rumbled by heading north, but soon, no other traffic appeared. She prayed the red car was busy chasing ghosts along the dark road.

"I've been wondering about the phenomenon," she whispered, staring straight ahead into the night.

"Yeah, that's all I've been thinking of. Any ideas?"

Hannah shifted. "There's obviously more behind this, Matt. Who have you told about your experience?"

"Well, there's Wendy and my friend Tony in mathematics. I kinda mentioned it to Gunar, too, because I was jonesing for some time off the project, but that's all."

"And at least one other person does. The camo guy."

"Right, and... wait a sec, he spoke of someone else. Someone called *Stone.*"

"Hm, so perhaps this phenomenon isn't isolated."

Matt angled his body to face her. "Explain."

"Well," she started, "these events, where ESPers receive psychic impressions from objects, aren't unique to your family. Perhaps other researchers or interested parties want to exploit that information."

"Like the hidden message, or more powerful visions?"

"Yeah," she said, "exactly. Or you. Look, there's something big happening behind the scenes. Think about it. If you're able to read these patterns, imagine what else you could decipher from other objects?

He remained silent. She studied his face in profile. Then he said, "But the only experience I've had is with the photo. I don't pick up a..." he searched around, "...a coffee cup and see ghosts dancing on the lid."

"As far as you know, it's only the farmhouse. But suppose you *could* see other things. Read *other* impressions. You'd possess a power that would advance science in my field, for sure, but it could also be used to exploit, to undermine. Think about it. What if you could read a world leader's thoughts? Or weapons codes from a distance? Get it?"

"Sure, in a Jason Bourne movie, but does that happen in real life?"

"Matt." She leaned toward him. "There are forces of evil working in the world all the time."

"Forces of evil," he mocked. "please, Hannah, you've been watching too many horror movies."

"Scoff all you want, but in my worldview, the way I understand the universe, there are clear, opposing powers. That creep was clearly evil. Okay, maybe he loves his kids and his mother, but his intentions in the bush were not the makings of a Hallmark movie."

They sat in dark silence listening to crickets. Fireflies zig-zagged in a field across the road. A couple cars drove past on the highway.

"All I'm saying, Matt, is perhaps what you experienced is part of a much larger puzzle." Hannah sighed, then resolve filled her voice. "We need to understand if your dad had any knowledge of that, if he was caught up with the wrong kind of people. Maybe that's what led to his death. In fact," she suggested, "perhaps his death wasn't accidental at all."

The black shadows playing across the highway and fluttering through the windshield may have caused fresh insights to flood her mind. Or the talk of Matt's dad and his death contributed to her lucidity. Most likely, the realization of the evil that prepared itself in the corners of the night, waiting patiently, routinely appearing in her dreams pushed Hannah toward a new revelation.

She watched Matt's shadowed face in the security and protection of the car's interior, and the urge to embrace him overwhelmed her, to take his hand and bring the comfort and security of the bedroom floor to her consciousness.

"Matt?"

"Yeah?"

She moved a fraction closer. "Are we going to be okay?"

"Yes."

"How can you be so sure? I mean, I place my trust and faith in God, and even then, I often worry about what might happen. How do you—?"

"I'm not a believer, Hannah, you know that. But I have faith in the fundamental goodness of people. That psycho in the woods? He's an exception. And if something or someone caused my dad's death, we'll find out and solve that mystery."

"You sound so confident."

He snorted. "I don't know about that, but we can't let fear dictate how we live." He hesitated. "Does that make any sense?"

His voice floated, sure and powerful, and Hannah leaned even closer. "Matt?" Their faces almost brushed together in the dark. She felt his soft breath, the immediate goose flesh whispering on her skin, and her own heart racing.

"Matt, I…"

He moved forward to kiss her, and she prepared to receive his lips. But a deathly image flashed deep inside her. She hesitated, and as he brushed his hand across her cheek, drawing her face toward him, she pulled away and turned to the window.

"I'm so sorry," she whispered.

EIGHTEEN

The Environs Near Edinburgh, Scotland
1843

ASH ROBERTSON TREADED CAREFULLY ALONG THE *stone path toward home from St. Andrew's church. He'd bundled his cap, anxiously protecting the three fresh eggs he carried. A hard rain drove in from the northeast off the ocean and surely they'd be in for a wicked, stormy night.*

A meeting of the parish elders and the congregation unfurled according to his father's prediction: a lot of talk, frustration, and misunderstanding. The Free Church was being established, and the great Disruption overran the village on the outskirts of Edinburgh.

He greeted Chevy the neighbour, waved at others in the warmth of their homes, then gathered on his doorstep. His parents' sharp voices drifted in harsh pulses from inside the house, and he wondered how much longer the split in the Church would keep tearing families and the community apart.

He pushed the door open, and they stopped their heated discussion.

"Ah, wee lad, come here a bite, will ye?"

"In a moment, Pa. Look what I brung from Mrs. Stanstead!" He lifted his cap to show off the eggs.

"Lovely," his mother said, "please take 'em to the kitchen and mind the supper I'm preparin'."

Ash took the eggs and placed them in a bowl before returning to the living room. His parents stood in front of the warm hearth and the dwindling fire.

Lionel Robertson watched the flames catch and dance in the fireplace. There'd been talk in the streets of a split coming, but now, as the Disruption solidified, it caused families to divide along the lines of worship.

Lionel picked up the dangling conversation as Alice left for the kitchen. "The Free Church! Seriously, love, what is that all about? It's an affront to God Himself."

He nodded at the fire, signalling he'd made his point. Then, returning his attention to Ash, he asked, "What's the news from the parish hall, lad?"

Ash threw back the tangle of dirty blonde curls and approached the fireplace. "Just like you expected, Pa. There's confusion and anger everywhere. But one thing's for sure. The Free Church is here to stay."

"Well, that settles it," he roared, straightening his shoulders. "I don't think we can live here much longer. Who would ever have thought the Church of Scotland— of Scotland!—would be ruined like this."

Alice joined him, wiping her hands on her apron. "I know an' all, my love. Even here in this house. See how the lads have taken a shine to that charismatic preacher, followin' his words, brawlin' with their friends. I canna figure what to make of it." She reflected a moment and slid beside him, eyes transfixed on the sputtering blaze.

"But Lionel, our family's been here for many a year. Our roots run deep. We canna just up and leave and—"

"Aye, but sure it fits a pattern. Da warned me of their doings, my grandparents did, too." He lowered his voice. "That group's been operating a long time, sowing dissension everywhere. And now, they're not only in Edinburgh, but inside the Church." The fire sparked and hissed. "Is there no stopping the... what is it they call themselves again... the Sodality of Truth?"

"Oh, we can, dear, we must. How far the Free Church has spread its terrible tentacles is a mystery, but my gut tells me the others are behind it an' all. We must live where they aren't, to protect the—." Alice rubbed her hands together and stared at Ash. "Oh, I don't know. We'll talk later."

"Mark my words, love, and mind my intentions."

She smiled. "We've always been a team. That'll never change, but I'll think on this and gather meself. We canna leave without plannin' and thinkin' an' all." Alice glanced furtively at her husband, then returned to the kitchen.

A minute passed as Ash stayed close to the fire, beads of rainwater still dripping from his clothes. Then he looked at his father. "I'm still gonna go, Pa. You understand that, eh?"

He nodded sadly.

A month ago, after announcing his departure to make his own way as a man, their immediate reaction was one of fear. Lionel worried he'd be left with too much work, and would have none of it. Alice smiled but kept her thoughts hidden.

"Aye, I've come to that realization, laddie," he said. "I don' like it and s'pose I never will, but you... well, you were always different. Did ye notice that, son?"

Ash thought about his older siblings on their own, either starting families or moving to the city for work. But *he needed more, something other than settling here. No, he realized that leaving was necessary. An urgent calling deep within compelled him to pursue a new path, divorced from the Disruption, and far from... them.*

"Pa, you're convinced the dark ones are behind the split in the Church?"

"Indeed, I am. We've spoken about this, eh, I've told you all I know about them an' all. And now, I see their work again." He placed his thick hands on Ash's shoulders. "You must flee, certainly. My selfishness wants you to stay near, with us, one day take over the farm. But you an' I share the gift, eh? You and I... well, we jes' know."

Ash nodded. The last time he sensed something else, someone else's thoughts when he touched certain objects, was fresh in his mind.

He envisioned things others had no clue about. An invisible world only he and his father could observe. None of the brothers or sisters did. They chastised his foolishness, made him the family pariah. But his pa never did.

"None o' my friends can sense things, either."

"No, that's understandable. Very few share the gift." He paused. "But now, before ye leave in the morning, recognize these are dangerous times, wee Ash. I must give you something to take and hold dear wherever you go."

Lionel pulled the dusty trunk from the corner by the hearth and pried it open.

"This old thing," he said, "has kept our treasures safe for many years. When me ancestors come north from London during the Great Fire, they bought this chest and it's been with the family ever since."

He swung the lid free and the rusty hinges groaned.

"What's in there, Pa?"

"Oh, mostly your ma's keepsakes. Look here. Her

weddin' dress." Lionel smiled, his eyes disappearing into the gloom. "I wager she could still wear it an' all, even after birthing you lot."

Ash touched the material in wonder.

"But this," he said, reaching for an object buried under the dress, "is the one thing you must take and, promise me lad, keep safe. Then pass it down to that future child of yours." He winked. "You'll know which one."

Ash blushed and knelt beside his father as he pulled out a parcel wrapped in an old blanket. After unfolding it, Ash found another piece of clothing. "What is that?"

"Aye, well, that's the question, eh? T'is a mystery where it come from, but it's been with us for a long time. Here, have a look."

Lionel peeled it apart. The garment was an ancient robe, thinned from the years, and cut for a short man. Dark splotches stained it here and there, and a lavender stripe ran along the hem in a herringbone pattern.

"Now, tell me what you see."

Ash reached out and gathered the garment. Immediately, his fingers warmed, and an awesome power surged through his body, unlike he'd ever felt before.

"Pa, it's... I canna say."

"Aye, you have the sight, heh. You and me, m' lad."

The boy held it, turning it over, upholding then refolding the robe before him. His eyes grew wide.

"Pa?"

"Aye, son, you see it an' all. Now, mind my word. Take this, and no harm shall come to ya. Keep it safe from the others, the ones in the shadows. You understand what it can do?"

"I do, Pa. Clear as your face."

"Good. Now, no more talk."

THE FOLLOWING MORNING, ASH ROBERTSON GATHERED HIS simple pack as the sun broke through thick clouds in the hills. A few raindrops pattered in the lane. He'd have to run to catch the carriage to Edinburgh, then the train to Glasgow. He wished his parents well. Alice shed a few tears, but her face radiated with joy. He hopped on the carriage bound for the city, and was dropped off at the railway station.

As the train lurched through the countryside, Ash fell in with a young family from the coast, also heading west. The husband was about the same age as James, his second oldest brother. His pregnant wife had just turned 20, the man said. Their rosy-cheeked child fussed on her lap.

"So, leaving for Canada?" Ash confirmed over the grating of the steel wheels and the whining bairn.

"We are, me and Mary and wee Darroch. Gonna start a fresh life away from all this."

"You talkin' about the Disruption?"

"Not only. The famine, my friend. Have you not heard an' all? The peasants in Ireland are starvin' to death in the streets. The British are doin' naught to help 'em. Me cousin who comes from Lake District, tells me them folk ha' taken to cannibalism jes' to stay alive. Whate'er you do, mate, don' be goin' to Ireland. Imagine, havin' to eat…"

The toddler shrieked. Mary tried to comfort him with no luck. Ash, knowing what to do, reached across the aisle, and touched the lad's forehead. The boy immediately settled.

"Oy, see now Mary, this fella knows summat about bein' a da." Then his eyes sparkled, and a smile crossed his face. "Say, maybe you'd like to travel with us to the colonies? The Telegraph sails in the morning from Glasgow if you're innerested."

Ash considered the idea. He hadn't planned to cross

the Atlantic; thought that Glasgow would give him an opportunity to work and make his way in life. But Canada...

He prayed to the Lord for wisdom and guidance, and his mind found the Book of Proverbs.

There are many devices in a man's heart; nevertheless the counsel of the Lord, that shall stand.

A moment later, assured of what to do, he said, "Aye, Canada. That's a bonny adventure. The Lord willin', I'll be on the Telegraph when she sets sail in the mornin'."

NINETEEN

DAWSON PULLED INTO A MOTEL OFF AUTOROUTE 40 near Beaconsfield on the West Island of Montreal in the dead of night. Hannah had dozed after reviewing their notes from Boston Township, but never fell into a deep sleep. It seemed like the events in the bush had all happened a lifetime ago. He parked outside the shabby, paint-peeled office, nudged Hannah, and went inside to book a place for the remaining few hours of darkness.

They were in luck. The droopy-eyed manager had one room left at the end facing the highway. Dawson wondered about how he'd pay for this after slapping his credit card down, but the most important thing was to meet with Charlie Denton and uncover any clues at McGill that could help them solve the mystery of the farmhouse photograph, and possibly reveal who else might be interested in whatever message it contained.

Hannah said nothing as she followed him to the room, clutching her overnight bag. He unlocked the door and swung it open, fumbled for the light switch, and entered.

There was only one bed.

Hannah froze in the doorway.

"You take it, Hannah. I'll sleep in the car."

"No, no, stay here. I'm used to being on the floor." She smiled demurely—her voice soft, full of fatigue—then grabbed a thin pillow and held it to her chest.

"Forget it. You take the bed and I'll camp out. It'll remind me of the fishing cabin my dad used to take me to."

They washed up and prepared for sleep without invading each other's privacy. Dawson grabbed an extra blanket from the wardrobe and settled down by the dresser. Hannah wanted to review the day before turning off the light, but he was bagged and, within moments of his head hitting the pillow, fell sound asleep.

MORNING BROKE WITH SUNSHINE BLASTING THE ROOM. Dawson stirred, rubbing his eyes and stretching. He sat up, blinking in the harsh light and, surprisingly, found Hannah on the floor beside him, curled up under a blanket. When he stood and checked the bed, he knew it hadn't been slept in.

He quietly showered and dressed, and as he left the bathroom, Hannah was awake, gazing out the window, the thin blanket wrapped around her shoulders.

"You did it again," he said.

"Yeah."

"Have any bad dreams?"

She hesitated. "No, not this time."

"Well, that's good news."

"Matt, listen. I didn't have the nightmare because I joined you before falling asleep." She grabbed her clothes from the end of the bed and disappeared into the

149

bathroom.

AFTER CIRCLING MANY SIDE STREETS AROUND THE congested McGill campus, Dawson lucked out and found a parking spot on Aylmer Street, a couple blocks from the main entrance on Sherbrooke. His phone said 11:15. He locked up and they strolled to the university, taking in the racket and sights of the big city.

Hannah scanned the area. They'd seen no more of that red car or any sign of the creeper from the bush, and Dawson considered the man gone. No one, other than their colleagues in London and Charlie Denton, knew their whereabouts. That provided a large measure of comfort. Hannah strolled beside him, gazing up at stone and glass buildings jammed together.

"Not much green space," she said.

"First time I've been here, but I've seen old photos. This place used to be a cow pasture in the country. Hard to believe how much has changed."

They studied the campus map located by a row of benches, found the building where the geology labs were, and headed off. Charlie had said to drop in any time, that he was always fixing equipment or prepping labs, and anyone in the department could track him down.

They entered the building, and the dusty smell of old paper, stale air, and spilled coffee floated in the scholarly mist. Groups of chattering students milled about, and some of them gazed at the obvious newcomers. Hannah quickly spotted the right hallway, which they followed to a small, open lab with lots of smog-scarred windows along the far wall. Inside, a short man with thick, salt and pepper hair hovered over a wooden tray of mineral specimens. He wore a tattered and stained navy blue smock and glanced up as they entered.

"Charlie?"

"Yes, yes, welcome! You must be Grey's son, Matt!" He brushed his hands together and greeted them. "Evidently you found the place okay. Pleasant trip?"

Dawson was immediately struck by the man's warmth. "Yes, and thanks again for seeing us on such short notice."

Charlie invited them to grab a stool at one of the benches. "Oh, sure, no problem. I knew your dad real well. Real well."

"How far back did you two go?"

"Well, let's see... we first worked together on a survey near Big Trout Lake, must be 30 years ago. He hadn't met Beth yet. Yes," he said, eyes sparkling, "it *was* in northern Ontario. He was surveying, and I was at the base camp for a couple weeks helping the crew with some technical equipment. I liked him right away. Not your typical field geologist."

Dawson smiled, imagining his dad as a young man. "What was he like?"

Charlie cocked his head as if sifting through weathered memories. "Well, over the years I got to know him like a brother. He was a quiet, generous man. And so proud of you, Matthew. Talked about you all the time." His face darkened. "But there was something else."

"What do you mean?"

"Not sure how to put this." He scratched his chin with a thumb. "He seemed real thoughtful. No, that's not quite right. Sad, maybe? He'd get these distant looks and disappear... emotionally, like... missing out on a conversation the guys had around him. Hard to explain."

Dawson and Hannah shared a knowing glance.

"Still," Charlie said, "I had a lot of time for Grey. Solid man." He slapped his thighs. "Well, you must be eager to see the leftover junk. Let me show you the stores and you can muck around there as long as you like."

He led the way down the sticky hall. They arrived at a steel door, which he unlocked and swung open.

The gloomy storage room had no windows and dim fluorescent lighting. It was the size of a small seminar room, lined with shelves running floor to ceiling with two massive worktables in the centre. Dawson recognized the equipment in there: a buffalo gun for seismic work, a couple of proton magnetometers and VLF generators, mag loops, and crates of specimens.

"The stuff from your dad's project is in this corner," Charlie muttered, pointing to the far end. "I haven't looked at it in years, but if I recall, the field notes from the scientists and students are in these boxes." He pulled a couple off the middle shelf. "There's a bunch more underneath, too. God knows what's in them."

"Thanks, Charlie." Dawson tossed his backpack on one of the worktables. Grinning at Hannah, he asked, "Shall we get to it?"

She nodded and rolled up her sleeves.

"Well, I'm down the hall if you have any questions, so I'll leave you to it. Got a crop of second-year mineralogists coming to the lab shortly." He turned before exiting the room. "Just swing the door closed when you're done."

"Will do."

Hannah smiled and dug into one of the boxes Charlie had dragged out, pulling worn books, maps, and musty field notes out and stacking them on the table.

After an hour of picking through the dusty remnants of the project, Hannah crawled under the bottom shelf and slid the last two remaining crates out. They'd found nothing with his dad's name or handwriting, and Dawson got discouraged.

"I guess this is it, eh?" Hannah said as she struggled to lift a crate on the table.

"Yeah. Any more blanks and we'll have to rethink our next move."

"But you already *know* what to do next, Matt."

He didn't need to think long. "Pick up the photograph again."

The box Dawson poked through was filled with bags of rock specimens, a couple of field books that a *Sheila McWhatters* had scribbled notes in from survey lines north of Kirkland Lake, and a handful of half-used spools of trail marker tape. Nothing from his dad. He leaned over beside Hannah, close enough to hint at attractive danger, but she didn't back away.

"No luck here, Matt," she sighed, lifting moldy folders and topo maps out. "We may be—". Her hands stopped.

"What is it?"

"Hang on." Hannah swept aside an envelope overflowing with stained reports and pulled out two odd-looking field books. These were leather bound, no larger than pocket notepads. She wiped their covers off. Both were inscribed with the initials *GGD*.

"Oh my god," he whispered. "Grey Gareth Dawson."

Dawson tried opening one, but it was sealed, petrified as if the pages and cover were glued together. "What the—" Hannah struggled with the other. It wouldn't open either.

"They must've got soaked at some point, probably out in the field. Never dried properly, and after all that water and time, well, they're shut tight. Not even a steam bath could fix these."

"Still," she said, brushing dust and dirt blotches off the book, "no question these were his, and they're unlike any other common field books we've seen. So my guess is they're definitely personal journals." She held back a smile, then hugged him before catching herself, and backed away awkwardly.

Dawson only half listened. His mind was already in the physics lab at Western. The experiment he'd established with Wendy used a tomographic arrangement to decode coherent information on a quantum level. But what if they reconfigured the equipment to image the interior of the journals? They'd have to tear down Gunar's work and rebuild the apparatus to isolate individual pages, and Gunar would vent a spleen if he found that out. Still, the imaging technology existed back at the lab.

"I have an idea how to read these notes."

"Tell all, Mr. Dawson."

"Using the scanning equipment in the physics lab. I'll text Wendy and ask her to map it out." As he sent messages and pictures of the journals to Wendy, Hannah poked around the room. At one point she'd perched herself on a stool and bowed her head.

Wendy: *Gunar's not happy you didn't show up for some meeting. He's planned a lab demo with other profs next week. Better return ASAP.*

Dawson: *leaving in a few minutes. Will be back tonight. I'll talk to him in the morning.*

Wendy: *reconfiguring the equipment will get us in deep trouble. Not sure I can do that?*

Dawson: *I'll take responsibility. Please, I need to uncover what's in these notes.*

Several minutes lapsed before her return text— *okay*—and Dawson thanked her. "Better clean this crap up and say goodbye to Charlie."

They returned everything to the boxes and organized the shelves better than they were before. Hannah stuffed the two leather journals into her pack.

"I can't wait to get home and shower. There must be decades of dust covering this gear," she said, gazing back at the room from the hallway.

Dawson ran his fingers through his locks. "I know what you mean." He flicked off the light switch and stood in the doorway, staring into the darkness.

Hannah waited, but he didn't move. "Don't worry, Matt, we'll get these unstuck."

"It's not that." Dawson reflected on the morning's work. "Something Charlie said earlier struck a chord."

"What?"

He searched her eyes. "When he talked about my dad... I never remembered him saying he was proud of me, or that he loved me. I'm sure he must have because we did all kinds of things together, but I just don't remember him ever saying the words. Strange, isn't it? In this case, maybe actions don't speak louder than words." He faced her, struggling with the emotion flooding his body. "I guess it would've nice to actually hear the words."

Hannah placed her hand on his back. "I won't pretend to understand what you're feeling," she said in a low voice, "but if it helps, for the longest time I felt worthless and unloved even though my parents said they loved me all the time. That feeling of shame had no basis in fact, logically, but it didn't matter."

He gave her a puzzled look.

"I wound up searching for acceptance with a bad crowd in high school. Skipped classes, got into all kinds of trouble. It may surprise you to know that I wasn't always a Christian. I didn't grow up in a church and my parents weren't believers. They still aren't."

They stared in silence at each other, lost in shadows spilling from the darkened room. Dawson asked, "But obviously you came through it, I mean, look at you now."

She smiled, lowering her head, and he felt her radiating warmth.

"I've learned a few truths over the years. You may not want to hear this now, but the thing about people in our lives is, no matter how much we love them, eventually we'll either leave them, or they'll abandon us. I lost someone really close to me when I was 18. But no matter when, it happens to all of us."

"Oh, thanks. That's a real comfort." He smirked playfully.

"Still, that's the point, Matt. I found someone who will never desert me. Ever. And you can, too. I accepted Jesus shortly after Emily's death, and my whole life has changed so much."

Dawson's innate defensiveness stirred and snuffled, and *that voice* felt like telling her to get bent with all this God talk, until another thought wedged into his head, shunting his defiance away... a tiny idea, the seed of potential. He gazed into her haunted eyes and, after mysteriously losing his natural tendency to lash out, wondered *what if she's right?*

TWENTY

"WHAT DO YOU MEAN THEY'RE NOWHERE TO BE FOUND?"

Stone evaluated Florian Lamont through narrowed eyes as they met in a booth at the Talisman bar. He never cared for the man, but Lamont had proven a trustworthy foot soldier with a solid record of violence for similar operatives in The Sodality. Until now.

"Well, they must've gone somewheres other than returning here, Mr. Stone. That's the only explanation I got."

"Tell me exactly what happened after your failure at the survey site."

Lamont recounted spotting them in Temagami at a grocery store. He'd followed the pair along the highway but lost sight of them in the dusk, figuring they'd show up again in London. He drove non-stop and parked outside Dawson's apartment building and waited, but they never arrived.

"Could he be with this girl, this Hannah King?

Staying overnight at her place?"

"No, sir. When I realized Physics Boy was MIA, I circled back to her basement apartment. She lives in a residential house south of here. I knocked on the door, but the lady who owns it said she'd gone for the weekend and hadn't returned."

"Perhaps they stopped at a hotel along the way for some fun and games?"

"Possibly."

Stone sipped his tea and reviewed the glyphs in front of him. *Slippery little bastard.*

"What do we know about this girl?"

Lamont wiped a bead of sweat from his cheek and opened a pad. "She's in neurosciences. A grad student. Sketchy background. Abandoned as a young kid. Adopted by a couple in Scarborough." He flipped through the pages. "Did her undergraduate work at York University and is part-way through her doctoral program."

"What's her speciality?" he asked, wondering if one of her professors might be a suitable candidate for recruiting.

Lamont cleared his throat. "Some weird subject called psychometry." He looked up. "I don't have the details."

Stone realized the connection. Dawson was deliciously ignorant of the photo, had no sense of its history or power to change the course of human progress. But she might.

"This girl, Ms. King, is of great interest to me. I'm confident The Whisper will want to know all about her."

"Mr. Stone," Lamont uttered, lowering his eyes, "I have failed The Sodality."

Stone cocked his head and inhaled deeply. The smell of the bar—ghostly cigarette smoke and booze—soothed him. "Maybe not. At some point, they'll return. When they left on Friday, they took overnight bags only, yes?"

"Correct."

"Then they likely stopped along the way. Go back and stake out Dawson's apartment. When he shows up, take another shot at securing the photograph."

"Understood." Lamont pushed toward the edge of the seat in the booth, preparing to leave.

"Oh, but now I want them both. Alive."

Lamont nodded.

"You just had to pull a knife and go all-out Rambo, didn't you? Had to scare them for personal entertainment, hm? So filthy and unnecessary."

"I apologize. Don't know what got into me. I thought they'd come with more easily if I threatened 'em."

"Never underestimate those two again. And next time, no weapons."

"Yes, Mr. Stone, I won't fail you."

The man rose, and Stone reached out and stopped him. "No, I should hope you've learned a lesson."

Lamont slinked out of the bar, and Stone returned to his tea and notes. There was simply no alternative now but to report directly to her.

He taxied back to the downtown hotel and sat at the tiny desk in his room. Silence enveloped the entire floor except for the soft sounds of a vacuum cleaner at the far end of the hallway. Stone punched in her number and waited. Within a moment, she answered. The woman's voice was barely audible. Clicks of the encrypted signal punctuated the connection and he wondered casually where she might be lurking today.

"I have some news on the Dawson file."

Stone briefed The Whisper. She remained silent while he explained the weak excuse for not possessing the old photograph and why he had yet to discuss the phenomenon with Matt Dawson.

After a moment's pause, she asked, "What of this girl?"

"Yes, Hannah King. As I said, ma'am, she's also a grad student at Western and is helping the young man interpret the incident, according to Lamont's report."

"But...?"

"Well," he cleared his throat and looked out the window at the parking lot below. "Ms. King is an unknown complication. Her understanding of the photo's power is unknown and, if Mr. Dawson ever clarified his thinking and discovered it, the significance to The Sodality would be impressive. But I assure you, ma'am, she will be taken as well. The two are apparently inseparable but once back on campus, they're obliged to return to their studies and old routines."

"I see." The Whisper paused, breathing lightly. Stone knew enough not to interrupt her when she was considering a plan. After a moment, she continued. "What is the next step?"

"Lamont is staking out Mr. Dawson's apartment. When they arrive, he'll alert me. Also, I'll notify another of our clients at Western and apprise her of the situation. Ma'am, I assure you they won't go unnoticed the minute they appear."

"You assure me," she whispered, letting her words float across the line.

Stone gulped. "I—I'm confident that both targets and the photograph will be secured within 24 hours. See, ma'am, I now have a better, more fulsome understanding of Mr. Dawson's pressure points. And those for the girl shortly, too. They'll no longer have a choice but to come to us."

"For your sake," The Whisper purred, "I hope so. Do not disappoint me. You're only as useful as your last task, and we've been searching many years for this photograph. My personal interest is…" She hissed. "Exquisite."

"Understood. I'll call when I have something new to report.

"Oh," she continued, raising her voice ever so slightly, "please make sure that Dr. Gunar, the recent addition, does not become a problem. His profile is less than ideal."

"Of course."

He listened to her breathe without saying a word, waiting for any additional instructions. Then the connection ended.

Stone placed the phone on top of the desk and paced around the room. *This is getting complicated quickly, but nothing I can't handle.* He opened his laptop and scanned the client base and master list they'd built for The Sodality in this region. All the hundreds of names and occupations to review, all the code words used in case some hacker ever gained access to the database. All with multiple encryptions.

He sorted by institution. Under the University of Western Ontario, the algorithm had isolated half a dozen researchers. The one he remembered, the woman he defiled and recruited several years ago, was fourth on the list: Dr. Catherine Gardner, the Dean of Graduate Studies.

"Catherine," he said to the endless night. "it is time we met again."

TWENTY-ONE

THE TWO STUDENTS TOOK TURNS DRIVING FROM Montreal to London along Highway 401. The events of the past few days caught up, and Dawson dozed whenever Hannah took a shift behind the wheel.

She remained awake throughout.

For the first couple hours after leaving the city, they reviewed their observations. Hannah made copious notes and studied his dad's journals, frequently trying to pry them open but with no luck.

Dawson walked through the tomographic configuration he'd asked Wendy to set up in the lab, discussing how by using subatomic particles to pass through the books, he hoped to delineate and image each page and recover the information contained on them without having to open the journals at all. More primitive methods like steaming or bathing the journals in a chemical solution were rejected because of the potential impact on whatever may be written inside. He couldn't take the chance of destroying that. No, tomography was the right method. The only question was whether he could adjust the apparatus to scan the books and define each page to the necessary resolution.

When they arrived in London in the middle of the night, Hannah drove straight to her basement apartment. She grabbed her gear from the trunk and began walking away. Dawson leaned against the driver's side door.

"So, meet you at the lab at seven?" he asked.

"See you there, Matt." She hesitated a few feet from the car. Dawson wondered if he should say something more. They'd enjoyed a great vibe during this time, despite the apparent, unknown danger and her hesitation to get closer.

Hannah's shoulders dropped. "Oh," she said, "I forgot. I still have the journals." She eased her pack down on a patio stone and pulled the books out.

"Yeah, we'll need these." He tossed them onto the passenger seat. "Okay, well, thanks again for your help, Hannah. I…"

"Yes?"

He hesitated. "I'll see you tomorrow. Have a good sleep."

An odd mix of fatigue and disappointment clouded her face. Then she turned and stepped down to her basement digs. Dawson started the car and took off.

Idiot.

MIDNIGHT HAD COME AND GONE LONG BEFORE DAWSON pushed his apartment door open and flicked on the lights. The air inside had grown stale, and after sliding the window open to the balcony, he showered, changed into sweats and flopped on the sofa. Within moments, he'd fallen asleep with two thoughts racing through his mind: the technical details of the tomographic experiment to image the pages in the journals, and Hannah's smile when she'd found them. *I hope the nightmare takes another night off.*

The next morning, Dawson doubled up the stairs to the second floor lab in the Physics building. He carried a coffee cup in one hand, *The Study of Psychometrics* in another, and his backpack was slung over his shoulder. Hannah was already there, and she and Wendy chatted softly outside the lab as he loped down the hall, almost spilling the drink.

Hannah wore a white blouse and jeans, and her hair was up again. She smiled warmly and his heart pounded anew.

"Shall we get started?" he asked.

Wendy unlocked the heavy door, entered first and turned on the fluorescents. "Matt," she said, "Gunar's going to swing by this morning and I don't know what to tell him."

"No worries, I'll talk to the grumpy professor. He's likely bent outta shape over the analysis for his experiment. But this is far more important."

"To you, maybe," she muttered, and immediately looked away.

"Wendy, I'll manage Dr. Gunar. Don't worry. Now," he continued, walking around the workstations and eyeing the newly configured equipment, "is this ready to go?"

Hannah hadn't moved from the door. She stared tentatively at all the machines.

"Come on in, Hannah. Throw your stuff here by my desk."

She dropped her bag and retrieved a notebook.

He led her to the back of the lab where a pair of massive tomographic plates were aligned in a separate, sealed compartment. "This is where the magic happens," he said.

Hannah studied the arrangement. "Explain how this all works again?"

Dawson checked the parameters on the machine. "These two surfaces transmit subatomic particles back and forth to each other. When I put an object in this hollow cube," he grabbed the container and showed it to her, "particles pass through and we measure the changes in velocity caused by differences in density. By adjusting the particle wavelengths, we can slice the target into layers of varying thickness."

"Okay, and you think if you can pare it thin enough, you'll image what's actually on each piece of paper in the journal."

"You got it." He took one of the two journals and placed it inside the cube. "We can see the results unfold on the monitor."

Hannah grinned. "This equipment is remarkable. I can already see how it could really help in my own studies." She moved so Wendy could adjust the placement of the journal. "I had no idea," she continued. "Funny that we'd be working on similar projects and yet not recognize the similar links."

"Stove-piping," Wendy said as she closed the housing and checked all the connections. "I saw a lot of it at Boston College. Seems to be the way research is done, in stovepipes."

When Dawson was satisfied with the placement of the equipment, he said, "Let's see what we've got here."

Hannah peered at the overhead monitor closely. "I've seen these CT scans work on mice. We've used them in some neuroscience research, but I've never seen this equipment used on pieces of paper. What about the resolution?"

Dawson twisted the gain controls and prepared to

irradiate the journal. "I'm assuming each piece of paper is about 5 micrometers thick, which is pretty standard. The scanner resolution is around 40 micrometers, so we might pull out what's on a page. The real challenge is managing the noise. We'll need some major league filtering to actually see any writing, and then, to decipher letters and words. I doubt we'll be able to separate one side of each page, so that'll be a trick."

Wendy pulled a stool up to the signal processor and ran a test pattern through the computer. A series of images appeared on the overhead monitor. "It's calibrated, Matt. We're ready to go."

Dawson checked the time on his phone. The machine required several minutes of sampling in order to figure out the signal-to-noise aspects of the journal pages, and the analysis itself could take hours depending on the quality of the images. He hoped to complete scanning both books before Gunar poked his head through the door.

He killed the overhead lights so that only a couple of incandescent lamps illuminated the lab. "All right. I'm engaging the scanner."

Dawson flicked the switch to the machine and immediately adjusted the beam coherency. At first, nothing but white noise showed on the monitor, but after several minutes, the book itself resolved into a three-dimensional image.

"So far, so good. Now, let's see if we can slice this even thinner."

He and Wendy continued fine-tuning the equipment, tweaking the filtering and attenuators until a cluster of pages appeared, but they were all dark except for random bands of white around the edges.

"Try tightening the beam, Wendy," Dawson said. Hannah moved beside him, holding her breath.

But after several agonizingly long minutes, the scanner was unable to resolve the journal pages any finer than 200 micrometers, definitely not enough to image individual words, and the intense noise in the data prevented determining anything more than a few letters and parts of field sketches.

"Unfortunately," Wendy said, "that's as good as we're going to find with this one."

Dawson wrinkled his brow. "Let's try the other journal. We can come back to this one later, but I'll need Gunar onside before then."

Wendy shut down the beam and opened the housing. She replaced the first journal with the second, then secured it again.

This time, when they fired up the equipment, the images appeared much cleaner.

Hannah said, "That first book must have been dropped in the mud, but this one's surprisingly better." She studied the monitor. "Look here," she announced, pointing to a corner of the image. "I can read it!"

Dawson traced his finger along the top of one of the pages shown on the monitor.

"Amazing," he whispered, fingers trembling. "Wendy, try to resolve each individual page. I'll adjust the filtering to clean up the noise." He smiled at Hannah. "Sometimes tweaking the tomographic images is like tuning an old-fashioned radio."

After a few minutes, they could read almost every page. Wendy quickly toggled from one to another, skimming over some of his father's handwritten notes. In a peculiarly guilty way, he felt as if he intruded on his dad's private thoughts, but the loftier beauty of the objective scientific method enamored him and over-ruled his personal concern.

"Wait... hold up, Wendy."

A page fluttered by and Wendy switched back. Something caught his eye, and when they retrieved the page, the word was plain as day: *farmhouse.*

Hannah gasped. "He's talking about your photo, Matt."

"Sure seems that way. Wendy, try to clear up the rest."

After adjusting the attenuators and performing some rudimentary filtering of the data, the entire page leapt clearly into view.

October 13, 2005.
Boston Township

Just completed another full day of surveys along the line for the project. Cold, miserable weather, but all going well. Some curious findings with the proton mag. But here's the situation. I found in my stack of papers, the one reserved for random observations and maps, an old photograph of a farmhouse. A post-it note was stuck to it in my mother's writing, saying I must share this too with Matthew when he's older.

What to do? I picked up the photograph and the damn thing bit me with heat. Got the blisters to show for it. Need to tell Beth. Always suspected something when I got these weird impressions from picking up different things, but this one, well, all I can say is... ha! Don't know what to say.

The image flickered, and Wendy fine-tuned her controls. Dawson and Hannah stared at each other. He instinctively raised his fingers in front of him. "Oh my god, this is it... what we've been looking for. This ability is genetic. Passed on through... at least three generations."

Hannah reached out reassuringly and touched his

shoulder. When the image reappeared, Dawson read out
loud.

Well, that's one thing. But after I got through
with the ghosts and the waving hands, the movement
that emanated from within the photo, I was
overwhelmed with a sensation that it was trying to
communicate. I have this feeling of danger... a
warning? Can't put my finger on it. Will explore it
later, but for now I simply recognize a strange
sense.

8:07 pm
Okay, I had supper and gave this more thought.
Couldn't get the stupid thing out of my mind. The beer
isn't helping. I was in the hotel bar finishing my meal
and watching baseball on the big screen. Making some
notes to myself.
Then it happened.
The message crystallized. Not so much spoken
words, but this inner feeling again, rising from the pit
of my stomach. My hands began shaking
uncontrollably.
And I knew.
In a flash, a stock-still moment floating before
me, I understood the meaning. I have to get home, tell
Beth. What do I say? Everything? No, can't do that,
she'd lose her mind with worry. I can tell her about
the image, but not the message. I don't know where
to turn. Thought this was all there is, but I was
wrong.
The message.
The message.
The only way to describe it in words is the
following: within this photograph and apparently my
genetic code, there's a power so immense, so
immeasurable that it could change the course of the
entire world.
For better.
Or worse.

TWENTY-TWO

D AWSON CURSED UNDER HIS BREATH,

"Matt, please," Hannah whispered.

He turned to her, eyes narrowing. Then he realized he took the Lord's name in vain; distant scenes of a dusty upbringing and sporadic Sunday School attendance where he learned, for some reason, he shouldn't do that. "Right, sorry about that." He pulled a stool over to the worktable and sat in sombre reflection.

Wendy continued grabbing screenshots of the images, then she and Hannah joined him. The image of his dad's hand-written note remained on the massive monitor in front of them. Light shadows danced across the table.

"He unquestionably felt the same thing," Dawson concluded. "Mum was right."

Wendy asked, "Matt, what's going on? What is this all about?"

He looked up, scratching his scruffy cheeks. "I don't know, but we've stumbled into a great big mess." He stiffened his back. "Come on, let's scan the rest of the book."

"But Matt, that's just it."

"What?"

Wendy confronted him with her deep brown eyes. "There is no more in the journal. This was the last entry. The scanner shows a bunch of pages, but they're all blank."

"Nothing more?" Hannah asked.

Wendy shook her head.

"But," she said, "can we run a high-res scan on them anyway, just to make sure?"

Matt concurred. "Short of another session between me and the photo, this is all we've got."

Wendy's mouth twitched, and she toyed with her pen. "Let me do a page by page check of the remaining ones," she offered, moving toward the equipment. "I'll continue scanning. Something might pop up." She suddenly stopped and checked her phone. "Oh, crap."

"What is it?" Matt asked.

"Gunar will be here in half an hour and he's expecting a report on the data analysis I haven't completed yet." She paced back and forth beside the table. "Oh, no..."

"We'll set up his configuration again," Matt said, "but not until we've finished checking all those remaining pages."

Hannah turned to Wendy, "Can we quickly investigate?"

She appeared not to be listening. "He's gonna hand me his lunch, Matt. You have standing here, but I just started a couple weeks ago. I can't go up against him." Her voice rose as panic set in.

But Dawson was determined. "We're wasting time. Look," he said, tabbing through various screens on his computer, "here's a file of some earlier preliminary results he hasn't seen yet. Show him these. That'll keep him busy for a few days. But," he added, "we must see the rest of the book now.

Wendy bit her lip, then slowly returned to the attenuators and filters. "Okay, let's do it." She continued scanning the journal while Dawson and Hannah watched the monitor in frozen silence.

Nothing else appeared. Page after page of empty space. The odd smudge here and there, likely due to noise in the system, possibly finger marks or other stains, but no writing.

Several minutes passed, and he was close to giving up when, just before Wendy shut down the experiment, more writing appeared.

"Whoa, hang on. There's something in the margins."

She tweaked the equipment, and the pages fluttered by on the screen. Then Hannah noticed it, too. "Looks like a name."

Wendy fine-tuned the apparatus until the markings cleared up. Indeed, words appeared in the smudges: *Dr. Christopher Rathbourne* followed by *LU* and another word they couldn't resolve. The closest they deciphered were two letters: *N* and *R. Neuro something?*

"Do you see it, Hannah?"

"Yeah, sure do. That name's familiar."

"Wendy, can you google this guy Rathbourne, please?"

Wendy jumped to the computer and ran a search. He was in there all right. "Dr. Christopher Rathbourne, Laurentian University, Department of Neurosciences." She read in silence a moment longer, then said, "Matt, you won't believe this."

He and Hannah watched over her shoulder as she scrolled through various pages.

"Look at all the journal citations. There must be a hundred. I don't understand these topics, but the sheer volume where he's first author…"

Hannah tapped Matt on the arm. "Time," she said.

"Okay, we can follow up on his publications later, but let's shut this down and set Gunar's experiment up."

They sprang to action and turned off the scanner. Wendy lifted the table top apparatus and returned it to the equipment shelf. Matt wheeled the monitors from Gunar's experiments and placed them front and center in the lab again.

"Listen," Wendy said, pushing a box of gear back on the shelf, "if he finds you here, he'll totally vent a spleen, especially if he sees *you* in the lab, Hannah. No unauthorized persons, you understand."

"I'd better go, then."

"Me, too," Dawson said. "Look, Hannah, what do you think about the findings? Like, I got a million questions buzzing in my head. And what did Dad mean about this message changing the world? And how do these visions run in the family?"

She grabbed the journals and stuffed them in her backpack. "Well, I don't teach till this afternoon, so if you want to hit the library, I can show you some background material. Might give us something."

"Okay, let's scram." Dawson swung the lab door open and peeked along the corridor. A few first-year students were hanging around, laughing. "Wendy, I owe you big time for all this."

She nodded, but her face held traces of delicate betrayal.

"I'll make it up to you, I swear."

Hannah stood outside in the hallway. Her head darted back and forth. "Come on, Matt," she urged.

But Wendy's look hurt him, a reminder of his

inability to keep his word. In his heart, something changed. He'd promised to return yesterday, and he hadn't. Now he promised to make amends. But the words rang hollow. He looked her in the eye and lowered his voice.

"Wendy, this mystery fills every waking moment of my day. My Mum's worried I'm about to die, I'm seeing visions I can't explain, and there's some psychotic bush man stalking us, too. I have to do this, Wendy, so I honestly can't say when I'll be able to help. I'm also a complete idiot for pretending otherwise. But I must solve this first, because I'm no help to anyone while this psychometric business hangs over me like the sword of Damocles. I'm sorry."

Her mouth opened momentarily, but no words came.

"See you soon."

He exited the lab and heard that dreaded voice, the familiar clacking of the professor's footsteps on the marble flooring.

Gunar yell-talked to someone around the corner and was clearly heading this way.

"Quick, Hannah, follow me!"

They dashed in the opposite direction down the corridor, slamming through the doors to another stairwell. He spotted Gunar turning the corner with a couple of bootlick students trailing behind.

Hannah was halfway down the stairs. "Is he there?"

"Uh-huh, but we're good." He caught up, and they raced down both flights, then jogged from the building.

The pair headed straight toward Weldon Library and casually mingled in with dozens of other students, all criss-crossing in various directions along the outdoor plaza.

"Matt," Hannah said, catching her breath. "You've gotta talk to him. Don't leave Wendy alone to do that."

"Yeah."

He pointed to a concrete bench, and they sat. Then he pulled out his phone and emailed the professor.

"What'd you say?"

"I told him something important came up. A family matter. And that Wendy had some preliminary results to review." He turned to her. "It's lame, bordering on a lie, and I guess he'll crap on me anyway. But he's the least of my worries."

Hannah sighed, and a magnificent smile broke out on her face. "With all the excitement, I almost forgot to tell you something."

"What? What is it?"

"Last night, I was so exhausted from our trip, but I dreaded going to sleep because of... this creep in my nightmare."

"And?"

She looked deeply into his eyes. "This'll sound super corny, and it's not my intention to weird you out or anything, because I'm still trying to process things..."

"Say the words, Hannah. What happened?"

"I fell asleep, *in my bed*—not on the floor, you'll be happy to know—thinking of... of you and our little adventure. And," she added, "it was an awesome night." Her face beamed.

"No nightmares?"

"Not a one." She lowered her head. "Okay, full on corny now, but when I'm near you, I feel... protected. Safe. And not from anything you do or say. Just from being around. Weird, eh?"

He grinned, marveling at the minor miracle, and instinctively leaned closer. They hugged, neither prepared to pull away. After several moments, he finally released her and said, "Come on. There's work to do."

THE MONOLITHIC WELDON LIBRARY CONTRASTED sharply with the historical limestone buildings on campus like an architectural hemorrhoid. All smooth concrete, with few windows. Not what Dawson envisioned as a centre of knowledge in such a prestigious university. But what the monster lacked in aesthetics, it made up for in volumes of books and access to online journals.

He and Hannah found a clear worktable and staked it out with their backpacks. Dawson pulled out his laptop and flipped it open. Hannah remained standing, gazing around, hands on hips.

"I'll be back in a few minutes," she said, and skipped away to the stairs, heading toward the forest of publications.

Dawson scanned his emails. Sure enough, Gunar had sent several over the past 24 hours. Their contents were predictable, and he deleted them. Charlie Denton also emailed, saying it was a pleasure to meet him and that he hoped they'd found something helpful. Dawson responded with a quick *thank you.*

A text message from his mother blinked. She was checking in, and he texted immediately: *all good mum. Back on campus and into the research.*

He didn't bother specifying the nature of his investigation.

When he glanced up, Hannah approached with a stack of books in her arms. She dumped the pile in the centre of the table.

"There you go," she announced. "Scan through these and you'll be in better shape."

"What gives?" he asked, glancing at the covers. "*Psychometrics for Dummies?* Seriously?" He laughed.

"See, that's the problem with this field. Because it's considered a fringe science and the mechanisms and methodologies haven't been perfected like those in your world, all kinds of crackpots dive in, spewing garbage."

"How so?"

"Well," she said, sitting down, "take the *Dummies* book. It's basically a manifestation manual. You know, think hard enough about something, and you can manipulate the future. All that *Secret* nonsense?"

Dawson nodded. "Yeah, I never paid attention to any of that. While there's little harm in positive thinking, too many guys lose themselves in this sorcery. Placing way too much faith in it, know what I mean?"

"Interesting choice of words... sorcery...," she said, leaning back. "But never mind. You need to understand the principles behind the phenomena. *Dummies* is okay if you stick to the historical aspects. These others are better. At least the authors attempt to take a serious scientific approach to the subject."

He picked over them like a smorgasbord.

"But," she added, "the professor your dad mentioned isn't here. He's written books, of course, but I think we'll have more luck with the online journals."

They logged in and scoured the various academic sites. Hannah knew the ones to focus on that shared a modicum of respect in her field as well as the social sciences. Over the next two hours, they'd downloaded a dozen articles, half of which were authored by Dr. Rathbourne. Dawson's head spun with the mountain of additional information.

"Hannah, look, this is great, but we need to do something. Like, visit Laurentian and talk to this professor. Learn what his team is up to and whether they've heard of this photo business before."

"I agree, but there are practical implications to consider, like, I teach this afternoon and again on Thursday morning. I can't just up and leave, and I doubt you can either."

Dawson clenched his jaw. He'd been prepared to ask Wendy to cover the undergrad labs for him, but that wouldn't be fair. "I've got a class tomorrow and Thursday morning, too, but we could leave after that. The weekend again? We could go to Laurentian on Friday, meet with Rathbourne and show him the photograph then. Perhaps he can interpret the visions? A geology buddy of mine and his wife live there, so we could crash at his place, and—" He suddenly caught his breath.

Hannah was fixing her hair on top of her head. A rare beam of sunlight filtered through the prison-like compound and caught her golden highlights. He was mesmerized by her honest beauty.

She looked up. "Okay, but there's two things, right? There's the psychometric part—what we're looking at now—but there's also the hidden message, the power your dad alluded to. Where do we even begin with that?"

"Wait a sec," Dawson said. He tabbed through various screens on the laptop until he found the journal he wanted. "Yeah, here it is. *Applications of Psychometrics Beyond Sensory Impressions.* Rathbourne authored it, and he discusses hidden worlds, multiple universes, and how limited our knowledge of science truly is."

"Show me," Hannah said, dragging a chair closer.

Dawson scanned the article until he found the passage that examined black and white holes, the multiverse, and whether some*one*, or some*thing*, had observed our universe into existence at the Big Bang. "I don't know how this relates to the photo or my dad, but lots of these researchers feel psychometry is a portal to another dimension... a spiritual realm. This Rathbourne guy says his studies led him to the possible existence of God. Not solid, incontrovertible proof that God exists, but all evidence and theories point that way according to him." He turned to her. "I wonder if the message Dad got came from another dimension... a spiritual realm?"

"Interesting," Hannah murmured, smiling, "but I already *know* God exists."

"Touché."

Dawson continued reading the journal findings out loud until Hannah interrupted. "Would you like to hear about it?"

"'Bout what?" he asked, eyes fixed on the screen, half paying attention.

"My faith."

He stopped and looked at her with a brittle mix of curiosity and defiance. "Hannah, you know I don't really believe that stuff, right?"

"Sure, all the more reason to stay open-minded." She brushed a loose hair behind her ear.

Dawson was intrigued, but he suspected Hannah would bombard him with the salvation speech and come to Jesus thing. He had no desire to roast in Hell like the YouTube preachers warned him about, so he pushed that thought away. *No Jesus, no Hell.* "Maybe I'll just stick with this, if that's alright with you."

She smiled and agreed, and they returned to the literature search. Sometime later, Hannah suddenly checked her phone and began packing up. "I gotta get to the classroom."

"Oh, right," he said, unable to hide his disappointment. He cleared his throat and stacked the books together, closed the laptop. "So," he said, "thanks for your help today. And I'll contact that prof at Laurentian about meeting with us."

"Okay, great." She tossed her pack over her shoulder. "I guess I'll see you around?"

He hesitated, suddenly caught in a high anxiety moment. "Sure. Listen, I was kinda hoping, er, we could possibly get together and review these notes some time. In case there are...connections...in the data, like." He grinned awkwardly.

"You're funny," she giggled. "Are you asking me out on a date, Matt Dawson?"

"Um, yeah... I guess I am." He exhaled and relaxed.

"Well, you have an entirely scientific approach to it." She smiled and hurried toward the exit.

He watched her leave, then sighed. *Another missed opportunity?*

"The answer's yes, by the way." Hannah called from across the open lobby by the main doors. Several heads turned.

"Hm?"

She motioned for him to call her later, then pivoted and vanished.

TWENTY-THREE

DAWSON WAITED OUTSIDE DR. GUNAR'S OFFICE, rocking on his heels. He checked his phone—the fifth time since arriving—wondering what took the professor so long. He pressed an ear to the closed door and thought he heard hushed whispers. *Perhaps he's with someone?*

Wendy left the lab an hour ago for the day. She'd been spending crazy days in that sour air covering for him, and now that he'd re-engaged, she needed some chill time. He agreed to work that evening as soon as his meeting with Gunar was done.

The professor's email was curt: *See me in my office at 6:00. Don't be late.*

He checked his phone again: 6:15. The thought of ditching and heading to the lab crossed his mind. If Gunar wanted to talk so badly, he could locate him there. But just then the door clicked open, snapping him back from his reverie.

"You may enter now, Mr. Dawson."

He followed Gunar inside and squeezed into the chair facing his massive desk. The tops of his kneecaps touched the front of it and he grimaced when he hit a corner.

"You've been a traveling man, Mr. Dawson. Running all over the country, hm?"

Dawson refused to answer, staring at a pile of undergraduate lab reports and hand-written notes on the man's desk. Something amidst the clutter caught his eye. Gunar had doodled around the word *Sodality* and a series of bullet points he couldn't decipher. The professor brusquely dragged a few papers over it.

"Stay focused, please. Seems while you were vacationing, you abandoned Wendy and left her to cover for your absence. Even I, Mr. Dawson, would never have bladed a colleague like that, let alone a prized student. I pull strings to bring her in, a rising star in the field, to assist you in finishing up your results before she gets her own lab. And what do you do? You leave." Gunar shook his head. "Do you have anything to say for yourself?"

Dawson cleared his throat and inhaled. "Wendy picked it up fast, sir. I was fully confident she'd handle the work while I investigated the mystery around my father's death. I was gone the weekend, which is my time, and—"

"And you were gallivanting around Montreal yesterday." He narrowed his gaze. "That was on *my* time."

Dawson's jaw hung open. He quelled the rising defiance, that inner voice that desperately wanted to tell this asshole to piss off. Instead, he swallowed the burning embers within and faced the professor.

"I was pursuing this other line of enquiry... the one I told you about last week. Remember, when I asked for some personal time?"

"Oh, I remember, to be sure. It seems you're treating my work as secondary to your flights of fringe science fantasy."

"It's not—" Dawson's voice rose, and he composed himself. "It's not fantasy, Dr. Gunar. Sure, there's a lot of strange ideas in psychometrics that lean toward *woo-woo* thinking, but we also uncovered some good, sound science. Do you want to see?" He reached for his backpack.

"No, that's quite all right. And, to be fair, I'd like to understand what you experienced. In fact, that was the basis of the meeting you missed with me yesterday." He leaned forward on his desk. "I still want to know more about what's got you so... distracted."

Professor," he started, "why the sudden interest? I mean no disrespect, sir, but what I saw in that photograph has nothing to do with your experiment."

"Oh?"

"Right. It implicates my father and how he died 13 years ago."

Dawson recounted snippets of what he and Hannah observed in his mother's basement, and finding the two journals at McGill. He kept the run-in with the bush psycho and the tomographic scan of the books to himself.

"I have a colleague who has expressed profound interest in your observations," Gunar said, locking eyes with him. "An ally in a position to help you, if you're interested."

Dawson straightened his back. His knees dug farther into the front of the desk. "Yes, I am. Who is it? Someone here?"

"Patience, Mr. Dawson. You see, all I mentioned to him was this... psychometric experience you had, and he wanted more details. That's why I scheduled our meeting that you blew off. That's why I'm talking to you now."

The hairs on the back of Dawson's neck bristled. Something didn't add up. "We're still trying to figure out the mystery. In fact, I'd like you to reconsider my request for time off, sir, to study the phenomenon more."

Gunar leaned back, placing his palms face down on the desk in front of him. The corner of his mouth twitched.

"See, me and my friend Hannah, well, we came across some fascinating information about the effect and I'd like to go to Sudbury on Thursday to meet the researchers at Laurentian and, if it pans out, I want to pursue it. I've already been in touch with Professor Rathbourne at the Laurentian Neuroscience Lab, and they're expecting me Friday morning."

Gunar sat in stony silence.

"I can trade off with another TA to cover my teaching, and even though Wendy's new to the project, she's wicked smart and is already pulling results out of the data, and—"

"That'll be quite enough, Mr. Dawson," the professor whispered. A slick grin crossed his face and his eyes darkened. "I am not prepared to give you any time off. And let me be clear: if you fail to carry out your teaching responsibilities in the labs, and refuse to report to my project, then I'm going to seriously look at pushing your thesis completion date out. Again."

Heat rose in Dawson's cheeks and he slouched back in the chair, his mind spinning about how he could still show this professor at Laurentian the photograph and maybe get his help on solving the mystery of his father's death and what this apparent world-changing power could be. He refused to tip off Gunar about that. The man would laugh him out of grad school. Physics + psychometry = professional ridicule.

"But I'm a fair man, and willing to give you the benefit of the doubt. So hear me well." Gunar leaned on his elbows, inching closer to Dawson's face. "I want everything you have on this photo effect, understand? Everything. Your notes, what you saw in your father's journals, what you did over the weekend. Who you spoke with at McGill. All of it." He narrowed his gaze. "And, naturally, I need the photograph. Not a copy, though. I must have the original, the one I suspect you're carrying with you right now."

Dawson gulped. The anger continued percolating, and he gripped the chair like a vise. His knuckles turned white.

"If you're willing and able to do that, I'm prepared to let this little sojourn of yours slide. Yes, I know. Very generous."

Dawson worked his jaw muscles but refused to speak.

"Hand over everything and get back to work on my project, then I'll forget the past week ever happened."

The wall clock ticked loudly as he sifted through Gunar's words. There's no way he could comply. Not now. Not when he and Hannah were getting closer to finding the truth. But he also had a responsibility to Wendy, to finish his thesis work and graduate with a PhD under his arm.

Am I willing to forfeit my future over this?

"Do you agree with the arrangement?"

Dawson lowered his head. "I'll get everything back after, right?"

"Of course, once you've finished the experiment and begin writing up your thesis. I'll return it all then, but not before. We can't afford any more distractions."

"Who is this colleague you want to share it with?"

"That," he sneered, "is none of your concern."

Dawson stood and grabbed his pack, then edged toward the door. He turned. "You'll have it all first thing in the morning."

TWENTY-FOUR

STONE ROLLED HIS BLACK SUV TO A STOP IN FRONT OF the Physics building and unlocked the doors. Gunar waited for him inside the lobby. He pushed through the doors, trotted down the concrete steps and slumped into the passenger seat.

"You're late," the professor bellyached.

Stone ignored him and hit the gas. The vehicle peeled out of the turnaround and raced down Campus Avenue, heading for Richmond Street.

"Where are we going?"

"Please, I ask the questions."

They drove silently northward to the city's fringe and continued through farmland as the sun set. Stone focused on the road ahead, never making eye contact with Gunar until he pulled off on a secondary county road and stopped on the shoulder.

The professor had squeezed himself against the passenger window like a crayfish in the rocks. Stone shut off the engine, removed a small notepad from his jacket pocket and faced the man.

"What can you tell me?"

"Now, just a minute, Stone, what's the meaning of dragging me out here? If this is how you're planning to—"

"Yes? Conduct our business?" He picked his teeth with his tongue. "When we spoke earlier, you had a million excuses why you failed in the one task I gave you. All you had to do was secure your student's work. That's all. I thought for a man in your position, that would have been simple. Apparently not."

Gunar squirmed. "I already told you, Matt Dawson is no ordinary student. He's, well, unpredictable."

"Hm, I see," Stone sighed. "So what is it you couldn't wait to tell me over the phone? Has something changed?"

"Yes," the professor said, "I have assurances from Dawson that he'll send me everything tomorrow morning."

"Everything? What does that mean?"

"The notes he's made, the father's journals... anything related to this psychometric excursion of his."

"And the photograph?"

"Yes, that, too."

Stone smiled in the gloomy dusk. "Excellent."

"So what happens now?"

Stone started the engine and hit the headlights. "Now I return you to the campus." His eyes narrowed. "And you, my friend, if what you say is true and Matt Dawson sends you everything I want, you will become more recognized and richer than you ever thought possible."

Gunar turned his gaze away.

"I detect a conflict. That is what you want, no?" His voice grew sharper, his initial soft-spoken manner now replaced by a compelling intensity. "Why can't people have what they honestly desire? Worldly treasures are available to all, to make everybody happy; yet how many truly claim what they're owed?"

The physicist cleared his throat. "Yes, that's what I want... to leapfrog my idiot colleagues who are out there being interviewed on network television, writing best-selling books on bullshit for the masses. I want the recognition I deserve, and the wealth that's due me." He narrowed his eyes. "I want it all."

"And you shall have it," Stone answered cheerfully. "My friends are prepared to publish the preliminary findings you cobbled together. Quite a nasty piece of excrement, we both know, but who reads these boring articles anyway?"

"I'm sorry?"

"Oh, come now." He spun the car around and headed toward the city. "You'll be lucky if a handful of researchers actually skim your abstract, but that's irrelevant. What's important is that you'll be published in a prestigious, recognized journal, with validation from other respected scientists just like you. And," he added, "my partners will make sure that you, Professor, become as well-known as De Grasse, or Kaku, or any of those other ridiculous pop experts." He grinned. "Even that Bill Nye the Science Guy." He chuckled.

Gunar grew silent.

Stone continued. "All this is predicated on your handing over Dawson's research the moment you get it. Please don't bother reading it. The content is not your concern. Just don't fail me again."

As they approached the northern edge of the city, traffic picked up and Stone focused on the road. They drove in silence toward campus, and soon he pulled up in front of the Physics building, basking in well-lit glory. Gunar opened the door.

"Oh, one more thing before you go, Professor."

He poked his head back inside the car.

"If you fail me, if you don't send me Dawson's work by noon tomorrow? Our agreement will be... shall I say... permanently altered. You'll be lucky to teach high school physics in Butthole, Wisconsin."

"I won't. I promise."

"Promises are a cheap commodity, Professor."

Gunar sneered and slammed the door shut.

If he only realized how close he came to—

Stone's phone pinged. He read the incoming text message: *I'm ready.*

He gulped. For her to appear on one of his active cases was a rare occasion, and he admitted that, yes, he was nervous. It could mean a promotion like last time, he thought, or a far more sinister matter. He raced along Richmond Street, heading south toward the downtown core, then pulled into the visitor parking lot at the Marriott hotel.

When she asked—and he used that term loosely—to see him, her request floored him. For The Whisper to travel to this fetid urban armpit, something extremely important must be going down, and for whatever reason, Matt Dawson's work was in the middle of it.

Although he did not know The Whisper's true identity, stories circulated throughout the levels of operatives around the world. Some believed she was a diplomat from a European country. Others were convinced she operated as a software vendor for a dummy company in California. No matter. Whenever she spoke, everyone listened.

He was no exception.

He rode the elevator to the 12th floor and padded down the heavily carpeted, dimly lit hallway. When he reached her door, butterflies raised holy hell in his gut. He lifted his hand to knock and felt it shaking.

Stone tapped twice with his knuckle. Momentarily, the door creaked open just wide enough for him to enter.

The only other time he'd met her in person was in Buenos Aires several years ago. Similar circumstances. He'd been engaged in pulling down a high-ranked politician so one of their own could assume more power. She'd arrived to oversee the final preparations, then congratulated him on his work. Since then, they'd only ever spoken by encrypted phone or text. Never video. Never in person.

The room receded in complete darkness.

"Come," The Whisper said, her voice barely audible.

Stone sensed at least one other person with them other than the operative who let him in. Possibly someone in the corner, but it was difficult to confirm. The curtains were drawn except for a pencil thin strip that allowed a sliver of light from the city to enter. Just enough to find his bearings. He was assaulted with the scent of lilac.

"Shall—shall I sit?" he asked.

"Remain standing," she said, "this shan't take long. I'll get straight to the purpose of my visit."

Stone caught her outline on the bed. While his eye adjusted to the gloom, the petite figure leaned against the headboard, appearing tinier than he remembered. The light and his trepidation played tricks with his eyes.

"Do you have the photograph?"

He cleared his throat. "I'll have it tomorrow morning, along with all the boy's notes."

"Tomorrow..." The word hung in the dark. "Tomorrow..."

"Yes, ma'am, you see, the professor—"

"Please, Stone, I have no interest in that little man." She excelled in the fine art of cynicism.

"Of course."

"Now," she continued, "this is far too important to leave in the professor's hands. Dawson does not understand what he possesses, and after that debacle in Kirkland Lake with the fellow you sent to retrieve it, my trust in you has been… shaken. I have never questioned my faith in you before…until now."

Stone's heart sank. He fought the uncontrolled urge to urinate.

"But you've grown soft, Mr. Stone. You've had it too good. I've seen it happen to others in this business, and we've had to part ways. Still, I like you, and I see a bright future if you regain your focus."

"Ma'am?"

"To make up for your fellow's misfortune, and for the delay in bringing the goods to me, I want you personally to oversee the operation. I'm reassigning your other cases. Dawson and the photograph are your only priority. Do not allow the professor to dictate when you'll receive the material. Retrieve it yourself."

"Yes ma'am, but…"

Her breathing pattern increased. *Wrong thing to say.*

"But *what*, Stone, please… spit it out."

"It's been years since I've been a field agent, and I…" He gauged her reaction by the sharp inhale coming from the bed. "Well, never mind, ma'am. I shall take care of this personally."

"Good." She shifted her soft weight, and the bedcovers rustled. "By the way, I received intel from our operative in Sudbury that our restless young physicist is planning a trip to Laurentian University to discuss his… visions. Curious, isn't it?" She paused. "Now I want to make sure he hasn't hidden the photograph. He's a slippery fish, Mr. Stone. Don't simply assume he always carries it with him. Go now. And don't disappoint."

Stone eased his way toward the door, stopped, then

gathered the courage. "Since I'm becoming more involved, what is so important about this photograph? Is it historical?"

She purred on the bed, leaning up. "If you only knew. Suffice it to say, I've been after this little treasure most of my career, and I also have a personal score to settle with Mr. Dawson. Now go."

He caught the placid movement of a hump in the corner. An arm pulled the door open, spilling him into the silent hallway in a blind stumble. The door closed, and he swore he heard a muffled cry.

TWENTY-FIVE

London
1666

GIDEON STOMPED ACROSS THE THRESHOLD AND slammed the wooden door shut behind him.

"Make haste, Molly, grab the children. We must leave."

His wife placed her sewing needle down on the wobbly table beside her and stood. "I don't understand."

"There's no time to explain. Not here, at any rate. Another fire's started, and the wind pushes it our way. Greater than all the others. Flared up on Pudding Street and we're in its path. Tarry not, love, we must flee at once."

He threw some belongings into a bag and leaned out the back window. The young ones played in the backyard, oblivious to the sudden stench of a foreign smoke, one not produced from coal in cookstoves. One that raged with a *ferocity once limited to Lucifer himself.*

"Children, come quick!"

They left the garden and ran to greet him.

"A fire's a-comin'. Make haste and grab a change o' clothes and a blanket."

Heather protested. The youngest didn't understand, but the faces on the older ones turned grey. They'd grown accustomed to sporadic burns and knew with the wood houses and drought this season, the flames would race through them like apocalyptic horsemen.

"Ellie," he said, "mind the young one, please."

Her eyes grew wide, and she nodded. "Come along, Heather, we'll make a game of it." They trundled off to the bedroom.

"Molly," Gideon said in a low voice, "we mustn't forget the cloth."

"Aye," she answered. "I know where 'tis and I'll bring it wi' me." She opened the trunk, unwrapped the quilt and pulled the folded material out. "Let me sew it quickly into my shawl, so's not to be noticed." She sat and re-threaded her needle. Gideon handed her the cloth, and she promptly went to work.

He placed his hand on her shoulder. "I think I knows who started this blaze."

"Oh?"

"It began in the bakery on Pudding. But the owner, well, I suspect he's one of them, Molls. A keeper from The Sodality."

She shuddered and touched her lips.

"Aye," he continued, "they must know we're here. Somehow over the years they've figured out where we be."

"And the fire?"

"Deliberately set to smoke us out an' all. Now, we have no choice. They put sentries at the roads leading out *of London."*

"That's normal," she said, "to prevent the lootin' and thuggery."

"True, but if them soldiers be part of The Sodality too, they'll be lookin' for us and the cloak. You know that to be true, eh?"

Molly's brow furrowed, and she focused on her work. The children staggered back to the living room one by one, each carrying a modest bag. Heather whined, but Ellie kept her in line and distracted her with a song.

"Give me a few minutes, Gideon."

He corralled the youngsters outside and set them straight in the lane. "We all stay together, mind. No runnin' about." Then he returned to the house, threw some of his and Molly's belongings into his own travel bag, and placed them by the door. Then he grabbed his coins from the safe box and stuffed them in a pocket. Across the city, flames stretched over the entire west end, licking the sky. Neighbours gathered in the street as well. Some had the fortune of a cart. A few had horses.

Molly appeared, wearing the shawl and carrying a basket of food. She locked the door, shrugged, and threw Gideon a useless smile. He nodded.

The family walked north toward the wall at Bishopsgate, one of the main entrances to the city. Ellie kept the young ones in line and happy to be on an adventure. Gideon knew their good spirits wouldn't last and prayed someone with a wagon would appear.

"Where will we go?" Molly, at his side, glanced at him with large, soft eyes.

"Reckon north as north can get. The fire is devastating, but The Sodality is far worse." He spat in the dirt, felt his pockets for his pipe and tobacco. "Maybe as far as Scotland."

"Oh, sweet heavens. I never seen Scotland," she

fussed. "I hear it's cold as the devil, and with winter coming an' all."

Gideon stopped her and gathered the children around. "We must, Molly. Besides, you an' me and this lot, well, we're strong. We stick together, no harm can come to us." He smiled warmly. "Move along, now."

They passed through Bishopsgate without incident, and as they reached the outskirts of London, the crowds thinned. Many remained to fight the fire, but Gideon knew it was futile. With an abnormally dry summer and a gusting wind, the flame would devour all the wooden structures in its path. They stopped at a hill crest where pockets of other families gathered and gazed toward the city that Gideon could only describe as a nightmare from Hell. In the distance, men shouted and women screamed. He glanced at Molly, who pulled the shawl close around her.

They continued heading north, and the road narrowed to a cruel trail when they arrived at a ragged clearing with a few others. Here, another group of sentries flanked the path, talking with the travellers. A handful of constables waited at the side, guarding a couple of young thieves who had clearly tried to escape with loot.

When it came time for Gideon and his family to pass, a tall sentry with broad shoulders held his hand up and asked, "Yer name?"

"I'm Gideon Lancaster. This be my wife Molly and these are all mine." He swept his arm, indicating the children huddled behind him.

"Possessions?"

"All's we have is what's in our bags, sir. No time to gather anything else for the fire." He gazed around. "Have ye seen anyone with a wagon, perhaps?"

The sentry eyed him suspiciously. "Why'd ye be wantin' a wagon, Mr. Lancaster? Planning to travel for a spell, are ye?"

"No, no," he lied, "just to help the young un's, you understand. We plan to wait out the fire in the hills and then pray our modest home is spared." He smiled thinly. "You have any children, sir?"

The sentry ignored him. Instead, he motioned to two others to check their bags.

"I tell you, sir, there's nothin' in there but some clothing."

"We'll see," the man growled. "Too many's been grabbin' their fill on the way. We won't have that."

"I understand perfectly."

When the soldiers had finished rifling through their belongings, they checked Molly's basket, removed a cloth containing a ham and plucked a couple of apples from it as well. She remained silent, but Gideon could tell from her eyes that her heart broke. A finer woman he could never meet. Then the young man reached for her shawl. She tightened her grip on it. Gideon clenched his fists, a movement that the lead sentry didn't miss.

"Easy there, Mr. Lancaster. Let the lad have his fun, eh?"

Molly gulped and dropped her hands. The fellow slowly eased the shawl open, letting it fall off her shoulders. Gideon prayed they wouldn't notice his family's cloak crudely sewn within as a liner. But the fellow's attention lay elsewhere.

"Lovely," he whispered under his breath. He reached out. Gideon stepped forward, catching the man's eye. Molly shook her head and with courage he'd seen in her more than once, she pulled the shawl back up around her and stared daggers at the youngster. He smiled awkwardly and backed away.

"An' feisty, to boot!" he cackled.

The sentries conferred. The lecherous one bit into an

apple, taunting Gideon while he did so.

"All right, Lancaster, off ye go."

The family passed through the checkpoint, their pace picking up. When they'd traveled about twenty feet, the sentry called out, "Oy!"

Gideon twisted slowly, putting a phoney smile on his face.

"Mind the highwaymen if you're headin' for Clerkenwell. They's be everywhere tonight."

Gideon exhaled, nodded his head and shouted, "Aye, that we will. Thank you, sir." He took Molly's arm, then marched purposefully along the path. Another family from the lane awaited them ahead and when they met, Gideon said, "Mind if we travel together, mate?"

"I were thinkin' the selfsame thought meself. Strength in numbers, eh?"

"Aye, to be sure."

They chatted as they moved en masse, the children poking each other and playing sing-song games. As night fell, they approached Clerkenwell, encountering many other refugees who'd created makeshift shelters along the road. Gideon found a spot for his clan under a copse of pine trees and rested. An orange glow rose above London. Heather trundled over and fell in his lap.

"Da, I'm tired."

"Me too, Hezzie. Me and your ma, too."

Molly doled out portions of food and leaned back on her elbows, watching the other families cope in front of them. After a time, she raised her head and met Gideon's eyes.

"Scotland, ye say?"

He stared ahead, grim-faced and resolute. "Aye."

She thought a moment longer. "Then Scotland it shall be."

TWENTY-SIX

HANNAH'S INTUITION SOUNDED THE HIGH ALERT IN THE form of an internal shriek. After teaching her class and checking in with Curious George, Radioboy and the others in the bullpen, she met briefly with her advisor to update her on what she'd been up to and where this side project might lead in terms of her own research into psychometric methods and processes. Then she rode the bus that night from campus to her basement apartment and, while walking along the street from the bus stop to her home, she couldn't shake this belief that someone, somewhere, watched her every move. The paranoia, if that's what it truly was, bordered on debilitating.

She paused to let a car pass before crossing the street, then peered into each corner, every bush, checking the dancing shadows between houses, watching every distant vehicle that rumbled by, certain that at any moment *he* would appear. The image of that seductive worm from her nightmare shattered her mind, and she shuddered. And all the while, her heart twisted like a tortured leaf in a cold, fall breeze. She placed her hand over her chest, over the cross tucked between her breasts, lowered her shoulders against the night, and raced home.

She passed under the streetlamp two doors down from her place, and the bulb flickered out. As someone who frequently experienced Street Light Interference, she was used to that happening, but this evening, after all she and Matt had been through the past week, the fresh darkness unnerved her. Hannah pulled the phone from her pocket and flipped on the flashlight function, hurried down the concrete steps and unlocked the door leading to her apartment.

Once inside, she flipped on the lights and dropped her bag on the bed. Then she latched and bolted the three additional locks she'd installed. Her notes were scattered everywhere, so she organized them in piles on the covers... some from the trip to Kirkland Lake, others from the morning in the lab when they imaged the pages in Matt's father's private journals. Finally, her own musings she kept in a separate file.

Hannah boiled a cup of herbal tea and chilled in front of her laptop at the small desk. Each of the dozen crosses she'd placed around the room, some on the desk, others hanging on the wall, comforted her. Over in the cramped kitchenette, two larger ones split the space above her tiny breakfast nook.

In the middle of the storm, I know you, my Lord, are with me always.

She opened her laptop and created a new file for her ideas and began jotting down random thoughts as they came to her.

· *A powerful world-changing message*

· *Matt's past, leading to psychometric phenomena apparently crossing several generations*

· *Mystery of the photo events. What were the ghostly figures communicating? A warning?*

· *Is Matt's life in danger...*

She highlighted that one.

· *Did his father really die from a heart attack or was it provoked?*

· *Who was that creep in the woods?*

· *Who is that worm in my nightmare?*

· *Are they somehow related?*

Hannah recognized the act of scientific discovery was much like the creative process: iterative, additional information revealing itself as one works through it, and no guarantees of success. Her own research project into psychometric methodologies offered glimpses of what might happen at the interface of affected humans and various subsurface layers of targeted objects that some argued was more art than science anyway.

Without question, Matt had a psychometric gift and had reached no limits to it yet. Every time he experienced the event, he learned something more, and whenever that happened, he also grew more concerned, diving inside his own thoughts, leading him down a path toward... *where?*

She added one more note to consider:

· *how can I help him?*

The personal feelings that quick-stepped in her heart were an unfamiliar complication. She had only known them twice before: once for Danny in grade 10—a whirlwind teenaged affair, crashing in a dramatic heap when she apparently got "serious"—at least that's what he'd said. But she recognized now it had more to do with her skipping school and self-sabotaging. Then there was Robbie. Beautiful, sweet Robbie. Her first intimate encounter...

Shortly after him, she accepted Jesus as her personal saviour and slowly turned her life around. And now, she couldn't possibly abandon the only sustaining strength she had, the only power that kept the creepy seducer in her nightmare at bay.

Her phone pinged, and she glanced at the screen.

Matt, needing to talk.

She thumbed a response: *what's up?*

Matt: *Can I call you?*

She answered yes, and in a moment, her phone chimed.

"Hey, you asking me out already?" she cajoled, but inside, something more rumbled. She didn't understand it intellectually. She *sensed* it.

"Hannah, I spoke with Dr. Gunar a little while ago. He's threatening to shut me out of his experiment completely unless I hand over everything to do with the photograph... notes, images, the works."

"He can't do that, can he?"

"Not sure, but it's his research grant, and he's been on my ass to finish up the trials and get the analysis done. He says he may be forced to push my thesis to next fall."

She leaned back in her chair, staring at the small go-to silver cross hanging on the wall behind her laptop. "What does he want with the photo? It's not even in his area of research. What we're investigating has more to do with my department than yours."

"Exactly. Still, he's threatening this and I really gotta finish up, I mean, I owe it to my mum who's supported me for so many years, and despite not having a clue about what to do when I'm finished, I can't hang around Western the rest of my life."

"What did you tell him?"

"You must understand, Hannah, he had me. If I don't hand everything over, he'll make my life a living hell. But if I do, we may never discover the hidden message in the photo. And you know how I feel about my dad's death, how it must've been more than a heart attack." He paused. "I wish I knew what to do."

"Matt, please listen to me. Did you agree to give it all to him?"

"Hannah…"

"Oh no, you did."

"I—I agreed I would. First thing tomorrow morning."

Hannah sighed. She understood the dilemma facing him and had no advice to offer.

"But after plugging away in the lab mulling it over," he continued, "I'm not sure I can go through with it. Will you help me out?"

She closed her eyes and said, "Matt, will you pray with me?"

His voice hardened. "Hannah, please—"

"Listen, whenever I'm messed up and confused, I turn it over to God, let him take the problem, and then I wait and listen."

"Uh-huh and does he always answer?"

She pursed her lips. "Not in the sense that I hear voices or anything like that. Often I don't recognize his work until later, like years later some time."

"Hannah, I need to figure this out before the morning."

"I don't think God works that, but pray with me. It couldn't hurt." She put him on speaker. "Sit down, get comfortable, close your eyes, and I'll say the words for you… for us, too."

Silence permeated the connection. Noises in the background like muffled street traffic floated by. Finally he answered, "Okay. But I'm not a believer, right?"

"I know, Matt. Anyone can pray."

She opened a prayer to God, thanking him for everything he's given her, praising him for her health, her studies, for bringing Matt into her life and giving her an opportunity to put what she's learned into practice. Then she said, "Lord Jesus, please be with Matt. Help him through this crisis with his professor. Give him a chance to find the wisdom he needs to make a decision that's consistent with your will for us on Earth." She listened for a moment. He remained on the line. "And Lord, be with him now. Be with me tonight. Bring us both the peace that only you can provide. I pray for these things in Jesus' name. Amen."

She opened her eyes and gazed at the crosses in front of her, breathed deeply, feeling the air fill her lungs and push through her body. She almost forgot that Matt was still on the line until she heard more sounds, like papers rustling or perhaps the phone itself scratching across clothing.

It was strange that he hadn't echoed the word. Other non-believers she'd prayed with accepted the courtesy, and would mumble it. So she waited for him to speak.

He never did.

AFTER AN AWKWARD SILENCE, WHERE DAWSON STRUGGLED with his next move, he finally thanked her, hung up, and gazed over the city from his balcony. Something about hearing her voice in prayer touched him beyond any intellectual assessment of his situation. But his hesitation to add "amen" when he didn't truly believe got the better of him. And this foolish stirring in his gut, rising through his heart, compounded the moment. Was it concern over his own hypocrisy that caused him to fixate on her, or some ancient, fragile longing?

He returned to his apartment and walked through to the kitchen, grabbed a glass of water, and flopped on the couch. After opening his laptop and reviewing the notes he'd made on the phenomenon, he overcame his defiance and gave it a shot.

God, if you're real and out there, you know I struggle with the idea of a supernatural creator. But I'm willing to keep my mind open.

Moments later, whether the path forward came from divine origins or his own ruminations, he didn't care. All that mattered was that he knew *exactly* what to do.

Thank you, Hannah.

Dawson grabbed his laptop and took it to his makeshift workstation at the dining room table. He entered *old farm house photographs black and white* in the search engine and scanned through the mountain of images that sprung up. He remembered Gunar had already seen his photo, had held it in his hands, so he wanted to find one that was similar to his.

It took an hour to land on a reasonable match. He downloaded it to a stick and bolted from his apartment.

Walmart was still open, and he arrived at the photo centre with time to spare. When the file he carried was printed out on actual glossy photographic paper, he couldn't believe how real it felt compared to his. Shiny image, grainy, and nothing but a farmhouse in a wide clear space. He crinkled the corners and folded it here and there, giving it the impression of age and handling. Back in his apartment, he placed it beside the original photo and only someone extremely familiar with his would see that this new one was a close, but fake, reproduction.

Dawson smiled. He made himself a cup of tea and, once steeped, he dipped a rag in it and rubbed it randomly across the fake photo to give it even more age.

Perfect.

Then he returned to the table and pulled up the notes he'd made. He copied them into a new file and reviewed each line, throwing in random terms and ideas that had little to do with his genuine observations. He rewrote his

Dad's journal notes into stream of consciousness gibberish.

When he'd finished, it was after two in the morning. He leaned back, saved the file, printed it out, and placed it all in an old folder with the mocked up photo. Then, he grabbed some of his dad's field notes he'd brought with him from home, some maps that had nothing to do with his work on that survey—not even close to Kirkland Lake—and arrayed it all on the kitchen counter.

Before heading to bed, he set the alarm on his phone to wake him first thing in the morning. He'd be ready.

He drifted off to sleep, a quiet, deep, unfamiliar peace overcame him, and he reflected on Hannah and her prayer. She'd asked God to give him wisdom to do what was necessary to further God's kingdom on Earth. Something like that, anyway. He didn't understand what that meant, not having read or understood much in the ancient King James Bible his mother had given him when he left home, but he trusted Hannah with an open mind. Now, as he lay in the darkness of his room, almost too excited to see the day end, he knew in his heart that his plan for tomorrow was precisely the right thing.

MORNING ARRIVED LIKE DEW ON A PETAL. THE ALARM softly chattered away, and Dawson forced his eyes open, stretched and sat up in bed. Half an hour later, he was out the door, jogging toward campus, the package for Gunar safely tucked in his backpack, beside the actual photo in a separate envelope. He still wondered if the creeper from the northern woods might turn up. The stranger was apparently willing to harm him and Hannah before they understood the hidden message, so the man would require little effort to find his apartment and rifle through it if he desired. Or grab him walking to Western and dissect his pack.

I'm an idiot. Didn't even check the parking lot for

that red car.

He searched the roads, then ducked onto a side street and followed a random path to the campus, mentally preparing to ask Hannah to help him out with his plan.

Outside the coffee kiosk at the Unicentre, he texted her: *I've made a decision.*

Moments later, she replied: *And?*

Dawson: *I'm giving Gunar a package.*

Several minutes passed before she responded: *Where are you now?*

Dawson: *Starbucks. Unicentre*

Hannah: *I'll meet you there shortly. On the bus.*

He ordered a Pike's and found a spot at a plastic table bathed in sunlight. Fifteen minute later, Hannah appeared. She looked like she hadn't slept a wink. Her hair was up, but tousled as if she'd been in a hurry. She noticed him across the massive court and joined him. After setting her pack on an empty chair, she slumped down. "Do you have it with you?"

Dawson lifted his bag from the table, exposing the folder and sliding it over.

She opened it, raised the photograph to the light, then paused and said, "Is this the right...?"

Dawson grinned like the Cheshire cat.

Hannah shook her head incredulously and began reading his notes. In a matter of seconds, she smiled.

"Sneaky."

"Yeah. What do you think?"

"The photo is so close, it's... eerie."

"Finish reading. I'll get you a coffee."

She nodded and plowed through the folder. When he returned with another cup, she thanked him without looking up. Several minutes later, she closed the folder, trapping all the lies within the covers.

"An impressive ruse," she whispered. "Where's the

actual photo?"

He tapped his pack.

She took the lid off her coffee. "When are you seeing Dr. Gunar?"

"First thing. He gets in his office at eight."

"And what are *we* going to do?"

"If you're still up for it, we'll leave for Sudbury today."

She reached over and took his hand, locking her shadowed eyes on his.

"Hannah, are you okay?"

"I—I had a tough night. Wrestling with my demon again."

He took her hand. "I'm so sorry. And here I am asking you to leave with me today. I'm such an idiot." He studied her face. "What can I do to help?"

"Matt, I'm with you in this. One hundred percent in. Yes, I can leave today. I'll be with you in Sudbury, and I'll be with you when you uncover the hidden message. In fact," she withdrew her hand and pulled some papers from her bag, "I may have figured out a clue."

Dawson looked around nervously and checked the time.

"Excellent. What did you find?"

She leaned on the table. "Well, I've been going over your dad's journal entries, and I discovered some really interesting stuff. More like thoughts or possibilities, actually. I haven't figured out yet *what* he was trying to say, but still..."

"Awesome," Dawson said, focusing on the students shuffling in. "I've thought of little else, so tell all."

"See, the issue is incomplete thoughts and words with little context." She cleared her throat. "Your dad mentioned an object, something passed down to him he didn't understand. But he didn't specify what, and we don't know what he was referring to."

"I just assumed it was the photograph."

"Yeah, that makes sense, but the way he describes it, referencing an object outside the photo, leads me to think he's talking about something else entirely."

Dawson chewed his lip, scanning the food court, looking for anything that didn't look as if it belonged there. *I'm imagining villains in the shadows.*

"So the question is: what object?" She tilted her head and he caught her gaze and smiled.

"If you're asking me, I wouldn't have a clue."

"I *am* asking you, Matt, and I think you must know. But maybe you don't realize it yet."

He thought about his family, growing up and poking around the basement with his dad. His mind went through an inventory of the dusty junk in the workshop, his geology tools, his old ham radio equipment. Nothing jumped out. He couldn't ever remember his dad pointing to something as a family heirloom being passed down from generation to generation. In fact, his mother hadn't either.

"What do you say, Matt?"

"Nothing's ringing any bells, but I'll keep racking my brain." He checked his phone again. "Well, we can talk more on the trip, but right now, I gotta book. I'll drop this package off to Gunar, then I've got to square away some things with Wendy. Could you leave at lunch?"

"Sure. Maybe we can swing by my place and I'll grab a change of clothes on the way."

"Sounds good. Let's meet back here at noon."

They stood and shouldered their packs, then wandered away toward their respective buildings. As they reached the point where it was time to separate, she stopped him.

"Tell me something, Matt, and be honest, okay?"

"Sure."

"I know it's sometimes hard for guys to find the right words to express their feelings, so I won't go there. But I'm curious. What's really driving this? For you, I mean."

He kicked the gravel and said, "I had a truly peaceful sleep last night, and other than the anxiety over handing Gunar a pack of lies and solving this secret, I've never felt more alive. What's driving this?" He paused, searching the sky. "Everything."

TWENTY-SEVEN

AT PRECISELY 8:07, STONE'S PHONE PINGED. A MESSAGE from Dr. Gunar flashed across his screen: *I have what you're looking for.*

Stone dabbed his lips and set his coffee down on the little white saucer in the hotel restaurant. He texted that he'd meet him outside the Physics building at 9:00 and that he didn't want to wait. The professor acknowledged the meetup. Stone returned to his toast and marmalade and observed the other guests loading their plates at the buffet.

Animals.

Lamont's earlier text suggested Dawson had left his apartment for campus, alone, and that he would search the boy's place for the photo. He had yet to report back.

When he pulled up in front of the building on campus, Dr. Gunar awaited him at the bottom of the steps, holding a blue folder. Stone rolled down the passenger side window and leaned over as Gunar approached and handed the package to him.

"Thank you, Professor. Have you looked through it?"

"Briefly, just to confirm the photograph was included. You'll see he's provided some of his father's field notes. Somehow related, I suppose, but I didn't read them, as per your instructions."

"Very good, Professor," Stone mused. "See, we're coming to understand each other very well." He leafed through the folder, glanced at the photo, and then placed the package on the seat beside him. "If there's anything else I need, I shall let you know. In the meantime," he stretched his neck, "you can expect to hear from two journals over the next 24 hours about your submissions."

"Submissions? But I haven't reviewed anything yet. How can you—"

"Professor, please. It has all been arranged. The referees will contact you, and you will answer their questions. When you're finished, good things will appear in your life, starting with your bank account."

"I don't understand.

"Of course you don't. Nobody does. But remember, this is what you wanted. Recognition. Fame and fortune."

"Sure, but I thought I'd have to actually give you tangible results, at least some interim findings I've been working on and—"

Stone patted the folder beside him and grinned. "You already have, Dr. Gunar. Now, be a good little scientist and keep an eye on that Dawson fellow. I want to know exactly what he does and where he goes today."

"But I'm not a—"

Stone rolled up the window, nodded at the babbling professor, and drove away. His request that Gunar keep an eye on Mr. Dawson clarified one thing in his mind: the professor had no idea his star student planned a trip to Sudbury. *Sneaky fellow.*

THE MINUTE HE'D RETURNED TO HIS HOTEL, HE ASKED the front desk to make sure he wouldn't be disturbed. Then, in his room, he opened the folder and reviewed each item.

The first was the photograph. This appeared to be exactly as described to him by others in The Sodality, previous operatives who had heard of it. A simple farmhouse in the middle of a prairie landscape. Quaint, he thought. Although, this one didn't quite sit right with him. He expected something older, time worn. This print had too many recent creases, not enough old ones, and the backing paper had yellowed little with age. Still, the photo itself was last century and black and white, and the farmhouse was what he expected. The experts in data analysis could confirm its authenticity.

Then he studied Dawson's notes. Again, some observations struck him as inconsistent, but Noetics was not a topic he understood well. So what he read made sense on a superficial level, and there was a thread of logic behind the descriptions. Finally, he leafed through his father's two field books from various surveys. He stopped frequently to study the sketches of terrain outcrops, strike and dip angles, copious side notes about numerous minerals.

But it didn't add up. He could understand having an incomplete knowledge of the photograph. It was, after all, the pièce de résistance, the prize The Whisper sought. And Matt Dawson's notes, well, who knows what rattled around in that young brain of his, being pumped up with physics and mathematics and other scientific endeavours. So he could look past the seemingly nonsensical yet logically presented narratives.

However, the journals were off. Stone knew that Dawson's father spent some of his last moments at the Thompson Hotel in Kirkland Lake in 2007. One of his closest colleagues had been in that room, and shared more than the formal report to the Council, including The Whisper's involvement.

Grey Dawson, he understood, had been surveying the lines in Boston Township, the same territory where Lamont encountered the boy and the girlfriend last week. But these notes were incomplete. Yes, he mentioned Kirkland Lake, some bullet points on survey techniques, but these were written well before his death. Plus, there were references to Geraldton, Ontario that stuck out like a bent nail. He entered one of the latitude and longitude positionings in his browser, and the area north of Hearst was pinned. Nowhere near Kirkland Lake.

What is going on?

He removed the portable scanning device from his satchel and illuminated the photograph. That's when he saw the disconnect come alive.

The photo was a fake.

Either Gunar had tried to pull a fast one—something that would not end well for the professor—or conversely, Dawson had duped the ugly professor.

"Interesting young man," he said aloud. "So full of surprises."

Then, the realization he needed to check in with The Whisper at noon struck him. He didn't have what he'd promised.

He punched Gunar's number into his phone, but it went straight to voicemail. For the first time in months, a cold bead of sweat appeared on Stone's forehead.

The operative had to think fast.

The Whisper told him to get personally involved, and he had the perfect occasion to take charge, pick up the boy—possibly the girl, too—and subject him to the truth test. *Yes, that's the way we do it.*

He closed the folder and stuffed it in his satchel. Time

to return to campus and track down Matt Dawson.

HE PARKED BY A FOOTBALL FIELD AND HIKED THE HALF kilometer to the cluster of science buildings as the brittle sun shone through a gathering of clouds scorching overhead. Stone sauntered along a fine gravel path, fitting in seamlessly with the tweedy academic crowd, attracting ineffable stares of scrabbled undergraduate girls.

When he emerged at the Physics building, he marched directly to Gunar's office. The door was locked, but his teaching schedule was posted beside it. Indeed, the arrogant physicist was in class until noon, 45 minutes away.

So he did the one thing he'd avoided: he planned to confront Dawson in the lab and beat the special photograph out of him if necessary.

His shoes clacked along the floor as he walked purposefully toward Dawson's room. An aimless pod of students in the hallway watched him. Probably not used to seeing a well-dressed person in these parts, he thought, grey socks and granola eating crowd that they are.

Outside the research door, he read the signs, ignored them, and knocked.

In a moment, it swung open heavily and a young Japanese girl in a freshly pressed white coat poked her head out.

"Yes?"

"Good morning. I should like to speak with Matthew Dawson."

"I'm sorry, sir," she said nervously, "but Matt's not here."

Stone narrowed his eyes and clenched his jaw. He may have already left for Laurentian, but being the clever sort, he could have hidden the photo in the lab. "That is unfortunate." He smiled. "Do you know when he'll return?"

"Oh, you just missed him, and he won't be back until next week sometime." She paused. "Are you here for one of the demos Dr. Gunar planned?"

That was a gift.

"Why, yes, I am. Thought I'd come by early for a private walk-through." He stepped toward her. "May I?"

The pretty girl hesitated. "I'm not supposed to let anyone in without Dr. Gunar's permission, and he didn't mention any guests coming..." She struggled with the decision, then resolved it. "I'm sure he won't mind, but I'd rather wait until he's back."

"I promise not to touch anything," he purred. "Please, you can leave the door open if you're at all concerned."

He recognized the look on her face, that twisted uncertainty between duty, desire, and fear, so he poured on the charm. When she was close to capitulating, his phone pinged. Stone glanced at the screen, recognized the number, and gulped. "Excuse me a moment."

He stepped away and called.

"Do you have the package?" she rasped.

"I have the material the professor says he received from Dawson, but, er..."

"Yes?"

"It's inauthentic. In fact, it's all rubbish." He was met with silence.

"Where are you now?"

"On campus, about to get into his research lab. Dawson has apparently left for the day, but I may find what I'm looking for here."

The Whisper breathed lightly into the phone. "Mr. Dawson and Ms. King are heading to Laurentian. Our op at the university alerted me to a rendezvous there tomorrow morning, Mr. Stone. Now, forget about the lowly professor. I want you to investigate the lab, then follow Mr. Dawson and the girlfriend north. It's time to bring them both in for a chat, and our friend there provides the perfect opportunity."

TWENTY-EIGHT

THEY MET OUTSIDE THE UNICENTRE. DAWSON BROUGHT Hannah up to speed on handing the package to Gunar and then checking in on Wendy.

"I'll bet she's the furthest from being happy about you taking off again, eh?"

"Yeah, and I feel rotten about that. I promised her yesterday I'd be around to help, and make sure Gunar got his results analyzed. But now?"

"Uh-huh," she said as they headed down Oxford toward Western Road. "You know, you can always change your mind. We could go next week, or—"

"Not a chance. Look how close we are. Besides, if I hang out here, Gunar or this mystery publishing partner of his will have questions about the photo, and I—"

She grabbed his arm. "Who's this other guy?"

"Funny, he didn't mention a name. Just that some other researcher expressed interest in the work. That's all."

"Not sure I like the sounds of that, Matt."

They continued hiking through a crowd of students until they reached Sarnia Road heading west.

"We'll take the side streets to my place," he said, glancing down the road.

They hurried through the residential area, ducking around the manicured lawns and quiet crescents, until they emerged by his apartment building.

Hannah adjusted her pack. "Matt, I wonder if this colleague is associated with the character who attacked us in the woods. The one who was following us. Remember the psycho mentioned a name?"

He stopped dead. "I hadn't considered that, but if that's the case, we sure as hell better move. If Gunar's tied to the bush creep, we're in deep trouble."

They rode the elevator to the apartment and after he'd unlocked the door; he swung it open and invited her in.

While he packed an overnight bag with fresh clothes, Hannah wandered around the living room. She called out, "Hey, look what I found on your bookshelf."

He stepped out of his bedroom, folding a shirt, and saw her silhouetted by the window. She held the Bible in her hands and waved it.

"Oh, that. Yeah, my mum insisted I take it wherever I go."

"But you're not a believer?"

"No, but she maintains I may need it someday, and I wasn't about to make an issue over it." He dropped the bag on the sofa and zipped it up. "My dad might have been religious. Not sure, but he used to quote these God sayings from time to time."

"Did your parents go to church?"

"Once in a while at Christmas and Easter, mostly. They'd drag me along, but I remember little except snacks afterward and being a shepherd in a play."

She cracked open the cover. "It's your dad's, see?" The dedication read to Grey Dawson, 1975.

"Cool."

Hannah continued leafing through while Dawson collected a few things from the kitchen. "So, have you read any of the Good Book?"

"Me? Nah. Well, I tried once but couldn't get past all the cultural rubbish and laws and who begat who." He returned with a couple apples and stuffed them in his pack.

"It's not easy," she said, "but I had excellent teachers to help me understand. Still, I hear what you're saying."

He looked over her shoulder as she flipped through the Gospels.

"So tell me, Hannah, what was the turning point for you? I mean, when did you decide to become a…"

"A Christian? Do you really want to know? Because it's not a two-minute conversation." Her smile disappeared, as if a painful memory stabbed at her. "Sorry, Matt, I'm not ready to share it all yet. Hope you don't mind."

"Not at all. But how about the thumbnail version?" he offered.

"Why do you ask?"

"Curious, I guess. You're smart and a scientist, yet here you are trusting an invisible God who demands worship and punishes those who think bad thoughts. I don't understand."

She inhaled deeply. "Okay, try this on for size." She closed the book and held it in front of her, then met his eyes. "If you want to learn about *this* God, answer one question: who do you think Jesus really was?"

"Hm. An inspired, charismatic teacher?"

"Was he not also God's son?"

"I can't wrap my head around that."

"If you're right, if he was only a moralistic teacher,"

she said, "then nothing in this book matters. It'd be just another piece of self-help mind mush. Remember, *he* claimed to be the Son of the Creator of the Universe. That's a bold statement, so if he actually wasn't, he must've been a total lunatic. Charismatic, sure. And one hundred percent crazy."

"Sure, I guess so."

"It's gotta be one or the other, Matt. There's no in-between." Her eyes widened, and she patted the Bible. "But if he actually *was* the Son of God, then what?"

"I—I don't know."

"Think, Matt. If he really was God among us, then everything he did, everything he said, this entire book, is the *truth*."

Dawson felt the heat rise to his cheeks and a nervous grin spread across his face. "But does it have to be either / or?"

"Yes, it matters because we deserve more than platitudes and images of fluffy sheep and humble shepherds and a moralistic cafeteria where we pick and choose what suits us. If he truly was God on Earth, that's what changes people's lives. Knowing he was here, and that he sacrificed himself so we could have eternal life in paradise, well, that's pretty amazing." She handed the Bible to him, eyes gentle and radiating hope.

Dawson accepted the book and leafed through it roughly, then shrugged and returned it to the shelf.

THEY LEFT THE APARTMENT AND DROVE TO HER PLACE. She hopped out of the Yaris in front of her home, and he asked, "Shall I wait here, or...?"

"No, come on down. Nothing special, I'll warn you. It's a basement room after all, so it often feels like a cave."

He accompanied her down the steps and, after she unlocked the door, he followed her in. Thin daylight flowed in from a tiny window to his left near a small kitchen, but when Hannah flicked on the lights, he froze, mouth agape.

The place was filled with crosses. He noted her desk immediately in front of him, her bed to the right with a dresser, a couple of chairs stacked against a far wall, and the kitchen lit up to expose a burner, coffee maker and a toaster oven.

"Wow, there sure are a lot of crosses," he said, gazing around.

"Criticizing?"

"No," he hurried, "simply observing."

She eyed him suspiciously, then pulled a bag from under the bed, flung it open and began sorting through items in her dresser. Dawson moved close to her desk, noticing the photograph of a young woman in a park.

"Who's this?"

Hannah looked up and said, "My birth mother."

Dawson picked up the frame and studied it. "Definite resemblance in the eyes, the hair." He stopped cold, turning white. "*Birth* mother? Oh, I'm sorry, Hannah, you're a... an..."

"It's okay, Matt, you can say the words. I was adopted as a baby, but before you go all Harry Potter on me, understand that the couple who raised me were the only parents that mattered. They didn't want to tell me when I was young, but when I turned 16, they said I had a right to know." She zipped up her bag and placed it on the floor. "They were amazing. Sure helped me through some rough teenage years when I struggled with my identity. I treated them like crap, but they never gave up believing I'd come through it okay, and they'll always be Mum and Dad to me."

"How did you find your birth mother?"

She grinned. "Wasn't that hard, actually. The internet

is a wonderful thing, and these days adoptees can locate their parents. Took me a few months, but when I saw that picture of her, well…"

He returned the frame to the desk. "What's she like?"

Hannah approached him and grabbed some notes from the drawer. "Couldn't tell you. We never met." Her face darkened. "Before you go there, Matt, I've chosen not to either." She gazed around the room. "Ready?"

They climbed the steps, and Hannah tossed her bag in the back seat. "I need to tell you something," she said, as they got in the car.

"What's up?"

"I, ah, I have little money, not enough for a hotel or anything like that, and I don't want you to feel obliged, so if you can cover for me, I'll pay you back next term when I get another loan installment. Does that work?"

Dawson pulled away from the curb and headed south. "No worries. I told you about my geologist friend, Jackie, who lives in Sudbury, right? Met him during my undergrad years. I already checked with him and he said we could stay as long as we need."

Her face tightened.

"It's all right, Hannah, he and his wife have a big old house in the country. Lots of room. Tons of privacy."

Her shoulders relaxed, and she leaned into the seat.

Once they merged onto Highway 401 with an endless stream of cars. He checked his rear-view mirror. No trailing red cars. A bunch of crossovers and a pickup truck and an SUV, but nothing suspicious.

That all changed several hours later at a greasy burger joint south of Barrie. He recognized it again: the black SUV, parked at the other end of the massive lot, skulking in the long afternoon shadows. Two men sat in it, watching him. He thought he recognized it from London. May have seen it taking the 400 in Toronto. Figured it was cops on highway patrol.

But maybe it wasn't.

"HE MUST HAVE THE PHOTOGRAPH WITH HIM," STONE remarked from the passenger seat of the sprawling Suburban. "The sweetheart in the lab squealed about not knowing where it was. You sure he didn't hide it in London?"

Flavian Lamont, hands gripping the wheel, burped quietly and said, "I told you, I checked his dump thorough-like when he left this morning and again after him and the girl went to her place. And no evidence of a safe deposit box either." He fetched a soft drink from the cooler in the back seat. "Explain to me again, Mr. Stone, why is it I can't take that asshole out behind them garbage bins right now and pound the crap out of him?" He sneered with his crooked mouth and broken teeth. "I owe him one… and that ugly girl, too."

Stone sighed. He couldn't believe he got ordered to do field work, sullying his hands with this uncouth creature beside him. *What a waste of my time and talent.* He watched Dawson and the girlfriend return to their car carrying a bag of food and drinks. "And you're certain it wasn't in Hannah King's place?".

"Please, Mr. Stone, I checked her hole and her office at the university. Put a real good scare into a couple of her pals. She don't have it." He slurped from the can. "Actually, I'd rather take her down first while the peckerhead watches. Yeah, that's it. Make her pay for chuckin' rocks at me."

"Lamont, The Whisper wants this young man alive and in one piece. Harming him or Ms. King is off the table. You see," he mused while drawing circles with his index finger on the car window, "the photograph is apparently only a tiny part of this puzzle. We must secure

Matt Dawson as well, and that means making sure he goes to the Neurosciences Lab tomorrow. The Sodality covets the photo's power, but I suspect one is useless without the other."

"Huh, sounds a bit wimpy to me. Not like the old days where we took care of business and collected what we wanted."

"Thank God for that."

"I can't for the life of me figger out what's so important about a stupid photo."

Stone sat up, eyeing the targets in the Toyota. "No doubt. Now listen, you just do what you're getting paid for and leave the strategy to the grown-ups, understand? I'll brook no showing off like you did in the woods last week. You deserved that hit in the head."

The Yaris eased toward the highway on-ramp.

"Time to go, Mr. Lamont."

Dawson sped up and merged with the north-flowing traffic. Lamont did likewise, ensuring he remained far enough behind not to be noticed.

Stone punched a message on his phone: *target heading north. Exact destination uncertain. Most likely Sudbury as per op stationed in situ.*

The Whisper responded: *Watch him carefully. Track his every move. Only engage once they're on campus at LU.*

He acknowledged the text and slipped the device back in his jacket pocket. The traffic thickened, and the operative craned his neck, peering farther up the road.

"Lamont," he said, "Are you sure you haven't lost them?"

The driver chuckled. "Look, I know what I'm doin' here. Let me worry about tailin' them and you worry about whatever it is you fuss about... fingernails or hair or whatever." He smiled at his own jab.

Stone made a mental note to himself. He would remove Lamont from service the moment Matt Dawson and the precious photograph were turned over to The Whisper.

And he would enjoy seeing his lard ass roast.

Soon, now. Soon.

TWENTY-NINE

THE SOUTHERN OUTSKIRTS OF SUDBURY WERE CLOAKED in darkness, and the two students were guided by the reflection of city lights in the harsh night sky. The drive up highway 69 from Orillia was uneventful. Much to Hannah's concern—one she wouldn't dare voice for fear of making it happen—was that Matt had apparently forgotten about the car he claimed had followed them most of the way from London. But in the smothering dark, they couldn't be certain, and her anxiety continued rising like a thermometer on a spring day.

In God I trust and I'm not afraid. What can mere mortals do to me? In God I trust and I'm not afraid...

He veered left, heading down Long Lake Road, away from the downtown core, away from Laurentian University where they'd meet Professor Rathbourne in the morning. Hannah played with the cross around her neck. There were few lights along this road, in the middle of nowhere, but she trusted Matt and felt safe beside him.

Finally, after passing a couple of small lakes glistening in the moonlight, he pulled onto a gravel side road for Chief Lake. A listing overhead streetlight marked the intersection. It winked out as they passed.

"Almost there," he whispered, for the car was eerily quiet in the soft darkness. "You still okay, Hannah? I mean, with going to meet this professor tomorrow even with those guys following us?"

"I am," she lied, "but I'll feel better once we're in your friend's house and settled. This back road is pretty creepy."

They pulled into a dirt laneway beside an unpretentious bungalow. A couple of outbuildings dotted the nearby yard in the moonglow. One looked like an equipment shed; the other could have been an old barn. A lonely lightbulb shone over the building's door.

As Matt parked the car by the house, away from the road, she noticed, the porch light blinked on and a thin, scraggly man with a down vest and hawkish grin waved from the doorway. Joining him was a petite, athletic woman with broad shoulders and blond hair pulled into a ponytail. They exited the Yaris and stretched. Hannah marvelled at the quiet here in the country.

"Well, look who came for a visit!" Jackie slapped Matt's back and they shook hands.

"Hey good to see you, Jackie... Colleen." She hugged him and said, "Welcome."

"Meet my, er..."

"Hi, I'm Hannah," she interjected, stepping forward. "I've heard a lot about you."

He greeted her, then stared dumbfounded at Matt. "Gee whiz, Mattie, what's up?"

"Tell you all about it inside. Hope you don't mind, it's been a hell of a week."

"Sure, sure," he said, collecting their bags, "but

Hannah, answer me one thing."

"Yes?"

"Ya look like a *normie*, so what are ya doing hanging with this old fart stain?" He cackled and led them into the house. Hannah snorted and glanced at Matt who rolled his eyes and smirked.

Although September lingered like a long kiss, winter's hush crept around the corner and as Hannah entered the bungalow, she was struck by an inviting, thick smell of wild meat and fresh bread. A cheery fire blazed in a heavy stone fireplace, and an old black lab, whose best years were clearly in the past, swished its tail from bedding near a picture window.

Colleen welcomed them in with a warm smile. Hannah relaxed immediately, admiring her Aran sweater, noting her thin fingers.

"You must be hungry," she said. "Come and make yourselves at home. Jackie, fetch our friends something to drink, and I'll check on the stew."

Jackie was like weathered barn wood, rough around the edges, likely due to his work as a geologist. But he was outgoing and gregarious—unlike her—and Matt slipped easily into a guy's conversation.

Jackie grabbed a couple of beers and offered them around. Matt took one, but Hannah passed, preferring tea, and they sat by the fire as Matt recounted the story of the photo and the mysterious message. The dog, Boomer, wandered over and nuzzled her hand. She petted him and rubbed behind his ears.

When Matt paused, Jackie leaned forward, cradling his beer. "Quite the tale, Mattie. And you, Hannah," he said, turning to her, "ya got some expertise in this paranormal field?"

She nodded. "I study psychometric phenomena as part of my research. But I haven't experienced anything similar, so we're hoping this researcher at Laurentian might shed some light on it."

"There's something else," Matt added, lowering his voice. "I'm sure someone followed us out of London. Kinda lost track once nightfall came, but a couple of weirdos are likely trailing us."

Jackie fell back in his chair, staring at the floor. Colleen spoke first. "If that's true, they'd better be careful." She stood and headed for the kitchen. "Hey, let's eat and then get you two settled."

The game Hannah smelled when she'd entered the home was moose meat stew prepared in a slow cooker. She had a large helping, and between that and the warm bread and home-made blueberry pie, her eyelids quickly grew heavy. Being in a strange house, she knew the creep in her nightmare would likely make an appearance, so in an uncanny twist, Hannah simultaneously ached for, and dreaded, much needed sleep.

After Colleen pointed out their rooms and laid out fresh towels, Matt and Jackie spent the rest of the evening rehashing war stories of their undergraduate days at Laurentian—most comprising practical jokes, oddball characters, and tales of woe in the laundry rooms. Hannah listened with an amused heart. *So, here are some stories about the young Matt Dawson.* She wondered about the hinted at, yet unspoken, exploits.

The conversation soon turned to sports, so Hannah joined Colleen and Boomer in the kitchen. While they tidied up, Colleen said, "It's clear you like him, Hannah, and just as obvious he likes you, too. Are you two a..."

"Oh, no, we're not." She frowned. "It gets complicated for me." The men's laughter filtered in from the other room.

"I don't know Matt all that well. We'd hung out as a gang back in the day, but this much is true." She wiped her hands on a dish towel and filled Boomer's bowl with some scraps. "Jackie would give his life for your Matt. Wouldn't ever say so, being a guy, but I can tell by the way he admires him. Those two were always different, maybe that drew them together. Funny how you can sense these things in your gut, eh? Even though nothing's said, you still know."

Matt's warmth and searching mind had exposed something most profound in her bones that, try as she might, she'd never find the words for.

Hannah mused, "Perhaps that's what poets are for. Maybe words are just too heavy for understanding the heart."

"Could be," Colleen said, drying a plate, "or perhaps the most important things are the hardest to say. Like those shameful memories we bury, because words are incomplete and diminish the experiences. But God knows." Her gaze bore into her soul.

Hannah gulped as a flood of dusty past sins and failures broke against her heart, especially those behaviours before finding Jesus, the ones that led to… She stared, bewildered at Colleen, feeling smaller than an innocent child, and she fought the tears welling up from a mysterious source.

SHORTLY AFTER, THEY RETIRED TO THEIR ROOMS. Hannah read briefly from her pocket Bible, then turned off the light and waited. Within half an hour, the entire house was quiet, but she couldn't—wouldn't sleep. So she crept to the window and peered outside, searching for any movement. But unlike that night at Matt's home in Haileybury, she sensed no one out there. The feeling of being watched had dissipated.

Hannah yawned, slipped back under the covers and closed her eyes…

...The crooked trail was fresh and the blue sky overhead spread out forever. Hannah poked along, admiring the towering trees and lush ferns that dotted the path like garland. When he appeared, the magnetic smile had gone.

"You..."

"We meet again, Hannah."

She straightened her back defiantly. "I won't listen to you anymore," she said.

The Seducer shoved his hands deep in his pockets and gazed around expectantly.

"Did you hear me?" She stepped toward him.

"Hannah, I'm not here to invite you anywhere today." He grinned, showing off his perfect, white teeth.

"I—I don't understand? Every other time we met along this trail, you begged me to follow." Then she pursed her lips and narrowed her gaze. "I know who you are."

The man laughed. "Well, of course you do!" He turned his back to her. "No need to follow, sweet Hannah. Do you understand why?"

She stood rooted in place, mouth agape, her cheeks flushing. "Why?"

"Because you're already mine," he hissed. "Tell me, Hannah, have you ever touched the centre of your own sorrow?" He sneered, his dark eyes glowing like dying suns. "You will."

The Seducer continued hiking along the trail, until he disappeared in the brush like mist at daybreak. Her mind filled with overwhelming dread, and every instinct screamed to run for safety. But despite the danger she knew lay ahead, inexplicably, she placed one foot in front of the other in a desperate attempt to catch up.

To follow him...

The dream repeated over and over again, ending the same way each time until Hannah awoke in a cold sweat, gasping for air. Once she found her bearings, she leapt out of bed and had to find Matt, but when she opened her door, Boomer the dog startled her, staring up into her face and wagging his tail. Then he padded toward the living room. Hannah grabbed a blanket and pillow from the end of the bed and followed.

The fire had died down to whispering embers, a soft reddish glow casting hellish shadows from the fireplace. Boomer lay down on his bedding, head raised. She knelt down.

"Mind if I join you, tonight? Hm?"

The dog offered his ears for scratching, and she obliged. Then, throwing the blanket out over the floor and tossing down the pillow, Hannah curled up beside the lab and closed her eyes, waiting for elusive reason to kick in.

Whatever the message was from The Seducer, she'd figure it out in the morning. *You are my hiding place. You will protect me from trouble and surround me with songs of deliverance.* She repeated the prayer until her mind settled and she drifted into a deep sleep.

DAWSON AWOKE TO BOOMER LICKING HIS EAR AND snuffling in his face.

"Okay, okay, I'm getting up," he groaned.

He pet the dog on the head and threw on clothing. *That's what happens when you leave the door open.* He stretched and glanced out the hallway and saw Jackie and Colleen's room still closed up, but Hannah's wasn't. He peeked inside, but the bed was empty.

After brushing his teeth, he headed for the kitchen to make coffee and found Hannah lying on the floor near Boomer's bed.

"Ah," he whispered to the dog. "Now I understand."

He let the dog out to run and shuffled toward the kitchen, hoping not to disturb her. After searching a few cupboards, he got the kettle boiling and set out a couple of mugs. Hannah stirred by the window and sat up, hair tumbling across her face.

"I bet that wasn't comfortable," he chimed.

"Oh, sorry." She turned, startled. "No, but better than being in bed." She wrapped the blanket around her shoulders. "The nightmare came again last night. Worst one yet."

Dawson poured boiling water into the mugs and dropped in a couple of tea bags. They sat at the kitchen table while Boomer nosed a stick in the garden, distracted by something up the road.

"Do you want to talk about it?"

She sighed, staring at the mug, then said, "It wasn't quite like the others. The creepy figure was there, but he was... different."

"How so?"

"Well, normally he entices me to follow him. You know, straight out of a horror movie. Motioning me to come with his bony fingers. I did some research into dream interpretation once and this creepy character is a seducer."

"What, you mean like someone after you... *that way?*"

"Sexually? Don't think so. And, just to be clear, it's okay to say *sex* in front of me. I'm a Christian, not a prude." She smiled and sipped her tea. "No, the seducer is someone who's trying to get me to follow. He probably represents some evil, satanic figure but comes across as handsome and trustworthy." She hesitated. "But last night, the creep said I didn't need to follow anymore because I'm... I'm..."

"You're what? Tell me."

"That I'm already his, Matt." Hannah shrugged and yawned. "If he is a symbol of darkness, what does it mean that I'm his?" They drank in silence a moment. "Still, you want to know the worst part? I started following anyway."

Hannah shuddered, wrapping her hands around the teacup.

Jackie squawked from down the hall, interrupting their chat, and soon appeared in the living room wearing sweats, his hair all askew. He surveyed the place, and asked, "Where's the beast at?"

"Boomer? I let him out a few minutes ago." Dawson checked the window but didn't see the dog. "I'll call him in."

"Oh, no, leave him be. He loves being outside." He rustled around in the kitchen and pulled the coffee maker out from a cupboard and filled it with water.

"Colleen's gonna be out in a sec and, ya know, she'll want to see this crazy photograph. Kept mumbling about it in bed." He scooped out some ground coffee. "Ya got it with you?"

Dawson nodded and retrieved the folder from his pack in the bedroom. He placed it in the centre of the table.

Hannah reached over, flipping it open, exposing the innocent-looking prairie farmhouse.

"That's it, eh?"

"Yeah, the cause of my visions."

Colleen entered the living room dressed in jeans and a green plaid work shirt, and opened the door to let Boomer in. The dog immediately traipsed to the kitchen and sat beside Hannah.

"He's taken a shining to you," Colleen said. She fixed herself a coffee and joined them at the table. "So, let's see this thing." She took the photo in her firm hands and studied the image, then turned it over a couple times and ran her fingers along the perimeter. "You said last night that you're the only one who can see the magic, right Matt?"

"Yes." His stomach churned at the thought of putting on a freak show.

"Well," she said, snapping it on the table, "let's have a look."

Dawson sighed, and Hannah sat upright, clutching the blanket, nodding encouragement. He handled the photo by the edges.

Within microseconds, heat flowed into his fingertips. He winced as the burning sensation screamed through his hands like an electric shock, and the margins began swirling in what was now a familiar foreplay.

Monochrome hands wiped across the image. The farmhouse disappeared and the featureless faces bloomed out of the chaos. Several held their mouths agape, their sightless eyes apparently staring at him. The woman evolved to dominate the scene, her presence growing larger, filling the space in a grey mist.

What do you want? What are you trying to tell me?

The ghostly woman shifted, receding, then advancing.

What do you want?

The pain needling his hands was almost unbearable. Her eyes, like concrete orbs, fluttered as he mentally noted her features. The hair tumbled across her slight shoulders. And she appeared to be holding something in her arms. Her mouth formed silent words.

What do you want? How can I help?

Then Dawson's heart sank.

The image reformed in front of him, and a new figure replaced the mysterious apparition—someone he knew well. Her face lost the ghostly grey and muted monochromatic structure, morphing into an almost human form.

Dawson's fingertips burned beyond pain, but he refused to relinquish the photograph. The woman clearly held something, cradled it like a... like a baby wrapped in a thin blanket.

Oh, my God...

The image blurred. Other ghostly hands swept across the space, and he recognized who this was. Then Hannah's voice strained to reach him. A bead of sweat dripped off his face and plopped on the photograph.

He could hold it no longer.

His fingers trembled, and the photo dropped to the table. Dawson continued staring at the swirls and eddies dissipating along the edges, the apparition and her entourage folding back into the mists, replaced by the farmhouse on the prairie landscape.

"Matt!"

Hannah shook his shoulder. Immediately, he recognized his surroundings. The image had gone.

Jackie and Colleen both stood beside him with horrified expressions. Hannah's face showed a frightening mix of terror and helplessness. "Matt, what happened?"

He gulped. "You—you saw it?"

Hannah nodded. "Only the glowing edges."

"I didn't see anything," Jackie whispered, "except you kinda freaking out."

Colleen remained silent, but her eyes narrowed.

"Just the glow, Hannah?"

"Yes" she whispered, "why?"

Matt brushed the sweat from his forehead. "Because I saw way more this time. Seems the more I handle this thing—when I can actually see stuff—the more it reveals." He faced Hannah. "You'll never believe who was there."

"Tell me."

He didn't know how to frame the words and began

doubting his own eyes. If the others had only seen part of it, perhaps he'd been hallucinating. But, no, the woman was there, cradling a baby in her thin arms.

"Who did you see?"

"Hannah," he gasped. "I saw *you*."

Hannah pulled back, leaning against the chair.

"Say that again, Matt, really slowly."

"*You*, Hannah, and that's not all."

He lifted his mug and took a sip with trembling hands. "You were... *it* was holding a baby, a tiny child, wrapped in a blanket, and I got the distinct message, like an understanding running through my body, that the child was..." He gulped.

Hannah's lips quivered as she gripped his arm. A haunted, nervous look passed behind her eyes. "What, Matt? What about the child?"

He stared intently at her, fighting back a sudden urge to cry. "The child was dead."

THIRTY

"I'M TELLING YOU, STONE, WE SHOULDA GRABBED 'EM IN the middle of the night. No fuss, no muss. And none of this waiting around pissing in the wind."

Florian Lamont slurped his coffee, threw his head back on the headrest in the Suburban and exhaled for dramatic effect.

The operative ignored the remark. He refused to engage with this inbred idiot. *What is it with these heavies? Are they clueless about what The Sodality stands for?* He peered around at the tree cover where they'd parked a few hundred meters from the bungalow. All seemed in order. It had taken a while to pick up the trail last night after getting caught in traffic in Orillia, but once on the highway, Lamont spotted them quickly. Stone had to admit that, despite the man's impatience and finger lickin' good attitude, he was rather skilled at his trade.

"Tick tock... tick tock..."

"That's enough, Lamont. In the fullness of time, you

shall have your exercise. But if you could think a step ahead, you'd realize that picking them up now and escorting them to the university would not be... satisfactory. We want to know more about who they meet, too."

The driver wheezed. "Yeah, sure, whatever you say."

Stone eyed him suspiciously. "Would you care to inform The Whisper of your concerns?" He grabbed the phone and offered it to the man. Lamont refused.

"Very well," he said, "we'll continue to do it my way." He watched the quiet house in the distance where Matt Dawson, the photo, and the girl spent the night. "I imagine they'll be leaving for the university soon."

"Uh-huh."

"Not to put too fine a point on it, but that couple are unknown variables. Without further intel, the risks are uncertain." He turned to his partner. "I don't like uncertainty."

"So we wait?"

"So we wait."

Stone's phone pinged. A message from The Whisper: *update?*

Stone: *targets holed up in a house south of the city. Will follow and report.*

Whisper: *understood.*

He slipped the device back in his pocket and pulled the coffee from the cup holder, eyes fixed on the bungalow.

They didn't have to watch long.

The homeowner, the scruffy one, exited the front door and headed off to the machine shed, followed by the blonde. Lamont sat up straight. "You sure they didn't bug out in the middle of the night?"

"I'm confident they are exactly where we left them. They attempted to hide that wreck of a car behind the house, but its nose is sticking out through the cedars." He fished a pair of miniature binoculars from a bag at his feet and handed them to Lamont.

"Ah, yes." He paused, then his arms and shoulders stiffened. "Heads up, Bossman, we've got more activity."

Stone replaced his cup in the holder and squinted into the morning sunlight. "So we do."

Dawson, the girl, and the dog exited the bungalow and wandered around the side, presumably preparing to leave.

"Getting ready to go, I'd say," Lamont mumbled.

"Stand by. We don't want them to spot us."

Scruffy and the blonde woman returned to the front doorstep and stood, hands in pockets.

The Yaris rumbled to life and inched around. They shouted and waved to each other, then the car scooted off in the opposite direction, toward the main road.

"Say, Stone, how's about we shake down the happy couple in the house, hm?"

"No. We've had this conversation. Not our job."

"But what if they left the photo there for safekeeping?"

He sighed. "I highly doubt our boy would do that given the purpose of their trip here, but we'll find out soon enough. Fire up the engine. They're going to Laurentian. And our man is waiting for them."

Lamont grinned, exposing his missing tooth.

THIRTY-ONE

"HOW DID I GET IN YOUR VISION?" HANNAH CHEWED ON A piece of toast as they wound along the back road.

"Great question. I was about to ask you the same thing. Is it accepted in psychometry for people to appear in others' visions?"

Hannah swallowed, bit her lip and said, "Well, there's so much we don't know, and finding common ground or some scientific basis to hang these observations on is elusive. But characters appearing in dreams is more the realm of psychology."

He glanced at her. "Is that like the seducer creep in your nightmares?"

"I guess so."

A thought struck him. "If these events are connected, like, your appearance in my vision along with your different nightmare last night, then what's up with this dead baby?"

Hannah trembled. He'd never seen her this way.

"Tell me more about that, Matt. Let's see if you missed anything, no matter how random or insignificant it seems. I gotta admit, that's got me shaken."

As he drove, Dawson recounted his observations again: the shifting apparitions, the primary one emerging holding a child, the waving, brushing hands in sweeping motions, and the cloth that the baby was wrapped in, and his emotional response to this awareness that the woman looked eerily similar to Hannah. Then, there was the dead child, and the vision ended.

"Interesting, but I don't see any obvious connection between that and my nightmare, do you? I mean, she wasn't a seductress, was she?"

"Didn't seem that way. But can you feel the clues changing? Like, between your altered nightmare last night and my evolving paranormal event, we learn new stuff. This morning with the baby, for instance, and the…" His brow furrowed and he stopped cold.

"What is it?"

"Funny. That blanket wrapped around the child. I think I've seen it before somewhere."

"Describe it to me."

Dawson thought for a moment. "Well, it was hard to tell from the vision. Everything in that world has weird colours. But there was an odd, familiar pattern on the cloth. Sort of like two ribbons, about an inch in width, in a pattern. Yeah, a herringbone style."

"Wait," Hannah cried, "I remember that, too!"

"What?"

"In your mum's basement. I'm sure some of your dad's equipment was wrapped up in a cloth that fits your description."

Dawson's mind returned to that day they went through his dad's journals and old field junk. He had seen it there. He also remembered, when he was a kid, his dad keeping the cloth safe, and telling him that it belonged to his father and had been in the family for years, and that he'd used it when he was a baby. Never talked about it. Dawson assumed it was an object that got passed down rather than trashed. The thought that this same material, wrapped around a dead child, had entered his vision caused a random surge of terror to rise in his bones. *This is the warning. Death must be the danger.*

He said to Hannah, "Your life might be in peril if your holding the dead child is an omen. Or, if my dad encountered the same vision, and he died a couple days later..." He gulped. "We need to send our regrets to the professor, drive straight to Haileybury and find that cloth."

"Right now?"

"There's no better time. We can grab it and be back here later this afternoon. That blanket has Big Clue written all over it." He handed Hannah the phone and she sent a message to the professor.

"Let's go."

THE SUBURBAN ROARED TO LIFE, AND LAMONT DEFTLY spun it away from its cache up the road. Stone told him to maintain normal speed to avoid any more suspicion among the ball cap and pick up crowd that lived out here in the bush.

When they arrived at Long Lake Road, the operative glimpsed the Yaris heading toward the city. Another car passed and then Lamont eased onto the road.

In the emerging sunshine, Stone noted the bristly area. Craggy hills and outcrops. Dwarfed trees, no doubt from the reforestation program this region had indulged in since he was a boy. A smattering of tiny lakes.

The car between them and Dawson turned off, leaving no one but the Yaris up front. But it suddenly accelerated and bolted like a skittish deer. *He must have seen us.* His phone pinged and the message from The Whisper was short: *they're going to Haileybury. Stop them.* "Take them now, before they enter the city. We'll escort them to the university."

Lamont grinned. The Suburban hammered into another gear and shot ahead. Shortly, they approached the Yaris's rear bumper and Stone saw the girl in the passenger seat waving her arms.

A wide clearing on the shoulder, designated as a truckers rest stop, loomed in the distance.

"Up ahead," he said to Lamont. "Let's block them over there and have a little chat."

Lamont sped up and the Suburban pulled alongside the Yaris. Dawson glanced at Stone, a pained expression on his face. The operative pointed to him to pull over.

But Dawson clearly had other ideas. He slammed on the brakes and instantly fell behind. Lamont cursed, twisting his head around and slowing.

"Bastard," he muttered.

The Yaris had stopped.

Lamont arced the car in a wide, dangerous U turn in front of oncoming traffic. Horns blasted as other vehicles swerved to avoid him. Lamont swore and accelerated. This time, the Yaris crossed into their lane, screaming toward him.

"Matt, what are you doing?"

"I'm using the only weapon we have to get these guys to quit."

Hannah threw her arms out against the dashboard.

Dawson continued speeding up. The overworked engine whined as it revved higher and higher. "Hannah, you know that kinetic energy is just as deadly as any other, and right now, this old Yaris is a 3000 pound killing machine." He gripped the wheel in both hands as the

Suburban refused to yield.

"Matt, stop!"

"I got this," he shouted. His back straightened and his resolve hardened.

The two vehicles raced toward each other in a chaotic game of chicken. The distance between them smeared by. Horns blasted, filling the car with a furious symphony.

"Matt!"

Dawson jerked the Yaris to the right, squealing and swerving into his proper lane, spinning the wheel to compensate for drift. He glimpsed the two men in the black Suburban and recognized the driver immediately: that psycho from the Kirkland Lake woods.

The other man in the passenger seat had leaned over to grab the steering wheel, but the Suburban traveled too quickly for the sudden change in direction. In the rearview mirror, Matt saw the machine spin, unable to overcome its massive momentum, then fishtail as the driver tried to wrestle it under control.

But it was too late.

In a flurry of dust and gravel, the car rode up an embankment and scraped along a bare outcrop. The windows along the passenger side exploded.

"Lord, you watch over me. Lord, you watch over me."

Dawson immediately slowed and pulled over. A handful of other cars and pickups on the opposite side swerved past the immobilized Suburban. A couple stopped, hazard lights flashing. Dawson threw the Yaris in park and jumped out, peering back at the wreckage in the early morning sun. The effect of hitting that outcrop had been immediate. The granite protrusion had sheared the side of the Suburban, peeling it back like an orange. When the vehicle had finally, mercifully slumped to a stop, it's right half dangled from the back end, tethered only by some cables and dumb luck.

People ran toward the wreck. A woman spoke into her cell phone, then pointed in Dawson's direction. He didn't know what to do. Part of him rejoiced that those goons got what they deserved, but guilt over his own actions burdened him, too. Then the driver of the twisted Suburban emerged, holding his head. And finally, the other passenger crawled from the driver's door, gazing around until he spotted Dawson. Their eyes locked.

"Matt!"

He turned and hopped into the car. Hannah was in tears and shaking. He leaned over and tried hugging her, but she pushed him away.

"They're both okay, Hannah."

"Thank God," she gasped.

He managed to hold her while the shaking ceased, then said, "Let's get out of here."

STONE AND LAMONT PUSHED THE GOOD SAMARITANS aside and dusted themselves off. Other than Lamont's bloody nose and wounded pride, they were both intact.

And furious.

Stone retrieved his satchel from the back seat, slinging it over his shoulder and said in a most understated manner, "That was a shit show."

"I can't wait to get my hands on that little bastard's neck," Lamont growled under his breath. "That's twice he's bested me. No more."

They began marching toward the city as first responders rounded the corner. Within moments, a car rolled up beside them and offered the pair a lift, which the operative readily accepted. The driver, an elderly woman, suggested they go to the hospital, but Stone refused. Instead, he asked to be dropped at Science North. As they drove into the city, his phone pinged.

The Whisper.

He updated her and then, when they reached the science centre, he and Lamont thanked the woman and exited the vehicle.

"What do we do now?" Lamont asked.

"We mark time until a local operative fetches us. Then we follow them."

After several minutes, a white van pulled up and the side door rolled open. They hopped in.

It was pitch black inside. Stone and Lamont found their seats and exhaled. Strangely, the driver exited and walked away.

He noticed immediately the overwhelming scent of lilac, and froze.

A disembodied voice floated from the dark depths.

"It's good to see you again so soon, Cornelius."

THIRTY-TWO

"YOU COULD HAVE KILLED THEM," HANNAH SAID IN A firm, low voice. The Yaris had fallen into a new rhythm as they drove east on the highway toward North Bay en route to his mother's house in Haileybury. Morning sun had given way to thick clouds rolling in, threatening rain.

"Yes."

Confusion and disbelief wrestled with her need for peace. His reckless behaviour was terrifying. She brushed a strand of hair away from her eyes. "You almost killed *us*."

"I—I'm sorry, Hannah, I wasn't thinking straight."

"Matt, please. Don't apologize if you're not even sincere about it. Don't spew words thinking that's what I want to hear, and once you say them, I'll shut up." Her voice rose. "We have to call the police. You caused an accident and fled the scene."

His annoying defiance was resolute. "Not a chance! Didn't you recognize the driver? The same psychotic asshole who threatened us on the survey lines? The bush man you brained with a rock, remember?"

She jerked her head around, fire in her eyes. Her mouth opened, prepared to retaliate with both barrels. Then she inhaled deeply and turned away.

The next half hour passed in silence until Sturgeon Falls appeared in the distance. Matt needed to stop for gas. He pulled into a Petro-Canada, filled the tank, and bought two coffees from the shop. Hannah remained in the front seat of the Yaris, muttering to herself.

After getting behind the wheel again, he asked, "So... what do you want to do?"

"Call the police," she insisted through clenched teeth.

"Can't do that."

She sighed with exasperation. "If you won't, then I will." She took the phone from her pocket, but he reached over and stopped her.

"Wait, I'll call, but first, let's get to my mum's place and find that blanket, okay?" He softened his tone. "Look, I screwed up. I honestly don't get it, Hannah. It's like sometimes I can't recognize myself. The right thing to do stares me in the face, but I continue to mess up. Worse, I dig in, you know? Like I've been doing with you." He took her hand. "I'm so sorry."

She gazed into his eyes, feeling his sincerity this time.

"Hannah, we've come this far. I've got to know the truth, the message, and what's so important about this cloth, and why my dad and I can sense weird things. Then, there's the creeps following us, and what they want with the photo. As soon as we're done here, I promise I'll call the cops."

A moment passed, and Hannah stuffed her phone away. "Matt, I believe you, but don't promise me anything, okay? You don't exactly have a solid record of doing what you say you'll do. "

At least he was smart enough to remain quiet. There

was a time for both words and for silence, and what she struggled with now were conflicting emotions requiring the latter. Even if she mastered the mental inertia to argue with him, she refused to, placing it all in God's hands where it belonged.

They pulled back onto the highway, racing toward North Bay. Hannah thanked him for the coffee and, having turned everything over, finally relaxed and let peace return. While she didn't admit it, she too wanted to find the truth, and whether the events of the past couple weeks somehow related to her nightmarish past.

"It's human nature to do stuff we know is wrong," she said, out of the blue after several minutes of silence.

Matt responded, keeping his eyes on the road. "How so?"

The space between them that had grown and thickened, slowly relented. "Mind if I use an example from the Bible?"

"Nah, maybe I'll learn something."

She sipped the coffee and grimaced. "In the Book of Romans, the Apostle Paul talked about this. He couldn't understand why he kept doing things when he knew intellectually that it was wrong. And those behaviours he realized were good, he avoided. In other words, he asked himself and us why we keep doing what we know we shouldn't do?"

"Sounds pretty messed up."

"Well, if you mean he was a human with weaknesses, you're right. Before Jesus redeemed him, he was a ruthless murderer. A persecutor."

"Yeah, I seem to remember Paul was a big deal. So what did he do?"

Hannah, grinned. *A big deal...* "Well, this is the point. On his own, there's nothing he could do, because this paradox, this misguided thinking, is *sin*. We *know* how Jesus would act in those circumstances, yet we do other stupid stuff. The alcoholic's drinking destroys his life, ruins his family, but he keeps doing it. Or the student buying an essay online and passing it off as his own. He knows he's not honest, but does it anyway."

"Sounds rather hopeless. But isn't it a matter of time and psychological research before we find answers? Like, isn't that what counsellors and psychiatrists are for? You know, find the underlying reasons, get some tools to deal with them?"

"What if everything we learned and tried, failed?"

Matt thought for a moment but had no response.

"See, the point Paul made wasn't just that he understood us, but that only one solution worked."

"What's that?"

"To live in the Holy Spirit a hundred percent of the time, and trust that God's plan for us is unfolding exactly, precisely, the way it should."

"Yeah, okay, but what *exactly, precisely* does that mean? What does it even smell like?"

She ignored the cynicism. "That's what each of us needs to figure out. Look, there are no shortcuts, Matt. We all must do the work before coming to our own conclusion. Once you've done that, you may reject the whole idea of a Creator, and that's fair because at least you're not doing it out of ignorance. However," she softened her voice, "what if you considered the evidence and concluded that, yes, there actually is a living God who can help us live better, more rewarding lives. Where we don't break promises, or lie, or cheat, or..." She shuddered as Emily's cold face flashed before her eyes.

They continued driving in silence. Hannah's burden was relieved, having shared a biblical idea. And she'd given him enough to add a dash of wonder to his mathematical view of life.

"Hannah," he finally said. "Someday I'd like to learn more about this faith of yours."

STEFAN GUNAR SLUMPED AT HIS CLUTTERED DESK, holding his head. He felt like he was the only one on the floor this early Friday afternoon. The hallways were dark and silent, an overcast sky contributing to the gloom. His office hours were over. Only the most dedicated students remained, including Wendy Sakamoto, recovering in his lab after that odd encounter with the mysterious researcher poking around the project. And what was the deal with a cryptic text from an idiot calling herself *The Whisper*? No doubt, one of Stone's Sodality types keeping watch.

How did I let it come to this?

He sighed deeply, recalling his discussion that morning with Wendy about the experiment, about Matt Dawson, and this fellow who'd questioned her and who sounded an awful lot like that asshole Stone.

What have I gotten myself into?

Gunar had reached a lonely milestone in his quest for a reclaimed career, for recognition, and over the past hour, his mood ranged from anger, to fear, to panic, and finally, to the cusp of humility. The last time he experienced an emotional riot happened when Shelly walked out to chase after some tax lawyer in Vancouver. Couldn't blame her for wanting to be in British Columbia, but leaving him for a tax lawyer? She'd announced it on a rainy Thursday evening when he arrived home late from a lecture. Her suitcases sat by the front door. Shelly was in the kitchen smoking a cigarette, drinking wine, dressed to kill.

After her calm declaration, he felt no remorse. Didn't try stopping her or raising a fuss at all. He simply shrugged and said, "Okay." And that was that.

However, after a couple of weeks, her absence gutted him. He'd fallen into a deep, haunting depression lasting over a year, driving him into a pit of bitterness and cynicism. Reflecting back, he realized that's when his career got completely derailed. Sure, it had been stagnating for some time, but that's when he stopped trying and resigned himself to mind-numbing grunt research, infilling for the true scientists. His emasculation was complete.

He pounded the desk, wishing he'd never met Cornelius Stone.

Yet, his capacity for learning remained, if only he'd apply it. If only he found a topic to get jazzed about like in the old days. The way Dawson was about that ridiculous photograph. If only...

The laptop was open on a page showing his bank account balance. He noted again the recent deposit of $25,000. Stone said to expect that, along with a promise to see two papers published over the coming weeks.

But the findings were second-rate garbage, and whether anyone would actually read them didn't matter an iota: he'd know. Now that the covenant with The Sodality was real, he couldn't escape his obligations. And it appeared he'd put Dawson's life in jeopardy, and Wendy Sakamoto's, too. Possibly even his own.

It had to stop.

He needed to find a way out and to make things right. And for that to occur, he must come clean with Matt and Wendy. He'd also have to somehow terminate this unbreakable covenant with Stone.

Now he'd always admired Catherine Gardner in Graduate Studies, and knew she'd been through the publishing wars and funding battles just like him, and had emerged unscathed. In fact, her entire career rocketed along the fast track.

She may have a solution for The Sodality's conditions.

He pulled up her email address and began typing.

Catherine,

I must speak with you on an urgent matter. Available today?

He paused. Where would he start? In some obsolete corner of his mind, a thin, persistent voice spoke, imploring him to share everything, and do whatever was necessary to protect his students and reset his career honestly.

Stefan Gunar reflected on his predicament, and with each passing moment, his need for academic redemption grew.

He signed the email, pressed the send button, and released the breath he'd been holding since his wife's total rejection. What surprised him was Gardner's immediate response. Her words made his heart sink.

Stefan,

I've been expecting to hear from you. A mutual friend says you've got a couple of papers coming out...

THIRTY-THREE

"MATT... HANNAH... I'M SO GLAD TO SEE YOU, BUT what are you doing back here? Why aren't you at school?"

Beth stood on the front porch out of the rain, hands on hips, as they closed the car doors. Dawson hugged her and kissed her on the cheek, but she seemed aloof.

"Like I said in my text, Mum, there's something in the basement we need to find. In Dad's stuff."

She wrung her hands nervously together. "Well, I must admit I'm a bit surprised. Come on in before we all get soaked, and I'll get you some lunch." She led them into the house.

In the hallway, Dawson said, "We'll visit in a minute. Just have to check something that could solve this puzzle." He neglected to mention the two creeps who chased them down in Sudbury.

Hannah descended the creaking stairs and turned on the light. "I remember exactly where it is." She entered the workshop and pulled a tattered cardboard box out from underneath a shelf. They huddled close as she rummaged through the carton. "There."

Dawson saw the old cloth. It was muddy and frayed, with a couple of grease smears.

"You had this as a blanket when you were a baby?" she smiled. "Gross."

"I know, it's pretty sketchy now, but Dad was adamant about not throwing it out. I guess he found another use for it down here. But I remember keeping that ratty old thing until I was about six. Then it disappeared."

He lifted it up, and the object—a piece of radio gear— wrapped inside tumbled out. After setting the portable antenna tuner on the floor, he spread the cloth out on the workbench. "What do you think?"

"Is this the same blanket from your vision?"

He examined it, swinging an overhead lamp closer to inspect it. "Yes, I can guarantee that. Same pattern." He lay his hands on it.

That's when it began.

Warmth immediately flooded through his palms and up his arms.

"Hannah?"

"What's happening?"

"I—I sense something in this… a power flowing out like nothing I've ever known."

"Same as the photo?"

"No, not even close."

His breathing grew shallow. No blisters this time, only a comforting, powerful force radiating from the cloth. Then a new vision appeared, the blanket acting as a canvas for the bizarre, unfolding scene.

"What do you see?" Hannah stood beside him. Their shoulders and arms brushed together. "Sweet Mary!" She jumped away.

"You feel it, too?"

"I do..."

But her voice melted into the auditory background, like a distant echo over water. Dawson found himself in what he could only describe as an ancient Roman city at dusk. People rushed past, grabbing their belongings and running. Shouts and screams descended from the distance, flames leapt from what appeared to be a seaport, with multiple wooden ships ablaze.

And unlike the farmhouse phenomena, Dawson was *in* this vision, playing a role he didn't understand...

"Quick, Valerius. Hurry." A woman grabbed his arm and forced him through the crowd toward a massive building. Words in a foreign language hung across the entrance. Latin and Greek.

"He's ordered the destruction of the Library," she said. "We mustn't lose the treasures, even if he thinks they're all gone. They have great value."

She darted around more stone structures, ducked through alleyways, avoiding the rush of people heading the opposite direction. They approached the Library from behind. Roman soldiers scattered the onlookers with spears while others entered the building, setting fire to the massive heap of scrolls and maps it contained.

"What is happening?" he asked.

"They're burning it all down, Valerius," she stopped and eyed him suspiciously. "Didn't you hear the edict? Theophilus has ordered its complete destruction. He wants to eliminate anything remaining that's not strictly Christian, but he doesn't know, and now everything's burning."

Another group of soldiers rolled in with torches and wagons.

"Our treasures are still inside, and these brutes don't

care. Now hurry!"

She crept through the crowd and approached the side of the Library. Several holes had been smashed in the walls. Dawson watched the soldiers move about, gathering papers and furniture and dumping everything in the centre of the great hall. The woman motioned to follow.

"In there?"

"Yes, they don't understand what they're doing."

When the Roman guards looked away, she led him inside. They crouched behind a stone table.

"It's in the storage area below, remember?"

"Sorry, I—"

She shook her head with disbelief. "Come, follow me."

Smoke permeated the room and burned his eyes as the woman drew him down gloomy marble steps into a subfloor opening. Strips of light pierced through cracks in the flooring above, illuminating the hanging smoke.

"Quickly now," she whispered.

They approached a massive wooden door. It was barred with a bronze lock. "Find something to smash it open."

Dawson was swept up in the moment's panic. He searched the floor and found a jagged stone splintered off the ceiling. It weighed several pounds and was pointed at one end.

"Let's try this," he said.

He raised his hands over the lock and threw them down. The contact made an unholy racket, but the latch held fast.

"Try it again, Valerius!" she urged.

More shouts and noises drifted down from the main floor. Heat from the fire above bathed them and sweat poured from his face. After raising the stone again, he brought it down anew, but the stubborn lock still resisted.

"Please, keep trying. The treasure is more powerful than anything imaginable. We must protect it."

He inhaled, raised the weapon and, with an angry force he didn't know he possessed, slammed down with all his might.

The locking mechanism shattered. The woman wriggled it free from its clasp and threw her weight on the door to open it.

Inside the sub-chamber, stale air greeted him. He could see nothing. Airborne dust and smoke filled his lungs, and he coughed. When their eyes had adjusted, she rifled through several crates.

"What are we looking for?" he asked.

She laughed in a nervous, anxious way. "Don't be silly," she said, and continued with her search. Dawson waited by the door, monitoring the staircase for anyone coming down. An orange glow cast hungry shadows from the top of the stairway, and his immediate thought was identifying an escape route.

"Found it." She grabbed a clump of material and stuffed it under her dress. "Let's get out of here."

"How? I mean, the fire and—"

"Have faith, Valerius. We are protected now."

They ran toward the stairs and began climbing slowly, looking above for soldiers. The heat from the flames was immense, hot enough to cause the bronze on the stair rail to glow an odd amber colour.

But he didn't feel it.

The woman gained the main floor and motioned for him to follow. The soldiers had abandoned the Library. Roars and shouts from the crowd outside drowned out the crackle of the burning scrolls.

But he seemed immune to the surrounding, ravenous flames, devouring everything combustible in their path.

The woman calmly took his hand and walked

cautiously toward the massive hole in the wall where they'd entered. It was blocked, however, by searing heat.

"Fear not, Valerius, my love," she said and smiled. A sense of inner peace overcame him, the likes of which he'd never experienced.

She stepped through the firewall, and he followed. He lost sight of her momentarily in the thick smoke. Then they emerged on the opposite side. The evening cool embraced him and he inhaled the clear air deeply. They continued barging through the crowd of onlookers onto the streets, and finally, into a narrow stone house where they fell to the ground, exhausted.

Sweat poured from his forehead. He slowly gathered strength and looked around, his gaze falling on the woman. He felt he should know her. There was a distant familiarity in her manners and features: the long hair, the high cheekbones. But he couldn't place her.

When she raised herself, she smiled broadly.

Matthew?

He heard a voice, as if underwater... someone calling his name. He went to the window and peered outside. No one was there. Crowds of strangers across the square poured out into the hills, moving like waves from the city. Firelight glowed from the hills, and off the clouds overhead.

"We did it," she said, coming up behind and wrapping her arms around his waist.

"I—I still don't understand what it is we did."

"Valerius," she said, turning him around. "You are so mysterious today." She reached into her skirts and brought out the piece of salvaged clothing from the Library. It appeared to be a blanket or cloak. "This is more important than anything you'll ever own. Touch it." She handed the material to him.

He gathered it in his hands. Immediately, power

surged through him and he felt as if everything turned inside out, every belief subverted, dusted off, replaced, cleansed, restored. He stared at the woman.

"Ah, you remember now."

"I—I do," he said, tears filling his eyes. He scrutinized the cloth and realized it was someone's garment. In the dim shadows, it appeared to be a long beige tunic with purple or navy stripes running along the edge in a herringbone pattern.

"Matthew, please!"

That voice again...

"Matt!"

Dawson's vision evaporated. He was again in his mother's basement, hands resting on the patch of blanket. Someone grabbed his arm. Hannah.

"Matt, please come up here."

His mother's voice, dripping with terror.

Something wasn't right. Multiple footsteps crept along the floorboards, and muted voices floated down the stairs.

"They found us, Matt," Hannah whispered. "I just know it."

A voice bellowed from above the basement stairs. "Don't make us come down there, Mr. Dawson. You won't like what happens to your mother."

His eyes widened, and he searched Hannah's face. Her mouth dropped open. "Wait, what did you see, Matt? You look... different."

He nodded, unable to process the clarity and meaning of the vision. "I have to help my mum," he said, and grabbed the blanket.

"No, give it to me." She stuffed the cloth under her loose-fitting shirt, camouflaging it against her body.

"Let's go.".

When they entered the kitchen, the two men from the Suburban eyed them with menacing looks. The creeper from the woods leered over his mother, who sat at the table, shaking. The other man, the passenger in the car, smirked.

"Ah, we finally meet in person. Properly this time."

"Leave her alone, and get the hell out of this house," Dawson growled, fists clenched.

"Of course," the well-dressed man said, "but first, let me introduce myself. My name is Cornelius Stone and my colleague here is Flavian Lamont. I believe you've already met."

The psycho from the bush grinned at Hannah and pointed to his head.

Hannah gulped.

"There's someone else I'd like you to meet. She happened to know your father intimately."

From the hallway shadows, a hooded figure emerged. She was petite, standing ramrod straight. When the kitchen light splashed her face, Dawson immediately recoiled. The creature appeared wraith-like, a gaunt, burned demon with deathly dark eyes and a scent of lilacs.

In her bony, crooked fingers, she held the farmhouse photograph.

"Matt Dawson? Meet The Whisper."

THIRTY-FOUR

"ARE YOU RESPONSIBLE FOR THIS?" HE SAID, GLARING AT the creature with the hidden eyes. "You're behind almost killing us?"

"Clever boy," The Whisper croaked, remaining in the shadows of the hallway. "But only partially. We belong to an organization as ancient as recorded history, and I am but one of many."

Dawson's stomach flipped as the woman stood completely still, her scarred face shrouded by the hood. His feet would not move, as if she'd cast a powerful spell on him. Confusion rushed through his bones until he felt light-headed and feared losing his balance. *What madness is this?*

Hannah grabbed his arm and moved beside him.

"Ah, the helper, Ms. King," the woman hissed. "Yours is an interesting story. Perhaps not as important historically as Mr. Dawson's, but curious nonetheless. Tell me, do you still have the nightmares? Do you think of her often?"

"H-How do you know? Who are you people?"

The Whisper smiled in the afternoon gloom.

Stone took up the conversation. "We are members of The Sodality of Truth, Ms. King."

"The what?"

He ignored the question. "We have existed in one form or another for thousands of years, and have but a single goal: to expose human beings for the sinful, hypocritical worms they are."

Hannah gasped and squeezed Dawson's hand. None of this made sense, but he was determined to protect his mother and Hannah with all his mind, body and soul.

Whoever these Sodality creeps were, he'd get them out of his life no matter the consequences.

"What does this have to do with us?"

The Whisper brought a corner of the photo to her darkened face and dragged it across her ruddy cheek.

"In short, my dear Mr. Dawson," she said, "everything. What you may not realize is we've been searching years for this photograph. Personally, I've sought it for 13 years. How's your math?"

Dawson prickled with rage.

Stone added, "We knew your father had hidden it, but had no clues where, except it wasn't in this house." He turned to Beth. "Apologies, ma'am, but our people visited your home shortly after Grey's death. Just to look around, you understand. The only item of interest to us was that photograph."

"But...but why?" Dawson asked.

"The photo itself is worthless, as you likely suspect," The Whisper said. "Just some dead relative's homestead on the prairie landscape. It has no value, no meaning except for one thing."

"What's that?"

"The message. You see, Mr. Dawson, the photograph is only a guide, a pointer to the veritable treasure we seek." She moved a little farther into the kitchen light, revealing the lower half of her face.

Dawson gasped at the sight of the burn scars, the mutilated mouth and throat.

"I do not wish to shock you with my appearance. Did you realize your father did this to me? No? Well, we have a saying in The Sodality: the father's sins shall be punished through all generations. That means you must pay for his brutality."

Dawson swallowed and took a tentative step forward. "Roast in Hell, you witch."

Stone backhanded him across the face, stinging him with its force. "I can understand why Mr. Lamont here wants to have his way with you... teach you some manners, you self-important—"

"That's enough, Cornelius." The Whisper rasped. "There's time for that later." Turning to Dawson, she continued. "We've been after the photograph's secrets for decades. That, and other such objects throughout humankind's history. In fact, our operatives have been following your family line since the time of Christ. The genealogical records are quite detailed, but the tale of the treasure and its power is not so well-documented. And now, we have one of the best clues to reveal what we seek."

"And... what exactly is that?" Hannah asked, her voice pitching higher than normal.

The Whisper straightened. "All in due time, my dear. First, we must decode this photograph, and apparently only Mr. Dawson is capable of doing that since, well, his father unfortunately passed away."

The cold realization hit hard like a two by four to the gut, and his mouth dropped.

"What did you do?"

"Come, come," The Whisper said, "surely you figured out he did not die from natural causes."

"You... had something to do with his death?"

"Indeed," she said, "I was there when it happened. Right after he did this to me. His death was not intentional, rest assured, but accidents do happen."

Beth couldn't contain her emotion any longer and broke down crying. Dawson and Hannah both moved to comfort her, but Lamont prevented them with his thick arm blocking the way.

"Let her cry it out," The Whisper suggested, her voice barely audible over Beth's grief. "She'll be fine in a moment."

"What happened to my Dad." Dawson demanded, his wrath rising.

Stone glanced at the shadowy figure. "We gave him a chance to come clean with the photo. Asked him nicely, but he lied, saying he'd destroyed it, the liar." He slipped his hands in his back pockets. "When it became clear he wouldn't divulge its whereabouts, our technician attempted to... encourage him to talk. He refused."

"You bastards. *You* murdered him."

"Well, we had no choice," Stone mused. "Think it through, Mr. Physicist. The only logical action to take was to squeeze him. In the end, it was too much. Such a waste."

"But the coroner said he died of a heart attack."

"Indeed, he likely did, but not before much pain and suffering."

"Why wasn't that part of his report?"

"Oh, well," The Whisper conceded, "we knew the man, understood his passions and desires. It took little convincing to welcome him into The Sodality."

Dawson lunged at the woman, but Lamont

intercepted and slammed him to the floor.

"Such anger, and for no logical reason," Stone sneered. "For someone well-versed in logic, you show a surprising amount of chaotic impulses, *human*."

Dawson pulled himself up and wiped a trace of blood from his mouth. "I swear you'll pay for this if it's the last thing I do." He stood definitely, fists clenched, breathing hard. Tears streamed down Hannah's cheeks. He tried consoling his mother but again, Lamont refused to let him near.

"Well, that's ancient history now," The Whisper croaked. "We have more important work to do." She held out a gnarled hand, the one containing the photograph. "Take this and read it."

He eyed her suspiciously. "What if I rip it up instead?"

"You won't," she said, "I could threaten harm to your mother or your pretty girlfriend here, but have no need to. You want to discover its secrets as much as we do. In fact," she mused, "I predict by the end of tomorrow, once we've determined where the real treasure is, you'll wish to join The Sodality permanently."

"Never."

She licked her grotesque lips. "We shall see. The Sodality doesn't simply *take*, Mr. Dawson. It *gives*, too. Anything you want. Just ask that smug professor of yours."

"You... you got to Dr. Gunar?" He knew Gunar's behaviour had been strained lately, pushing to publish results that hadn't been vetted or reproduced. Now his behaviour in the lab and Wendy's cryptic text messages made sense. They gained his cooperation by giving him something in return.

The Whisper motioned for him to take the photograph while staring coldly at his mother.

The temptation to tear it up almost overwhelmed him. But he could not risk anything happening to his mum, or Hannah, and besides, this Whisper creature was absolutely right: he wanted the truth, and his quest for knowledge over-ruled the growing desire to destroy. In the end, he could never go back to the way his life was before the first vision, so the final proof of the phenomena was paramount.

Dawson took the offered photograph, held it out front, and waited for the ghostly story to unfold.

THE WHISPER COVERED HER FACE MORE BY PULLING THE hood over it, and slipped around the table to watch Dawson. He raised the image to his face and focused on the edges, looking from one side to the other, his gaze following the perimeter like he'd done previously.

Nothing happened.

He sighed with frustration, adjusted the object in his fingers, anticipated the needles of heat. But after several silent minutes, he glared at the woman and said, "It doesn't seem to be working right now."

"Commit yourself and try again." Her voice had become hard.

He concentrated more on the centre of the stark farmhouse set against the backdrop of an infinite prairie landscape. He wished for the apparition to appear, for the swirling of the edges, the faces with no pupils, the child wrapped against the woman's—Hannah's—breast.

Still nothing.

Dawson exhaled and claimed, "It won't work." He faced the woman. "You realize I can't just force this to happen. Sometimes it reveals things, other times I get nothing. This is one of those times."

Stone voiced his annoyance. "Then concentrate more, Mr. Dawson!"

The Whisper froze him with a glance, saying, "I know all about psychometric events and the unreliability of the method. You touch this with your fingers, I note. Interesting." She returned to the hallway shadows. "But other options to decipher the message exist and are at our disposal. The professor at Laurentian is already aware of this. Did you appreciate that?"

"Wait, what professor?"

The Whisper shrugged.

"You mean…" Dawson hated that she teased him toward the inevitable conclusion. "How do you know about Dr. Rathbourne?"

The woman grinned crookedly.

She had no way of knowing about their aborted visit to the Neurosciences Lab that morning unless The Sodality could intercept text messages, or… but that didn't add up.

"Matt?"

He read the truth in Hannah's eyes.

"He's one of you," she said.

"Indeed," The Whisper responded. "And soon, we'll return to Sudbury and meet with Christopher in the morning. That'll give you time to *try again.*"

"I'm not going anywhere until you let my mother and Hannah go. They have nothing to do with this," Dawson threatened, a rebel's edge creeping into his voice.

Stone said, "Your mother, perhaps. But Ms. King has been involved from Day One and is responsible for bashing Mr. Lamont in the woods." He nodded at his scowling colleague.

"I owe you for that," the big man growled.

Hannah moved closer to Dawson's side.

"So listen up," Stone continued. "Mr. Lamont will stay here with Beth to make sure you don't try any monkey business. If there's even a hint of deception, she dies. And you two will come with us."

Dawson straightened up and struck a defiant pose. He'd dealt with bullies before and learned the only way to stop them from doing harm was to confront them with force. "And if we refuse?"

The Whisper said, "Don't test our resolve, Mr. Dawson. No good will come of it, you can rest assured."

He chewed his lip and held his tongue. The reality of the situation quickly imposed itself and he reluctantly surrendered to their demand.

"Once you have what you want, you'll let us go."

"Of course," the crone whispered. "The moment we have the photo's secret, we'll have no further use for you, your mother, or your little girlfriend. You'll be free to carry on with your useless, insignificant lives if you so choose."

Dawson caught the hint of a smile across her mismatched lips from the shadows.

"But you must cooperate at every step, and in particular, with Professor Rathbourne. Is that clear?"

Hannah squeezed his hand. "We have to do what they say, Matt."

He hated giving in so easily. "How can we trust them to keep their word? Look at what they've been doing? What they did to my dad."

Despite the chilling situation and uncertainty of their future, a warmth and peace radiated from her face and through her hand to his. "Have faith, Matt, that this will work out exactly the way it should. The way it must."

"Ah yes, you are the religious one," The Whisper purred. "Interesting. You invoke faith in God, which is truly fascinating."

Hannah refused to acknowledge her.

"Well then, there may be a larger role for you after all."

She turned and continued. "Mr. Stone, gather their phones and prepare them for the journey. I'll be in the van."

Stone held out his open hand. Dawson hesitated, but Hannah pulled her cell out of her pocket and handed it over. He did likewise.

"I appreciate your cooperation. See? That wasn't so hard." He nodded at his partner. "Nice and easy, eh, Mr. Lamont?"

The man grunted and tightened his grip on Beth's shoulder.

"Now Ms. King, approach."

Hannah complied, and Stone drew a thick zip tie from his jacket pocket and placed it around her outstretched hands.

"Your turn, Mr. Dawson."

Matt clenched his jaw, but he came forward and held out his wrists. Stone bound them snugly.

"Such good cooperation. Now, you will both come with me. Need I remind you of the consequences if you attempt an escape?"

Dawson stared at his mother. Her eyes were red and puffy from crying, but she smiled bravely and said, "Go with them, Matt. I'll be okay. Please do whatever they ask. I couldn't live if something happened to you."

A lump grew in his throat. "We'll be back soon, Mum."

Then Stone marched them out through the rain to the van. The woman sat deep in the rear, hidden in the blackness, breathing gently. He covered their heads with thick hoods, and pushed them into the seats. The smell of flowers was overwhelming, even through the dense material.

"Why these hoods if we're going back to Sudbury?" Dawson coughed.

"You're a clever sort, Mr. Dawson. You'll figure it out."

Hannah whispered, "So we can't tell anyone later where you're taking us tonight?"

"Ah, the young Ms. King gets a prize."

He felt disoriented inside the pitch black hood. Once the vehicle pulled onto the highway and maintained a constant speed, the sensation of floating was even more pronounced.

No one spoke. Dawson brooded with his emotions, sinking further into dangerous thoughts, desperately worried about his mother and concerned about what Dr. Rathbourne might do. He fought to crawl out of the mental gravity well, reminding himself that he had enough to process without resorting to full-on self-reflection. Then he felt Hannah's bound, warm hands rest on his.

"It'll all work out, Matt," she whispered.

The sensation of having an invisible conversation with her, with no visual context, was a mental curiosity as if he spoke to himself and a disembodied voice responded. It reminded him of those chats in the dark tent with his dad, just before he fell asleep.

"How can you be so sure, Hannah?"

"You know, Matt. I have faith that God knows what he's doing here, and I don't have to figure it all out myself. Trust that his plan is unfolding exactly the way it's supposed to."

"Even if people get hurt? They killed my father."

"That's the funny thing about belief. You either have it or you don't. But Matt, listen. I've learned none of this is real, that we've never belonged here, see?"

"I don't understand."

"Okay, do you ever wonder why you're here, like why this life is such a struggle? When a fish is in water, it's fine, doing its thing. But bring him on land, and he struggles to survive because he wasn't built for that environment. Do you ever think we weren't made for *this* world? That we belong somewhere else? And perhaps that's why we find life such a challenge?"

Dawson considered the idea and her logic.

"I believe," Hannah continued, "that we're the same. We weren't meant for this evil place. Our true home is elsewhere."

"What, like heaven?"

"Sure, if that helps you understand." She paused and her fingers found his. "I need to tell you something. Before I came to the Lord, I was having a difficult time processing my adoption and school and normal teenage crap."

"You mentioned that. Skipping classes and falling in with a bad crowd. Lots of kids do that and turn their lives around like you did."

Hannah whispered, "Matt, I became infatuated with a boy, Robbie. He was a year older and kept an eye out for me. Anyway, he was my first love, Matt, and I didn't know what I was doing and long story short, I got pregnant."

Matt swallowed hard as a swirl of anger and jealousy bubbled inside. "What did you do?" he asked curtly.

"After I found out, I absolved Robbie of all responsibility. You know, he was strong and determined to do the so-called right thing by me, but deep within, that wasn't a solution either of us wanted. I told him I was getting an abortion, dropped out of school, and went to give birth at a home in Toronto."

Matt's shock wrestled with his disbelief in the moist heat of the hood. "You're... you're a mum," he said matter-of-factly.

Hannah sighed. Minutes passed. "Well, around the twentieth week, the doctors told me the baby had all kinds of congenital problems with her heart and lungs, and unformed kidneys. They said she wouldn't live and asked me about terminating the pregnancy. I thought long and hard about that, but just couldn't. Not because of any moral or political reason though; it just didn't feel right for me."

"What... happened?"

Hannah's voice shook. "I gave birth to Emily on a humid August afternoon. I held her tiny body against me, stroked her back. Oh Matt, she was beautiful. Her little fingers grabbed mine, you know? She knew my voice." A moment passed. "Then, in the middle of the night, a nurse woke me and said that Emily was in physical distress and that it was time. They brought me to a private room where I held her and sang *You Are My Sunshine* to her. Remember that one? Anyway, her ragged breath was soft and warm against my neck. It fluttered like the sweep of butterfly wings, and I swear some nights I can still feel it. But she didn't squirm like before. I lifted her limp arm and stared at the nurse, and she nodded and stroked my hair. A few minutes later, Emily passed away."

Matt heard her whimpering beside him. Her hand gripped his hard.

"Emily lived for seven hours and twelve minutes. She would have turned six last month. I've told no one about her outside my family. Except you.

"Anyway, I went home two days later, and shortly after, a counsellor told me about Jesus and introduced me to some young people who helped me get back on track. He's the only reason why I can accept Emily's death and not lash out at everyone or self-sabotage anymore."

A hundred questions screamed inside Matt's brain. Finally, he cleared his throat. "Why are you telling me this, Hannah?"

"Because, Matt," she whispered, "I don't want any

secrets standing between us. The truth is, I'm falling in love with you."

THIRTY-FIVE

MATT DAWSON HAD NO IDEA WHERE THEY WERE. HE thought he recognized the winding road from Haileybury to North Bay, and the more or less straight highway from there to the outskirts of Sudbury, but once in town, Stone took hard rights and lefts and stopped so frequently that he couldn't perceive where they were in the city.

Hannah's confession lingered in his mind and he felt a visceral stew of pain and sadness, tempered marginally by her desire to remove any secrets between them. This only added to his heightened anxiety surrounding his mother's welfare, and what might happen at the Neurosciences Lab. The question that also plagued him was whether Emily's death had found its way into his visions.

The van finally rolled to a stop, and the engine shut down.

Dawson and Hannah were led up a couple of steps and inside a building. Distant, muffled traffic tempted his ears through the hood. Then, the cover was yanked away.

Darkness permeated the room. A sliver of light bisected the flooring in front of him like a cubist abstract. His eyes were used to the pitch black in the hood, so as he quickly scanned the place, he saw furniture silhouettes: a sofa, some chairs in an otherwise empty gloom.

They were in a house.

Stone removed Hannah's hood and she rubbed her eyes with her bound hands.

The Whisper lurked in the foyer shadows. "We'll attempt another reading of the photograph in the morning. Mr. Stone has some food and water for you, then you'll rest."

After they'd snacked on stale muffins, the operative led them to separate rooms. He attached a thick chain from Dawson's bound wrists and locked it around the bed frame, then left with a grunt. Dawson lay on the mattress in darkness, listening to the heavy rain pound ancient rhythms on the roof. The curtains were drawn, and although his body ached for sleep, the events of the past day played vividly in his mind.

He knew little about this biblical God Hannah spoke of, but had faith in his own human abilities and understood his obligations to prevent The Sodality from harming his mother. He toyed with several thought experiments to get out of this mess without any harm coming to her.

Again, that distant, distracted thought of Hannah and her child.

She told him she was falling in love, no doubt at least in part a reaction to these events surrounding the phenomena. He also felt something warm with her. He enjoyed her company. They worked well together, despite their theological differences. Could he ever be so open and honest? Would he find the courage to share his jumbled emotions with her? It seemed obscene to leave those questions unanswered, abandoning them to the black, but the answers weren't prepared to come to him now. Not even halfway.

AFTER A FITFUL SLEEP, DAWSON AWOKE TO THUDDING footsteps in the hallway. It could have been the middle of the night or early morning—in the absence of light, he'd lost all sense of time.

The door creaked opened.

Stone entered, unlocked the chain and said, "It's time to uncover this message."

He guided him into a large room. Despite the curtains being drawn throughout the house, a faint glow surfaced from the windows. Morning.

In the gloom, Stone ordered him to sit at the table. Moments later, Hannah appeared followed by the woman, her face mostly covered by that same hood from yesterday. They nodded at each other, but the operative kept them apart.

"Release his wrists, Mr. Stone."

The man drew a pocket knife and sliced through the zip ties. Dawson rubbed his wrists. Although they hadn't been tight enough to restrict blood flow, they left indentations in his skin.

"Mr. Dawson, we shall try again, hm?"

The Whisper lay the photograph in front of him, then disappeared into another room. She pulled a distant curtain open to allow additional light to filter through the space. Dawson stared at the photo.

"I don't know if I can do this," he said, "I mean, it doesn't feel right."

"Regardless," the woman croaked, returning. "You shall try. There is no harm in that, is there?"

He refused to answer.

"And you will continue to cooperate, yes? Now,

focus on reading the message contained within."

Hannah's eyes widened. She sat across from him, her wrists bound in front of her, and her hair falling loosely over her shoulders. Despite the desperate circumstances, she was the most beautiful woman he'd ever seen.

"I understand what I have to do," he said, resignation in his voice.

He inhaled sharply and picked the photo up by its edges.

This time, as he held it, warmth surged through his hands and the edge of the image swirled around the perimeter.

He expected the appearance of the faces, the apparitions in the photograph, the dominant woman holding a dead child.

But they refused to reveal themselves.

Only the rolling, glowing edges appeared.

His fingertips burned, but he clutched the photo and focused on seeing the other images. Minutes passed, and he could not hold it any longer, releasing it on the tabletop, grabbing his hands together and rocking back and forth on the chair to squelch the pain in his blistering skin.

Hannah said, "There was something. I saw the glow."

"Indeed," The Whisper rasped, "I noticed that, too." She floated about the room to stand behind Hannah. Her entire body was in darkness, but Dawson caught glimpses of her shiny, beady eyes.

"What else did you see, Mr. Dawson?"

The now familiar nerve-ending pain exploded on his fingertips. "Nothing more this time," he said, perplexed by his own trembling voice. "Only the swirling pattern around the perimeter."

"Try again," the woman rasped in a hard, low voice.

"I—I can't. My fingers are burned too badly."

Stone shifted his weight and grabbed his shoulder.

"You heard The Whisper," he growled. "You will attempt another reading or I'll send a wake-up text to Mr. Lamont."

Hannah interjected. "Please, Matt, can you try once more? I've been praying for you all night."

He scanned her face in the gloom and blew into his fingers. "All right," he conceded, "I'll give it another shot."

Dawson concentrated on the image in front of him, then lifted the photo by the edges and raised it to his face.

The margins had gone completely cold. No eddies. No searing heat. Several minutes passed, and he finally placed it down.

"It doesn't seem to be working," he concluded.

Stone said, "Shall I send the text?"

"No," The Whisper mused, "Not yet. In due time, if he fails to cooperate…"

"I've done what you've asked," Dawson argued. "If it's not responding, I can't control that."

"Perhaps," the woman whispered. "Your subconscious mind may be interfering with the paranormal phenomenon. But once you're in the professor's lab, his equipment will detect what you refuse to see."

"What do you mean?"

"She's talking about Dr. Rathbourne's research apparatus, Matt. Is that right?"

The Whisper nodded. The operative bound Dawson's wrists with a fresh zip tie, then grabbed the photo and slipped it into an envelope. He produced the hoods again and slammed one over Hannah's head. Then he forced the other on Dawson, replacing the odd comfort of the morning gloom with complete darkness.

Stone hauled him from his chair. A door opened and a rush of cool, damp air encircled his body. The rain had stopped, replaced by the dank air of approaching fall.

Someone held his arm. A light touch. Hannah? No, he was used to her, and this was ice cold.

The Whisper.

"There are no secrets from the professor, Mr. Dawson," she wheezed. "Once you've been capped, all shall be revealed."

THIRTY-SIX

IN THE MASSIVE VISITOR PARKING LOT AT THE BOTTOM of a craggy hill at Laurentian University, Cornelius Stone pulled the van to a stop far away from other vehicles and potentially curious eyes. Thick clouds morphed overhead, threatening more rain, and a fierce northeast wind groaned through the stunted pines encompassing the campus.

Stone opened the side door, tore the hoods off the students, and ushered them out. He glanced around calmly, then pulled the knife from his pocket and sliced through the zip ties. The Whisper slinked out of the rear. Her cowl hid most of her face.

"See this, Mr. Dawson?" Stone held his phone up to the boy's eyes with a text message he'd composed the night before. "Read it aloud for all to hear."

Dawson scanned the note. He stared at the operative with fire in his eyes, then read, "Mr. Lamont, you may do what's necessary."

The man lowered his arm. "This phone doesn't leave

my hand, Mr. Dawson. If either of you gives the slightest indication that we're more than a couple of researchers and students, I press the send button. You look at any other person here with anything more than a cursory glance, I press the button. Understood?"

The young physicist scowled but after a moment's reflection, said, "Let's get this over with."

They marched toward the main path and climbed the steps leading to the enclave of buildings.

When they arrived at the one marked *SCIENCE 1*, Stone opened the heavy door and checked the information sign by the elevators. The desired Neurosciences Lab was in the lower level, so he motioned them down the stairs with Hannah, subdued and apparently lost in her thoughts, leading. Dawson and Stone were directly behind her, followed by The Whisper.

As they wandered through the basement hallway following the signs to the lab, one of the overhead lights flickered as Hannah passed underneath it. Dawson glanced at her.

Stone, attuned to noticing the extraordinary, found this odd. "Something on your mind, Mr. Dawson?"

"Nothing I can repeat to you," the boy muttered.

Still some fight in that lad. Once they'd secured the message and the clue to the whereabouts of the power they sought, he'd talk to them about joining The Sodality. Both would make a fine addition, once their minds were cleansed.

After walking down another long corridor, they arrived at an orange wooden door leading into the professor's lab.

There was no handle on the entrance. Instead, a peephole peered at them and, as the sign suggested, Stone knocked.

Muffled voices inside grew louder, and the door

swung open to reveal an oily-skinned student with large glasses in a cerulean blue lab coat. She introduced herself as Mara. "We've been expecting you," she said in a mousy voice. "The professor is so excited to meet you, ever since he got Matt's email." She studied Dawson, running her gaze over his entire body. "Come, make yourselves comfortable."

The anteroom was similar to any other university office Stone had visited when he met clients on their turf. Overcrowded, stuffed with papers and furniture that had probably never been replaced since the campus opened in the 1960s. Three walls were lined with books and tattered paper journals of all sorts. A tiny kitchen area led off the far end. On the wall immediately opposite them stood a thick, imposing steel door with a bar handle that reminded him of an industrial freezer: the actual lab chamber itself.

Mara guided them to a round table where she invited them to sit. The Whisper, as was her custom, remained standing, her face in shadows.

"Professor Rathbourne will be out shortly. In the meantime, tell me about your experience with this... what is it again?"

Stone pulled the photograph from the envelope.

"Ah, fascinating," Mara gushed. She studied the photo. "An old farmhouse. Intriguing." She removed her glasses and brought it to her face. Her eyes darted across it. "Where was this taken?"

"Saskatchewan," Dawson offered.

"Yes, highly intriguing. The professor will want to study this." She leaned back, replacing her glasses. "And what happens when you touch this?"

Dawson filled her in on his psychometric experiences. When he finished recounting the most recent occurrence of shadows in the photo earlier that morning, the steel lab door groaned and whooshed open. Stone recognized the stocky, barrel-chested man emerging wearing a dress shirt and tie, and carrying a tablet in his hand. His jet black hair stood in contrast to the stark white lab coat he also wore.

"Ah, Professor Rathbourne," Stone said. "We meet again."

They shook hands, then the operative introduced the students and, motioning to The Whisper hovering by the bookshelf, said, "I believe you two also know each other."

The Whisper nodded. "You look well, Professor," she croaked.

Rathbourne said nothing, but turned immediately to the table where the others were sitting.

"Hello, Matt. I apologize for being coy in my emails with you, but it was the only way to ensure you'd come visit my lab."

Dawson's face was set with shock.

The professor read his concern. "I understand you're not part of The Sodality, but never mind all that. I'm sure you'd like to know more about what your vision means when you handle this old photo, hm?"

The boy refused to speak, opting to pout and fold his arms across his chest. Stone flashed his phone in front of him.

Dawson eyed him with pure hatred. "Yes," he spat. "I want this to end. Take the stupid thing and do whatever it is you do." He glanced at Hannah. "We just want to leave."

The professor stared at the young woman and cocked his head. "Hannah... what's your involvement in this?"

"I'm helping my friend figure out the message in the photo and how it relates to his visions."

"You are a student at Western, too?"

"Yes, I study psychometry in the Neurosciences Department."

"Well," Rathbourne laughed, slapping his thigh, "this is most excellent. Most excellent. Tell me," he asked, moving closer to her, "what got you interested in neuroscience?"

She straightened her back. "I find ESP and psychometric phenomena beyond curious."

"Really. That's all?" He stared into her eyes and studied her face until she nervously turned away.

"Mr. Stone? I propose setting up the experiment for both of them."

He eyed him suspiciously. "Why the girl? She doesn't truly have the gift."

"Please, don't tell me my business," he said with a smile. "She may not have the same kind or degree of ability as Matt, but I sense something there, regardless. I insist we read her as well."

"Wait a minute," Dawson protested. "You have the photo. What more do *we* have to do with anything? Don't you just put this into some magic box and decode it?"

Mara chuckled. "If only it were that simple."

"No, you see, Matt, the photograph is but an object. In my world, everything that gets touched carries messages. Even now, you're imparting a psychic impression on the table through your touch. The photo is the medium, and we will discover its secrets, but it's your sensory ability to decode it—even partially—that fascinates me. Now," he said, turning to his assistant, "prepare the intake survey for both of them."

Mara scurried away down a dim, narrow hallway.

"And you two shall come with me."

THIRTY-SEVEN

THE SUDDEN TEMPTATION TO GRAB HANNAH AND BOLT from the lab was an offshoot of not only renewed courage, but also, an emerging plan, even though he realized the scheme was more fragile and vulnerable than a baby's breath. The only hesitation restraining him was what Lamont might do to his mother. He couldn't live with himself if his actions caused her any harm.

They followed the professor along the hallway and entered a cramped meeting room, and he hated that The Whisper *knew* he yearned for the truth about the message. The combined effect was simultaneously profound and ridiculous.

"Please, make yourselves comfortable," Rathbourne said, motioning them to enter the room and sit at a modest round table. "Despite what others in The Sodality might do, Mara and I are not like that. Our interest is strictly in science, the research. No harm shall come to you from me."

Dawson took a chair facing the door. "How did you ever get involved with them?"

"Of course, that's a long story, but when Cornelius approached me several years ago, my investigations into the God Mind had limited funding. I was ridiculed by my colleagues around the world for my *X Files work,* they called it, but I knew it was worth pursuing."

"You mean, the truth is out there?"

"Yes, something like that. Anyway, I needed little convincing. The Sodality funds my research, and I inform them of the findings, and when prospects who show a propensity for the paranormal come along... well, I make introductions." He paused, licking his lips. "I apologize for the subterfuge when you contacted me, but that's one of the prices I pay to keep working. They were extremely interested in you, by the way."

The professor opened a wall cabinet and withdrew two thick documents from a stack. "These are a series of questions for the Minnesota Multiphasic Personality Inventory. They're designed to measure several psychological factors, but most importantly for us, they provide a sign of your openness to paranormal activity." He dropped one in front of each and provided them with pencils. "As you can see, they're all true or false statements. There are 328 and the exercise should take you about 45 minutes to complete."

Dawson read the first question: *I like mechanics magazines.* He looked at the professor and snickered. "Mechanics magazines?"

"Yes. Some questions may seem outdated now, but they still have plenty of value. Again, it's all true or false. If mechanics aren't your thing, then you answer 'false'. No need to overthink this."

Dawson raised an eyebrow. "Will you be staying with us?"

"Oh no, I have other materials to prepare. You two fill out the documents on your own." He stepped to the doorway. "And feel free to chat among yourselves if you like, but please, not about your answers. Understand, too, that you'll be under surveillance. The Sodality will hear and see everything you do."

Hannah shrugged her shoulders and lifted a pencil.

"Wait until I give you the signal to begin. You'll hear my voice through the intercom in a few minutes." He pointed to a speaker on the ceiling. "Questions?"

Dawson shook his head and folded his hands on top of the test.

"Very well. I'll complete my checklist and notify you shortly." The professor exited and closed the door.

"This is odd," Dawson muttered. "Do you understand what this assessment is for?"

"I've come across it in my department. My advisor mentioned it in passing, but I've never taken it."

He read through some questions on the top page, conscious of The Sodality's gaze into the room. He struggled with an idea hammering at his brain, and chose this moment to explore it. "I've been thinking about what you said earlier."

"Oh?"

"You know," he hinted awkwardly, dancing around the subject in his mind. "The Jesus thing."

She smiled. "You mean whether or not he was real."

"Uh-huh."

"And what conclusion did you draw, Mr. Dawson?" Her voice had a soothing lilt to it, filled with comfort.

Where does she find the ability to accept what's happening?

"Not sure I've landed on one yet."

"Hm. Tell me what you're thinking about, then."

He raised his hands to his face in an ironic prayer.

290

"Well, lots of smart scholars have studied the Bible for centuries and have decided there is a God, and that Jesus was God among us."

"And?"

"Others discount all religions as nefarious social instruments designed to keep the masses oppressed, to gain personal wealth. Like those Sunday morning preachers who talk about God wanting us to be rich and how we deserve all these blessings."

"I put little stock in those characters."

He eyed her cautiously. "And then there are the natural philosophers and quantum physicists."

"What about them?"

"Well, I'm no philosopher, but when I consider the origins of the universe, for example, I wonder what happened *before* the Big Bang? Like, there was nothing? I don't even know what *nothing* means at that scale, but logically, someone or something observed nothingness into reality."

"Sounds a lot like God. *In the beginning there was chaos.* That's a big part of the Bible and what God does… he takes chaos and brings order to it. A bit like a cosmic physicist, maybe?" She grinned.

"Perhaps, but I just don't know. I mean, I can read what Jesus says about morality and living a good life, and I like that stuff. But all that salvation business and going to hell… I struggle with that."

Hannah cocked her head. "Let me ask you this. Assume for the sake of argument that Jesus was real and actually was the son of God. If that's true, then the Bible is accurate because he said so. As a result, we must conclude there *is* a heaven and hell, and our salvation lies in accepting that Jesus paid for our sins on the cross and died the death we deserve so we could live the life he deserved. The ultimate sacrifice. Taking our place when we don't earn it at all. Wouldn't that make him pretty awesome?"

Dawson wondered. "I suppose so."

Silence fell over them for a moment. Then Hannah continued. "So intellectually, you pursue science in order to bring chaos to disorder. You work out equations to explain it, thought experiments to expand it. You talk about constants and conditions and free-body diagrams and accuracy to certain decimal places. But what does your heart say?"

He turned and gazed into her eyes. "What do you mean?"

She smiled warmly. "It's the sunset thing again, Matt. When you watch the sun go down, do you think about light refraction and wavelengths and the rotation of the Earth, and the dew point? Or, do you marvel at the awesome beauty of our sun dipping below the horizon, and how whoever created this must have had a painter's eye?"

"Honestly, I don't know. I want to understand nature, look under the hood and see how it ticks. What you describe is more about appreciating the surrounding beauty with the faith that nature's designed this way for a purpose even if we can't explain it. So we don't have to figure out what the design is for, or what our role is in its function. We can appreciate the beauty for its own sake."

"Yeah." She agreed, "that's the heart. Something that hits your senses." She whispered, "You have a strong sense of the intellectual Jesus struggle. Was he real and did he honestly believe he was the son of God and perform miracles and such? But would you like to know Jesus at the level of your heart?"

That innate defiance snuffled in his gut. He tried suppressing it but failed. "Oh, I don't think so, Hannah. That seems beyond me right now."

"Okay, then how about praying with me?"

"I can do that."

"Great, and as I pray for us, open your heart fully, not just your mind."

"I'll try."

Hannah raised her hands and bowed her head. She closed her eyes and Dawson did likewise, focusing on opening his heart to whatever message may appear.

"Lord," she began, "thank you for watching over us, for all the strength and insights of your will. Thank you for giving me some time with Emily, and Matt, and for opening his heart and mind to your word. Thank you for bringing us together. Lord, if it be your will and if it advances your kingdom on Earth, please keep us safe from The Sodality and from all the other temptations surrounding us. We ask that you be with Beth and give her strength. Please help us understand you and give us the courage to do what's right in your eyes at all times. I pray for this in Jesus' name. Amen."

"Amen," Dawson echoed.

Hannah's eyes filled with tears as she turned away.

"Matt? Hannah? You may now begin the test."

COMMIT YOUR WAY TO THE LORD; TRUST IN HIM, AND *he will act.*

Hannah repeated the psalmist's line as she and Dawson waited in the tiny room for the professor to return with their paranormal assessment results and readiness for the experiment's next phase. He'd told them it would take a few minutes to compile their answers and offered a snack and coffee. Both refused.

Presently, Mara poked her head in the doorway. "Follow me," she said.

Hannah rose and stepped into the corridor. Matt followed.

"What happens next?" he asked behind her.

"The professor will explain it all. There's nothing to fear," Mara replied.

"Are you one of *them*?"

Mara glanced over her shoulder with a funny look. "Of course."

They entered the darkened anteroom where the others waited. Stone sat at the table eating a muffin. Dr. Rathbourne huddled over a computer monitor, and The Whisper skulked in the shadowy corner by the bookshelf, working her phone.

"Ah, our guests have returned," the professor said. "Please, have a seat."

Hannah pulled up a chair and invited Matt to sit beside her. He appeared distant and exhausted. Her heart pounded as he brushed against her shoulder.

Stone angled his body to face the professor. "We're all here, Rathbourne. May we see the results of the preliminary assessment?"

"Yes, quite," he said, placing a hand on the monitor. "We've run your responses through the algorithm and, as we suspected, Matt, you have a high level of psychometric ability. As well, your defiance and skepticism are above average, but we can normalize the experiment easily enough to accommodate those."

He began pacing. "What we didn't expect is what we learned from you, Hannah."

"Me?" she asked, startled.

"Yes, yes, you see, I sensed you had a capacity for reading objects, or possessed other paranormal inclinations, but we had no idea how gifted you truly are."

"Me," she said again, this time with her own dose of skepticism.

"Fascinating," the gravelly voice in the shadows whispered.

"Of course, I'll need to confirm this preliminary finding with the experiment, too, perhaps after we're finished decoding the photographic message."

"Forget it," she said weakly.

The professor eyed Stone, who wiped his hands on a napkin and pulled his phone from his jacket pocket. "What applies to Mr. Dawson also applies to you, Ms. King. You shall cooperate fully with the professor."

Hannah's heart sank. It was sickening that they forced Matt to participate in this psychic experiment, but now they wanted her, too?

For we walk by faith, not by sight... we walk by faith, not by sight.

"I have no choice, then."

Rathbourne parked himself beside her. "Tell me, Hannah, do you have vivid dreams? Ones that you're convinced are real?"

"Sure, I guess."

He leaned forward. "Well, you know how when we dream, there's a part of us that realizes we're dreaming. Often, something fantastic or magical happens to remind us that, even though there's an element of realism, our brains recognize it isn't true. You have those?"

Hannah bit her lip. "Not dreams. Nightmares."

"Ah." The professor clapped his hands together. "Yes, of course, nightmares. And tell me, are they the same over and over?"

"With minor variations, yes."

"And you've had them how long?"

Hannah wrinkled her brow, wondering where this was going. "Since I was a child, I think. I became aware something was different with me when I was seven or eight." She paused, tempted to say more.

"And?"

She exhaled deeply. "I've been to shrinks and healers

and pastors and shamans… you name it. No one has made them go away."

"They come every night?"

"Mostly when I'm stressed or in a strange place. Like last night." She lowered her head, shuddering at the image of the beautiful creeper in her mind, motioning at her with his bony finger. Hannah peered into the professor's face and detected a hint of sincerity.

"Perhaps there is a connection. And if there is, I might be able to help you."

Hope stirred within her, a distant promise that he could accomplish with science what no other had before: rid her of the seducer.

She said, "Do you think—"

"Enough." The voice interrupted from the darkened corner like fingernails on a chalkboard. The Whisper stepped forward. "Time is short, Professor. Do what you wish with the girl after we have what we came for."

Rathbourne, locking his eyes with Hannah, slowly nodded. "Yes, of course, ma'am." He stood and turned to Mara. "Do we have results from the photographic reading?"

The lab assistant punched the keyboard and the farmhouse, surrounded by shades of the colour spectrum, appeared on the large overhead monitor. Hannah approached the screen. She studied the image and said, "How are you reading it?"

"Quantum tomography."

She glanced at Matt and caught his jaw dropping. "Similar to x-ray tomography? CAT scans?"

"Similar in concept only. We look for variations in an object, but rather than trying to image the interior of it— like a typical CAT scan—we attempt to delineate the auras, the surrounding EM fields. They often yield insights into the person or persons who handled the object in the past. Like when a gifted one touches a pair of gloves and can sense, quite accurately, what the original wearer was doing, where they lived, their physical attributes."

Matt stepped forward. "You can learn all that from this?"

"And much more. Unfortunately," the professor added, turning his attention to the screen, "this particular image is rather muddled. Mara, is that the best filtering we can do?"

"Yes, Professor."

He drew a pencil from the work desk and pointed to patches of reds and oranges in the image. "All this nebulous area, particularly around the edges, shows that multitudes have left their psychic imprints on the photo. I was afraid of that. Too many touches. Makes it impossible to delineate the desired message from the noise." He faced Stone. "I'm sorry. We've run up against the limitations of the equipment."

"So… we're done here." Matt stated, glaring at The Whisper in the corner. The witch remained silent.

Hannah moved beside him. "What else does he have to do? You've got the photo. You've got our assessment results. What more is there?"

The wraith floated along the tiled floor. "We're not finished at all, Mr. Dawson." Under the cowl, the corners of her mouth raised a hair's breadth. Hannah gulped. A shudder tore up her spine. The Whisper nodded to the massive steel door protecting the inner chamber. "The actual experiment comes next."

THIRTY-EIGHT

Dawson held his tongue during the questioning, studying the room, but now he stood and confronted the shorter man. "Professor, remind me again of what this experiment of yours is. We investigated your work back at Western, but it's still unclear what exactly happens in that room." He threw his chin toward the steel door.

"Why yes, of course, Matt. Keep an eye on the large monitor above the desk. Mara, bring up the notes on the process, please."

The assistant punched the keyboard, and in a second, a slide show flashed on the screen. The first image was that of a head covering that reminded Dawson of an old-fashioned leather football helmet or aviator's cap. "I've seen that before," Hannah said, "in the literature and in one of your books. It's a... an EM transducer of sorts, isn't it?"

"Yes, Hannah, that's it exactly. The client wears this on their head. The electrodes, or transducers situated around the temporal lobes, allow me to send weak electromagnetic signals into the brain, to stimulate the neurons. This allows the subject to experience what I call the God Effect."

Matt raised his hands defensively in front of him. "Whoa, professor, I'm not sure I like the looks of this. Besides, how does this headgear help with analyzing the photograph?"

"The photo is but an object, Matt. An important one, to be sure, but inert nonetheless. What makes it significant is *your* ability to read some psychic impressions imparted on it by your relatives or others who have come in contact with it." The professor motioned to Mara, who skipped ahead to another slide featuring the EM spectrum outlined with colour-coded bands.

"I recognize the spectrum, but what are those lines?"

"Ah, yes, the colours represent the ranges of frequencies where most of the clients who have undergone the experiment tell us they experience the God Effect. It's the sensation that their awareness is expanding, that they perceive a divine presence and have visions about what they call the true nature of humankind and the world."

Dawson's defiance rose like a geyser, and he fought to quell it. His impression was that Rathbourne was some out-there *woo-woo* fringe scientist experimenting with people's emotions. "I suspect any hallucinatory drug might have the same effect, Professor."

"Perhaps, but not quite this. We've had atheists come in, skeptical like you, and leave the lab with a religious experience, a conversion, if you will. Several have dropped their careers and taken up ministry. It's rather remarkable."

"So you want me to put that thing on and...?"

"The process is simple." Mara pulled up a new slide showing the interior of the steel-door chamber. It housed two large chairs, like he'd seen at a dentist or an old school barber shop. A thin light shone in the centre of the room. There was nothing else but the pitch black walls.

The professor smiled. "The client sits in a chair and we fit the electrode cap on their head, make sure the transducers work and so on. Then, after running through our preliminary equipment tests, we dim the light and begin administering tiny currents to the client's brain. The resulting cranial activity is recorded here," he pointed to the computer, "and we note those frequencies where massive responses are seen."

"And you can see God from that?"

"We determine the frequencies that work the best on each client, but the real magic happens in the chamber, and when they come out and debrief us on what they envisioned, then we attempt to correlate that with the brain's responses."

"What exactly do these people experience?" Dawson's curiosity rose.

"Some, their childhoods. Others see colours or hear music. And, yes, some are convinced they've met God."

"Interesting, but what does that have to do with me and the secret message?"

The professor appeared confused by the question. Dawson looked at Hannah and shrugged. She said, "Is it because you believe the message may hide in Matt's subconsciousness, and by stimulating the proper neurons with the true frequencies, he could access it?"

"Yes, that's it precisely, Hannah. That's why we're doing this. There's a school of thought that believes psychic phenomena are genetic... that messages are passed on from generation to generation through DNA. Personally, I suspect that may be true but haven't found a suitable client yet to test the theory." He stared at Dawson, scrutinizing him. "So the more information we gather, the more reliable the results. The analysis of the photo was inconclusive, but Matt's interaction with it will yield what The Sodality requires. I can almost guarantee it." He gazed around the room. "Shall we begin, then?"

Stone flicked his hand. "Yes, get on with it."

"Very well. Matt, if you'll follow me."

THE PROFESSOR HELPED DAWSON INTO THE MASSIVE recliner, and Matt shivered. The chamber was several degrees colder than the anteroom. And dark. Thin light overhead cast a pale glow, and harsh shadows cut across the professor's face as he adjusted an electrode on the cap.

"There," he said. "Finally got it." He looked up and smiled. "Matt, this doesn't hurt at all. Once I stimulate the neurons, you may feel some slight warmth, but that's all. It's rather comfortable and relaxing."

Dawson allowed the man to secure the headgear and pull the straps tight. "How long does this take?"

"That really depends on what you see. I should say as well that you're free to leave any time. No one is in here holding you against your will." He pursed his lip and averted his gaze.

Is he trying to tell me something?

"But I wouldn't recommend leaving. Those people out there are deadly serious about their mission."

Dawson lowered his voice. "Then why do you stick with them?"

A forlorn, distant look crossed his face. "Ah, my research. It's all I value in life. They fund my work and I get to meet interesting individuals like you and Hannah." He adjusted the back of the cap. "The Whisper in particular is poisonous."

"I've noticed."

Rathbourne held Dawson's head in his hands as he performed a final inspection. "There, you're all set. In a moment, the light will slowly dim and blink out. Try to remember everything that comes into your mind during the process. Even the smallest of details may be significant. Mara will come and get you when we're finished."

The professor exited the chamber and the solid door whooshed and clacked behind him. The room suddenly grew deathly quiet. Dawson's heart hammered methodically against his rib cage.

He closed his eyes and focused on relaxing. When he opened them again, the light had dimmed and the space was pitch black. He was surrounded by darkness, and heard nothing at all except his own breathing.

Dawson gripped the chair rests, staring ahead into what seemed to be an infinite abyss.

Something appeared in the distance.

A faint reddish-brown sphere, like Mars on hazy summer nights. It began pulsating. He definitely felt a surge of energy reach into his head. The Professor hadn't lied: warmth trickled against his temples...

The old farmhouse shimmered. Not in the photograph, but on the prairies itself, in colour, as if he had been present when the picture was taken. He surveyed the flat landscape. Nothing but grass flowing in all directions.

Wait.

In the distance, a rising dust trail.

Someone approached.

A traveler soon arrived and dismounted. Suddenly, three young children and their parents appeared and flocked around him.

The young horseman brushed the dirt off his coat, grabbed a small black kit from a saddlebag, and addressed the mother.

They nodded at each other. Their lips moved, but he heard no voices. The two grownups and the rider marched into the farmhouse. Dawson followed like a curious apparition.

Inside, in a corner of the great room, a baby lay in a crib, covered with a blanket. The man held the woman close while the traveler—a doctor, it seemed—examined the child. After several minutes, he shook his head.

A wave of hands flashed before Dawson's eyes. Ghostly figures darted back and forth, as if the souls of the world mourned with silent screams. Then, they slowly dissipated into a new scene, one that was also familiar.

The woman—Hannah!—held the child, clothed in a blanket against her breast. She stared directly into Dawson's eyes, pleading with him, holding the baby out as if begging him, imploring him to touch it.

He gulped, recoiling at the thought of accepting the corpse. But the Hannah-woman insisted until she—it—finally disappeared in a misty wash of swiping hands...

Everything returned to darkness.

THIRTY-NINE

"What the hell is going on, Professor?" Cornelius Stone hovered over the researcher as he monitored the brain waves on the overhead screen. "What do all these signals tell you?"

Stone clenched his jaw. He'd grown tired of this painstakingly slow and bizarre process, and wanted to uncover the answer from the kid's photograph and complete the mission. Then he could return to his proper lifestyle recruiting suitable candidates.

He knew The Whisper well enough now to recognize her patience was running thin, too.

"Please, Mr. Stone, let us do our work. This isn't something that's easily revealed. Need I outline all the possibilities that the experiment must consider?"

"Just hurry," the operative said, hands on hips. "We don't wish to stay here any longer than is absolutely necessary."

"Of course." The professor increased the time scale

range on the incoming signals. "Matt has returned from his vision, based on these new observations." He pointed to the right-hand side of the graph. "Despite the shift in EM parameters, his response is stable." He turned to Stone. "We won't get anything more from him now. Mara," he said, "please attend to the client and bring him back out."

The professor shut down the electro-magnetic wave generator and sighed.

"Well?" Stone asked. "What can you tell?"

Rathbourne studied the graph on the monitor, muttering to himself, then said, "We'll need to hear from Matt himself about what he experienced, but his mind was extremely active. Off the charts, in some cases. Here," he marked the screen, "and here."

"But you can't say what he experienced, correct?"

"That's right, Mr. Stone. Only Matt can."

The Whisper shifted her stance in the dark corner. "I grow weary of this."

The professor refused to budge. "You both understand the process and recognize the results are open to interpretation."

Mara emerged from the chamber with Mr. Dawson. Hannah went to him, placed her hands on his shoulders and studied his face. Stone admitted to himself that the boy appeared different, almost as if he'd seen a ghost. Clearly, something happened in that lab, and he was determined to find out what.

They sat him at the table and circled around. Stone faced him directly, and The Whisper glided slightly closer. The operative pulled out his cell phone and texted Lamont.

Stone: *update please*

Lamont: *No change. All good here.*

He pocketed the device and leaned forward on his elbows.

"Well, Mr. Dawson, what did you learn? And I remind you to tell us everything."

In a moment, the young physicist spoke in raspy and low tones. "I saw more of the images from the photograph," he started. "Same as before, the swirling motions and eyeless apparitions. Like when I held the actual photo in my hands." He paused a moment, gazing off into space. "I also saw the woman who looked like Hannah, holding out her child. The body was completely hidden by a blanket, like I had as a kid. And her eyes..." His voice cracked. "Those stony eyes bore into my soul. I see them even now." Dawson's hands began trembling.

The professor scribbled notes on a small pad. He looked up and asked, "What else did you notice, Matt? Any changes in your own mood? Your own thoughts?"

The boy shook his head. "I was terrified of this woman." He glanced sheepishly at Hannah. "Actually, more fearful of what she asked me to do."

"What was that," Stone demanded.

He gulped. "She wanted me to take the baby from her. But it was dead. Still, those eyes... she begged me to take it."

Hannah King, appearing more upset and frightened, asked the professor, "What could that mean? What is Matt seeing in there?"

Rathbourne cleared his throat and reviewed what he'd done on his side of the chamber, adjusting the micro frequencies of the EM band, noting where Dawson's brain activity soared, and where it regained its baseline. When he finished, Stone turned to The Whisper. "This tells us nothing more."

"Indeed," she croaked from the shadows. "Professor, is there any other way to interpret the message from what he's seeing? What could this dead child or this—Hannah woman—symbolize?"

Rathbourne returned to the computer station and scrolled through the various squiggles. "To be honest, I've seen nothing like this before. Matt's activity is beyond the scale. There's definitely a connection between him and the invisible realm. It's curious he's able to reproduce the vision he had while touching the photograph, and that shows it clearly left a psychometric impression on him. But I've reached the extent of what my equipment can do. Perhaps we could attempt another reading in a week's time, but in my experience, that won't likely yield any additional information." He cocked his head. "Or possibly…" The professor turned to Ms. King. "Hannah, you mentioned seeing something in that photograph as well, yes? When you handled it, I mean."

"Sort of," she answered, "but only when Matt touched it. A reddish glow came off the edges. I couldn't see what Matt witnessed."

The professor's demeanour changed. "When you grabbed it, though, you sensed nothing."

"No. It's just another old picture of a farmhouse."

He immediately tabbed through various screens and landed on a page with a histogram. "Yes, interesting…" he muttered to himself.

"What is it, Professor?"

He ignored Stone's question and studied the graph.

"Professor Rathbourne," Stone continued, "I won't ask again."

The researcher raised an eyebrow. "I have an idea. These results from the initial MMPI questionnaire show that Hannah's mind is also extremely open to paranormal activity. And the fact that he sees her in the vision… well, at first I discounted that as transference because he knows her, so she appears in the images. Frankly, that's fairly common. But, I wonder if there's more to it. If we put them together in the chamber, perhaps their minds could work collectively to solve this puzzle."

Stone grinned. *Of course, there must be a connection with the girl.* "I thought Mr. Dawson alone could have been the answer, but it makes sense the girlfriend plays a part in it, too." He glanced at The Whisper and recognized the slight upturn of her crooked mouth.

"Well, Professor, I'd say you'd best get on with it."

Hannah protested, but Dawson took her hand and smiled. "I want to discover this secret, Hannah, and why you're part of it. The process is painless, and together we might finally sort this out."

Stone scraped his chair back as the professor asked the two students some additional questions. He meandered toward The Whisper, breathing in her aromatic lilac.

The Whisper's breath came rapidly, rattling at the base of her throat. "If this doesn't work," she mused, "we may have to cut our losses and charge our own people with dissecting the photo."

He squinted into the shadows of her face. Her eyes were hidden under the hood she wore, but her visible mouth was set in a thin, firm line.

"Understood."

THE VIEW OF TREES AND THICK, LUSH LAWNS WAS THE first thing Stefan Gunar noticed when he entered Catherine Gardner's office in the Faculty of Graduate Studies that afternoon. She stood behind her desk, talking on the phone, but waved Gunar to sit on the sofa by the expansive windows overlooking the pristine campus. He wiped the sweat off his palms.

Catherine finished her call and hung up. "May I get you anything, Stefan? Water or coffee?" She swung her office door closed.

"No thank you, I'm good."

"Wonderful!" She sat in a large leather chair across

from him and leaned forward, as if she'd fallen off the cover of a fashion magazine. The dark blue business outfit complemented her well-cut greying hair.

"You mentioned you'd like to chat and said it was urgent, so what's on your mind?"

Gunar licked his lips. "I'm not sure how or where to begin, but I need your advice."

"Let me guess," she said, steel-grey eyes boring into his soul. "You're concerned about your upcoming papers."

"Yes."

"And worried that they may not be suitable for publication, and yet…"

He cleared his throat. "Catherine, I don't think they're even close. The results are preliminary and inconclusive at the moment."

"We're talking about your quantum encoding experiments?"

"Yes, but how did you know?" He scrutinized her angular face. Catherine was sharp and had risen through the administrative ranks quickly, but he had no idea she followed his research.

"It might surprise you to hear that, since you joined us, I've taken more than a passing interest in your shop."

"Joined us?"

She narrowed her gaze. "You know what I mean, Stefan." A delicate silence filled the office. "I'm talking about The Sodality."

More sweat formed on his palms and he gulped.

"Are you surprised?" Catherine leaned back into the massive chair, holding his gaze.

"May I ask, what do you know about this Sodality outfit?"

"I've been with them for several years. Cornelius Stone is my primary contact, and he pushed my career forward and helped me achieve all this." She waved an arm indicating the prestige of the corner office.

"Did he ask you for something in return?"

"Of course."

"May I enquire what that was?"

She cocked her head and thought. "Each of us has our own skills and experiences that are valuable to The Sodality. In your case, I suspect it's quantum research. For me, I helped them identify and secure some ancient artifacts from my colleagues in Anthropology. In exchange, I got tenured and fast-tracked." She paused. "You joined a couple weeks ago?"

"Yes."

"Have you received funds?"

"I have, but I'm uncomfortable with this."

She raised an eyebrow. "Why?"

"To be honest, Catherine, I don't feel I've earned anything. I mean, my research is progressing—it could always move along quicker, but we're on track now."

"With your new student, Ms. Sakamoto?"

He straightened up, surprised that she'd known about Wendy. Then again, she was Dean of Graduate Studies.

"I keep tabs on those who are... with us," she said.

"Did you ever feel guilty about your involvement with this organization? I mean, it appears somewhat shadowy and sinister. Like, why don't they operate openly?"

"Stefan, I have no interest in their inner machinations. They have their reasons for working the way they do and, as long as I get what I want, I could not care less. You read the clause in your agreement, no doubt. The one referring to non-disclosure of any Sodality business with those outside the organization?"

"Yes."

"Well, Cornelius may even frown on us having this

chat right now. But I told him when he contacted me—"

"Wait, he's spoken with you?"

"Of course." She leaned forward again. "There are many of us on campus. I'm only aware of a few personally, but my sense is we're much larger. Keep an eye on those faculty members who suddenly shine. That's a major league clue."

Gunar frowned and wiped his forehead.

"Still, there's something else bothering you."

"I'm afraid so. Catherine, I don't think Stone is so much interested in my research as he is in one of my students."

"Matthew Dawson?"

He nodded. "Mr. Dawson experienced an extraordinary psychometric phenomenon."

"Ah, yes, I understand now why Cornelius would be excited by that."

He continued. "Well, I feel guilty about sharing Dawson's work with them, and Ms. Sakamoto tells me the other day that he's taken off to Sudbury, basically abandoning his own research, and The Sodality... well, they've gone after him. I haven't heard from him despite my emails. Neither has Wendy."

"I understand," she said, adjusting herself on the chair. "And because of your actions, your student may be in danger? Is that it?"

Gunar sighed heavily. "Yes."

"Feeling a modicum of guilt at the beginning is normal, but I assure you, it passes." She paused, then her gaze narrowed. "You're not thinking of trying to leave us, I hope. Their covenant is one hundred percent binding. It can't be broken. When you commit to The Sodality, the arrangement truly is forever. Better learn to embrace it."

"I was hoping you'd help me. Maybe stop the publication of those papers before they bring shame to the school. And since I discovered you're with them too, perhaps you could tell them to leave Matt Dawson alone."

A knock sounded, and the door opened. A short, well-dressed man poked his bald head in. "Your budget meeting starts in a few minutes, Ms. Gardner."

"Thank you, Paul." She stood and smoothed her clothing. "I'll be right there."

Gunar prepared to leave.

"I won't get involved in your business, Stefan, but I'm confident of what Cornelius would say in a situation like this because I've overheard him before."

"What's that?"

"Three things. One, the agreement cannot be changed. Two, The Sodality demands fierce loyalty in exchange for the riches they provide." She guided him toward the door.

"And the third?"

Catherine lowered her voice, leaned over, and whispered in his ear. "If you can't abide the first two, there's only one other option. The final one."

"What's that?" he asked nervously.

She held his shoulder. "Late on a moonless night, when you plumb the agonizing depths of your sorry soul, you're convinced that you're different from everybody else. Special."

He gulped as the bile rose in his throat.

"But you're not."

Catherine smiled curtly and brushed her hair behind an ear. She said cheerfully, "It was a pleasure seeing you again, Stefan. Give my regards to Mr. Dawson. Tell him..." she paused, then a smile crossed her lips. "Tell him I'd like to meet him for lunch soon, will you?"

ON OVERCAST DAYS LIKE THIS, AS SUMMER FADED AND fall took hold, it was difficult to read the sky. When Gunar pulled into his driveway, hit the button to open the garage door, and parked inside, he didn't know if it was two o'clock or five.

He contemplated Catherine's third tenet.

And knew exactly what to do.

While still behind the wheel, Gunar drew his laptop from the satchel on the passenger seat and opened up his bank account. He stared at the inflated balance, then began the process to transfer funds. The algorithm prompted him for an amount to enter, and Gunar typed $25,000. The cursor hovered over the confirm button briefly, but his resolve was steadfast.

He pressed send. Almost instantly, the transaction was confirmed.

This'll help him out with his student loans.

Gunar considered himself to be a good man, despite his ambitions and failures, his lies and arrogance. He had his faults like anyone, but fundamentally, he strove to do right. This afternoon, the guilt he'd carried with him about endangering Matt Dawson and Wendy Sakamoto led him to find a way out of his agreement with The Sodality. His own solution.

He tapped the button on the remote control and the garage door clacked shut behind him. In a minute, the overhead light winked out. Gunar opened the car windows and closed his eyes. *Perhaps this will make up for the pain I've caused.*

He thought of Shelly on their wedding day and turned the ignition over.

FORTY

THE RECONFIGURATION OF THE GLOOMY CHAMBER comprised repositioning the second oversized chair so the solitary ceiling light shone between the two. The professor had the pair sit and relax while he placed transducer caps on each of them. Hannah fidgeted, asking lots of questions and wearing her brooding skepticism on her sleeve, but Dawson, having been through this once, assured her the process was actually soothing, refreshing. She inhaled deeply.

"It'll take me several minutes to set up the experiment with Mara so we can adjust your inputs independently from each other. You may feel a slight tingling around your temples while we do this, but again, it's harmless. Please relax and concentrate on the photographic image as you remember it. When the light above you dims, the procedure will be starting." He couldn't contain his excitement, smiling and rubbing his hands together. "Well, I have great hope this is what we've been missing.

Good luck." The professor swung the heavy door closed behind him.

The black walls and soundproof nature of the room immediately caused Dawson to close his eyes and focus on his breathing. His heart pounded at a slower rate this time. He relaxed his shoulders and waited.

"Matt?"

"Hm?"

"I've been thinking about God and science, and something occurred to me. Wanna hear?"

He glanced at Hannah in the gloom.

"Sure."

"Okay, here goes." She bit her lip. Dawson noticed the rise of her chest as she gathered her thoughts and realized, here, in the chamber, how beautiful she was and how much he enjoyed her company. It seemed cowardly to leave that observation unspoken, abandoned to the shadows.

"If I understand the Uncertainty Principle, when describing a particle, we can't fully measure its momentum and location simultaneously. We might determine one, but there'll be uncertainty in the other and vice versa. "

"Yeah?"

"But sometimes the Principle refers more to an observer effect. Like, nothing we see is completely true because the observer is biased and, in fact, *changes* what we're trying to measure. So there's a hint of uncertainty in everything we think is real. Is that right?"

"Yes. A famous double-slit experiment in physics shows the effect."

"Okay, so does this mean that we can't prove something is real until it's *observed into* existence? And even then, we can't be certain of the object's innate truth either."

"Wait," Dawson said, grinning, "A tree exists in a

forest or outside on campus even though I'm not standing in front of it right now."

Hannah shifted in the chair. "How do you know?"

"I just... Okay, I saw a pine tree in that green space beside this building as we came in today."

"Ah, so the probability you'll find it later if you go out the same door may be high, but you can't be a hundred percent certain it'll still be there."

Dawson considered her point, but before responding, she added, "So what convinces you the laws of physics here are true everywhere?" She giggled. "I told you I've been thinking about these things."

Dawson smiled and said, "Uh-huh. Well, I believe the laws of physics are the same everywhere because that's logical. The universe isn't random."

"But it could be, right? I mean, we haven't even begun to map the entire universe yet, never mind the multiverse."

"I suppose, but everything so far suggests an order, an underlying logic."

"Wait, did you feel something?" Hannah leaned back in her chair. A warm wave surged around Dawson's left temple.

He recognized it from the previous procedure. "Yeah, just chill. Won't be long now."

They remained silent, and then Hannah continued. "The laws of physics... suppose you drop a ball over and over again. It falls to the ground because of gravity, and since it falls consistently *here*, you believe gravity works the same *everywhere*. That's inductive reasoning."

"Right."

"But it doesn't *prove* the existence of gravity everywhere, or that dropping a ball will happen the same way every time, everywhere."

"Perhaps, but I have faith in the scientific laws and in

a logical universe."

"As do I."

"Wait a sec," he said, "I thought you put your faith and trust in God."

"I have always leavened my faith with reason, and since God created everything, including science, they're kinda the same thing. Look, the Uncertainty Principle applies to faith, too. I'm certain God exists with all my heart and soul; therefore I must be uncertain about all my daily ways. I can't seek control of my life and have faith because that would be playing God. I have to trust that because God is real, then everything that happens is for his purpose. Let God be God. But, if I'm certain that I'm in charge of my own destiny, that if it's going to be then it's up to me, well, then God is nothing more than a mysterious, archaic idea. In other words, Matt, you can't truly believe in God and think that you're in control of yourself and your environment."

Another brush of warmth nudged him, this time on his other temple. It lasted only a few seconds.

"But how are God and science identical?"

"In a very real sense. Look," she continued, "suppose you draw a circle around the Earth and say, gravity as we understand it works here inside the circle, but according to Godel's Incompleteness Theorem—"

"Godel's what?"

"Oh, Matt, surely you've heard of Godel. Don't put me on like this. He proved any statement like the law of gravity requires an external observer to exist. No statement alone can prove *itself* to be true."

He grinned sheepishly. The fact was, he'd never heard of this Godel business before.

"Anyway, within the circle, you note gravity is consistent. Now suppose you're still an observer and you expand the circle to cover the solar system and you say, yeah, gravity works the same inside here, too."

"Makes sense from what we understand."

"But you can't deduce that it's the same way *outside* the circle."

He furrowed his brow. What she said made his head hurt. "For the sake of argument, sure, until we go beyond the solar system."

"Ah, so now if you encircle the entire universe, then…"

A cold realization dawned on him. Hannah's argument was leading him to a major conundrum. "Then, since the universe is everything by definition, anything outside the circle must be… boundless."

"I think so, too."

He gathered his thoughts and focused his mind on the problem. After considering its different possibilities, he said, "Okay, if the universe began as a Big Bang, then something *outside* the universe must have… *observed* it into existence."

"Why?"

"Because there's order and logic, cause and effect, and information in the DNA of living things. Like Rathbourne thinks about the hidden message. That must come from somewhere."

"In other words," she said, "whatever's outside the circle is not only boundless but also consciously bringing order to chaos."

"You're talking about God."

Hannah's voice lowered to a whisper. "Well, it's impossible to prove it's God, but also impossible to disprove. I have faith that the boundless, rational entity that brought order to chaos and gave us DNA from nothing is God. The Creator. The Word. That's what the Bible says. And as a social scientist, it makes perfect sense to me."

Dawson shook his head in wonder as the warm sensations in his temples grew, then faded. "Admittedly, I know little about this, but I always thought the Bible was about sheep and donkeys and keeping everything really clean." He paused. "And roasting in hell if you're bad."

She snorted. "There is truth in that, too. What God wants is to show us his love for what he sees and gave certain people insights into the invisible world. Why is it Einstein kept talking about wanting to know God's thoughts? Perhaps his pursuit of science was his way. But others experience different callings, unusual phenomena. Music, art, even business. What if," she continued, "God sent a message to the world, and he chose your family and all your ancestors to carry it in your genes, to discover it at some point, and to share it with others?"

"The secret in the photograph?"

"Well, that's a breadcrumb along the trail. The Whisper understands the photo only points to something else." She grunted. "Mm, felt it that time."

Dawson considered her words, her logic, the flow of the argument that brought them both here to this room. How it related to the vision of the woman holding the dead baby, and a prairie farmhouse remained a mystery.

The overhead light flickered and dimmed until he lost his senses in the complete blackness of the chamber. "You ready, Hannah?"

"Yes," she whispered.

"Then let's find out what the secret message is."

FORTY-ONE

HEAVY DARKNESS AND LOSS OF SENSORY PERCEPTION overwhelmed Hannah as she reclined in the immense chair, staring at nothing.

The thick black reminded her of night and the inevitable terrifying dreams that often accompanied her. Instinctively, she closed her eyes, bathing in the warmth of the EM waves kneading her temples. Like Matt said, it was relaxing, and her heart rate decreased as her breathing grew deep and full.

She focused on Matt's vision. The glowing edges. What she perceived as the shifting images around the perimeter of the photograph. Her mind turned to the farmhouse, and within the vision, she scanned its dimensions.

A rush of energy urged her to peek.

Euphoria swirled throughout her body and her eyes popped open. And there, on the opposite wall, stood the mysterious farmhouse...

...but this time, it appeared to be real, as if she stood on the prairie, warming her face in the hazy sun, hearing the grassland shift and ripple like water on the ocean. She smelled cooking and a wisp of smoke rose from the building, something she hadn't seen before in the photo.

"Hello?"

No answer came.

"Anyone home?"

She inched closer to the house and peered into a window but saw nothing definitive inside, just shadows of objects, perhaps a table and some chairs. A painting on the wall. Overhead, clouds quickly gathered like she remembered in movies, covering the sun as the wind grew more intense. Toward the horizon, dust kicked up, and the grassland chugged wildly.

Hannah tested the door handle, and it turned. She pushed and leaned inside.

"Hello?"

The air continued to boil, so she entered the house and closed the door behind her.

The place was empty. She walked through the main room, hearing her footsteps on the worn, wooden flooring. A fireplace and hearth sat against one wall. A couple of bunk beds rose against another. Toward the back was a short hallway. She crossed the floorboards in that direction.

She reached the corridor and peered into the gloom. That suspicion of being watched emerged, powerful and present. She gulped and peered around. A kerosene lamp squatted on the mantle. She grabbed it and the box of matches, then ignited it after a couple of false starts and trimmed the wick to cast a warm glow throughout the room.

Outside, the wind now howled, sounding almost

human, like a woman's high-pitched cry of anguish. Like a—

"Matt?" This time, her voice was barely audible. Had she actually spoken in the chamber or only inside the vision? No one else was present in the farmhouse, but she wasn't alone.

Hannah raised the lamp and entered the dark hallway. Nests of cobwebs hung in the corners. Long shadows splayed across the floor and up the bare walls.

"Who—Who's there?"

Then a human form emerged from the gloom, leaning against a doorjamb. The thin face and bony fingers. The death-carrying, serpent eyes.

"Hello, Hannah," he purred. "I've been waiting for this moment a long time." He checked his fingernails. "You have too, I imagine."

"How did you—?" Confusion smothered her mind. The man, or demon, or whatever it was from her nightmares had appeared here, in Dawson's live action prairie scene.

"Where am I?" she asked.

"Oh, quite safe, if that's the real question. Sure, you've been having fun with your boyfriend's photo, playing Sherlock Holmes, running away from the bad guys..." He drew his body up straight. He stood well over six feet with sunken cheeks and hollow eyes.

"The Lord will keep me from all evil. He will keep my life. The Lord will keep me from all evil—"

"Ah yes, Christian, pray, pray, pray. Maybe God will save you," he snorted. "Or maybe there is no God, have you considered that?"

"He is real."

"Your boyfriend doesn't think so." The figure slinked around, shrugging. "So where is this God? We've been waltzing for years, you and me, and where has God been?

Missing. In. Action."

"No," she whispered, "He's with me. Just because he doesn't intervene all the time doesn't mean he's abandoned me." The seducer slithered toward her. Hannah shifted, digging deep to find a shred of courage. And within that moment of confrontation, she snarled, "Whoever you are, I'm not afraid of you anymore."

The figure smiled pitifully. "Yes you are, Hannah." He stretched out his crooked hand. "But I can make all the bad stuff disappear. Your sinful past. The poor child. Emily, yes? Do you miss her? Join me, and together we'll bring peace to all the hurting people of the world. But we must hurry."

"No."

"Isn't that what you want? To help others? Be a suffering servant like your weak saviour?" He snorted and began pacing like a caged animal. The seducer had become more agitated. Impatient. Perhaps Matt's nearby presence threatened him.

Emily's glazed eyes appeared in her mind, but Hannah buried the horrid memory. "You're frightened," she said, stiffening her back. "What is it you're afraid of?"

"I fear nothing," he growled. "But I'm growing tired of this, and there's work to do. Join The Sodality, and we shall bring truth and enlightenment to this evil world."

This was no mere nightmare, she thought. The seducer knew of The Sodality, and of Matt.

She gulped. "I refuse."

"But I'm afraid you have no choice." He approached her, squeezing her out of the hallway and into the main room again. "I chose you a long time ago for this work. Have you not recognized your abilities to manipulate matter? The shattering of lights, for example?" He grinned, displaying his perfect teeth.

Hannah recalled the first moment she caused

streetlights to flicker or self-extinguish. How she believed this was coincidence until she realized her power extended far beyond chance happenings. The seducer seemed to be a link, an interlocutor between her deepest fears of abandonment and being completely alone in the world, and a sense of purpose and community with The Sodality. Or with God?

Is this what I'm supposed to do? Who is behind The Sodality?

"Help me, Lord, show me the truth, show me the light. Please, God, tell me what to do!"

"It won't do you any good, Hannah. He's deaf, dumb and blind." The man lurched forward. "Come. Follow me. You'll be able to see her again, the way she was meant to be."

From deep within, his words triggered a reaction so visceral that at first, it startled her. How dare he take the Lord's words and twist them? He staggered toward her and now loomed only a few feet away.

She inhaled deeply, feeling a new power surge through her body. Her back stiffened, and she stood taller.

"No."

Something in her voice sounded foreign, amazing and commanding, as if the word itself was disembodied, bubbling up from a source of immense strength.

"I said no!"

The creature stopped in his path and narrowed his dark, lustrous eyes.

"Don't you dare defy me, Hannah King. You won't like what happens next."

But she stood her ground, refusing to budge as the figure floated within inches of her face. His fetid breath filled the shadowy space, and she shivered in the cold radiating from his grey skin.

"You may not get this," she said, "but I finally do.

And you've reminded me of what being a follower of Jesus truly means. To let go of inconsequential worldly pursuits. To obey and trust only him and what he commands about loving my enemy."

"Such rot," the seducer hissed. "You believe all that crap? It hasn't helped you much, has it? You must be a particularly special brand of loser." He sneered in her face, but Hannah refused to yield.

"I understand. You're afraid."

"Bah!"

Her eyes softened as the full force of the true God's love filled her body, and she understood what it meant to be one of the elect. "Here," she said, setting the kerosene lamp on the floor and presenting her arms to him. "You are loved. Come and let me embrace you."

"What is this sorcery!" the figure screamed, slinking back a step.

"Not sorcery," she whispered. "Only love. Let me share the power of his love with you."

"Nonsense, Hannah King! There is only The Sodality. It is the only truth in this world."

She shook her head at the creature as he reeled away. Hannah held her arms out. "I forgive you."

The seducer clutched at his chest. "No... No..." He shrank, smoke hissing from his body. His thin flesh continued withdrawing, exposing the bony apparatus underneath.

"Come," she said, her heart bursting with a love she'd never fully understood until now. *I am truly with Him, and He is truly with me.*

The figure dropped to the floor, continuing to melt in a cloud of ash. A thick orange glow encircled him, just like she'd seen around the edges of Matt's photograph.

"It's not too late," she said, but the man had already morphed into a grotesque, oozing hump.

It was over.

Hannah closed her eyes, thanked Jesus, and prayed for the man's soul. Then, she remembered where she was, somehow located within Matt's photo, inside the farmhouse itself.

But there was no more left for her to do here. Nothing more to fear, ever. Hannah grabbed the lantern, trimmed the wick, and extinguished the flame...

In that instant, she was back in the chamber staring into the black surroundings. Something had changed in this encounter with the seducer. She'd been able to tap into a huge reservoir of overwhelming grace.

Then she remembered.

Matt's cloth from his mother's basement was stretched across her torso, and she fingered the old blanket tucked inside her shirt.

FORTY-TWO

THE SOLITARY LIGHT IN THE DARK CHAMBER WINKED ABOVE them. Matt Dawson, jaw clenched, gripped the armrests, refusing to believe he had seen nothing new. As he reviewed the experiment—the dimming of the chamber followed by what seemed like hours of darkness with no farmhouse vision, Hannah's soft voice floated in.

"Did you see anything, Hannah?" he asked, continuing to stare at the black wall in front.

"Yes, Matt, and it was... beautiful."

Before she explained her own experience, the door swung open, and the professor entered, brow furrowed, rubbing his hands. The recognizable whiff of burned circuitry followed him like body odour.

"Are you okay, Hannah?" He seemed more focused on her, passing by Dawson brusquely and releasing her from the skullcap.

"I am, Professor. I was just about to tell Matt how amazing my vision was."

"Yes, yes, I knew something happened from the EM readings and brain activity." He turned to Dawson. "But you, Matt, not so much. I suspect little appeared to you based on the flat baseline we recorded?"

"Yeah, that's right. Zilch."

"Well," Rathbourne continued as he guided Hannah from the chair, "Not exactly nothing. The apparent synergy between you two in here manifested itself in some powerful equipment surges out there. Fried a couple of secondary power supplies. We'll replace those for the next round."

"Next round?" Dawson asked.

Rathbourne and Hannah joined him as he swung his legs over the side of the chair and allowed the professor to remove the transducer cap.

"Yes, Matt. More studies. These are the most exciting findings we've encountered in seven years. It's hard to put into words what your presence here together truly means."

"Don't forget, we're not here for you. My mother's being held hostage so those two freaks can find whatever they're searching for." He paused, scrutinizing the man. "Why are you really involved with this group? I know you talked about funding, but seriously, wouldn't good science overcome cultural biases? Others do it that way."

Rathbourne sighed, glanced at the chamber door resting ajar, and lowered his voice. "It's challenging, Matt. I don't care what The Sodality's mission is. Never have. Oh, Cornelius Stone found me at an international workshop years ago, started chatting about wealth and a faculty position at one of the big western schools, but I honestly wasn't interested in that. All I've wanted to do since grad school was research like this, trying to understand how naturally occurring EM waves and other phenomena influence how we think and feel, and if they can be used to distil information coded into our genes." He paused a moment, scratching his head. "Do you really believe I'm one of them? No... No, I'm more aligned with you two than any antiquated principles The Sodality follows."

"Why not leave?" Dawson asked. "Help us escape and come with us."

But the professor simply shrugged in resignation. Then, raising his voice, he said, "Let's hear about that vision, Hannah."

They exited the chamber and gathered around the table. Dawson felt more relaxed and rested, more at peace this time with the process, even though there was no revelation that time. Stone glanced at The Whisper who had shifted closer to the group, her face still mostly hidden, but now the bony, gnarled hands hung at her side.

"The professor informs us, Mr. Dawson," she murmured, "that your experience was non-existent." She approached him and angled her head up slightly, revealing her horrid, burn-scarred cheeks and nose. "Is this true?"

"Yes. I tried, believe me, I want this to end, too, so I can get home and see my mum. But it didn't happen."

"With the photograph, perhaps, but this morning you witnessed several interesting events in that room without the presence of the photo." She turned to the professor. "So what changed?"

The man rocked on his feet, scratching the side of his head. "What Matt says is true. This has always been an experimental science. It's incredibly difficult to reproduce all the conditions necessary for a reading of this sort. But," he said excitedly as his face beamed, "Hannah's readings were ridiculous. You saw what happened to the equipment."

Over at the computer rack used to house the experiment, Mara had crawled under a metal cabinet and was removing the damaged power supplies.

"I did that?" Hannah asked. "How can that be? I'm not the one with the—"

"That, my dear," said the professor, "is what I'd love to know, too. Come, look at your brain activity." He pointed to the large monitor that displayed a timeline of all her readings.

"How long were we in there?" she asked, studying the output.

"Approximately 18 minutes. Bet it felt a lot shorter, hm?"

"And strangely longer." She peered into his face. "It's a paradox, this experimental arrangement, isn't it?"

"Indeed. Some have called it that and more."

Stone sighed in disgust. "Please, Professor, let's get on with this. You can have your little mind-meld later, all right?"

"Of course, of course. Hannah," he said, "sit down and describe everything about your vision."

She took a chair at the table. Dawson stood defiantly beside her, keeping an eye on Stone and The Whisper. As Hannah discussed the farmhouse and howling wind, he formulated a plan to capture these two creeps and hold them until his mother could be freed. He'd noticed the longer they all stayed together, the more relaxed The Sodality became. Even the broken crone who preferred the shadowy background, watching everyone from afar, had merged with the group. Hannah could take her down given her athleticism, he thought. Stone might be a bit tougher. He noted the man's build, the broad shoulders and square jaw. He'd be a greater challenge, and he's the holder of their phones.

"Then I met the creep, the seducer, from my nightmares," Hannah said, staring directly at the professor. "This character has been part of my life since I was a child.

But he was in Matt's farmhouse, creeping around in the shadows." She threw a glance at The Whisper. "When he confronted me, talking about... about what The Sodality does, I found a source of power I've never experienced."

"What, you mean *God*?" Stone snorted.

"Yes, that's exactly what I mean. God, Mr. Stone. And he was there with me."

She continued describing the scene in the farmhouse, how rather than trying to evade the creep, Hannah offered to embrace and forgive him, inviting the seducer to join her in the warmth of God's love. It was all a bit much for Dawson to digest, but he'd grown abnormally fond of Hannah, and her easy manner of talking about God and Jesus was compelling.

And *real*.

If he tapped into that power the way she did, perhaps he'd become a believer, too. But then, his entire life would require a massive change. There's a *Quo* for every *Quid*, he thought, and becoming a Christian carried an immense cost.

Could I ever pay that price?

Stone's commanding voice interrupted his thoughts and stopped Hannah's debrief cold. "What's that inside your blouse, Ms. King?"

Hannah instinctively pressed her palm against her chest and glanced at Dawson. Her eyes widened as the realization stung hard, stealing her breath.

"No use trying to hide it. Come on," he demanded, "hand it over."

Then Dawson remembered, too, and glimpsed it.

A tuft of the cloth they grabbed from his mother's basement peeked out between the buttons on Hannah's blouse. She'd hidden it there before The Sodality stormed the kitchen. Held it for safekeeping. But now? Is this what the photographic breadcrumb pointed to? What The

Whisper truly coveted?
    Panic exploded through his body.

FORTY-THREE

"ALLOW ME, CORNELIUS," THE WHISPER EXULTED. SHE glided over the dimly lit room and drew up beside Hannah, who quickly stood and backed away, knocking the chair on the floor. Stone positioned himself between Dawson and Hannah and stared him down.

"My oh my," the woman rasped. She grabbed an edge of the cloth between her bent thumb and forefinger and slowly tugged it loose from beneath Hannah's shirt.

Hannah peered at Dawson, her face an assortment of terrifying emotions. But rather than allow his anger and fear to hold sway, an extraordinary sensation washed over him. A thin, almost imperceptible voice suggesting everything would work out exactly as it should. He smiled and immediately, her shoulders dropped and relaxed.

"Do you find something amusing, Ms. King?" The Whisper asked as she wrenched the remainder of the material out.

Hannah ignored her, straightening her back and

glancing at Dawson.

"Ah, of course, your mighty protector will save you from all harm, hm?" She spread the cloth out on the table before the others.

"What the hell is that?" Stone glared, hands on hips. "It looks like a filthy old dish towel."

"Indeed," said The Whisper. She zeroed in on Dawson. "Where did this come from? And you will tell the truth. I know when a man is lying." Her skeletal fingers clutched his arm. They were surprisingly strong and unusually cold, as if no blood ran through her veins.

"It's part of an old blanket from my childhood," he said, refusing to offer anything more. No, if this creepy Sodality wanted to make ridiculous links between his moth-eaten swaddling cloth and whatever rattled around in their heads, that was their thing. Not his.

The Whisper fingered the cloth, lifting up a corner here and there, studying the odd herringbone pattern along one of the edges.

"This is ancient. Why were you hiding it, Ms. King?"

Hannah pursed her mouth, glaring at the woman defiantly.

"Mr. Dawson, then? Why was your girlfriend carrying this rag in her shirt?" She bent over and smelled the cloth on the table. "Hm?"

"We found it in my mother's basement," he conceded. If the truth could indeed set him free, then the truth it shall be. "It was wrapped around an old piece of radio equipment my Dad used. I don't know why."

"Ah, your father." She touched her cheek. "And when you held it, supernatural magic happened, yes?"

Rathbourne darted about the room. "Oh my," he repeated in rapid succession. "Oh my, oh my. Perhaps this was also a factor in Hannah's revelation. And you, Matt, sensed visions from this, too?"

334

Dawson glanced at the professor, then returned to the shadow covering The Whisper's eyes. "Not in the chamber, no. Earlier, in another paranormal event, but completely unrelated to the farmhouse photograph." His gaze dropped to the floor.

The Whisper held the cloth against her face. "So thin," she wheezed, "yet not overly soft. Not like one would expect a blanket to be." She spread it out again. "Curious." Then, turning to Dawson, she said, "Tell us all about this other vision."

"No, Matt," Hannah cried.

"It's okay. I'm not afraid of this witch."

The Whisper froze. "You speak with misplaced bravado, Mr. Dawson. But you'll regret such disrespect. Now, enlighten me as to what you saw when you touched this filthy rag."

Dawson relayed as much as he could remember from the ancient Roman scene in which he apparently played a role by rescuing a linen cloak from destruction of the Library at Alexandria. He had no idea what it meant, and said so, but since it wasn't related to the apparitions in the photograph, he dismissed any possible connection.

But there was a link. The blanket in which the dead child was wrapped by the Hannah-woman in the farmhouse had the same herringbone pattern as this old cloth lying in front of them. Dawson was not prepared to reveal that finer point.

"This is most interesting, don't you think, Cornelius?"

"It is, but I sense the young man continues to withhold important information."

"You can think whatever you like. I've told you what I know."

The Whisper sighed. "A lie of omission, Mr. Dawson, is still bearing false witness. And you?" she poked a crooked white finger at his chest. "You are a liar."

An awkward silence filled the room. Mara had finished repairs to the monitoring equipment and now stood by the computer console, wiping down her glasses. Stone drew closer to The Whisper like a grand protector. Hannah inched toward Dawson, and he placed his arm around her waist.

Stone pulled the phone from his pocket. "Our patience has run out. You either tell us everything, and I mean *everything* associated with that snot rag and the stupid farmhouse, or else Mr. Lamont finally gets to satisfy his many cave-dwelling urges." He dangled the phone in his palm, preparing to send the text. "Do we understand each other?"

Dawson eyed the man shrewdly, assessing his options. As long as his mother's life was in jeopardy, he had no choice but to capitulate. He closed his eyes briefly. *Lord, help me. Give me the strength to believe.*

"Well, Mr. Dawson?"

His shoulders slumped, and he exhaled. "I'll tell you all of it." He brushed a hand through his hair. "We clued in to this blanket early yesterday morning at my buddy's house. I touched the photograph and after the initial hand swipes and strange ghosts, the woman in the vision presented me with the child wrapped in material that had the same pattern... this one." He pointed to the off-colour band along the cloth's edges. "It looked vaguely familiar, and Hannah, well, she remembered seeing it in the basement with Dad's stuff. So we raced back to Haileybury."

"And that's why you canceled our appointment," the professor said.

Dawson nodded. "I don't know why we didn't leave the rag there when you all showed up. I knew it had something to do with the mysterious message, but couldn't connect the dots. I needed more time to process the evidence. Anyway, Hannah grabbed and hid it in her shirt. We figured when this business with the photo was done, and you let us go, we'd try to put the puzzle together." He squeezed Hannah's waist. "And that's it. That's everything."

The Whisper who had been stock still during Dawson's confession, said, "I believe you." She inhaled deeply a couple times, her sunken chest rattling beneath the cloak. "So all along we've been assuming there was a clue in the dead child. Isn't that right, Mr. Stone?"

He nodded, staring at the cloth on the table.

"But it's not about the child, after all. The message here is not about a corpse." She traced the perimeter of the blanket with a gnarled finger and glared at Dawson. "It's about this... this ancient, worn piece of filth that one of your ancestors saved from the destructive fires of the Alexandrian purges.

"Ancestors?" he asked, but The Whisper ignored him.

"Now, the only task remaining is to resolve the significance of the rag, and," she faced both Dawson and Hannah, "we can determine that ourselves, with our own historians who are so well-versed in antiquity."

"Do whatever you want. Just let us go." Dawson's voice sounded worn and beaten. He wished this all to end so he could get home to his mum again and spend time with Hannah.

The Whisper sneered. "Oh, but you misunderstand, Mr. Dawson."

"What are you talking about? You got what you wanted."

"Oh yes, these two artifacts—the photograph and this old cloth—belong to us now and shall be stored with all the other curious objects The Sodality has found through the ages." She sighed. "But that's not what I mean." She edged closer. His nostrils filled with the scent of lilacs. "Since we have what we came for, and cannot risk you squealing to the police, we cannot let you go."

"What?"

"I apologize for the deception, but it was necessary to secure your cooperation. However," she said, picking up the cloth and folding it neatly, "we have no further need of you two."

Hannah gasped.

"And, you're no longer welcome in the Sodality. We shall all return to the safehouse now, and then Mr. Stone will, how shall I put this delicately... he shall remove all the pain you've ever known, and all the pain you ever will."

FORTY-FOUR

MATT DAWSON CHASTISED HIMSELF FOR ACTUALLY believing these Sodality creeps would keep their word. He'd encountered enough scientific thieves masquerading as researchers in the university and at conferences to know that most people only look after themselves. So he should have known better.

Hannah tensed beside him. He stared at the gloating face of Cornelius Stone and the crooked maw of The Whisper. Of course, they'd betray his trust. Of course they would. The rage that had slowly festered in his gut roared to life and ripped through his body. He clenched his fists and grit his teeth. The anger, like a black, waking beast, invaded his thoughts and took over his mind.

The hell with forgiveness.

He dropped his arm from Hannah's waist and lunged at Stone, smashing the table aside and upending a couple of chairs. He swung at the man's head, barely missing, but his momentum caused him to stagger sideways. That gave the operative enough time to reposition. Dawson hadn't fully respected the man's fighting ability. The only times he had ever fought were in grade school and a hotel bar once, and those weren't much more than wrestling. He realized, facing Stone, that he was seriously over-matched.

But that wouldn't stop him.

He lashed out at the operative with a full swing, immediately followed by a second punch to the gut that caught Stone just below the ribs. The man grunted and fell back, grimacing.

"It's been a while since I sullied my hands in a good old-fashioned beating, Mr. Dawson," he said through clenched teeth. "This is normally Lamont's business, but I'm rather enjoying the dance." For a big man, he moved nimbly and drove out a leg, catching Dawson in the kidneys and sending him tumbling to the floor. But he rolled up immediately and pivoted in time to duck as Stone launched a round of punches. The last one caught him on the jaw, radiating numbing pain. His mouth filled with blood.

"Is that... all you got?" Dawson spat and wiped the slop from his lips. He shot a cursory glance at Hannah standing with the professor near the chamber door. She held a hand to her face, and her eyes were fixed on The Whisper. The crone had slowly backed away from the fracas, inching toward the main entrance, holding both the photograph and the cloth.

Dawson welcomed a fresh wave of adrenaline and rage. He head-faked Stone, then dove for the diminutive woman, missing, but forcing her to return to Stone's protection. In the chaos, her cowl slipped off her head, revealing the full ugliness of her melted face and patchy tufts of white hair.

After pulling himself up, Dawson studied her hard facial lines, the brutal scar across what remained of her forehead, and the cold, lifeless eyes.

That provided the operative with time to re-engage. Within milliseconds, the distance between them disappeared, and he struck with incessant fury. After absorbing several punches to the body, Dawson felt the dull, heavy pain of a leg kick to his thigh. Then, spinning around, another blow behind his knees crumpled his legs.

He scrambled to rise but could find no purchase, and the sharp pain of Stone's knee and body weight stabbed the small of his back, squeezing the air from his lungs. A cold steel blade pressed against the side of this throat.

Stone grunted into his ear, "I was surprised you hadn't tried this earlier, Mr. Dawson." The blade scraped against his neck. "But fortunately, I'm a patient man and you, my friend, did not disappoint."

He grabbed a mitt full of curly hair and snapped his head back. "Now get up slowly, or I swear I'll end you right here in front of everyone."

"Matt, stop!" Hannah screamed.

Dawson, clenching his jaw, overflowed with burning hate. Hannah insisted that everything happened according to God's will. That's what she said. And he almost believed her. Almost understood the need for dictators to wreak havoc on the world, or for creepy lowlife criminals to manipulate innocent people. Almost understood there was a reason, a cause behind the effect of mass murders and evil.

Almost.

But now, in his clouded, rage-filled mind, he saw no reason why a so-called loving God would allow *this* to happen. With a sudden thrust of strength, he fought to escape from Stone's grip, and tried to wriggle free.

But the man held on fast.

"Still a bit of fight left in you, hm? Well, let's eliminate that right now." Stone slammed his face into the floor and the impact stunned Dawson, jarring a couple of teeth loose and snapping his jaw, sending torrents of dizzying pain through his entire body, and spewing a torrent of fresh blood from his mouth.

But Dawson's resolve was strong. Through his bleeding, crushed face, he growled, "Screw... you."

Stone released the young man's hair and smashed his fist into Dawson's temple. His vision blurred and black speckles appeared.

"Stop this!" Hannah begged.

Stone grunted and shifted his weight. "Had enough, you little puke?"

"That will be all, Mr. Stone," The Whisper rasped. "He's done."

The operative shoved Dawson's face into the floor one last time for good measure before hauling him to his feet and slamming him down on a chair like a rag doll. Hannah rushed over and held his head against her chest. "You animals," she cried. "I pray to God you'll both rot in hell for this."

The Whisper grinned under her hood. "Perhaps one day we will encounter divine retribution," she mused. "But not today." She slipped the cowl over her head, then motioned to Stone, and he pulled fresh zip ties from his pocket. Before binding Dawson, Stone drew his phone.

"Mum?" he whispered.

"Relax. I won't relieve Mr. Lamont of his own fun with your dear old mother. No," he sneered, "but I do want her to see what her only child, the would-be hero, looks like now." He snapped a photo and sent it off.

Professor Rathbourne appeared beside them, holding a wet cloth out to Hannah. She began the grim task of cleaning Dawson's face. When she touched his jaw, he flinched, but wouldn't give The Sodality the pleasure of knowing his pain.

"You are strong, Mr. Dawson," The Whisper said in a hushed voice. "Very much like your father that way. Now, we have what we came for and there's nothing more to accomplish here. Let us retire to the house and, in a beautiful and pathetic ironic twist, you shall witness first-hand where your father took his last breath." She grinned. "I'd say that's a rather fitting end to this business, wouldn't you, Mr. Stone? Like father, like son?"

The operative narrowed his eyes and flexed his fingers. "Indeed. I most definitely would."

FORTY-FIVE

"WAIT, PLEASE," THE PROFESSOR INTERJECTED. "WE HAVE an opportunity to discover something never observed before."

Stone snorted. "What are you mewling about, Rathbourne? We've got this rag. This is what Mr. Dawson's photo pointed to, and now we're going to analyze it and, if necessary, destroy it. Or," he mused, "perhaps there's an archaeological purpose it might serve. Either way, we are done here."

Dawson inhaled through his nose. He suddenly felt tired and beaten and ached to clean up and grab some painkillers for his pounding jaw. Still, in the corner of his mind, buried beneath the shards of stinging humiliation, he found a spark of hope... something gently reminding him of... *of what?*

"Please, ma'am, hear me out," the professor continued. "I don't believe this cloth, this blanket is the final answer."

The Whisper sighed. "What are you talking about? If this is some kind of scientific trickery to grab some free research, I'm not interested."

"No, I assure you, it's not. Let me explain."

Rathbourne approached the table, picking up an overturned chair on the way. "Let's consider the evidence." He ran through facts as he understood them: Dawson's apparent genetic ability to psychometrically read the photograph, but only to a certain extent. The apparition in the image suggested a connection to this cloth and to Hannah. And the cloth was somehow tied to antiquity. "But," he said, "we have no idea what that link is."

"And this is important *why*?" The Whisper hissed. "Is it not sufficient to know the cloth holds mystical power? My clients will offer millions on that basis alone."

Rathbourne furrowed his brow. "Well, beyond the academic interest and pursuit of knowledge which, by the way, The Sodality prizes," he flashed a quick grin, "there is the secret that the amalgam of these things presents. What if," he asked, "this cloth offers even more compelling visions to ESPers? What if it points to something omnipotent they carry within their own genetic code, and this cloth is the key to unlocking it?" He stared at Stone and The Whisper. "Could that not be worth... billions?"

Hannah scrunched her brows. "Professor, are you saying there's more here than the old blanket? That this," she pointed to the cloth in The Whisper's hand, "is *not* the end of the story?"

"That's exactly what I'm suggesting, Hannah. And," he turned to her, "you provided the clue."

"Me?"

"Yes, yes! Before you entered the chamber for the procedure, you told me you'd experienced nightmares as far back as you could remember. And not just random hauntings, but the same terrifying dream over and over: an invitation to join some sinister man."

She cocked her head. "That's true."

"And now? After the experience?"

She straightened. "I feel much better. I mean, what these creeps did to Matt sickens me, but I'm surprisingly full of peace, as if witnessing the seducer's demise in the nightmare signaled an end."

"Right. Initially, I believed that was from your first time in the chamber, and that certainly had an impact on your ability to visualize your nightmares. But there's more." He pointed to the blanket. "You had that with you. We know those with psychometric abilities can read all kinds of impressions from specific objects, and your test proves you have that ability too. But you didn't read the cloth as much as the cloth read you. And the power to overcome your deepest fear was unlocked, I propose, through channeling that material."

Hannah gulped, catching Dawson's gaze.

He groaned, stretched his jaw slightly, and struggled with his words. "There... may be truth... to that. When I... read the cloth in mum's basement... it was extremely clear, profoundly real. Not like the vision in the photo. I was also *in* my vision."

"Ah yes, of course." The professor turned to The Whisper. "I believe this holds a power the likes of which we have never encountered in psychometry. And Matt is the key."

Rathbourne, rocking on his heels, concluded, "There's a way to discover the truth here, ma'am. This cloth clearly has at least one psychic impression on it that Matt has read." He rubbed his fingers together. "With the help of our equipment and procedures, we'll determine what's ultimately behind it: the source of power that both he and Hannah were tapped into." He eyed The Whisper carefully. "Is that not what you truly covet?"

"Why this fool?" Stone asked, arms folded across his chest.

"Mr. Stone," he said, dismissing him, "if Hannah with her limited psychometric ability could achieve what she saw, imagine what Dawson might tell us. His test scores, may I remind you, are unheard of." His eyes widened as he continued. "If we run one more procedure in the chamber, this time with Matt in physical contact with the cloth like Hannah was, well, my sense is we'd finally learn why this old rag as you call it, is so important to his family and how it might affect the world forever."

Temptation is a funny thing, Dawson thought. The lure of lying to get something. The promise of intimacy in the shadows. *And these two creatures are not above it, despite their polished exteriors.*

He peered into the gloom of The Whisper's hidden face, dangling the prize. "I'm game," he slurred. "If there's nothing more, then at least we'll know."

The Whisper floated across the room and leaned into him. He caught glimpses of her dark, penetrating eyes sizing him up. Despite the pain in his body, Dawson clenched his fists. Then, the presence of something else enveloped him. The ache in his limbs vanished. He relaxed his hands.

What is she doing?

The Whisper drew back. "Very well, Professor," she rasped. "You have one shot at this before we take him and Ms. King home with us." To the pair, she grinned and added, "You may become one with The Sodality yet."

"Not likely," he gasped.

"We shall see. The Sodality can provide you with everything—*everything*—you could ever desire." She cast a look at Hannah. "Everything."

Dawson tried swallowing, but his throat seized. "It's far too late... for that."

"Au contraire," she purred. "There's no such thing as too late."

FORTY-SIX

"ARE YOU SURE YOU'RE UP TO THIS, MATT?" HANNAH stood nervously behind the professor as he carefully adjusted the transducer cap on Dawson's battered head. She and Mara had cleaned him up and given him Tylenol. In his hand, he held the piece of cloth that he hoped would bring clarity to the mystery and allow him to bargain for his and Hannah's freedom.

It took some convincing for The Whisper to return the blanket to him.

Despite the professor's belief that the material would liberate untold secrets in Dawson's hands, The Whisper only gave it to him when Stone assured her he would remain in the chamber with him—not attached to the procedure, but in the room nonetheless.

"Perhaps... it'll take my mind... off the pain," he slurred.

Hannah squeezed his hand and kissed him lightly on the cheek. He winced, but held the agony between his teeth.

"There," the professor said. "You're all ready to go, Matt. Again, I'll need to adjust the transducer inputs on the computer, and once the light dims, you'll be 'live', as we like to say." He smiled curtly, then scuttled out of the chamber, taking Hannah with him.

Stone, sitting on a hard-back chair he'd brought from the other room, watched him like a prison guard from the corner of the chamber. When the door closed, he said, "Looks like it's just you and me now, Mr. Dawson. If you try any monkey business again, your life is over. Understand?"

"You won't get a... a fight from me. I'm done."

Stone grinned, stuck his legs out and leaned against the wall, steepling his fingers.

Dawson spread the cloth out over his lap and ran his palm along the frayed edges. This piece had lost its elasticity over time and was paper thin. The herringbone pattern stitched into the material appeared to be hand sewn, perhaps reflecting its age. He recalled the previous vision, the destruction of the Library at Alexandria, and remembered that happened... sometime in the fourth century? And in that dream, he and a woman he apparently lived with had rescued a blanket—possibly this one—from the Roman soldiers bent on destroying it and everything else.

How did that implicate him with the photograph? If the farmhouse and apparitions pointed to this cloth and his ancestors, what was the source of it? And how were Hannah and the dead child involved?

The overhead light slowly dimmed. Stone murmured something from his perch, and Dawson quickly found himself bathed in black.

He felt the gentle heat of EM waves tickle his temples, and he stared where he knew the cloth was. He lay his palms on it and waited for a vision to appear.

Nothing happened.

He closed his eyes and desperately searched for something—anything—that he could envision, even though the burning Library had simply appeared through no effort of his.

Still nothing.

Several moments later, he sighed in frustration, shifting his weight in the large reclining chair and adjusting the cloth.

The vision he wished for remained elusive.

Electromagnetic waves pulsed steadily in his head. *Surely Professor Rathbourne realizes nothing's going on.* Dawson stared straight ahead and longed for the secret to be revealed so he could be done and move on, and that despite The Whisper's threat to kill him, he'd find a way to escape with Hannah and save his mother.

He pushed his thoughts to focus... wishing, hoping, cajoling, threatening to discover something—a hint of the extraordinary.

Still, nothing appeared.

Then Hannah's words returned to him: that God could handle his honesty.

He sighed deeply and prayed.

God, I don't know if you're real. And if you are, whether you're the God in the Bible. Hannah tells me to be honest, to come to you with everything... my fears and doubts, my hopes... so here I am. And to stop trying to control events myself and fix these problems on my own. She says to let it all go, the outcome, the future, my research, and to simply put you first.

Well, I don't even understand what that means.

But this much I've learned: I can't do this by myself. I took pride my whole life in my independence and resourcefulness and this is where that mindset brought me.

I need help.

I'm not asking for a miracle, or for you to appear and save us from these fiends. I get it. You don't work that way. But God, I pray for wisdom and understanding to meet you where you are, to recognize that even though everything here seems bleak, that whatever happens is your will for me, for the others. Help me to keep an open mind no matter what my role is.

Lord, I won't bargain with you. How does one negotiate with the Creator of the universe? No. I come to you, a broken man. If it be your will to reveal the mysteries of this cloth and what it means to the world, I pray you'll give me the courage to face whatever happens.

Hannah said I should pray for these things in Jesus' name. So here goes, even though I'm not sure whether he even lived... or if he truly was your son... whether I honestly believe or not. Still, I pray for courage, strength, wisdom and insight... if it be your will for me... in Jesus' name.

Amen.

The difference between having his eyes closed and open was indistinguishable. The chamber's architecture nullified all senses so the client could focus on the effects of the neuron stimulus without undue environmental influence. So when Dawson opened them, feeling at least on some superficial level better for having prayed, the reddish hue on the opposite wall perplexed him.

He recognized a new vision appearing.

And as before in his dad's workshop, he was firmly in it...

FORTY-SEVEN

"HURRY, DECIMUS. DID YOU NOT FEEL THE
EARTHQUAKE?"

Dawson peered around the grim terrain. Brutal, dark
clouds unfurled across the angry sky amid the sounds of
crying and wailing. He carried several articles of clothing
in his arms, and the helmet he wore crept over his eyes.
He stopped to reposition it.

"Decimus!"

He pulled on the chin strap, then gathered the clothes
and followed the trio as they marched through the
laneway toward a series of huts and tents. Along the way,
people ran past them while keeping their distance. Dawson
could not place this location, or his purpose, but there was
no mistaking what he was.

Dawson, or Decimus, was a Roman soldier.

"Halt," the other one said. "Let us divide the spoils
here."

They arrived at a fieldstone wall rising up from the

ground to Dawson's thighs. He poured the articles on top and wiped his forehead. The other three picked through them and made four even piles. While they engaged in the sorting, Dawson peered around.

From the hilltop, he saw few structures. A trail of burning lamps snaked through the paths away from the hill toward the outskirts of an ancient city. The air filled with shouts and cries, and the smell of smoke. Soldiers and civilians scurried about in a chaotic frenzy.

In the other direction, the rolling hills continued to the horizon, and pockets of sheep and goats dotted the landscape. He removed his helmet and placed it on the wall.

"Some of this material is of the highest quality," one of the soldiers growled. "My woman would appreciate that." He grabbed a tunic from a pile and threw it over his shoulder.

"Mind the greed, Rufus. There's plenty to go around." The leader continued dividing out the clothes.

The earth rumbled again, and some women screamed in the distance.

The centurion captain was nonplussed. "Just a tremor. Nothing more."

But something wasn't right. The two other soldiers looked about nervously, glancing at the approaching storm.

"Hurry," he said, "let's finish this."

The captain sneered. "Hey, don't let all this strange talk bother you, young Decimus. They all had it coming. Do I speak the truth, Rufus? Marcus?"

"Yes, Philo," the one called Rufus said. "Opposing Caesar is ill-advised."

Dawson eyed the gathering clouds. Strangely, the words came to him. "There is no questioning that. The law is clear. But tell me, did your heart not burn with the man hanging there? When you heard him speak?"

"No," Philo scoffed. "And yours didn't either."

"But—"

"Yours did not either, Decimus!"

The familiar rage bloomed in Dawson's chest, but rapidly dissipated.

Not from Philo's surly disposition.

Something else was in play.

Marcus, the quiet one, eyed Dawson suspiciously. "Quick," he said, "let's finish up and be on our way. I fear no man, but this storm carries an ill wind."

The captain inspected the four piles. In each were a collection of garments: a tunic, a bloody cloak, robe, sandals. One piece remained. A large, seamless chiton. Philo ran his fingers over it, inspecting it closely in the gloomy light.

"This is truly of the highest quality." He raised his head. "No seams," he said with admiration, "and I dare not cut it up."

The others agreed.

Dawson was beyond caring about the spoils on the wall. Everything had changed. He did not understand how, but the world he knew no longer existed. Between the structures winding along the lane, a young, dark haired woman stood in simple raiment, watching them from a safe distance. He stared at her, and she lowered her head.

"I propose we draw lots for this piece."

Rufus wandered off a few paces and pulled various pieces of straw from the ground. He turned his back, then presented the group with his fist. The straws appeared to be the same length.

"Short piece wins the garment."

Each soldier took their turn. Dawson picked the winner and claimed the chiton. The idea that they gambled for these articles of clothing sickened him, but he *dared not protest anymore.*

"Why so sad, Decimus?" Philo said, "You hold the extra prize! Here," the captain offered, grabbing one of the piles, "take this, too." He tossed the bundle at him and laughed.

The wind swirled and moaned through the hills. Philo looked skyward and said, "Come, let us away. Return to the barracks and prepare the night watch."

The soldiers gathered their winnings and marched down the hill toward the city. Dawson brought up the rear. The woman he'd seen earlier walked up and presented herself as he passed a small granary.

"Do you know who those belong to?" she asked. "Which of the… the men, I mean?"

He stopped. "I do not."

She stepped closer, cautiously. "May I look?"

Dawson was stuck by the high cheek bones. Her eyes were red and swollen, perhaps from the thickening smoke. "Do you require help?" he asked.

"No, at least, not the kind you can provide." She held out her hand. Dawson turned them over to her.

Fresh tears flowed across her cheeks. "These were his," she said.

"Whose? Your husband's?"

She shook her head, taking the chiton reverently and running it along her face.

Dawson noticed the material, the attention to the sewed hem. The herringbone pattern.

This cloth.

"Do you feel it?" she asked.

"What?"

"The power still flows. Even in death."

Dawson pulled the chiton from her and wrapped it around his hands and forearms. She watched him, her eyes wide in anticipation.

Although he could not place it, power flowed through this garment. He inhaled deeply and his insides burned.

He knew.

He burst into tears as guilt crushed him to his knees. The woman knelt beside him, placing her hand over his.

"He healed me," she whispered. "Even in death, he continues healing. Here," she said, unwrapping the chiton from his hands and wiping his face, "let him heal you, too."

She helped him stand and strode with him through the lane, down the hill. Shouts and mournful cries grew from the city, and lamps flickered everywhere. As they walked together from the enclave of structures, the full meaning struck him.

To his right, jutting up across the barren, lifeless hill like spindly black tree trunks after a raging fire, were dozens of crosses. In the clearing closest to him, three stood apart.

FORTY-EIGHT

THE SCENE IMMEDIATELY VANISHED, AND DAWSON regained his bearings in the chamber. Sweat dripped into his eyes and rolled down his face. He touched the cloth in his hands and, yes, the power surging through it, through his palms, and filling his body with warmth and a sensation he couldn't place but instinctively recognized as otherworldly.

The lab door burst open even before the ceiling bulb had flickered on. A shock of blinding light slashed his sight, and he turned his head away. The smell of burned circuits again—and more—assaulted his nostrils, and a shrieking alarm pierced his ears.

"Quick," the professor shouted. "We must leave!"

Dawson squinted.

"What's happening out there?" Stone pushed his way past Rathbourne, gazed into the outer room, then stormed back. He ripped the cloth from Dawson's hands and vanished. Dawson, still woozy from the revelation, processed the sights and sounds in front of him. Hannah cried out, and he yanked the transducer cap from his throbbing head.

"Professor?" His slurred voice sounded foreign.

"Matt, come right away. There's been a massive overload in the equipment and a fire broke out. Come on."

"Matt!" Hannah raced into the chamber. She pulled him from the test chair and they followed Rathbourne into the anteroom. What Dawson encountered could only be described as a chaotic inferno.

Water gushed from the automatic sprinkler's in the ceiling. Mara hunched over the primary computer console, ripping out cables and wires from it as the equipment erupted in billows of smoke.

"Leave it, Mara," the professor calmly ordered. "Follow me out right now."

"I can't! There's too much captured here... the data..." She stared at Dawson, then lowered her head as if terrified or ashamed.

"Let it go," Dawson said, "it's not important." He placed his hand on the student's forearm. Mara's face instantly relaxed, then she hurried after the professor through the main entrance to the lab.

The pain in his mouth rattled him, but somehow it dissipated. *The Tylenol must be kicking in.* "Where's Stone and the woman?" He scanned the room.

"They've already left, Matt," Hannah said, "and they took the cloth and the photo." She held her face as the flames roared. "I'm so sorry, Matt. I couldn't stop them."

Dawson grabbed her hand and pulled her toward the exit as the flames licked the ceiling and toxic yellow smoke poured over the equipment bank. The professor yelled from across the flaming barrier separating them from escape in the corridor.

He seized her shoulders. "We'll make it, Hannah."

She began protesting, but he placed his swollen finger on her lips and whispered into her ear. "I know we're protected, no matter what. You understand?"

She searched his eyes and her face relaxed. "Yes."

"When I say *go*, run as fast as you can."

Hannah nodded and pursed her lips.

Dawson struggled to draw a breath. The fire ravaged the remaining oxygen in the room, encircling them in a frenzied furnace.

"Ready?"

"Yes."

"Let's go!"

They tore through the fire. Flames attacked his exposed flesh, but he was calm and clear, filled with overwhelming determination.

Determination to save Hannah and his mother.

Determination to share the truth bursting in his heart.

Determination to right the wrongs of his life.

The pair burst through the firewall and tumbled to the ground on the opposite side. Matt lost his hold of Hannah's hand, but staggered onto his hands and knees and saw her. She lay supine near the concrete wall, fire ravaging her clothes. He rolled her over several times, ignoring the searing pain of his smashed jaw and his burning flesh as he extinguished the flame and dragged her smouldering body away from the encroaching inferno.

In the crosscut madness of screaming alarms and ghostly, plaintive shouts, the professor's shrill voice rang out in the distance, ordering students and shocked instructors to vacate the blazing building as Dawson staggered to his feet. It was almost impossible to see in the corridor through the thick, eerie smoke. An emergency strobe light flashed above the exit doors. Hannah coughed and choked.

"Matt?

Dawson knelt beside her and brushed the singed hair from her face. He smiled, lifted her up in his arms, and carried her to safety.

FORTY-NINE

"WHAT DID YOU SEE IN THERE, MATT?"

Hannah sat on the cool ground outside the *Science 1* building while firefighters doused the remnants of the blaze, and other first responders kept curious onlookers away. A paramedic had draped a thick wool blanket over her shoulders and patches of burned clothing. She'd also treated the minor burns on her hands and arm.

Dawson rested beside her under the ashen afternoon sky, cradling his knees, watching the emergency workers and paramedics move methodically, and scanning the campus for signs of The Sodality. Both operatives had disappeared. The painkillers they'd given him had taken effect, and his eyelids grew heavy. The malocclusion inhibited his ability to open his mouth too wide, but compared to earlier, felt strangely better. "The cloth was one of the garments Jesus wore at his crucifixion." His gaze drifted over the pines toward the bitter blues and greys of Ramsey Lake. "I saw myself there."

"Oh," Hannah gasped.

"Yeah, it was all real. *He* was real." Dawson was overwhelmed with peace and understanding. Healing power surged through his body. "In the revelation, I was a Roman soldier, and we gambled for his clothes." He paused, reflecting on the believing, raven-haired woman in the vision and how she'd opened his eyes to God's power. "The blanket is meaningless, Hannah."

"What? But I thought—"

"Sure, that it held an awesome energy. But just like the photo pointed to the cloth, the cloth pointed to something else... someone else... the *actual power* here. If I understand correctly, the soldier was a distant relative of mine. He had the piece of clothing from Jesus. And over the years, it was passed down through subsequent generations, until finally, my dad and I got it. But my sense is The Sodality will find it useless. What brings it all to life is the message encoded in my family's DNA and in the genetic code of others who have found their faith."

A police officer approached, carrying a notepad and talking into a radio. He stopped in front of them. "Thought you'd like to know, Matt, that your mother is fine. The Temiskaming OPP detachment says the man holding her disappeared." He offered a stiff smile. "No sign of your phones, but we'll set up a call with her as soon as we've taken her statement." He checked his notes. "Oh, and those other two you mentioned? This... Cornelius Stone and the other mysterious woman? I'm afraid there's no trace of them or a white van anywhere. But we have established a perimeter and we'll keep looking." He wished them both speedy recoveries, then marched away.

Dawson sighed as relief swept over him. That, mixed with the painkillers for his jaw, untethered his thoughts. His body finally relaxed, and he turned to Hannah.

"There's no way to know whether Dad understood the significance of the cloth and the photo, but from his notes, he'd started piecing it all together." He coughed hard, spitting smoke and ash from his lungs.

"That's what prompted the note about the professor in his journal," Hannah said, wincing as the paramedic inspected her hands.

"Yeah, I suppose. He got close, but The Sodality tracked him down and..." A rush of tears filled his eyes and the lump in his throat continued growing.

"There," the paramedic said to Hannah, "you're fixed up for now. I'd still like you to come to the hospital and get thoroughly checked. You, too," she said to Dawson. "That jaw won't heal on its own."

He smiled knowingly. "Sure, but give us a few minutes."

The responder gathered her supplies and returned to the ambulance.

"Hannah?" Dawson lowered his voice, wiping his eyes. "I don't understand why my ancestors were chosen. If the encoded message was that Jesus was real, and who he claimed to be, then why not just state that?"

She shrugged. "The Bible does say it clearly, but still not everyone believes." She grinned. "You didn't for the longest time, right? And the book sat on your shelf untouched. But just because you didn't believe in him, maybe that doesn't mean he didn't believe in you. Maybe we all come to this understanding in our own time."

Hannah was wise. And beautiful. Even when Jesus walked the Earth, performing miracles, many refused to believe he was the son of God. Dawson speculated about the spiritual message encoded in his DNA, the truth that had been released through the quantum awakening in the Neurosciences Lab, but it was something he felt in his heart, not in his head. Explaining it to others in words seemed... cold and futile.

Professor Rathbourne and Mara approached. Concern covered the man's face. "Matt, perhaps this isn't the best time, but when your psychometric vision began, our readings," he gaped at Mara, "were totally wild. Totally. What happened in there?"

Dawson glanced at Hannah, unsure about what to reveal since the professor remained part of The Sodality. The last thing he wanted was to invite those creatures into his life again.

"I'm feeling a little beat up, Professor," he whispered. "But... it was the most amazing revelation."

"Please, Matt, would you... ever consider exploring this with me again one day? I'll have to rebuild the lab and find an alternative source of research funds, and—"

Dawson raised an eyebrow.

"Yes, I'm going to break free from The Sodality. The covenant I signed," he lowered his voice, "is unbreakable. But there are always alternative solutions." He squeezed Matt's shoulder and the pair of psychometric researchers departed, chatting enthusiastically together.

Dawson worked his jaw, feeling the pain continue to dissipate. "I should go to the hospital."

"I'm coming with you." Hannah's eyes filled with tears.

They helped each other up, and arm in arm, wandered toward the ambulance.

He could never return now.

Sunlight broke through the cloud cover and momentarily bathed the campus in a flash of September warmth. Dawson peered into the sky, pushing the limits of understanding as his mind traveled through the solar system to distant stars. While he failed to grasp the extent of God's work in the visible domain, the unseen quantum world was his, too. When the limit of humanity's knowledge is reached, somewhere beyond the realm of space-time foam, God was *there*, and was *more*.

Boundless.

The paramedics prepared a gurney, and Matt stared with wonder into Hannah's tear-stained face, studying her as if she was a beautiful renaissance portrait. He followed the brush strokes that nudged across her hair, alighting on the hint of forget-me-not eyes, the splash of warmth on high cheekbones, and settling on her full mouth. In isolation, every micrometer of Hannah King shone with the stars, yet in the whole, betrayed a haunting hush of profound loneliness.

As if she never truly belonged here.

Hannah encircled him, wrapping him in her blanket and drawing close, like a cosmic interlocutor weaving the foundational fabric of God's entire creation.

Acknowledgements

As we often say in the writing workshops, while each of us has to do the writing alone, it takes a group to create a novel. I would like to thank the following for their insights, beta readings, thoughtful suggestions, and support throughout the writing of this novel: Gary Raymond Coffin, Peter Dyer, Pricilla Padaratz, Mike Marshall, Frank Kitching, Nicholas J. Forster, Styles Desbarats, Janet Edwards, Glen Packman, and my wife, Susan.

About the Author

David Allan Hamilton is a teacher-writer living in Ottawa, Ontario. He has edited and published numerous collections of stories from participants of the Ottawa Writing Workshops since 2017, helping hundreds of writers and novelists feel that sense of achievement from accomplishing their dream.

David previously enjoyed a career with the Federal Public Service and has been a contract instructor at Carleton University. He holds a B.Sc. (Honours) degree in Applied Physics from Laurentian University and a M.Sc. in Geophysics from the University of Western Ontario and has undertaken literary studies at the University of Sheffield. He is also a licenced ham radio operator. His own stories often combine his love of the natural world and the endless possibilities of science fiction.

You may wish to contact or follow David at the following:

Davidallanhamilton00@gmail.com
davidallanhamilton.com

Twitter: @DAllanHamilton
Facebook.com/davidallanhamilton

Thanks for reading!

If you enjoyed this story, please consider writing a short review on Amazon and Goodreads and let me know what you thought.

Other Novels by David Allan Hamilton

The Ross 128 First Contact Trilogy

An alien distress call, nervous world leaders, and scientific betrayal

September, 2085. Listening for alien signals is a welcome respite for Jim Atteberry, an English professor at City College who's marking a pile of boring undergraduate essays.

But when he detects a subspace distress call from the Ross 128 system, Jim becomes a pawn in a global scientific conspiracy bent on stealing the alien technology for political domination. Jim and his colleague Kate team up with Dr. Esther Tyrone at the Terran Science Academy to confirm his findings and warn the aliens. But are the Rossians truly in distress, or setting a trap for an ambitious, naïve Earth?

The Crying of Ross 128 is the opening installment in the Ross 128 first contact trilogy. If you like science fiction with credible stories, compelling characters, and mysterious aliens that will keep you guessing, you'll love author David Allan Hamilton's page-turning trilogy of near future alien encounters.

They have arrived...

Kate Braddock, a sexually ambiguous ex-Spacer, isolates herself on Luna. After detecting a faster-than-light ship en route to Earth several years ago, she now conducts geophysical surveys for a mineral resources consortium.

One day, she and a young intern, Mary Atteberry, discover an anomaly in the dust near the *Mare Marginis* that is clearly unnatural, and clearly alien. The purpose of the spaceship on Luna is unclear, but its origin is not. This is the same ship she detected in 2085... the same one that led to the destruction of the Mount Sutro comms tower in San Francisco... the same one that nearly got her killed: the Ross 128 star system.

Time is running out on Kate and Mary, and on the Echo to discover the truth behind the Rossians arrival in the solar system. Will humanity survive this first contact alien encounter?

The Echo is broken...

Janet Chamberlain, an aging field operative with the Northern Democratic Union—and Jim Atteberry's ex-wife—is compelled to undertake one last mission: to save their daughter Mary from those who will stop at nothing to scrape her mind for the alien secrets she holds. Chased by the ruthless Benedikt Winter of the Prussian Consortium, and coveted by Titanius CEO Clayton Carter, the Atteberry's search for a way to remove the alien Keechik's knowledge that is destroying Mary's brain.

But time is running out . . .

Against a backdrop of increasing global tension and deteriorating peace in North America, Jim desperately pursues a solution while Janet contemplates the unthinkable: kill their daughter to protect the future of all humanity.

As galactic warfare breaks out, the Echo is conscripted to offer Mary one last chance at life, but Winter is determined to seize both her and the ship to promote his own diabolical vision of the future. Can humanity survive these final three days of darkness?

Don't miss the shocking conclusion to the Ross 128 First Contact Trilogy!